Previous Titles

Detective Inspector Christy Kennedy Mysteries:
I Love The Sound of Breaking Glass
Last Boat To Camden Town
Fountain of Sorrow
The Ballad of Sean & Wilko
I've Heard The Banshee Sing
The Hissing of the Silent Lonely Room
The Justice Factory
Sweetwater
The Beautiful Sound of Silence

Inspector Starrett Mysteries:
The Dust of Death
Family Life

Other Fiction:
First of The True Believers

Factual:
Playing Live

www.paulcharlesbook.com

THOMAS CRANE PUBLIC LIBRARY
QUINCY MA

CITY APPROPRIATION

NOV – – 2012

A PLEASURE
TO DO **DEATH**
WITH YOU

PAUL CHARLES

A PLEASURE
TO DO **DEATH**
WITH YOU

A DI Christy Kennedy Mystery

Dufour Editions

First published in the United States of America, 2012
by Dufour Editions Inc., Chester Springs, Pennsylvania 19425

© Paul Charles, 2012

All rights reserved. No part of this publication may be reproduced or transmitted in any form or by any means, electronic or mechanical, including photography, recording, or any information storage or retrieval system, without permission in writing from the publisher.

This is a work of fiction. Except for public figures, all characters in this story are fictional, and any resemblance to anyone else living or dead is purely coincidental.

ISBN 978-0-8023-1352-2

2 4 6 8 10 9 7 5 3 1

Cover photo by Jay Graham - jaygraham.com

Lay Down Beside Me
Words and Music by Don Williams
Copyright © 1973 UNIVERSAL - SONGS OF POLYGRAM INTERNATIONAL, INC.
Copyright Renewed
All Rights Reserved - Used by Permission
Reprinted by Permission of Hal Leonard Corporation

Library of Congress Cataloging-in-Publication Data

Charles, Paul, 1949-
  A pleasure to do death with you : a DI Christy Kennedy mystery / by Paul Charles.
    p. cm.
  ISBN 978-0-8023-1352-2 (hardback)
  1. Kennedy, Christy (Fictitious character)--Fiction. 2. Police--England--London--Fiction. I. Title.
  PR6053.H372145P57 2012
  823.'914--dc23

                                                          2012001156

Printed and bound in the United Kingdom

Thanks are certainly due and offered to:

My good friend Donald Miller who introduced me to Half Moon
Bay while we were returning to LA
after a gig in SFO many moons ago.

Niall McIvor for his patience while sharing his
knowledge on stocks and shares.

Terry Fitzgerald for the editing and to
Duncan May for showing Kennedy what it's like
to drive on the other side of the road.

Steve MacDonogh for all your energy,
support and counsel; you're sadly missed.

Lilo O'Carroll for your bravery and ability to carve
out a piece of California for the O'Carroll clan.

Police Chief Don O'Keefe for your time,
insights, valuable information and hospitality.

Christopher May for arriving with the cavalry just in time.

Andrew Charles M.M. for always being my
template for the good guys in the books.

Catherine

This book is dedicated to the memory of

Nuala McGinley
whose passion for knowledge I always found inspiring.

and Cora Charles
who taught me by example.

PART ONE

PRIMROSE HILL

CHAPTER ONE

Kennedy had been awake half the night trying to find a comfortable position for, at the very least, a catnap. His back was so brutally painful in some of the positions he'd tried that he'd have settled for a gnatnap. Why was his back giving him so much jip recently? It had been four years since his near-death brush with a suspect in the then dilapidated York & Albany which, thanks to a recent make-over from the Gordon Ramsey team, was now enjoying a new lease on life.

Kennedy, on the other hand, could find little in life to enjoy these days. When we're fit and well we tend to take our health, and particularly our backs, for granted. He would have thought that a bad back would be the last ailment he'd suffer after being stabbed in the gut. At the time of the incident, both Kennedy's GP and Dr Taylor had assured him there'd be no long-term side effects from his wound. Kennedy now accepted that perhaps listening to a pathologist - who, as part of a medical profession in general, enjoyed a 100 per cent death rate with their patients - might not have been the best idea. It had been ann rea who'd suggested he visit an osteopath and who then had even taken the trouble to source him a real magician in that field by the name of Miss Chada. The osteopath in question was always referred to as *Miss* Chada.

In the early days, Miss Chada's magic fingers had worked wonders on his back, but recently, especially in the previous couple of weeks, Kennedy's back had gotten, if anything, worse - and perhaps even the worst it had ever been.

Kennedy tossed and turned, trying in vain to find a comfortable position to relieve the lightning pain mainlining his spine. He pictured his movements in his mind's eye. He imagined it was like a bizarre ballet, which was bringing tears to the eyes of the sole performer. He gingerly edged to the side of the bed and dropped his legs to the floor, hoping the momentum would help to right his torso, but all he got for his efforts was an even more excruciating bolt of pain in the small of his back and another thin coat of sweat.

He eventually managed to sit upright on his bed, temporarily incapable of further movement. Even turning his head slightly to his right to look at his clock brought tears to his eyes. Kennedy was now experiencing the pulsing of an oncoming headache. It felt as if someone were trying to carelessly drill from inside his crown out through the centre of his forehead, just above and between his eyebrows.

He couldn't lie.

He couldn't sit.

He couldn't stand.

He could find no relief.

It was only twelve-fifty a.m., but because he'd registered every single second since he went to bed at ten-thirty, it felt like it must be at least seven o'clock in the morning. He found himself trying to become preoccupied with the creaks and groans of his house; trying to figure out the source of the late night sounds. He focused on whether he was hearing a window rattle in the window-frame or was it a car having trouble finding a gear low enough to climb the nearby steep Primrose Hill Road. Somehow he had to find a way through sixteen hours of agony until his scheduled appointment with Miss Chada. The visit would surely bring him some respite, but then the price he had to pay, travelling to and from Unlocked, her Camden Market treatment room, might not make it as worthwhile as he'd been dreaming it would be since his last visit five days ago. He hobbled down the stairs grasping the banister for dear life. One floor took a full seven minutes to negotiate. He considered leaving immediately for Camden Market in the hope that, at his current speed, he'd make the less than a mile journey in the remaining fifteen hours and fifty-three minutes.

He went into his first floor sitting room - his book and television room - and all of a sudden he had a great idea. If he just lay down on the floor, maybe face down, surely the solid support of the floor would ease his pain.

Big mistake.

That position was even worse, if worse were possible. It took him five minutes of agonising manoeuvres to turn face up. It was certainly more difficult to get up than it had been to lie down, and he found himself involuntarily crying out in pain. He took to huffing and puffing deep breaths, like a mother in precious labour, and eventually made his way on to the sofa. From the previous evening, he already had his sofa piled with cushions, so he was able to find a suitable, straight-upright position, which afforded him a little respite from the pain.

He tried to read the book he'd started a week earlier, but he was still only forty pages into Ray Davies' *X Ray*, and he was desperate for a clear mind to finish it off. Now was definitely not that time. He replaced the book, picking up the remote to flick on first the TV and then, when he couldn't find anything to distract him, the DVD. Another flick of the remote, and the flickering shadows and unsympathetic sounds disappeared. He closed his eyes.

He'd found the magic relieving position: heels and knees tightly together, upper torso straight to the perpendicular, maybe a little curved, giving the spine its preferred "S" shape, head slightly bowed and eyes closed. He opened one eye. Another sharp twinge in the small of his back was enough to convince him he shouldn't risk a second.

Peace at last.

How typical it was of ann rea that she would find Miss Chada for him. He thought of how atypically she'd reacted at the end of his last case when a friend of hers was involved. ann rea had accused Kennedy of being a policeman first and her lover-cum-friend second. She told him she couldn't forgive him. Ever! She'd ordered him off her barge and out of her life.

Kennedy had hoped that when she calmed down they'd be fine.

Maybe not as good as they'd been, but with a bit of work they might be fine. Surely she'd have to see that Kennedy couldn't be held responsible for what other people did? Maybe she was just so traumatised by what her friend had done that she needed someone to blame, and Kennedy was there, right there, dead centre, in the firing line.

Kennedy had been wrong. They hadn't spoken since that fateful night. Clearly she hadn't just been over-reacting at the time. He'd rung her several times in her *Camden News Journal* offices and left messages, all of which were ignored. She hid behind the answering machine on her barge, a barge he frequently walked past in the vain hope of bumping into her.

He admitted to himself that he'd hoped she would at least ring him and tell him it was difficult to do this thing; difficult to break up with him. Kennedy wasn't used to breaking up and was ill equipped to deal with it.

He thought about how they'd met, how long it had taken them to get together. How absolutely blissful and spiritual their lovemaking had always been. He thought of how important and influential she had become in his life. He focused once again on the fact that it had been so typical of ann rea to have found Miss Chada when he needed help.

Mind you, he'd happily have swapped his original back complaint for his current one. Either his back was getting worse, or Miss Chada was not as effective as she had been at the beginning. Kennedy was convinced Miss Chada was aware of this fact.

She even seemed to Kennedy to be feeling sorry for him. Over the last couple of months, she appeared to be veering ever so slightly from their clinical relationship. She'd started to be very nice to him, smiling at him in a caring way, maybe even flirting with him more than a little, or so it appeared to Kennedy. Of course his feelings might have something to do with the fact that he was missing physical contact with ann rea.

Miss Chada - Kennedy didn't even know her first name. She was a brown-skinned woman, probably in her late twenties, thirty at the most. She was slim and trim (but not thin), with healthy long, straight, black hair. Not a speck of make-up was needed or ever used, and she had large, sad, brown eyes that drank you and your soul in, in one gulp. She was the type of woman who always looked alone but, at the same time, she seemed to enjoy her own company very much. She was not really the kind of person who'd start up a conversation off her own bat, and if someone tried to engage her, Kennedy reckoned, all they'd get would be monosyllabic responses. When Kennedy was lying face down on her special leather table and he wasn't preoccupied with the ache in his back, he'd think how bizarre it was for him to be lying in a state of near undress while in the company of a stunningly beautiful woman. And to top that, the arrangement had been set up by his (albeit ex) girlfriend.

Kennedy found that if he concentrated on Miss Chada and her work, it was as if the countdown to his next vital visit with her had kicked off, and he took comfort from the fact that the treatment was coming, as it were. He accepted that this state was a bit like how much better some ailing people felt the second they took their medicine, even before the miraculous cure had been able to work its way through their bodies. Knowing that help was on the way sometimes was as effective as the help itself. His recovering state of mind allowed his thought process to dally somewhere around the perfect body sheathed in Miss Chada's brilliantly white, starched uniform.

Kennedy dozed off at this point. He would pay dearly for the sleep by waking up the following morning at 8:43 with a severe crick in his neck. It was a price he was happy to pay.

Kennedy gradually came back to consciousness, alert enough not to make any drastic movements. Straightening up his head did cause considerable discomfort, but nowhere near the same degree as the previous evening. Kennedy had a theory that darkness always intensified one's pain. It was at that point that he tried to get up from his sofa.

He wished he hadn't. Another one of his late-night theories had come home to roost; the inactivity of the night also served to intensify the pain. He screeched out in agony.

He felt totally helpless and vulnerable, and he desperately needed to go to the toilet. The consequences if he didn't accept the pain for this chore were just too embarrassing to consider.

There were tears streaming down his face eleven minutes later as he crawled out of his bathroom and rested flat on his face on the landing for a few minutes. He was disturbed some time later (it could have been seconds, it could have been half an hour) by the ring of the telephone. He gathered together all his energy and willpower and made it to the phone just as it stopped ringing.

It was a Saturday morning and he wasn't due back at work until Monday morning, so it was unlikely to be North Bridge House on the phone looking for him. He thanked his lucky stars (Paul Newman and Barbara Parkins) that he wasn't currently working on a case. Superintendent Thomas Castle, sympathetic to Kennedy's back problems, was keeping his load light. Kennedy thought his superior might not be doing him any favours. He had too much time to think about things, like the thoughts he had been having about Miss Chada the previous evening. The phone rang again.

Bizarrely, it was Miss Chada. How was he feeling?

"I've had better nights," he replied.

"Are you still okay for this afternoon?" she enquired.

"Yes, but I…"

"What is it Mr Kennedy?"

"Okay," Kennedy began with a painful sigh, "I… my back, it's got worse… much worse…"

"I can hear," she sympathised. "Are you mobile?"

"Not very."

"I can come to your home. You wish Mr Kennedy?"

"But I thought…" he started, remembering an earlier, typically short conversation of theirs.

"I think I know you well enough to trust you, Mr Kennedy," she continued. It sounded like she was flicking through the pages of her diary. "Now find somewhere comfortable and supportive to sit. Place a hot water bottle in the small of your back. Soak in a hot bath. I'm booked up until after lunchtime. I can come to you at two-thirty."

"Good," Kennedy said, feeling a little better immediately. He wasn't sure if she'd heard him or if she'd already hung up.

Kennedy returned to his sofa, catnapped there through a couple more hours, then crawled back to the bathroom, ran a hot bath and, very gingerly, managed to lower himself down into the steaming water. The relief he found when he settled down into the bath compensated for the pain he felt while doing so. He kept heating up the water from the hot tap until, a lot quicker than he expected, he heard the doorbell ring.

CHAPTER TWO

It took Kennedy six minutes to flop out of his bath, towel himself as best he could, put on his bath robe, and hobble down, with the aid of his highly varnished banister, to the front door.

It took only five minutes for Miss Chada to help Kennedy into his ground-floor kitchen-cum-dining-cum-living area, sit him down straddle-like on her work chair, start to work on his neck and ease up his back pain.

Her fingers worked their magic so aggressively it was very clear she had neither time nor patience for his pain. She offered no sympathy to Kennedy, barely saying a word to him in fact. So focused was she on her task, it appeared as though she was exorcising his demons. Kennedy imagined how Lazarus must have felt.

After ten minutes intense work on his neck, Kennedy could feel the heat on his skin build up until he was sure it was scorched and most surely blistered.

"Do you have water to drink?" she asked. Her voice sounded like a shy whisper, slightly throaty.

"In the fridge," Kennedy mumbled from somewhere in the Twilight Zone.

"That feels a lot better," Kennedy said, gingerly rubbing his neck and half expecting his back to make him pay heavily for the cost of lifting his hand to such a position.

Miss Chada opened the door to the large Siemens silver fridge.

"Ah I see. No girlfriend?"

"No," Kennedy conceded. "Is it *that* obvious?"

"Boys only shop for one day," she replied, her eyes still doing a recon of his mostly empty shelves. "Boyfriend?"

"No," Kennedy said, making a feeble attempt at a smile.

"No one to take care of you?" she continued in her comma-less diction, as she searched the cupboards for two glasses, which she examined closely. "Very clean for single man. Very clean house."

"Thank you, and I live by myself."

She squinted sternly, destroying the incredible lines of the natural beauty of her nose and eyes. "But I still see a woman's touch in your house. Your curtains are too gentle for a man. Very tastefully done."

"There was...," Kennedy started. Kennedy thought of ann rea. There was no short way to describe ann rea and his relationship with her, so he didn't even try.

"Ah I see," she said, nodding knowingly, as she poured two large glasses of water. She walked back to Kennedy and handed him his glass. She was very light on her feet. She was now close enough for him to see she was quite flushed and there were several beads of sweat on her brow and below her eyes. Strong and all as he knew her to be, her massage must, of course, be as taxing on her as it was on her client.

She took a long swig of cold water and then held her glass up and cooled her brow and cheeks with it. The manoeuvre looked very sensual, although Kennedy was sure she was totally unaware of this.

"You're in very bad shape," Miss Chada said, "worse than I thought. You look poorly Mr Kennedy."

"Christy, please call me Christy."

She smiled; it wasn't a shared smile but a very private one.

"No, no, I didn't mean..." Kennedy began, fearing she might be thinking he was trying to get fresh with her. She probably had to put up with advances from patients all the time. She looked absolutely amazing. He couldn't remember ever thinking this before about her. In the last few minutes, they had spoken more than they had in the previous twelve months.

Miss Chada smiled again, this time a generous, shared smile. She always looked as if she were in her own wee world though. Kennedy had put this down to the fact that she needed to go to her own space to get her through manipulating other people's bodies to try and heal their various ailments.

"Please drink water," she began, avoiding addressing him by name. "I need to do some more work on your neck and back. You have music you like?"

"Ah, yes..."

"It will help distract you from my work," she began, and thought for a second before adding, "It helps me too."

These four words were the first words between them that could be interpreted as in any way personal in the year she'd been treating him.

"You put on the music. I'll bring in my treatment table," she ordered as she left Kennedy. As he stood up, he was shocked by how pain free his movement had now become. He went to his music room under the stairs and selected *Astral Weeks*, and soon the (perhaps) greatest forty-six minutes and five seconds of music produced in modern times was filling his house.

Even though it was a warm June day, Miss Chada still had her fresh white towels, which she layered over Kennedy and moved around him to accommodate the areas of his body she was working on.

She didn't speak for the duration of *Astral Weeks*, and as the final piece of music came to its abrupt end, she said, very, very quietly, "What was that? I have never heard anything like that before in my life."

She seemed genuinely overcome by what she'd been listening to.

When Kennedy explained the little he knew of Van Morrison's masterpiece, she asked if he would mind playing it again.

Again no words passed between them as they listened to the music and she worked, sometimes gently and other times violently, on his body.

The aches that had been troubling him were now slowly evaporating. He actually thought he could feel the stiffness and soreness leaving his body in waves of heat.

At every break, Kennedy half expected her to say, "Right. That is it. I need to be going now." But on and on she kept working at his body. She spent an extremely painful (for Kennedy) twenty minutes, bringing tears back to his eyes as she tried, and eventually succeed, in releasing the knots in his fingers and toes. Occasionally she would pause to catch her breath, cool her brow and have a sip of water. But all the while Mr Morrison cast his mesmerising spell around them both. By the time *Astral Weeks* concluded its second cycle, it was just before five o'clock.

"When did you last eat?" Miss Chada asked.

Kennedy struggled to remember.

"I thought so," she chastised. "Your body also needs food to help it recover. Your aura is still unbalanced."

Okay, Kennedy thought, *right there you just lost me.*

She made him sit upright on one of the kitchen chairs and started reiki treatment. He could feel the heat from her palms even though she never actually placed her hands directly on his head. He could physically feel a great weight lift off his shoulders.

"There," she said, "that is better much better. Now let's eat. I'm hungry."

She looked in the fridge.

Kennedy looked embarrassed. Did she not trust him to eat? Was he really in such a bad state that she felt she had to baby-sit him?

"Don't worry. I have an idea." She fetched her mobile from her black rucksack, punched in a few numbers very quickly and said something in a foreign language. The only part Kennedy recognised was his own address.

"Just give them twenty minutes. Then I guarantee you'll enjoy the best Indian food you've ever tasted."

"Good," was all Kennedy could find to say.

"You have shower I can use? I like to enjoy my food. I can't enjoy my food when I'm…"

"Of course; it's at the top of the house. I'll show you," Kennedy replied, kicking himself for reading too much into a simple hygiene request.

Kennedy escorted her and her rucksack to the top landing and pointed her in the direction of the shower, a half a flight up from his own bedroom. He disappeared into his bedroom to replace his dressing gown with a T-shirt and light black linen trousers. As he stopped to put his feet into his trousers, he found himself more impressed by the fact that his back appeared totally pain free than he was by the fact that a beautiful woman was naked and entering a shower about ten feet from where he stood.

Kennedy was down in the kitchen serving the Indian takeaway on to two large plates in the centre of the table when he heard her footsteps on the stairs. He thought she'd ordered enough food for a feast as he uncorked one of the two chilled bottles of wine in his fridge.

She was barefoot and wearing very expensive-looking Prada tracksuit bottoms with a vibrant blue sweatshirt. Once again, her face appeared flushed. Her long black hair still looked a little damp. Kennedy enjoyed a moment of feminine perfection and then scolded himself for ruining it with an, albeit brief, sexist image of her feeding him his food.

"You are very clean Mr Kennedy. Your bathroom is very clean. Your bedroom is very clean. Your house is very clean. Clean is good. I like clean," she smiled. "I am Sharenna, Mr Kennedy."

"And I am Christy," he said as he poured her a glass of wine, thinking if he had to pick one word, other than stunning, to describe Sharenna Chada, it would be "clean."

She was very polite; she always spoke in short comma-free sentences; she didn't talk much about herself save that her mother was a Fijian Indian, her father was from Malaysia, and she was born in Woodstock, just outside of Oxford. She was very passionate about her food and kept saying that she would need strenuous exercise to work it off. Kennedy pulled himself up short just as he was about to tell her he thought she had the perfect figure. He felt there was no statement surer to send her running for the front door. He was at least ten years older than her, for heaven's sake, and was this any way to treat a lady who'd given up her Saturday afternoon to massage away all his aches and pains?

Kennedy told her about ann rea - the whole story about ann rea.

"Men and women want too much from love," she said. "Our lives are bigger than love. What is love? Love is for when you're old and you've lost your passion. Love is companionship. Love is for when you witness your partner's body slowly age and unconditionally forgive them for it."

"Wow," Kennedy said.

"No, no. I see in your eyes Mr Ken... sorry... Christy. I see in your eyes that you don't believe this. Tell me did you ever feel a love which was stronger than what I was able to do for your pain this afternoon?"

"But we're talking about two different things."

"No we're not," she said forcefully. "The mistake men and women make is that they think once they fall in love they'll be in paradise. Then they realise that paradise is just a word. But look at you and ann rea. Once you fell in love you were lost. Love did nothing for you. Most people go through exactly what you went through. Unlike you, most people feel that to protect this big love or capture this mystical love they must get married or move in together. In order to develop as people we need to learn that 'loving' really is just a higher degree of 'liking.' Maybe if we can accept this fact we have a better chance of nurturing our relationships. If we accept this fact as a benchmark then we reach a good starting point."

"But that's so cyn…"

"If you don't dismiss me as being cynical about love I will show you Christy. I will really show you."

They were finished their food, and as Kennedy cleared it away, she opened the remaining bottle of wine from the fridge. She seemed to be noting and approving of the way Kennedy dealt with the dirty dishes and the remains of the food.

She refilled both their wine glasses from the new bottle, and Kennedy could see she was really enjoying their exchange. He suggested they move to the more comfortable sitting room, one floor up, and put on some music. She said she'd prefer he didn't put on a CD; she said music was for listening to, but right now she wanted to talk. She also added that it might be nice to listen to *Astral Weeks* again later.

The conversation was initially lighter than it had been downstairs, a bit of joking about Christy always calling her Miss Chada and she always calling him Mr Kennedy, a way, she said, to ensure she kept a distance from her clients.

"Do you have a boyfriend?"

"No," she whispered, "nor a girlfriend."

"Ever?"

"Oh Christy please. You mustn't patronise me either if I'm to show you. Just because I understand the shortcomings of love doesn't mean that I don't seek fulfilment."

"What is it that you're going to show me?" Christy felt compelled to ask.

"I will show you something bigger than love. I will prove to you that the love you so desperately sought with ann rea was quite possibly the reason your relationship with her failed."

Okay, Kennedy thought, *right there you've got me again.* He then refilled their empty wine glasses, finishing off the bottle.

"No more wine. We've had enough. You really need to be able to see.

To be able to feel..." she said as she, very quietly and sensuously, stood up in front of Kennedy.

There were no embarrassing movements, no feeble attempts at lap dancing or pulling shapes, exotic or otherwise. Even the self-conscious semi-smiles were noticeable only by their absence. Miss Sharenna Chada very gracefully removed her track suit bottom and blue top and stood before Kennedy, a proud, stunningly beautiful, firm-bodied woman wearing nothing but her white briefs.

Kennedy had never seen a vision like her in his life - no, not in person, nor on the small screen, large screen, nor even a photograph. He sank back into the sofa, his jaw dropping.

"No. No this is not it," Sharenna whispered, sounding a little disappointed. "My body is not it. Not what I wanted to show you. This is only an instrument."

In the fifties movies, this is where the screen would fade to black, and the last thing you would see in focus would be the romantic hero leaning over a bed, but with his foot still touching the bedroom floor. In modern terms, Miss Chada quite simply bonked Kennedy's brains out.

There was one moment when he realised the reason why Miss Chada had spent so much time, attention and energy working on his back; she had wanted him to be fit for their prolonged horizontal activity. She showed him in no uncertain terms (and repeatedly) the power and attraction of pure, unadulterated lust. To make sure Kennedy wasn't confused in what he was experiencing, she permitted no kissing nor offered cooing endearments.

They fell asleep in each other's arms and bodies, complicatedly intertwined, at one-twenty the following morning, both totally and exquisitely exhausted.

When they woke on Sunday morning at ten-thirty, she advised Kennedy that she couldn't possibly be seen leaving his house in daylight. So they stayed in bed all day long, where she continued to give practical and effective demonstrations on her theory, breaking only occasionally for food and for her to do some much needed maintenance work on Kennedy's back. She left at eight-ten on Sunday evening after he'd used the last of his energy and the last of his eggs to make her an omelette. This time though she was the one who immediately washed the dishes and tidied everything away.

She left him on his doorstep acting, Kennedy thought, for the benefit of the neighbours, more as a masseuse than a lover.

Did they grow closer? No, of course not.

Did they care for each other? Perhaps, but maybe only in the way a racing driver cares for his car.

Did they get to know each other better? Only physically.

Was the sex the best Kennedy ever had? Quite possibly.

Did he miss the "love" element? No, not so far.

Why him? That's what Kennedy would like to have known, but he felt it might be counter-productive to enquire at this stage in the proceedings. On top of which, just before nine o'clock, he fell, happily exhausted, into the best sleep of recent months.

CHAPTER THREE

The next time Kennedy visited his study, the green new-message light was flashing on his answering machine. He was enjoying his new mood so much that he ignored it and was on his way to the ground floor when the phone rang again.

Kennedy immediately had a flash of his parents up at their home in windswept Portrush. They could be reaching out to him. Although they were always extremely happy when he rang them, they never ever rang him unless it was about something important. He picked up the phone.

"Ah, Kennedy," the familiar voice announced confidently and loudly, "you're there. Right, my good man, I've decided it's definitely time for you to get back in the saddle again."

"Hi, sir," Kennedy replied, feeling his new mood of contentment evaporate as his superior, Superintendent Thomas Castle, continued, totally ignoring Kennedy's greeting.

"There's a body, Kennedy, quite close to you in fact."

Kennedy instantly had a flash of ann rea comatose on the canal bank by her barge.

"It's very bizarre, in fact," Castle continued. "This chap, it seems was… ah… indulging in some self-pleasuring activity, and either he used it intentionally to top himself or it all went horribly wrong and he accidentally killed himself. It's just the other side of the canal from St Mark's Church in Prince Albert Road, just by the bridge."

"Do you mean the house with the detached swimming pool?" Kennedy asked, as he thought once again of ann rea's barge on the other side of the bank and forty yards at most away from the house under discussion.

"Yes, that's the one. That's exactly where he was found in fact, in the building housing the swimming pool. Kennedy, your team are all there waiting for you: Dr Taylor, DS Irvine, and DC Dot King. I ordered them to do absolutely nothing until you arrive. We need to be careful on this one, Kennedy; we need to do it all by the book."

Kennedy never did it any other way.

"I don't recall who lives in that house," Kennedy said.

"No one famous, my man. I don't mean anything like that. It's just when the papers find out how he died, they're going to be all over this and…" Castle uncharacteristically hesitated.

"A politician?" Kennedy offered, trying to help Castle find his words.

"No, no, much more unpopular than that. He was a banker, an investment banker."

***

Detective Inspector Christy Kennedy could feel his confidence growing now; he felt physically taller. He knew Miss Chada was probably responsible for this, but Castle putting him back on a case - even though Castle had admitted he had no one else available - was exactly what he needed.

Kennedy quickly changed into black chinos, his favourite blue shirt, his black comfortable plimsolls and, just in case the temperature dropped, his insulated, black, unbranded windbreaker. His back felt good, but at the same time he was still slightly wary.

Five minutes later, he was standing on the Water Meeting Bridge, looking at the white Regency house with detached indoor swimming pool. The swimming pool building was located quite literally on the bank of the Regent's Canal. ann rea's houseboat was, at the most, a two minute walk, in the direction of Camden Market, on the opposite bank.

Already there was a considerable crowd gathered on the bridge and on the towpath on ann rea's side of the canal. If the amount of texting going on were anything to go by, the gawkers' ranks would swell considerably any time soon. Kennedy wondered if the unwanted attention might catch ann rea's eye or ear.

With the front gates shut the gawkers weren't going to enjoy much of a view though. The brick wall, on the street side of the house, was at least seven feet tall, and the canal bank was heavily overgrown with foliage and trees, including a grand chestnut which separated the corner of the bridge from the grounds of the house.

Kennedy quickly body-swerved his way through the crowd, flashed his warrant card to the constable on the gate (a new face to Kennedy), and nipped into the compact grounds of the house. Eagle-eyed Detective Sergeant James Irvine was the first to spot Kennedy. He quickly made his way across to his superior and shook his hand furiously.

"Ah, we missed you, sir. Absolutely brilliant to have you back in action again. The whole team thinks so."

Kennedy didn't take compliments well.

"It means we won't have to work on shit cases any more," Irvine added, deflating the compliment somewhat.

Kennedy's vivid green eyes smiled his thanks as Irvine led him towards the white stucco building that housed the swimming pool.

"Who found the body, James?"

"Jean Claude Banks, a Frenchman. He's the housekeeper, it seems," Irvine replied, in his usual dulcet, Sean Connery-influenced Scottish tones.

"A male housekeeper?"

"Just wait until you see him."

"The geezer who's trying too hard with the hair and the fake tan?"

"Aye, spot on, sir," Irvine said, breaking into a lopsided grin. "That's him."

"Right. I'd like to speak to him first, please," Kennedy said quietly, and then added as an apparent afterthought, as the ever-lively Detective Constable Dot King joined them, "before I see the body."

"Jean Claude," Irvine began, "this is Inspector Christy Kennedy."

Jean Claude Banks was sixty-plus, slim, dressed all in black except for a pristine white shirt opened a couple of buttons too many, the exposed wrinkled skin visible around his neck betraying his years.

"He's wearing his hair much too long for a man his age," Dot King whispered to Kennedy. "He's older than my dad!"

For all the sniggering, Jean Claude still had a twinkle in his eye and he looked very fit. In fact, he looked like someone who worked out in the gym every day of his life and who had no problem refusing the pick of the contents of the desert trolley. Equally, Kennedy thought, the Frenchman didn't look like someone who was suffering a great trauma over his boss reaching the end of his natural life.

Kennedy, his right hand unconsciously twitching furiously by his side, led Jean Claude away from the ever-growing team of Camden

Town CID Scene of Crime Officers, and they walked through the double-bay car-parking area alongside the swimming pool building. There was a covered cobbled pathway between the main house and the lower level swimming pool building.

"So, Jean Claude," Kennedy began, "when did you discover the body?"

"I came into zee house this morning as usual. Mr Mylan, he is not here. It was perhaps eight a.m. when I arrived to get zee day organised."

"So, you're not his housekeeper?" Kennedy asked, remembering Irvine's information.

"Zee housekeeper? Please, monsieur," Jean Claude protested, "*we* have a housekeeper, Mrs Cynthia Cox. She comes in Mondays, Wednesdays and Fridays."

"Right, I see," Kennedy replied. "She's not in the house now cleaning, is she?"

"No, Inspector Kennedy, she is not, how do you say, 'destroying zee evidence.' I rang her earlier and told her she would not be needed today."

"Good, Jean Claude. Good. Now, you were about to tell me how and when you discovered the body."

"Ah yes. I was surprised Mr Mylan was not in zee home. He likes to start his morning quietly with a bit of a workout - he has a gym just off zee pool. He usually gets up around six o'clock, goes over to zee pool for his workout, swims for thirty minutes, showers out there and returns to zee house at seven. He will then spend an hour doing his emails and getting up to speed before stopping for porridge, honey, and blueberries - *every* morning, zee same," Jean Claude said, sounding a little exasperated, considering his boss' current stone-cold body.

"Every morning?"

"Mr Mylan was in very good condition for a man his age," Jean Claude offered, by way of explanation.

"How old was he?" Kennedy asked.

"He was fifty-two, just after Christmas."

So Mr Mylan had passed over the big five-oh, Kennedy thought. In fact, Kennedy realised he was as far short of the big five-oh as Mylan was past it. He certainly felt a lot younger now than he thought he'd feel when he reached this age.

When Kennedy turned twenty, he'd thought he would feel ancient by the time he was honing in on the half a century, not out. Not out indeed, although he'd a very close call, and his hand instinctively went straight to his gut to try and trace the scar from his wound. Nonetheless, he was beginning to accept his father's approach to the ageing process: starting into a new decade is a lot like considering a new tenner. It's fine when you still have the ten-pound note intact in your pocket, but when you need to break into it, you're always shocked at how fast it disappears.

"How long have you worked for him?" Kennedy asked, consciously pulling himself away from thoughts about the unstoppable ageing process.

Jean Claude's eyes looked to the stagnant canal water, as he appeared to try and focus on Kennedy's question. "Oh…" he began but stopped.

In Jean Claude's pause, Kennedy spotted the rotund Dr Leonard Taylor exiting the swimming pool building.

"Christy!" Taylor involuntary shouted at that precise moment, disturbing the usual stillness of a crime scene. "So, Castle's got you back in the saddle again?"

"Sorry," Kennedy said, just as the Frenchman was about to continue with his answer, "we'll continue this later if you don't mind. I need to have a word with the pathologist before he leaves."

They hugged, although both men for different reasons were unable to circumnavigate the other.

"Something like that," he continued, now answering Taylor.

"How's the back?"

"Perfectly fine now," Kennedy replied, fleetingly thinking of Miss Chada.

"Sad to do this, Christy," Taylor said in a much quieter voice, nodding backwards in the direction of the swimming pool building.

"What can you tell me?"

"Well, it looks like he was trying to achieve higher self-gratification and it all went horribly wrong. I need you to take a look, Christy, so that I can move him and continue my examination."

With that Taylor led Kennedy back through the double glass doors to the swimming pool.

CHAPTER FOUR

Even though it was a fine June morning, the cool air still managed to drag clouds of steam from the hot water of the blue pool. How beautiful and pure a blue the walls and bottom of the pool had been painted struck Kennedy. He found himself concentrating on the power of this blue even at the expense of looking at the body. Once again he was delaying the inevitable meeting with death.

He could feel every single finger of his right hand flex and stretch to the extreme as he turned to the gym section of the pool. There, amongst the various pieces of apparatus, he spotted the deflated carcass of what had once been a human.

Kennedy stood and stared at the body. He had to go to the third person. It had to be Detective Inspector Christy Kennedy who was there now with the good doctor and the victim, one Mr Patrick Mylan. The Ulster detective really did have to distance himself to that degree to get through this. Otherwise he would go off on one of his "How can humans do this to each other?" tangents.

It would appear that the deceased - dressed in a white sleeveless undershirt, blue, red, and black striped boxer shorts and blue socks attached to garters - was in the throes of solo passion, the pleasures of which he appeared to be trying to heighten through strangling himself using a noose made up from a belt looped through its own buckle with the free end attached to a hook inside the cloakroom door. In his efforts to free himself from his predicament, he'd obviously kicked and splattered around, thereby opening the toilet door and displaying his pathetic last scene in all its sordid detail.

In death, the deceased looked each and every day of his reported fifty-two years. Although at the same time he looked slim and fit enough, the ageing process on his tanned skin betrayed his years. He had thick, longish, dyed black hair and was clean-shaven, with no embarrassing ear or nose hair visible. On closer examination, the front of the crown section of hair, at least, had obviously been transplanted; the betraying hairbrush-like clumps of hair were very visible at this close distance. He looked a couple of inches short of six foot. There were no visible marks or scars about the body. His hands and fingernails looked as if they were regularly manicured.

Kennedy stared and stared at the victim's body, but it was saying nothing to him. He needed to hear Mylan's voice. He found that the voice betrayed so much about the owner. Kennedy's mind had now clicked into its professional working gear, and he was very happy he could get on with his work of resolving the cause of death, rather than being distracted by the actual death of a human being.

On closer examination, the toilet and, in fact, the entire interior of the swimming pool building was hospital-ward, disinfectant-smelling clean.

"And the big question?" Kennedy asked, not realising until he'd actually spoken how loudly the echo of the room would amplify his words.

"How long has he been dead?" Taylor whispered. Even at a whisper, his words seemed to go skiing off across the steaming water and returned to them quite a few decibels louder.

Kennedy nodded as he glanced once more at Mylan's remains. It was clear to Kennedy how important the heart was to the body in its daily lifetime efforts to keep pumping blood to all parts of the body and keeping at bay the yellow, shiny hue currently evident on Mylan's body. It really was incredible how quickly the body started to destroy itself. The decaying process that threatens you all of your life takes total control of your remains immediately on your final breath when it sets about returning you to the dust whence you came. With his recent debilitating back problems, the Ulster detective had started, for the first time since he was a teenager, to consider his own mortality, and in doing so, thought maybe it was time to stop waiting around; not that he'd ever considering himself to be waiting around, but with hindsight…

"From the state of the body," Taylor offered, interrupting Kennedy's thoughts, "the rigor mortis has started to wear off, which happens after about a day and a half. The eyes are quite opaque, which shows us he's been dead for more than a day but not quite two. Equally, the eyes haven't started to bulge yet, which confirms it's definitely not three days. I'd think we'd be safe in saying our victim has been dead forty hours max."

Kennedy looked at his watch.

"Which would give an approximate time of death of around six p.m. on Saturday," Taylor offered, confirming Kennedy's maths.

"Give or take?"

"Oh, no more than two hours either way."

"Any notes?" Kennedy asked.

Irvine and Taylor both answered, "No," simultaneously.

"How does this actually work?" Kennedy asked.

"How does what work?" Taylor asked.

"You know, this thing about lack of oxygen giving you greater sexual pleasure?"

"Right, it's known as autoerotic asphyxiation or AEA. Supposedly you experience euphoria when you cut off the oxygen supply to your brain, and if this occurs as you're pleasuring yourself, then…"

"You have twice the fun, or double o' heaven, as we say in Scotland," Irvine offered mischievously.

When Kennedy didn't appear to get it, Irvine explained, "Well, sir, the first 'O' is the noose, and the second…"

"Okay, okay," Kennedy whispered, annoyed more at himself than his favourite bagman.

"I believe our American friends refer to it as 'The Choking Game,'" Taylor added very soberly.

"And is it true, do they, you know… feel better?" Kennedy asked, seeking an end to this part of the conversation.

"Well, all the reports start with the disclaimer, 'It is believed,'" Taylor offered.

"Is it common?" Kennedy asked.

"Statistically speaking, more than we're led to believe, and particularly with young people. The feeling is that a lot of what gets filed as young suicide cases are in fact attempted AEA incidents turned bad," Taylor said with a sigh. "The parents discover the body, feel ashamed, so they reset the scene and remove embarrassing evidence before the police arrive. All this serves to do is greatly distort the stats.

The authorities also seem happy with the cover-up approach. They seem to think if it comes over ground, there could be an epidemic. But really, as with all bogeymen stories, all that's really needed is the light of knowledge shone on it. *This can kill you*, is actually quite a powerful deterrent to the majority of people."

Kennedy recalled a story of a pop star dying under similar circumstances in a lonely hotel room in Australia. He wondered if in that instance the local police had ever considered the incident more a suicide than an attempt at self-fulfilment gone badly wrong?

Kennedy walked around the body, viewing it from as many angles as he could through the various exercising and fitness pieces of poolside apparatus; he was looking for something, a clue maybe, or even just a hint of what had happened. Yes, the SOCO crew would go through the scene with the finest toothcomb for evidence of fingerprints, alien hairs and materials, but what Kennedy was looking for was logic to the proceedings. Something out of place that would ultimately betray the real facts of what went on. One thing would be enough for him, but the lack of a suicide note would not be that one thing for the detective.

"He seemed to be serious in his search for fitness," Irvine offered, breaking into Kennedy's thoughts.

"And quite hard on his equipment," Taylor offered, pointing at wear and tear marks on the heavier gear and the deflated large orange exercise ball close to Mylan's feet.

"What's that used for?" Irvine asked.

"It's for back strengthening exercises," Kennedy replied, remembering some sweat-induced routines he'd been put through himself over the past year. Kennedy had found that aqua treatments had worked best for him, so he'd forsaken everything else. All else that was until ann rea introduced him to Miss Chada.

This is no time to be thinking about Miss Chada, Kennedy thought, as he noticed something.

Taylor immediately picked up on Kennedy's increased alertness. "What?"

"Maybe... can we take the body down carefully please?" Kennedy replied as he continued to examine Mylan's legs.

A couple of the SOCO boys helped Kennedy, Taylor, and Irvine unsuspend the victim. A couple of the girls, including DC Dot King, offered to help in the awkward manoeuvre, but Irvine waved them off. Kennedy wasn't sure if he was trying to spare their blushes or reclaim just a little of Mylan's lost dignity.

Due to the position of the body and the resultant livor mortis, Mylan's ankles, just above his socks, were very dark blue. The smell was unbearable. Kennedy always found this a little weird. Yes, he knew exactly why the decaying process produced such vile and gut wrenching stenches, but the fact was that even in death the body was still capable of well… carrying on, was the best phrase Kennedy could think off. And it was the exact timing of this process that enabled the likes of Dr Taylor to determine precisely how and when the victim had met his end.

"Is there a possibility that he could have died elsewhere and been placed here?" Kennedy asked, now gloved, gowned, and shoed up, as he closely examined the areas just above the calf of Mylan's legs.

"No," Taylor replied firmly, as he gingerly unbuckled the brown leather belt from Mylan's neck. "I was checking the body as we removed it, and there is no evidence of livor mortis discoloration elsewhere."

Kennedy seemed happy with this information.

Taylor handed the belt to Kennedy, who held out a transparent evidence bag from one of the SOCO team for Taylor to place the belt inside.

Kennedy examined the belt very closely, particularly the area around the punch holes. There were no evident wear marks around any of the holes.

"I don't think this was his usual belt." Kennedy passed the belt to Irvine and continued his close examination of the victim's lower legs.

"It looks like our victim didn't normally wear sock garters," Kennedy declared.

Irvine and Taylor looked at him, bemused.

"Okay," Kennedy started, "none of us ever put our socks on in exactly the same position every day, so if we wear tight socks there will be varying degrees of marks on our legs from the numerous sock positions. The oldest will have all but faded, and the most recent will leave clear, precise marks on our skin. Now these garters are much tighter than socks, yet each leg displays only one impression of the elastic."

Taylor crunched his chin up towards his nose. "And the point?"

"Well, either our Mr Patrick Mylan died on the first day he wore garters, or someone wanted to humiliate him in death."

"So, you think there's at least a fifty/fifty chance he didn't commit suicide?" Irvine asked as Kennedy stood and removed the plastic gloves with two loud snaps, which echoed across the still water of the pool. The detective hated the sensation of plastic so tight on his skin. It always left him feeling he needed to inhale deeply to catch a breath.

"I'd say there is a 100 per cent chance he didn't commit suicide. He's not going to want to be found like this now, is he?" Kennedy said.

"So you think he was murdered?" Irvine persisted in a stage whisper.

Kennedy was about to reply, but at the last moment pulled himself up short.

"I know, I know," Irvine said, "let's not get ahead of ourselves."

"Yes, precisely," Kennedy whispered. "Let's let the good doctor here take the body back for a post-mortem, and we'll start our investigation."

CHAPTER FIVE

Kennedy was happy to leave the swimming pool building, especially before the body was bagged. Although the necessary procedure still seemed inhumane to Kennedy, he didn't allow it to bother him any more. His mind was now totally focused on this particular mystery: the "how" and the "why," and then, if there was malice involved, the "who."

"Okay," Kennedy said as he and Irvine emerged to sunshine, "DS King and myself will question Jean Claude."

"*D'accord*," Irvine replied.

"Can you get someone to visit that row of houses at the foot of the garden? They've all got balconies. Maybe someone was sitting out there on Saturday reading the paper or listening to the football results on the radio and noticed something. Has anything useful been discovered in here yet?" he asked as they climbed the steps to the front door of the house.

"Not that I'm aware of," Irvine started, but pulled himself up very quickly and added, "but I'll go and check immediately."

"Good. Could you track down the house cleaner too and see what information she has. And maybe see where it would have been possible to buy men's garters. I can't imagine too many places having them in stock these days. We're very nearly two days behind on this one, James; it's vital we catch up as quickly as possible."

Irvine veered right and bounded up the stairs, while Kennedy turned left and headed toward the kitchen where he found DC Dot King.

"Right," Kennedy said, as he quickly looked around the brushed-chrome finished, ultra modern kitchen, "and who's with Mylan's man?"

"He was here a few minutes ago, brewing up a coffee for everyone," King replied.

"Could you do me a favour and go and find him, please?"

Head down, her mop of black curly hair obscuring her face and her thoughts from her boss, King speed-walked out of the kitchen.

Kennedy walked over to the back part of the kitchen, which opened out through the original back wall of the house into a conservatory. The garden beyond was small and wasted to pathways and paving. Due to the high, dense foliage along the left hand perimeter of the garden, Kennedy had totally forgotten how close they were to the Regent's Canal; it was just the other side of the overgrowth, in fact. From the conservatory, he could see the swimming pool building to his extreme left and, rising high above the trees, the magnificent St Mark's Church. Kennedy had once, in the company of ann rea, been there to a reading and talk by local author, playwright, and all round national treasure Alan Bennett. Kennedy was amused that the last time he'd visited a church had been for a non-religious, fund-raising event.

He wondered if he could see ann rea's multi-coloured barge from the end of the deceased's garden. Probably not. He considered whether or not her close proximity gave him a justifiable excuse to go and knock on her door and ask if she'd seen anything and then to ask, "Oh, and by the way, exactly why have you been ignoring me for the last few months?" Okay, maybe not. He found his mind drifted very, very quickly to Miss Chada and he was disappointed in himself for doing so.

He sat down in the one and only high chair in the conservatory; Miss Chada had instructed him to avoid low soft chairs for the foreseeable future. He studied the house whose garden bordered Mylan's tiny yard. The narrow balcony, with black iron railings and steep sloping roof supported with uprights from the railings, reminded him of some of the Brighton seafront houses. It would have been very easy for neighbours, maybe sunning themselves or reading the papers, to see directly into the conservatory where Kennedy now sat. He wondered how much Mylan used the room. He looked around the modern furnishings and spotted an uncomfortable looking grey ottoman, close to the garden-side glass wall. He noticed the distinctive pink hue of the *Financial Times*. He checked the date. It was the weekend edition, which meant that Patrick Mylan had been alive, well and reading at least on Saturday morning. Apart from the *FT*, the conservatory was incredibly tidy. He wondered if Banks had tidied the place up when he'd arrived. Then he had a flash: had the Frenchman also acted as though he were one of those concerned parents Taylor had been talking about, the ones who cleaned up any embarrassing literature from the scene of the crime?

"He's not in the building, sir," the young and enthusiastic DC Dot King said breathlessly as she returned.

Kennedy counted to seven under his breath. Instead of getting mad with his team, he forced himself to focus on Jean Claude Banks Could he, in some way, be responsible for the death of his boss? Had he returned to the scene of the crime to tidy up and ring the police as a demonstration that he couldn't possibly be the perpetrator and simply walked out of the house and away from the scene of the crime?

Kennedy was ultimately responsible for securing the crime scene. He knew it was his head on the block and not King's or Irvine's. If he screwed up, his boss, Superintendent Thomas Castle, would think he'd brought him back to a major case too quickly. But Kennedy could use as mitigating circumstances the fact that he'd solved the case in, he looked at his watch, less than twenty minutes. Surely that must be a record for Camden Town Criminal Investigation Department, maybe even for the whole of Scotland Yard as well? The butler *had* done it, and Kennedy had allowed him to slip out from under his nose.

But he was a Frenchman in London, for heavens sake; surely it couldn't be too difficult to apprehend him. Just send a couple officers over to the new sexy, but very poor use of space, Eurostar terminal at St Pancras. But, Kennedy wondered, why might the butler have done it?

"Do you think it was Banks and he's scarpered?" King asked, with a bit of a quiver in her voice.

Kennedy turned to face her, briefly glancing over her shoulder, back into the main part of the house.

"I very much doubt it," he said, leaving no room for debate.

"How can you be so sure?" King replied.

"Because he's just walked back in through the front door," Kennedy replied, barely above a whisper.

"Excuse me, Inspector," Banks apologised as he walked into the kitchen and put a brown paper bag down on the worktop closest to the coffee pot. "I just nipped up to Anthony's in Primrose Hill to get some sweet breads to go with zee tea and coffee for your team."

Just as quickly as it had drained, the colour returned to DC Dot King's cherubic face.

CHAPTER SIX

Within ten minutes, Jean Claude had coffee and tea on the go, and even better, at least for Kennedy, the tea was amazing. Not too strong, not too weak, and the chocolate croissants went down as an absolute treat. King nodded approval to her cup of black coffee and then at Kennedy. She sat at the table in the conservatory, removed her notebook, and elaborately opened it at a new page.

"How long have you worked for Mr Mylan, sir?" she started. The Frenchman looked to Kennedy as though disappointed it wasn't the inspector who was questioning him.

"I started to work for Patrick," he said eventually, pronouncing the second syllable of his boss's Christian name as though it was a description of a foul smell, "just after his fortieth birthday."

"That would make it twelve and a half years."

"Ah, nearly, Madame," he agreed, lighting up his face with a smile.

"Detective Constable will be fine," she replied; "and all this time you worked in this house?"

"Yes, Detective Constable, I arrived just after he had bought this house. He had just left Credit Suisse and needed a home with more space because he wanted to base his work here."

"What exactly did he do?" the young DC continued.

"He was an investor."

"For other people?" she pushed. Kennedy was content to remain quiet and observe.

"No, only for his own company, although sometimes he would give his friends, and myself, tips on where he felt would be a good place for them to put money."

"Were the tips always successful?"

"Don't you mean, 'Were any of zee tips failures, big failures, the type of failures…'" Jean Claude paused in consideration. He did a funny thing with his jaw - he kept his mouth shut and moved the bottom half of his jaw from side to side a few times - before continuing, "'…the type of failure which could threaten ones' health?'"

"Well, now you come to mention it."

"Ah, yes," Jean Claude replied. He smiled again, looking very pleased with himself in an Inspector Poirot kind of way, "They say that gambling can damage your health. But all I can tell you is that Mr Mylan's tips were slow burners, and if one troubled one's self to get involved and one was prepared to take a long view on zee project, then I believe one did well."

"Did you ever lose money on any of Mr Mylan's tips?" King asked, now sounding a wee bit impatient.

"I'd have to consult my portfolio for you, but overall I believe I am up, and doing better than if I'd invested zee same money on deposit at the bank."

Kennedy caught King's eye and gave her a brief nod encouraging her to move on.

"These friends of Mr Mylan's, could I please have their names and contact details please?"

"It feels so… it feels like a betrayal," Jean Claude started.

"Mr Mylan is dead, sir," Kennedy stated. "For the moment, the best we can say is that he died in mysterious circumstances, so all you are guilty of is helping us find out what actually happened; you are not being disloyal to him or any of his friends."

"Yes, Inspector Kennedy," Jean Claude replied, visibly moving into another gear, "Okay, let's see… his best friend - well, I suppose he had four very close friends really. They are all from zee Credit Suisse days. He was with Credit Suisse for a long time - over ten years I believe - and a lot of his acquaintances are from that time. Martin Friel and Tony Stevenson, then there was Roger Littlewood and his wife Maggie. Maggie was very fond of Patrick…"

Jean Claude left the words hanging in the air.

"Did they ever…" Kennedy started, needing this all spelt out. It was better getting the important facts right at the beginning, rather than amassing and chasing down misleading and potentially time-wasting leads.

"No, no, no, not fond of him in that way," Jean Claude replied, looking happy that Kennedy had taken the bait. "She cared about him. She was always checking to see if he was taking proper care of himself."

"We'll come back to this later, but for now, could you continue with his close friends?" Kennedy asked, nodding in the direction of King's notebook and her growing list of names.

"*D'accord.* Let's see, ah, Martin and Tony, Roger and Maggie, Nealey Dean..."

"Nealey Dean, the actress?" King interrupted, quite literally spitting out the name in disbelief.

"Yes, that's her. They were all around here a couple of weeks ago for dinner. In fact, that really was his ideal get-together: Martin and Tony and their wives, Roger and Maggie Littlewood, Nealey Dean and Tom Dickens."

"Nealey Dean and Tom Dickens are dating?" King said in disbelief, immediately looking as if she regretted her involuntary reaction.

"No, no," Jean Claude replied, looking happy to have some inside information to share. "I believe most of zee people around the table had hoped Patrick's attempts at matchmaking would stick, but neither the actress nor the singer seemed interested in each other in that kind of way, although they seemed to get on well, and they shared zee same sense of humour."

"And that's all Mr Mylan's friends?" Kennedy asked.

"Well, yes. I mean, of course he had lots of other acquaintances, business contacts and what have you, but zee group at the dinner table on Friday past would have been his inner circle."

"What about his own family?"

"He never shared the details with me, but I believe his mother died when he was young and he hadn't spoken to his father in over thirty years. I could be wrong about that though. I don't believe he has any brothers or sisters, but I don't know for sure. I think Maggie Littlewood knows a little bit about his early life."

"Girlfriends?" King enquired and then added immediately, "Boyfriends?"

Jean Claude Banks starred intently through the glass of the conservatory in the direction of the swimming pool building where Mylan's body had been found.

The Frenchman raised his eyebrows, moved his lower jaw from side to side, shook his head sadly for quite a few seconds before saying, "It seems he took no comfort from woman nor man."

"But did he have a girlfriend or a boyfriend?" King asked again, this time more directly.

Jean Claude arched his shoulders as if to suggest he wouldn't know.

"What were your working hours?" Kennedy asked, deciding to move on but at the same time wondering what he was hiding.

"I'd get here for eight o'clock and leave about seven in the evening on weekdays, unless he was entertaining. Sometimes on Saturday evenings, if he was entertaining, but Saturday during the day was always sacrosanct; that was zee time he wanted to be alone. I rarely worked for him on a Sunday, although I was always available when needed."

"And Saturday just past?" King asked.

"No, he didn't need me this weekend. He wasn't entertaining on either day, so I didn't see him at all."

"When was the last time you saw him?" Kennedy asked.

"Friday, when he returned from lunch. We went through his emails, and he said that was it, he didn't feel like doing anything that afternoon and he'd see me on Monday."

"How did he seem?" Kennedy continued.

"He seemed very happy to have a free weekend for himself. He was, how you say, in good spirits."

"You've no idea how he spent his weekend then?"

"No. He had a season ticket for Arsenal, but I don't know if they were playing at home. He was a loyal supporter. He was always saying they were a few seasons away from being great, but he'd been saying that since I met him."

"I believe their season is over, sir," King offered. "My Ashley is a supporter, and I think he was happy… well, happy that this particular season was behind them."

"Maybe we could trouble you to tell us what a typical day would have been for Mr Mylan?" Kennedy asked.

"When he was here, he got up around six o'clock, worked out and swam until about seven. He'd come back to the house, spend an hour on his emails, still in his dressing gown from his post-swim shower, have breakfast and read his papers from eight o'clock until about nine, and then he dressed."

"Okay, let's stop there for a moment," Kennedy said, trying to figure out the best way to word his next question. "Did he dress from habit, or would he have a variety of clothes he wore?"

"Sorry, I don't understand."

"Ehm, did he have a look? You know: a set of clothes, style if you will, that he was happy with."

"Ah, I see what you mean. Well, since he left Credit Suisse, he never wore suits or, how do you say…blazers, he never wore a blazer. He wore a clean shirt every day, varying colours, mostly blue, pink, and dark striped. He never wore a cravat, no I didn't mean a cravat, I mean…"

"Oh, you mean a tie," King offered helpfully.

"Yes, a necktie. Sorry, it's still zee simple words that elude me. He wore black, traditionally cut trousers, either a leather jacket or a wind-breaker, and polished loafers. He never wore a jumper or a cardigan, but he would wear an overcoat over his jackets in the winter."

"And socks?"

"Socks?"

"Yes. Some people feel more comfortable in more sober-coloured socks, and some people like their socks to be bright exciting colours."

"Ah, I see. He liked to wear black, dark blue, and brown socks, so you would say he liked to wear more sober socks."

"Right," Kennedy replied hesitantly. He still hadn't reached the point of this line of question, and he didn't want to accuse himself of leading the witness to where he wanted to go. "Ah…"

"One other thing," Jean Claude offered, while appearing to be deep in thought.

"Yes?" Kennedy and King asked in unison.

"Those elastic suspenders Patrick was wearing at zee time of his death…" the Frenchman hesitated.

"Yes?" Kennedy nudged gently.

"They were not his; well, at least I'd never seen him wear them before."

"Okay." Kennedy was pleased with himself but not showing it. "So we were up to nine o'clock when he got dressed - then what was his routine?"

"Then he'd go to his office and work through until around eleven-thirty, eleven forty-five."

"Would you be in the office with him?"

"Sometimes, not all of the times. It would depend on whether he needed me or not."

"For instance?" King asked simply.

"Well, Patrick would be on the phone, ringing around his contacts, checking out things, monitoring what was happening in the market. He spent a lot of his time researching new stocks, and that is where I would help him. Someone would drop him a name of a new potential invest-ment, and he would have me do as much research as possible on the company."

"Did he do well at it?" King asked. Kennedy subtly nodded his ap-proval to her.

"Well," Jean Claude started, his eyes now leading them in an arc around the house, "I believe he did very well in zee good days. He had some land in Ireland, a property in California, and a large coun-try style house in Nice. He and Tony and Martin had made quite a few robberies."

"Sorry?"

"No, no, excuse me, of course I did not mean robberies, I mean… killings. That was how Mr Mylan used to describe them, he would do a killing."

"Make a killing?" Kennedy offered.

"Yes, yes, make a killing, that's how he would say it. They would buy into companies when zee shares were almonds… No?" he added when he saw how blankly the Camden Town CID officers were look-ing at him.

"I think you mean peanuts," Kennedy offered.

"Maybe," Jean Claude said, looking very confused and sounding very French. "They would buy bulk shares very cheaply, and then as the shares rose, Mr Mylan would take out only his initial investment and leave the rest of his shares to mature. That's why he studied what was happening on the market so closely each morning, so that he would know when to sell. But he was happy to be cautious in these troubled times."

"Did he invest in currencies?" Kennedy asked.

"Never," Jean Claude said firmly. "I know he had euro, sterling, and dollar accounts to cover himself, but speculating on currency was not something that interested him."

"Okay, so we're up to midday?" Kennedy said.

"Yes. Mr Mylan would generally leave the house just before twelve…"

"For lunch?" King suggested.

"No, no. He was very, very keen on playing tennis. He tried to play every day during zee week, indoor or out depending on the season. This time of the year he would head over to the courts in Regent's Park, meet up with a partner or his coach and play a few games before lunch."

"Who would he play tennis with?" King asked.

"Mostly his friends - the ones I mentioned from the dinner party. Or his coach, or people he'd met over the years at the courts. He and Tony Stevenson played together a lot. Mr Mylan would frequently say Tony was superb at tennis. Mr Mylan was very, very serious about his tennis. Then he'd have a late lunch."

"With his tennis partner?" King again.

"Sometimes yes, sometimes by himself. I'd pick him up at the courts around two o'clock."

"Ah, so you were also his driver?" Kennedy asked.

"Yes, in recent times. I mean, I was at the beginning, but then because I didn't know London all that well, we hired a dedicated driver, but Mr Mylan wanted me to do it again. He said he didn't like anyone other than me being with him all the time."

"Did he have a regular place he went to for lunch?" Kennedy continued.

"Regular?"

This conversation was starting to remind Kennedy how he'd felt when he first came over from his native Portrush in County Antrim, Northern Ireland, all those years ago. Until that point, he hadn't realised he had an accent, let alone how strong it was. People would just stare at him blankly when he said something that, as far as his own ears were concerned, was perfect Queen's English. He quickly learned to have a list of alternates or wee trick phrases for the troublesome words. For instance, Wimbledon became "the place where they played the tennis," and "films" were "movies." The numbers three and eight were very difficult to understand in his strong Ulster accent, so he'd say, "One, two, *three*," and "You know, the number between seven and nine."

"You know: common, frequent, favourite," he offered.

"Ah, favourite," Jean Claude replied, looking relieved. "For lunch, he would generally go to his club, Two Brydges, in the West End."

"And then in the afternoon?" Kennedy asked, as King seemed content to scribble in her book.

"He'd get back here about three-thirty and do another three hours of emails, and then he'd check in with people to see what was going on. Most days I'd go home around seven, and he would have zee evening to himself. If he was entertaining, he would generally request me to stay around."

"And if he needed to go out?" King asked.

"He was happy taking occasional taxis; he said taxi drivers were the best people to learn from what was happening in the country."

"Do you know what he did when he was alone here in the evenings?" King asked, unable to avoid a quick glance in the direction of the swimming pool building.

"Do you mean did he entertain girlfriends?"

"Well, yes, I suppose so."

"I know not of that side of his life."

Kennedy found this hard to believe, while at the same time admiring the Frenchman's loyalty.

"Were you aware," King started off confidently enough and then faltered, "you know, when you found him this morning… were you surprised?"

"Surprised that he was dead?" Jean Claude gasped in shock. "Why, of course."

"No, I mean, surprised at what he appeared to be doing at the time of his death?"

"And what was he meant to be doing?" Jean Claude asked, now very agitated.

"Autoerotic asphyxiation," King replied.

"Ah, *mais oui,* this is no-thing for a lady to discuss," Jean Claude protested. "But I know nothing of such things, it is enough."

"What is enough?" King asked.

"It is enough of this conversation, please," Jean Claude said, and then turned to address Kennedy. "Please?"

"Okay," Kennedy said to the Frenchman's visible relief. "One final question: can you tell us what you were doing between the hours of four and eight o'clock on Saturday afternoon, early evening?"

"Let's see. I lunched rather late, maybe as late as three o'clock, so

I'd have been in the house until four-fifteen. Then I went shopping in Camden Market. I had a coffee and a maple Danish pastry at a stall near Camden Lock about five o'clock. I did some more walking around my favourite stores and second-hand bookshops until about twenty to seven, when I went to Baroque, had a few drinks, and then dined at Belgo at around a quarter to eight."

CHAPTER SEVEN

"Well," Kennedy whispered to Dot King when they were alone again in the conservatory, "we're making progress. Now we have one alibi to check and the names of seven people who can furnish us with information about Mr Patrick Mylan."

"He seems to me to have been a bit of a loner. I doubt if any of the seven will know a lot about his life, but if you put all their information together, we might…"

Kennedy just looked at her, not in an unkind way; more like a proud parent the second before their child encounters a slight trip-up.

"I know, I know," King offered immediately in her own defence. "I regretted the sentence the second I started it. Of course it's much too early to be making assumptions."

"Tell you what, while we're waiting for Mrs Cynthia Cox, I'd like to visit Mr Mylan's bedroom and study, see what we can uncover there."

Jean Claude was loitering around the entrance hall, which was tiled in checked black and white marble. He appeared to be willing everyone to avoid dirtying the hall or breaking any of the valuable-looking vases on the two dark oak baroque sideboards. Above both were large military style paintings. One depicted a battlefield in the heat and fire of conflict and benefited immensely from an inconsistent red hue. The other picture, of a similar size, was a straight on, full-length portrait of a soldier, perhaps even one of the soldiers from the battle scene, now fully decked out in his parade best.

Kennedy thought Jean Claude's movements were rather amusing: appearing to be shadow-boxing in silence, he was trying desperately to mentally will the members of Camden Town CID to be careful, very careful, in his boss' palace.

Jean Claude froze mid pose when he saw Kennedy approach him.

"Could you direct me to Mr Mylan's bedroom and office or study, please."

"Of course. Let me show you there."

"No, it's okay, just tell us where it is."

"I will have to open both the doors for you."

"Even the bedroom door is locked?" King asked, looking very surprised.

"I thought it was respectful to secure his private spaces."

When they reached the first floor landing, they discovered SOCO officers busy in two of the three rooms. The room at the front was a sitting room, with a good view of the Feng Shang restaurant boat across the road, sitting, as opposed to floating, in Regent's Canal. Also in view, just a matter of yards beyond the boat, was a magnificent bank of tall trees. The room had an extremely high ceiling with floor-to-ceiling windows elaborately draped with fawn material, puffed up here, there, and absolutely everywhere. Set up around the fireplace were a large coffee table and three chunky, uncomfortable-looking, fawn-coloured sofas. Opposite the fireplace was an antique console table, guarded on each side by a pale blue-striped Regency chair, and supporting a large vase of multicoloured flowers. The five large paintings in the room were abstract and perhaps all by the same artist. They looked to Kennedy like a paintings-by-numbers approach, where someone had mixed up all the numbers; the over all effect was a bit more Stallone than Picasso. Kennedy reckoned this might be a dangerous room to enter when you'd had a few too many, with more than a slight chance that the deep-pile cream carpet might enjoy a psychedelic transformation. All in all, Kennedy figured, apart from the obvious vile smell, such an organic change would be infinitely preferable to the works of art on the wall.

Kennedy felt there was no soul to the room. Except for the lack of magazines, it looked more like the waiting room of a very expensive doctor or dentist. It told Kennedy absolutely nothing about Mylan.

The back room was similar in décor, a lot smaller, but equally forgettable.

The third door off the landing, the middle one, was unlocked discretely by Jean Claude, and Kennedy and King entered it hesitantly, putting their latex gloves back on, careful not to disturb anything until the SOCO team had used their fine-toothed comb on it. If Kennedy had ever seen a tidier office, he couldn't remember when. The windowless walls were white and graced by a lone Shepard Fairey *Obama Hope* poster.

The matte-black desk, resting on two sets of grey "A" frame legs, was centred against the middle of the wall opposite the door. On the desk was a modern Apple computer. Two sets of grey shelves were built into the wall, either side of the desk. The files were marked either by years, various research items or various brand names, the most frequent of which seemed to be Airtricity and Nighthawk Energy. To the left of the desk was a smaller worktop of a similar style, accommodating a fax machine, a printer, and a hi-tech phone unit. There were two drawer units beneath, but not supporting, this top.

King continued diligently writing away in her notebook.

Kennedy sat in the Aeron chair by the desk and wheeled himself across the grey-painted pine floor to the drawers and started to check them, careful about bending his back. This line of thought led him again to Miss Chada, and he wondered if he would need to wait for his next appointment with her before he would see her again.

The first drawer, the top one of the left-hand unit, contained office supplies, pens, pencils, erasers, paper, envelopes, and elastic bands, all laid out as though on display in a shop. Next was a drawer full of telephone directories, and then a drawer of odds and sods, including a Tim Dickens *Best of* CD. As yet, however, Kennedy hadn't spotted a CD player. The bottom drawer was completely empty except for about a dozen bars of Green & Black's butterscotch chocolate.

Kennedy shifted his attention to the unit to his right. He pulled on the top-drawer handle. The front section, consisting of a pretty board with all four drawer-fronts, came away in his hand, exposing a shelf-less, empty unit. On closer examination, Kennedy discover a keyhole between the second and third drawer front, a broken lock, and catch and hinges ripped out with screws still intact from the right hand side of the unit.

"Get the SOCO to dust this one down," Kennedy said, stopping to sniff inside the vacant space to see if he could detect what might recently have been there. He got a whiff of something strong, but his memory bank wouldn't recall for him what the scent was.

"Slim pickings here," King muttered as she and Kennedy exited Mylan's office.

"Right," Kennedy announced to the waiting Jean Claude, who was still twitching nervously about what may be going on down below, "we're ready to see his bedroom."

The Frenchman walked them up to the next floor, where the ceiling was still high but not anywhere near as high as on the first two or ground floors.

There were four doors off the second-floor landing. From the back room, Kennedy could see an incredible panoramic view of the ever-buzzy Camden Town. The room, painted in off-white, had a double bed covered in a matching off-white eiderdown. There was a bedside table and wall-mounted reading light on one side only, the right. The bedside table and the thick pile carpet were in the same off-white, and on the bedside was a copy of *Vanity Fair* magazine and three books: *The Private Life of Chairman Mao* by Zhusui Li, *The First of the True Believers* by Theodore Hennessey and *Reporting America: The Life of a Nation 1946 - 2004* by Alistair Cooke. There were no drawers in the bedside table, no shelves on the walls, nor any photos, posters, or paintings upon the walls.

The next door was opened to reveal two members of the SOCO in their transparent-blue, head-to-toe suits, busy going through what appeared to be a bed-less room. Jean Claude walked past the third door and on to the fourth, dismissing the third with, "This one doesn't open from the outside," and unlocked the remaining door. Like the back room, the windows were smaller than downstairs, but enjoyed, in at least forty shades of green, magnificent views of the Zoo and Regent's Park through the tops of the trees. Kennedy noted that the inside of the locked door in the hallway had been rendered into the rest of the way giving him the sense of extra wall space in the bedroom. This room was dark, very dark, with a Japanese-patterned wallpaper with a base of woad blue. The floor was covered with a dark blue carpet, the pile so thick Kennedy felt as if he were walking through fluffy snow. The only thing absent was the sound of the crunch beneath him.

This room was in the shape of an inverted L with, in the toe, the door they'd entered by, a sitting room arrangement of smoked glass coffee table; two matching chairs, one of which was extended into a near horizontal position not unlike an airline's club class seat; a small bookcase just over half full of original Penguin Classics; and a small black box, about eighteen inches wide by two feet tall and two feet deep, which was plugged into the wall. Eventually Kennedy worked out that the entrance to the box was via the top. Inside the cooler/fridge he discovered several bottles of white wine, Champagne, still and fizzy

mineral water, two large wine glasses, and two unopened large tubs of
Ben and Jerry's Chunky Monkey ice cream. The gigantic bed was in
the other section of the L and covered by matching black silk sheets
and pillowcases. Kennedy wondered why there were no blankets. On
the wall opposite the bed was a large, flat-screen Sony television, and
on either side of that was what looked like two matching prints of the
same concubine pleasuring two different men in two different locations.
The prints looked very expensive and better from a distance.

On the other side of the bed, opposite the windows and sitting room
area, was a wall-to-wall, floor-to-ceiling, mirror. On close inspection,
this mirror was made of several mirrors of varying sizes. Jean Claude
demonstrated that each section was push-latch activated and, when
opened, revealed rows and rows of neatly hung clothes and drawers
filled with socks, perfectly folded shirts, T-shirts, and shorts, all neatly
stored in their own compartments. One section, the size of a small
wardrobe, was generously racked with various ladies clothes, which
were, as far as Kennedy's eye could tell, probably still store new. The
final mirror, the one closest to the television wall, was in fact a full-size
door and the entrance door to the bathroom.

The generously sized bathroom betrayed nothing of its owner. Part
mirrored and part white tiled, it looked - and was certainly decked out
- like a bathroom in a high-class hotel. Kennedy noticed what looked
like straight lines cut in the large mirror just about eye height above
the two Edward Johns and Co matching sinks. He pushed the mirror
gently at the intersection of one corner of these lines, and part of the
mirror sprang open, revealing a stainless steel cabinet with four shelves,
all neatly packed.

The bottom shelf had Nivea shaving products, two hairbrushes, a
Gilette G9 super dooper shaver with three spare cartridges of blades.
There was also a black canvas bag which King, safe in her evidence
gloves, unfolded to reveal a set of silver toenail clippers, fingernail clippers, small and large tweezers, two combs, a smallish pair of scissors
with curved blades, and a larger pair of scissors which looked like they
might have been a barber's.

Next shelf up was a glass containing three purple toothbrushes with
different textured bristles, Mentadent P toothpaste, mint mouthwash
and a bottle of stronger-looking Corsodyl mouthwash. Third shelf up
had neat rows of male creams and three tubes of Aloe Vera Gel.

The top shelf contained what Kennedy was really keen to see - Mylan's medication - which was a real disappointment. There was nothing stronger than a couple of packets of soothing Strepsils throat lozenges; several packets of Durex; a bottle of Night Nurse, with the matching Day Nurse; vitamins; a bottle of Ginseng capsules; a couple of packets of amoxicillin; a bottle of liquid echinacea; and a couple of dispensers of very expensive looking Royal Jelly capsules.

Kennedy could find nothing in the bedroom or bathroom to detain him further, so he handed it over to the SOCO team to see what they might unearth.

"From the outside, I was expecting the house to be a lot bigger," Kennedy said as he, King, and Jean Claude made their way back down the stairs.

"Yes, I agree, it is deceptive," the Frenchman declared. "There is some loft space if you'd like to view that," he continued with all the enthusiasm of a deflated estate agent.

"Of course," King replied immediately.

Jean Claude led them back up the stairs again and then along the landing towards the back of the house and there, just before the door to the back bedroom, was a full-length mirror. Jean Claude's delicate touch activated another push-latch, and the mirror gently swung towards them, revealing a steep, narrow, unpainted wooden staircase.

The Frenchman remained at the foot of the stairs as Kennedy and King ascended into the roof space.

King obviously thought they were on the verge of some great discovery because she physically sank on reaching the top step. The space was entirely empty. The floorboards were newly laid pine, perhaps a first step in an unfulfilled refurbishment plan of Mylan's. The loft was incredibly lacking in dust, as was not the case with most loft spaces. Kennedy walked over to the bay window cut into the roof and briefly took in more magnificent views of Regent's Park.

Kennedy turned and walked around the space. It seemed somewhat small for the size of the house, but the majestic red-brick chimney stack stole a good deal of the area. Kennedy figured that if the floor space downstairs was anything to go by, the stack must be in the middle of the house. This obviously meant that there must be a mirror image space on the other side of the stack. He walked over to where the red brick joined the recently painted triangle of white tongue and groove wood at the front. He could find no doorway, and he pushed the wood some-what self-consciously in the hope that another push-latch might be hid-den behind.

"Ah, here it is," King announced proudly from the other side of the chimney as she opened a door in the wood panelling and the smell of dust, age, and a draught of cool air hit them. The door was no bigger than four foot by two foot six. Once King found a light switch on the inside of the wall to the left, they discovered that this area probably hadn't changed since the house was originally built. There were no floorboards, just pieces of plywood haphazardly picking out a path way across the rafters to a large water tank in the middle. Where the back edge of the roof hit the rafters, more plywood was visible, this time forming a platform upon which various bits of discarded furniture and bric-a-brac rested in their last stop before the inevitable dump.

Disappointed but content that there was nothing further to be dis-covered, they retreated and found Jean Claude still waiting for them at the foot of the stairs. He appeared to be preoccupied by his image in the mirror-door.

"The house is more like a hotel," Kennedy began when they reached the front door of the house, Jean Claude having peeled off on the first floor, no doubt trying to ensure the SOCO team did not dam-age his precious ward.

"Sorry?" King asked earnestly.

"There doesn't seem to be any of the owner's personality invested anywhere in the premises. It's like…" and Kennedy paused to put his thoughts into words, "… a show house, which has been dressed for po-tential purchasers to come along and buy it."

"Yes, yes," King replied enthusiastically, "and the wife will say, 'It's got potential, but we're going to need to rip out the kitchen completely and fit a new one, and all the bathroom furniture needs to be dumped and replaced.'"

"Perhaps," Kennedy smiled.

"And the husband," King continued, "will pretty much ignore her until he discovers a room he likes, and then he'll say, 'Okay, just as long as I can have this room and do it out for myself.'"

"Right," Kennedy replied. "Can I assume you and your Ashley are flat hunting?"

"That's the problem working with detectives."

CHAPTER EIGHT

"When was the last time you saw Miss Dean?" Kennedy asked Detective Sergeant James Irvine.

He had borrowed his favourite bagman, who was now acting as his favourite driver, and they were making their way down to Marylebone to interview Nealey Dean.

Nealey Dean's name had jumped out at Kennedy for three reasons when Jean Claude had first mentioned her. The first was that she was an accomplished actress whose popularity was on the rise, thanks mainly to a series of entertaining cocoa adverts she was currently appearing in. The main hook of the adverts was that her new boyfriend was a bit of an old fuddy-duddy, and whereby she was loosening him up a bit by dumping his carpet slippers, cardigans, stuffed owls, antique ornaments, and what-have-you, he had successfully turned her on to the joys of cocoa. Allegedly, cocoa was now enjoying somewhat of a renaissance, thanks to the popularity of the adverts.

The second reason was that Miss Dean had been a witness on the case ann rea had christened the Sweetwater Case; the case which, in fact, had hastened the demise of Kennedy and ann rea's relationship.

The third, and perhaps most important, reason was that she was an acquaintance of James Irvine. In fact they had met on the Sweetwater Case and had continued to keep in contact with each other.

Kennedy liked to have a truth reference while working on his various cases. When you start out on a new investigation, invariably you are walking blind into a totally new world. There was a chance, albeit a slim one, but a chance nonetheless, that every single person involved had something to hide, maybe even together, and so they were going to lie to you. So, he would always try and seek out someone in a victim's group of people that he or one of his colleagues knew, someone, anyone, he could use as a truth reference; someone who could save him a lot of time.

"Ach, you know," Irvine replied.

"I don't know, James," Kennedy replied, slightly amused by his detective sergeant.

Irvine had the reputation of being a bit of a ladies' man, but having said that, he had four main characteristics in the romantic stakes: a) he was always falling in love, deeply, head-over-heels in love; b) just as often as he fell in love, he fell out of love; c) he never cheated; and d) he never told tales or swapped gossip on any of his ladies. He always seemed to fall for the flawed type. One of Irvine's ex-girlfriends, Rose Butler, a staff nurse at the Royal Free Hospital, had confided in Kennedy that she thought James was only interested in relationships that couldn't possibly work out. With Bella Forsythe, she certainly had a point. Dr Bella Forsythe was currently being detained at Her Majesty's pleasure for murdering, not just once but a few times. In fact, it had been Kennedy, Irvine, and the team who had been responsible for her being apprehended.

Irvine cleared his throat in a very self-conscious way.

"James, I'm not looking for gossip here," Kennedy said as they eventually managed to cross the busy Euston Road at the foot of Albany Street. "I just want to know how close youse are."

Irvine took a large breath of air, loudly, and started, "Well, you know, sir, it's at that stage where it could still go somewhere, but she's very, very busy. She's very busy with her career, and she has a very, very full social life."

"Were you aware she knew this Patrick Mylan fellow?" Kennedy asked, thinking that Nealey Dean fitted nicely into Rose Butler's view of Irvine's attraction to unattainable relationships.

"Um, no, but then again I wouldn't know most of her friends."

"And when was the last time you saw her?" Kennedy persisted.

"Well, funny enough, she actually took me to the theatre last Wednesday."

"Oh, what did youse go to see?"

"Some auld tosh that one of her mates was in," Irvine started, and then, obviously thinking that he might be sounding ungrateful, he added by way of justification, "Nealey thought it was 'hard work' as well. But we went to this great place in Soho for a bite of supper afterwards. It was great to see her again."

"How often do you see her?" Kennedy asked, thinking that from Irvine's last phrase it couldn't be very regular.

"Maybe once a week, when she's around."

"So that is quite serious, James?"

"Well, we'll see; she's a canny lass. I like her."

And Kennedy knew that was as much as he was going to get. Which was fine, because they'd just arrived at the corner of Weymouth Street and Marylebone High Street.

Nealey Dean lived on the fourth floor of a refurbished mansion block. The porter recognised Irvine immediately.

"Miss Dean is expecting you, Mr Irvine. She said I was to send you straight up when you arrived."

"Frequent enough a visitor, I'd say," Kennedy muttered under his breath as they entered the lift.

Her apartment door was already open, and a voice from inside called out, "Come on in, James."

Kennedy's brain raced through a few scenarios, all of them proving embarrassing for him.

Nealey Dean had the energy ann rea had had when Kennedy first met her. He wondered if his assumption that ann rea now had less energy had anything to do with the long, laborious process both of them had experienced as they broke up. On reflection, it seemed to Kennedy that they'd started to break up the moment after they'd first slept together. If only he'd realised that at the time, he could have saved himself four or five years.

Nealey bounced up to Irvine and flung both her arms around his neck, giving him a semi-passionate kiss. Irvine didn't try to shy away from the intimacy, but neither did he make a meal of it. Nealey acknowledged Kennedy's presence and didn't want to embarrass either him or Irvine, but both were definitely declaring that a relationship beyond friendship existed.

"Sorry, I just can't keep my hands off him," she giggled as she extended her hand to Kennedy. "I've heard so much about you, Detective Inspector Kennedy."

"Oh, Christy is fine," Kennedy replied, shocked at the strength of her grip and how vigorously she shook his hand. "It's weird, I feel like I already know you."

"Ah yes, as my agent is always telling me, 'the ever diminishing power of telly.'"

Kennedy was still trying to fit Nealey's cute voice to her body, but it seemed somewhat out of place. If bear cubs could speak, Kennedy imagined their voices would sound a lot like Nealey Dean's. She had obviously just been doing her workout because she was wearing thick black tights and a black spray-on top, similar to the nothing-left-to-the-imagination outfit that ann rea had sometimes worn. Miss Dean also had a large snow-white towel around her neck, and her blonde hair awkwardly crunched up into a black Beatles baseball cap.

"James, will you do us up some coffee, please - you know where everything is - and I'll go and have a quick shower," she said as she ran out of her large, tidy living room.

As Irvine did as he was bid, Kennedy wandered around the living room. In one corner, Nealey had her office set-up. On a cork notice-board were several business cards, a sheaf of paid bills, and a good few unframed photos. There was none of James Irvine but one with Nealey between two men, one of whom looked remarkably like the live version of the corpse he'd seen only a matter of an hour ago.

Nealey reappeared within five minutes, by which time Irvine was exiting the kitchen with a beautiful Quaker wooden tray bearing coffee for two, tea for one, and a few toasted cinnamon bagels.

"James, you're a gem," she declared, rubbing her hands together in glee. "I could get used to this."

She was dressed in a large, baggy, light-blue Nike T-shirt and loose fitting, black cotton trousers with white stripes down the sides of each leg. Her cheeks were quite flushed, her face was make-up free, and her shoulder-length blonde hair would be fully dry in about ten minutes. Her dark brown eyebrows intrigued Kennedy.

"Miss Dean…" Kennedy started, but was quickly interrupted by the lady in question.

"Nealey, please."

"Yes, sorry," Kennedy continued as he milked and brown sugared his tea, "I don't know if DS… if James mentioned the reason for our visit."

She shook her head "no" energetically.

"We've reason to believe you may have known a gentleman by the name of Patrick Mylan."

"Yes, I know Patrick," she replied immediately, a bit of the energy draining from her sparkling brown eyes. She was sitting next to Irvine on her country cottage style sofa, and Kennedy was sitting on a matching easy chair to the right of her permanently disused fireplace.

She set down her cup on the tray, and took Irvine's hand tightly in hers.

"Patrick ... is he?... I hadn't thought... ohmiGod, has something happened? I mean, when James said you wanted to come to see me, I figured it might be something to do with you researching the theatre... television even...oh-mi-God..." she babbled.

"I'm very sorry to have to advise you that Mr Mylan was found dead this morning," Kennedy said, stopping her in her tracks.

"OH-MI-GOD!" she said, betraying her Cockney roots for the first time.

"Jeez, James, I'll be scaring you off," she said when she regained her composure.

"Sorry?" Irvine asked, but with his Scottish accent the word sounded very big and important.

"Well, I first met you when you came to interview me about someone I knew, and he turned out to be a... ohmiGod... and now poor Patrick. I'm sure neither of you would be here if there wasn't something suspicious behind his death."

Irvine just patted her hand, while Kennedy asked, "How well did you know Mr Mylan, Nealey?"

"How well can you know anyone?" she began, sounding somewhat evasive to Kennedy. "I mean, now I know he's dead, it seems... like he will probably cut a bigger figure in my life. How did he die?"

"We think he might have committed suicide," Irvine offered, much to Kennedy's annoyance.

"Was there a note?" she asked, now turning to Irvine.

"We're still investigating," Kennedy cut in before Irvine had a chance to respond. "How long had you known him?"

"Woo, let's see." She swept her fingers through her hair, appearing to dishevel it, only for it to fall perfectly back into place. "Tim Dickens, who is a friend of mine, took me to a dinner party Patrick was throwing at his house. That must be nearly three years ago."

"The songwriter?" Kennedy asked, now recognising the third person in the photograph he'd just been looking at.

"Yes, that Tim Dickens," she replied as she smiled at Kennedy. "I can't believe Patrick would take his own life."

Kennedy and Irvine remained quiet, hoping she'd elaborate. Miss Dean looked more concerned than shocked.

"From the little I knew of Patrick, I wouldn't have put him down as someone who'd even consider taking his own life."

"Did you ever have a relationship with him?" Irvine asked.

"Steady on, James," she offered curtly. "That question seems a tad inappropriate.

"I'm sorry, Nealey, I didn't mean it in a personal way. I don't as a rule do jealously on exes. I was asking you in a professional capacity."

"I'm sorry, James. I mean, you've both just totally thrown me; I'm trying to come to terms with the fact that Patrick is dead."

The room fell quiet.

"Okay," she eventually said, slapping herself on her cheeks a couple of times, "right, right, background - you'll be looking for background."

"Yes, we'd be grateful for any information," Kennedy agreed hopefully.

"Okay, I knew Tim Dickens, the singer/songwriter." Nealey obviously noticed Irvine's eyebrows rise at her use of the word "knew," because she paused, didn't quite, but nearly, rolled her eyes. "I mean, I know Tim, he's a good friend, and occasionally I'll be his plus-one, or he'll be my plus-one at functions neither of us would want to go to alone."

"How long have you known him?" Kennedy asked, putting the question he knew was on Irvine's mind.

"Of course all of this was before I met James," and again she paused, and this time she smiled sweetly at the DS. "I was introduced to Tim by a mutual friend. I think they dated, but I'm not quite sure. Anyway, this actress, Suzy, was away on location, and she rang me up and asked if I'd do her and Tim a big favour by attending an award ceremony with him. He absolutely hated them but had to go to this one because he was being honoured. I was happy to. I had a slight fear that maybe it was his sly way of asking me out on a date - you hear all of these stories of rock stars or actors seeing photos of young actresses and then either using their fame to seek out the actress in question's telephone number and cold call her, or have their agent or a friend ring the actress on their behalf. But I really needn't have worried. Anyway, that's me, always looking at the other angle, but it was all cool. He was a true gent, a great storyteller, and absolutely good fun to be with, and even if he hadn't been such good company, the column inches the following morning were well worth it. We became friends, good friends, nothing more," and here she was addressing Irvine directly.

"And Mr Dickens introduced you to Patrick Mylan?" the relieved Irvine asked.

"Yes."

"Did you always see Mr Mylan while in the company of Mr Dickens?" Irvine pressed.

Kennedy felt Irvine just might be guilty of leading Miss Dean on to what he considered a safe path.

"Oh, no," Nealey replied. "Patrick was a collector; he liked to collect things, and he liked to collect friends, and sometimes like all collectors he even forgot where pieces of his collection had come from. I remember one famous dinner party where he'd invited both Tim and me separately and seated us as though he was trying to fix us up. Tim had to remind him we already knew each other. He was crestfallen when he discovered his little bit of matchmaking had failed."

"So, can we go back a wee bit, please?" Kennedy asked. "Initially you met Patrick Mylan when Tim Dickens brought you to his house for a dinner party. What I would like to know is how your own friendship with Mr Mylan started."

"Okay, I see," Nealey replied, running the long slender fingers of her right hand through her drying hair again, "you want to know how I got to know him well enough for him to invite me to dinner on my own?"

"Indeed," Kennedy replied.

"People who regularly give dinner parties are a lot like directors; they both love to have a large cast of people they can draw on. Sometimes, just like directors, hosts will invite people they don't even like, because of how it's going to help the mix on that particular occasion. Great hosts, like great directors, will ensure that every person there will be there for a reason vital to the mix; someone from the pop world, from the theatre, from TV or the cinema, maybe a painter, an athlete, a politician, some people from the real world, and maybe even a character or two from the underworld. If the host picks their cast intelligently, it will be a successful evening. If he or she doesn't get the mix right, the party will be as flat as a pancake. For instance, you can really only have one, possibly two at the most, celebrities. Then, perhaps most importantly, hosts and directors always need to ensure they have an audience present."

"So, Patrick Mylan added you to his potential dinner party cast list?" Kennedy asked, trying to pick the pace up a bit.

"In a word, yes, although he was more subtle than that. He's a very charming man is Patrick. He was never in the thick of it; he just liked to set it all up, put these parties together and sit back and watch all of the interaction."

"He just rang you up then?" Kennedy pressed.

"Well, no, he didn't *just* ring me up. He had more class than that. He rang Tim and asked Tim if it would be okay to ring me. Tim rang me, and I asked Tim if Patrick intended it to be a date? Tim said no, I wasn't his type."

"What did he mean by that?"

Nealey didn't reply. The smile drained from her face. She looked to Irvine as though she wanted him to save her. Irvine toyed with the pen in his notebook. So intent was he on her conversation that he was yet to put the pen to the virgin page.

"Ah, I'm not totally comfortable here, Christy," she whispered, in her cute voice, which made her sound very vulnerable.

"Why so?" Kennedy asked.

"Well, this is starting to border on gossip a bit, isn't it?"

"Nealey, at this stage we're trying to build up a picture of the victim, what he was like. We need to find out about him and his friends and see what happened to him. If we discover what happened was not self-inflicted, then we'll need to work out who did what to him and why. Somewhere in his life story, this information is waiting for us. And yes, bits of what we pick up will be gossip, but if we take an overview from the people who knew him, eventually a true picture will emerge."

"Thank you, Christy, that makes me feel a bit more comfortable. On the occasion in question, Tim told me I wasn't Patrick's type because a) I was too old for him and b) because I had a brain."

"How old are you, Nealey?" Kennedy asked.

"I'm thirty-three."

"Tim didn't mean that Patrick Mylan was into…" Irvine started hesitantly.

"OhmiGod no," she whispered. "You see, that's exactly what I mean about gossip getting out of control. No, Patrick liked his girls to be early twenties, late teens at the youngest."

"And the brain bit?"

Nealey squirmed a bit in her seat.

"Okay, eventually I talked to Patrick about this. He was quite open about it, to his friends I mean. Well, at least to me, so… I suppose what I'm saying is that this bit is not gossip. He liked to be with girls just for the sex."

Now it was Irvine's turn to raise an eyebrow.

"No. I don't believe he treated them badly, but I believe the limits of the relationship were clear to both sides. I say 'I believe' only because I've never really spoken to any of these girls. But it seems they knew what the relationships were about. When they were in his life, they were a part of his life. But there was a big part of his life, the social side, that they weren't involved in. They didn't live with him, but I believe they were taken care of."

"Were they like call girls?" Irvine asked.

"OhmiGod no, James, they were not call girls. It was quite the opposite in fact. Patrick knew his needs, and he wanted to have someone available to satisfy his needs."

"You mean he was addicted to love?" Irvine enquired, trying desperately hard to put a good name on it.

"No, James, I think he was addicted to sex, and I think he was addicted to sex because he'd never known love."

"Were there several of these ladies?"

"No, Christy, as I tried to explain, it wasn't like that."

"I see," Kennedy replied, but wasn't completely sure he did.

"In the time that I've known him, three years, I've heard of only two girls…I'm…"

"What?" Kennedy pushed when she couldn't find the words she wanted.

"I'm terrible, James knows this about me. I'm so intrigued about people and what makes them tick. It's probably got a lot to do with my work, but I do love to meet all kinds of people. It's never gotten me into trouble, but my father says that's more to do with luck than judgement. Also, I'll stick around probably longer than I should.

I always think if I meet someone just one more time, they'll reveal something they've never disclosed before, and I'll solve the puzzle of their personality. But anyway, what was I saying? I told you a wee white lie just there. When I got to know Patrick a bit better and he told me about this, I pushed and pushed until he let me meet his current girl."

"Oh," Irvine muttered, as he looked ready to use his pen for the first time.

"I mean, I pestered him on it. I just couldn't figure out why a woman would stay with a man if he was making it clear that he was only with her for one thing and one thing only. I was beside myself to meet such a person. Obviously, as far as Chloe was concerned, I couldn't let on that I knew the exact details of their relationship."

"Chloe?" Irvine inquired.

"Yes, Chloe Simmons."

"And how did you meet?" Kennedy asked.

"He invited me around for tea on an afternoon Chloe was scheduled to meet him. The plan was that we would overlap by five or ten minutes."

"And?" Kennedy prompted.

"She was stunningly beautiful, very English, pale complexion and beautiful dark brown hair. I think she'd just turned twenty, she'd a good figure. Chloe was funnier than you'd think a beautiful woman should be, and we rabbited away for about half an hour before Patrick started to get twitchy. I wasn't sure if he was scared we were going to become best mates, Chloe and I, or if he was in need of his fix, but he kept looking at his watch and nodding towards the door when he could catch my eye, so I left."

"Did you see her again?"

"What did you learn about her?"

Both questions were asked simultaneously, the first by Irvine.

"No, never, James. I think Patrick was shocked by how well we got on together, so I don't think anything would have been allowed to develop. We didn't enjoy anything more than a surface kind of conversation, Christy. She seemed okay. I think she was aware of how stunning she looked, maybe more sensual than beautiful. She seemed to have a great sense of her own body. Her dress sense was very classic, nothing tarty, but you were aware what an amazing body she had."

Nealey must have noticed something in Irvine that twigged her interest. "What, James? You don't think one woman can appreciate the beauty in another?"

Kennedy liked her spirit; liked the way she was so animated when she talked. She was stylish, she had class, she had the beauty she described in Chloe Simmons, but she didn't look fragile or flawed, which was often the case, Kennedy felt, in truly beautiful women. The detective also loved the way she was picking up on everything, even the unsaid, in the interview. He imagined it was just another example of her previously admitted inquisitiveness, her never-ending research of character traits and flaws.

Kennedy also noted that Irvine had the good sense not to enter an argument he could never win.

CHAPTER NINE

As Kennedy and Irvine were interviewing Ms Nealey Dean, DC Dot King and DS Allaway took Mrs Cynthia Cox into the conservatory to interview her as soon as she arrived at Patrick Mylan's house.

Cox and Dot King immediately clashed. Although Cox gave off the appearance of being a mumsy type, King's first impression was that this was just a cloak for the self-opinionated pain in the butt she really was. On top of which, she smoked like a chimney and insisted that the interview be conducted at the door to the conservatory, so she could hold the cigarette mostly behind her back and flick the ash outside.

Mrs Cynthia Cox, complete with wedding ring, had a chubby face, a French bob of badly dyed, blonde hair and was quite glamorously dressed for a housekeeper. She seemed to be in her mid to late forties. She wore a tight-fitting, blue, knee-length knitted skirt, a loose-fitting white blouse, and she carried a black micro handbag - probably incapable of housing more than her pack of 20 Rothmans and her pink disposable lighter. Her bare legs and arms were tanned, but her face was white. King reckoned she was most probably divorced, living on a settlement and using the cash from house-cleaning as pin money.

"Oh my goodness, Jean Claude will be very upset by all this business," Cox offered unprompted.

"And why would that be?" King replied, unconsciously echoing the hints of Southern Irish just about audible in Cox's accent.

"Oh... all these people in the house will drive him bonkers," she replied. "I have to keep reminding him that it's not *his* house."

"How long have you worked for Mr Mylan?" Allaway asked.

The cleaning lady took another deep drag of her lipstick-smudged cigarette, smiling sweetly - and falsely, King thought - at Allaway, using her free hand to fan away the smoke from her face.

"Well, I've been the lady of the house here through two owners now," Cox began proudly. "I started back when Carlton Davidson, an antique dealer, and his family lived here."

"Do you know what Patrick Mylan did professionally?"

"Well, they say he was one of these new breed of investors, but I'm afraid that doesn't mean anything to me. My father, he was a labourer, born and bred. He worked hard all his life on a farm, and you knew how he earned his money. He'd bring home his pay packet every Friday night to my mother, and you knew where you stood, didn't you? But investing, taking advantage of other people's misfortune, now that's no way to make a living, is it?"

"How did you find him?" King asked, thinking Cox was perfectly well balanced; she'd a chip on each shoulder.

"He was usually in here or in his office."

"No, not where, but how?" King continued. "I mean, how was he to work for?"

"He was a good boss because he was never late with his cash... with his cheques. Mind you, that might have more to do with Jean Claude than Paddy."

She laughed, more of a snigger than a laugh.

"Sorry?" King felt obliged to ask.

"No, it's just he hated to be called Paddy. I mean, he *was* a Paddy, just like the rest of us from the auld sod, but he felt he was better than that. He'd get into a fit if anyone ever referred to him that way. Jean Claude says he refused to have dealings with anyone who ever called him Paddy. He says the boss walked away from a lot of money over the years because of this."

"Saturday last," King started as casually as she knew how, "what were you doing in the afternoon, say between four o'clock and eight o'clock?"

"Oh that's easy. Saturday is my golden day off. I'm not beholden to anybody, well not unless overtime's involved," Cox sniggered. "I slept in - a wee bit too much red wine the night before - so I was running behind all day: late breakfast, later lunch. I'd say I started lunch around three o'clock. Left my house about four-thirty and went for a trawl around Camden Markets. I can get lost in there for hours. I just love their antique stalls, and you can still pick stuff up for a reasonable price.

I had a coffee and a doughnut; you know, there is this great doughnut stall on the way into the market. I find them impossible to resist." She went to pat her stomach but wisely thought better of it and continued, "Did a bit more browsing, had a quick look in at the opticians, just across Chalk Farm Road from the doughnut stall. Too expensive, much too expensive. Then I went to Baroque for an aperitif and then eventually to Belgo at seven forty-five for dinner. I'm afraid it was another late night."

King felt this woman could probably tell her a lot about Patrick Mylan, but she needed to find a way in. She needed to put her at her ease; to unlock the gossip Cox looked like she was raring to get off her chest.

"Tell me this, Cynthia," she began, trying another approach, "do *you* think Mr Mylan committed suicide."

"I think he was perverted yes, but suicidal no."

CHAPTER TEN

Kennedy knew he needed to have another chat with Nealey Dean, but he knew it was equally important he do so without James Irvine sitting nervously looking and listening over his shoulder. So Kennedy and Irvine bade their farewells and set the dials on their Ford Monster for North Bridge House, Camden Town, and the home of Camden Town CID.

By the time they reached the grand building, the oldest in the area and originally a monastery, most of the team had also returned, leaving only the SOCO officers remaining at Patrick Mylan's house.

There was a message awaiting Kennedy when he reached his office. Superintendent Thomas Castle wanted a word with him.

"So," Castle began, inviting Kennedy to take the chair in front of him, "what's the story with this Mylan fellow?"

"Well, it seems like it was set up to look like a suicide…"

"But you're not convinced?" Castle interrupted.

"Well, the body was positioned for maximum public humiliation."

"But surely if someone is going to take his own life, he's not concerned about what state he will be found in?"

"I'm not sure I agree, sir," Kennedy began, knowing he was working on nothing other than a hunch, based mostly on the fact that Kennedy felt the garters for Mylan's socks had been a plant and that the belt around his neck was not Mylan's usual belt. "When people take their own lives, they usually believe it's the only thing to do. Mylan, it appears, was well balanced; there is no medication visible in his bathroom. There were also quite a few signs that he was very vain: he had hair transplants, and we found several vanity products to enhance his looks in his bathroom. There was no note left…"

"But we know that fewer than half of suicide victims leave a note," Castle interjected.

"Agreed, but the point I'm trying to make is that I believe the victim would have been very conscious of how he would look when he was discovered."

"Could it have been an accident? A thrill-seeking device that went badly wrong?"

"Perhaps, but Taylor reckons death through autoerotic asphyxiation happens mostly to younger, more inexperienced practitioners."

"You mean that by the time they get to Mylan's age, they know what they are doing?"

"Something like that."

"But you're not ruling out an accident? I mean, at this stage you're not convinced either way?"

"Well, no," Kennedy replied hesitantly, "I'm not sure whether it was a suicide or an accident or an act of ill intent. I'd like to find out more about Mylan's background."

"Okay," Castle said, agreeing with Kennedy's approach and knowing where the conversation had been going since it started.

Kennedy suspected he was being indulged. He felt that if he had been in better health then, at the very least, he most certainly would have had to put up a better argument to be allowed to continue this particular investigation.

"And Kennedy," Castle added, with a genuine smile in his eyes, as Kennedy headed for the door, "we've missed you. I missed you. You're looking good again, slimmer and fitter. Welcome back."

Castle's attention to a file on his desk was a signal to Kennedy that they were done.

"Thanks, sir," Kennedy replied as he closed the door behind him.

***

"Did the SOCO guys find anything?" Kennedy enquired of DC Dot King as his team gathered in his office five minutes later.

"Nothing so far, sir," she began unhappily, looking at the blank pages in her notebook. "They've bagged a lot of stuff and removed it for closer examination though. They'll give us a shout if they discover anything."

"Okay," Kennedy said, strolling over to the "Guinness Is Good for You" noticeboard in the corner of his wood-walled office. He started writing names on a sheet of white foolscap paper and pinning it to his noticeboard.

"Okay," he repeated when he'd finished his task, "here is the list of people we need to talk to."

1. Tony Stevenson
2. Martin Friel
3. Cynthia Cox
4. Nealey Dean
5. Tim Dickens
6. Roger & Maggie Littlewood
7. His solicitor and or accountant
8. Miss Chloe Simmons

"Yes," King agreed, "I think Cynthia Cox has got a bit of information up her sleeve, but she was never going to spill it to me. I think she might open up to DS Irvine though."

Kennedy wrote Irvine's name down on the Cynthia Cox entry, happy that King had given him the perfect opportunity to interview Nealey Dean again, but this time with King and without Irvine.

"They're all friends or business associates of Patrick Mylan's, and we need to speak to them. We need to build a good picture of him and his life as soon as possible. I'm not sure how long the honeymoon period of my return will last with the super."

CHAPTER ELEVEN

DS James Irvine and DC Dot King met as arranged outside Tim Dickens' double-fronted, three-storey house in Leinster Mews, London W2. As King rang the doorbell, Irvine imagined it was probably one of several of Dickens' London rendezvous points. The songwriter's PA, the efficient and apparently friendly Alice Robbins, greeted them. The mews house, so spotless it looked as if it had been maid-cleaned every day, looked unlived in. There was lots of wood, glass, clean white walls, and Japanese opaque sliding screens. The house's only clue to its owner was the presence of a Yamaha Baby Grand piano in the first-floor, open-plan living room. The piano was guarded regally by a dark Gibson L100 vintage guitar resting in a stand to the right of the piano's keyboard.

Before she left them, the PA handed King and Irvine two small bottles of Perrier water; she didn't offer them a choice and she didn't ask whether or not they even wanted the water in the first place. Irvine reckoned it saved her the fuss of making them tea or coffee. King couldn't resist lifting the keyboard lid of the piano and attempting her party piece, "Our House."

"Ah, so you like Graham Nash then?" Tim Dickens said with a smile as he sauntered into the room.

"Well yes, I suppose, but it's the only song I can play," King answered, not embarrassed in the slightest.

"He's a very nice man is Graham. I mention it not as an excuse to name-drop, but because he's the exception in our business." Dickens took over King's recently vacated piano stool. He continued playing the song and singing along for a verse before breaking into a warm smile, closing the keyboard lid, crossing his legs, and turning side-on to face the members of Camden Town's CID. By this point, Miss Robbins had provided two white foldable chairs from a space under what Irvine thought must be the staircase.

"It's one of those songs all songwriters wish they'd written. The idea was so simple we all kicked ourselves for not thinking of it first, but Mr Nash beat us all to it, showing us, as he and the Beatles often did, that writing simple songs is anything but simple."

Irving thought Dickens was in his mid to late fifties. He was about five foot ten, slim, and was in good shape for his age. *No, scrap that,* Irvine thought; *Dickens is in great shape.* He looked and dressed affluently. His skin was clear and clean-shaven with only a few age lines to the sides and under the eyes. He wore black canvas flip-flops, loose-fitting grey trousers, a grey sleeveless cardigan, and a black shirt with the top button done up. He certainly had the air of a millionaire. He looked unhurried, safe and at peace in his own skin. Or maybe Irvine just thought he looked like a millionaire because the detective already knew he must be a millionaire.

"Do you still write songs?" Irvine asked.

Dickens smiled. It was a warm-hearted, gracious smile, which hinted at the tolerance of an often-asked question. He had brown eyes and a hairstyle appropriate for a man his age: well groomed, brown, dense enough to shelter his crown, with a tidy parting and the greyness of his years visible.

"I try," he answered. His English accent was obviously influenced by a good few years in USA. "Sorry, I wasn't trying to be modest. I enjoy writing a song. I take great pleasure from writing songs..." he paused to turn and look directly at King. "It's probably the thing in my life I take most pleasure from."

Irvine suspected he wasn't finished, that Dickens was used to holding court and enjoyed the drama of a good pause in his narrative. Kennedy had long ago taught his favourite DS to be patient, to always work at the pace of the subject on the first interview. If there was to be a subsequent interview, then you might want to rattle them along a bit or even slow them down to take them out of their comfort zone of considering each and every thing they said.

"But I'd also have to say I no longer have a record company or manager for my new songs. There's probably not even an audience for my new stuff for that matter. No one is banging on my door looking for new songs. There still seems to be a demand for the older material, no matter how many times it's repackaged, but nowadays, the music business is predominately a young person's business, particularly on the performing side. But writing songs is what I do, what I love doing, so I have to do it. I'll spend a good part my day writing."

"What do you do with the songs?" Irvine asked.

"Well, for my new material, I'm lucky enough to be with a great publishing house, Hornall Brothers. They're old-fashioned in that they get out there looking for covers for my songs. Pretty much, these days, placing songs is a lost art, but, as I say, I'm lucky enough that they still find homes for some of my songs. Tom Waits famously said his songs are like children. They get older, leave home, and go out and earn a living for him. I love Hornall Brothers because they give me a very good excuse to continue to practise my chosen art. Sometimes they even find me a movie project to write for."

"Do you still perform live?" King asked.

"Ah, no," Dickens laughed heartily, "and every time I'm asked to, I'll just dig out a recent live DVD of Tom Jones, and that's the only reality check I need."

"My mum and dad love Tom Jones," King protested.

"Exactly," Dickens laughed, "but I'm sure you're not here to interview me for *Mojo,* so this is probably a very good point to talk about *your* business."

"When we spoke to Alice, your PA, on the phone earlier, she said you were already aware that Patrick Mylan was dead," Irvine started.

"Yes, very sad, isn't it?"

"How did you find out?" King asked.

"A mutual friend rang and told me."

"And who was this friend?"

"A mutual friend of DS Irvine here and mine, a Miss Nealey Dean," Dickens replied, looking directly at Irvine.

"Right," King replied, writing something in her notebook as Irvine asked, "How long have you known Mr Mylan?"

"Whooa," Dickens more breathed than said as he turned to stare at the lid of the piano and then chose instead to turn around and lift his guitar. "Ah, let's see now," he continued as he absent-mindedly started to strum the guitar, "probably coming up to eight or nine years. Alice would know more accurately; she's great with dates and diaries and things like where I've got to be at noon. We can check with her when you're leaving."

"How did you meet him?" Irvine asked.

"John Stevenson, a great concert promoter I know, his brother Tony is involved in investments in some way or other, and Tony is a business acquaintance and friend of Patrick's. John invited me to drinks at Patrick's one summer evening. I didn't know if I was being lined up as a potential investment client or a future tennis partner."

"Do you play tennis?" King asked.

"Not a lot, and nowhere near seriously enough to share a court with Patrick."

"How well did you know him?" Irvine asked.

"Not very well, DS Irvine."

Irvine gave a "that doesn't really help" type of shrug, which Dickens must have correctly interpreted, because he continued, "I'm not being facetious. It's just I've been thinking about nothing else this morning since I heard the news, and I can't admit to being upset about the news. Over the last few years, I've spent quite a bit of time in Patrick Mylan's company. He was always pleasant and friendly to me and I to him, but neither would I claim that we made a connection beyond that with each other. You know, I haven't a clue what he worried about or what made him happy. I didn't know if he was single because there had been a big love of his life and she dumped him, leaving him scared for life. I sometimes saw him in female company, but again, I never saw him with anyone he seemed to really care about."

"Did anyone you know really care about him?" King asked, a sad tone evident in her voice.

"Maggie Littlewood cared about him, she and her husband Roger, but particularly her. She was always at him to look after himself better; nagging him to find a good woman and settle down and have children. She was always telling him that having children was the making of a man."

"Have you any children yourself?" King asked.

"In another life," Dickens replied without regret.

King looked puzzled.

"I married my first girlfriend when I young. We had two children. We divorced when my son was three and my daughter was one. She remarried quite quickly and had another couple of children, and she felt it was important that they played happy families. Her version of happy families did not include me being involved in my children's lives. I felt so bad about the break-up that I complied. By the time I came to my senses, my children had another father."

"So you never see them?" King continued.

"No. But look, that's my version of the story. If you spoke to my ex-wife, I'm sure she'd have a totally different slant on it. I think she felt I was living my life for material for my songs."

"So, from what you're saying," Irvine began, picking his words carefully, "Patrick Mylan wasn't exactly what you'd call a happy soul, was he?"

"Well, you know," Dickens replied, "it would be incorrect to claim Patrick was always down or dark. He'd laugh with the rest of the table. He seemed to really enjoy his own dinner parties. He loved playing tennis. I mean, he'd a real passion and a skill for it. He enjoyed playing more than needing to win every time he played, if you know what I mean. He wouldn't be overtly depressed. Does your question mean you think it might have been suicide?"

"That's what we're trying to ascertain, sir," Irvine said. "Were you aware of any trouble he might have been in?"

"From what I can gather, he did very well with his investments. Obviously we've all heard the stories about people losing millions overnight in the current climate, but he didn't seem to suffer much from the recession. Obviously Rodney, that's Rodney Stuart, his accountant stroke advisor in all things legal, would have a better handle on that area of his life."

"When was the last time you would have seen him?" King asked.

King always had her shopping list of vital questions she would work her way through without ever disrupting the line of the conversation. Irving's problem was that if he weren't careful - or was out without King or Kennedy - he'd find himself concentrating too much on the questions he felt he really needed to ask, making that his preoccupation rather than the answers.

"Let's see, the last dinner party I would have attended would have been a fortnight ago. We can also check that with Alice when you're leaving."

"And how did he seem?" Irvine asked.

"Same as usual. I didn't notice anything unusual. That particular dinner party would have been the first I'd attended for ages, so maybe there was a wee bit more catching up than normal, but apart from that, nothing to note."

Irvine hoped that his frustration wasn't showing to either Dickens or King, but he was learning absolutely nothing about Patrick Mylan, even from the people who supposedly knew him. On top of which, there didn't seem to be a lot of grieving going on in his circle of acquaintances either. Irvine couldn't help wondering who'd miss *him* if anything happened to him. He went through the people outside of his family who he hoped would miss him. He got as far as Kennedy, Rose Butler, Bella Forysthe, Nealey Dean, and then, try as he might, he couldn't think of a single person to hit the fifth finger.

The interview was running out of steam. King asked the only question left to be asked.

"What was I doing between the hours of four o'clock and eight o'clock on Sunday last?" Dickens recited her question back to her. "I believe I was here, working on a new song."

He started to finger a different set of chords from the ones he'd been aimlessly strumming for a while. He played several bars, humming a sad melody to his precise guitar work.

"I've been trying to catch this one for several months now, and I'd a bit of a breakthrough on Sunday. I started just after lunch and worked on it into the evening. I think I've cracked it. With any luck I'll get it finished this week. That happens to me a lot. I work on a song for ages - years on a couple of them - until something happens to make it all fall into place. Then it's just a matter of polishing it up a bit."

"What do you do first, the music or the lyrics?" Irvine asked.

"Both, I do them both at the same time, but nine times out of ten I'll finish the music before I'm happy with the lyric."

"Was there someone working with you - a producer, other musicians or technicians?" King asked.

"Ah no, the writing stage is a very solitary one. I find I need to be alone to have a chance of reaching the muse. But I think that's why I enjoy this part of the process so much. Well, more like this part of my life so much."

"So there'd have been no one with you between the hours of four p.m. and eight p.m.," King offered, it appeared to Irvine, as much for her notebook's benefit as for Dickens.'

"No one."

CHAPTER TWELVE

Kennedy's day was progressing more quickly than he wanted - well, more quickly than he wanted without producing any results. Added to that was the pressure that he felt that he was beginning to feel very ungallant in respect of his dealings with Miss Sharenna Chada. He wasn't exactly accusing himself of being a cad, and it wasn't as though he were avoiding her or not returning her calls. At the same time he felt in his soul that after how close they'd been on Saturday and Sunday, he should try and make some kind of connection. But how gallant was he really being? Was there not a chance, he asked himself as he tidied up his desk of two weeks' worth of junk circulars, that his interest was more lust driven?

He and Irvine were due to leave North Bridge House in ten minutes to interview Roger and Maggie Littlewood, who lived up on the borders of Hampstead. Changing his plan, Kennedy popped into Irvine's office and advised him he'd an errand he needed to run and that he'd meet him outside the Roundhouse in half an hour.

The closer Kennedy walked towards Camden Lock, the less confident he grew about his decision. How would she feel about his just turning up at her place of work unannounced? How would he feel if Miss Chada just nipped into the reception area of North Bridge House and asked Sgt Tim Flynn to show her through to Kennedy? Not great, he had to admit. They'd parted without making any further plans. Had that been intentional on her part?

Self-conscious as he was approaching her part of the hippie haven that was Camden Lock, he felt he had to go and see her, but he hadn't a clue what he was going to say. He toyed with the excuse of needing to see her because of his back ailment, but dismissed this out of hand. On careful consideration, he wondered if this was because he didn't now want to appear weak in her eyes. He wondered about this power she seemed to have to pull him towards her. Perhaps it could simply be put down to abstinence making the libido grow keener, but then he hadn't consciously abstained. No, he'd lost his mate. Could that be what this was all about? The fact that ann rea had left him?

Sharenna Chada was a truly beautiful and sensuous woman. Yes, there was something dark, lonely, and sad about her that Kennedy hadn't yet figured out, but her overwhelming, prevailing power was that she had been put on this earth to make love. Yet Kennedy had never been attracted to this type of woman before, and he admitted to himself that before he'd met ann rea, he'd probably have run a mile from someone with Miss Chada's silent power. She'd taken complete control; she'd seduced *him*. No matter how willing he'd been in the encounter, the bottom line was that he really had nothing to do with it. Maybe she'd taken pity on him due to the pain he'd been experiencing. Maybe the wine played a part. Maybe she too had been without a lover for just too long a period of time. Whatever the reason, she'd been the instigator, and Kennedy had most certainly been a willing and happy participant. As he walked across Dingwalls' crowded and multicultured courtyard, he admitted to himself that it had been the most exciting sexual experience of his life.

Kennedy entered the refurbished warehouse that housed the tiny reception area and suite of rooms that made up the Unlocked treatment centre. Unlocked was a long established massage centre that had developed its own successful line of oils, candles, and herbal remedies. After visiting Miss Chada the osteopath at Unlocked for several months strictly as a patient, it felt very weird walking back into here wearing a different cloak.

Jan, the friendly and talkative Scottish receptionist, spotted him immediately.

"Ah, Mr Kennedy, Miss Chada said if you came by today, even though you don't have an appointment, I was to disturb her." She paused to pivot one hundred and eighty degrees in her chair, reach up above her, open a cupboard, take out a crisp white towel, close the door, and swivel back around to hand the towel to another masseuse who Kennedy hadn't noticed standing behind him. Jan had her tiny reception laid out so she could do nearly everything from her swivel chair. "Let me just check here for you." She flicked through the pages of her large, well-used appointment book, swung back around and checked the clock above the cupboards. "Can you wait five minutes? I don't like to disturb her when she's with a patient."

"That'll be perfectly fine," Kennedy said.

"She's got a break before her next patient. Not long enough to fit in a session for you though. Would you like to try some of our herbal tea? It's brilliant, I'm really addicted to it, totally chills me out and makes me more mature in my dealings with the morons who still come in here expecting quick relief for a ten pound note."

"Do you get much trouble from them?" Kennedy asked.

She laughed heartily.

"You see this button here?" She swung around to her right and pointed to what looked like a doorbell attached to the wall at about the height of her computer screen. "If I'm getting any grief from them, I just push this as I warn them they'd better get out before Geoff and Diesel throw them out."

She laughed again, leaned across her crowded desk and whispered, "There is no Geoff, and there is no Diesel. The button isn't even connected. But it always works. I picked the names because of Geoff Capes. My dad was always a big fan of his. He could pull a truck by himself. I'm not really sure why he would want to, mind you, but he could, and he did it every Christmas on that *The World's Strongest Men* series. They've always got shows on like that at Christmas, haven't they? I mean, people are so bored at Christmas they'll watch anything, won't they? Diesel, that's after Diesel Van What's his name. Oh yes, Geoff and Diesel have come to my rescue on lots of occasions."

Jan excused herself as her phone rang. Everything she did was monitored by a security camera fixed to the ceiling. Kennedy noticed a wee red light pulsing on the camera and figured that it was at least connected and not part of the Geoff and Diesel scam.

Kennedy helped himself to a china cup full of herbal tea, which was brewing in a weird black oriental pot with a bamboo handle, on a small table just to the front of Jan's desk. The tea was very refreshing and seemed to blend seamlessly with the Tibetan music and scented oils wafting gently from somewhere behind the reception desk.

Jan finished the call and went about her business, completely ignoring Kennedy until they both heard a door open in the treatment rooms section. Kennedy wasn't completely sure, but he thought he could hear the sounds of *Astral Weeks*. He smiled.

A few seconds later, Miss Chada escorted an elderly woman through the reception area. She smiled and nodded to Kennedy as she offered the old woman up to the buzz of the courtyard.

"Ah Mr Kennedy," she said as she turned back into the room again, "will you come though please? Thank you Jan."

It was only when Sharenna turned to face Kennedy that he was hit by the full impact of her magic. He struggled to catch his breath. He could utter no word other than, "Hello," and held out his hand towards her. He felt it was quite a bizarre act, considering just how close they'd been barely twenty-four hours ago.

She intentionally missed his hand, choosing instead to gently grip his arm and used it to direct him towards her particular treatment room.

"I knew it was you from the music," Kennedy offered, wondering why he was whispering.

She squeezed his arm, leading him into her spotless white room, invited him to remove his shoes, as usual, and gently slid the door closed behind her.

"I'm sorry to come here to see you, I just didn't know…"

"I'm glad you did, Christy," she said quietly, patting for him to sit up on the side of her treatment table. She glided to the opposite side of the table and started to massage his neck and shoulders. "I was trying to work out how to see you. We don't have another appointment in the book. Oh goodness you're very tight. You've started work again?"

Kennedy nodded.

She was a pure magician when it came to hitting the right spots in his neck and shoulders. Kennedy felt his head dropping. She might well have the most amazing body Kennedy had ever seen in his life, but she was also an absolutely amazing genius as a masseuse, and her fingers quickly started to unlock the damaging fusions Kennedy knew would become more painful if left to their own devices.

"I had an enjoyable time with you," she whispered a little bit stiffly during a particular noisy part of the music.

Kennedy started to turn towards her.

Her hands worked away on his neck, refusing to allow him to turn.

Perhaps we are being watched, Kennedy thought.

She worked on for another five minutes and then broke the spell she'd been creating as she said, "I'm afraid that's as much as I can fit in for now Mr Kennedy. Don't forget to do the exercises I showed you. You need to take thirty minutes each day to help fix your own body. You're only back at work a day. Already I can feel it in your shoulders."

She returned her hands to his shoulders and showed him exactly where he was tightening up again. She helped him down from her table. She looked as if she were nodding a very discreet "no" to him as she did so.

Did she think he was going to try and kiss her? Were they being monitored? Kennedy clocked another pulsing red shadow on the ceiling like the one in the reception area. Luckily enough he saw the shadow before he'd actually looked straight at the camera and he was able to look away in time. *In time for what?* he wondered. What exactly was he feeling guilty about? What had he done wrong? Did he think ann rea was at the other end of the camera or something?

Outside the door to her room, Kennedy was putting his shoes back on again when she put her right hand into the pocket of her starched, snow-white, knee-length cotton gown.

"Thank you Mr Kennedy," she said, taking his hand and shaking it. "Please have Jan put another appointment in the book."

She smiled a little at him as she returned to her room, closing her door after her.

As Kennedy walked back towards reception, he closed his hand over the piece of folder paper in the palm of his hand, put his hand in the pocket of his dark blue windbreaker and left the note there.

"Yes," Jan began when she saw him again, "Miss Chada said you'd a very bad weekend and that you might drop in today. How are you feeling now?"

"Oh, much better," Kennedy admitted, passing his credit card over to Jan. "She's very good, isn't she?"

"I'll tell you this in confidence," she said quite quietly, sounding as if she and Kennedy were best mates, "she's by far the best we've ever had in here. I try them all, you know. Get them to work on me so I know which patients to put with which masseuses, and Miss Chada really is the finest I've come across."

"Can I book in my next session, please?"

"Yes, of course, the usual forty minutes... let's see," Jan said, as she flicked through the pages of her appointment book. "Today and to-morrow are totally out, fully booked. This week... now, let's see...you like to come in at lunchtime, don't you?"

"If possible?"

"Let's say Wednesday at one o'clock?"

"Okay," Kennedy said making a mental note. "Maybe I should stick one in for the following week as well."

Jan flicked on another seven pages. "Hmmm, I'll have to get back to you on that. She's got all next week blocked off for something."

Kennedy wasn't really paying attention to Jan; he was too preoc-cupied with the note burning a hole in his pocket.

Kennedy had five minutes before he was due to meet DS Irvine outside the Roundhouse. Once he'd turned out of the Market into Chalk Farm Road and the volume of pedestrians dropped by about 90 per cent, he removed the note from his pocket. It smelled of her distinct blend of aromas; the predominant one was clean. *Clean,* he chastised himself as he was nearly run over by a car pulling into the petrol sta-tion midway to the Roundhouse. *What the hell does* clean *smell like?* She didn't have the scent of someone who smelled hygienically clean, that was most definitely something else; this was more soulful. He thought about this as he opened the four-fold note. *Clean smells like Miss Chada.* A bit of a cop-out, he accepted, but that really nailed it for him. Her scents were intoxicating, soulful, and *clean.*

Her handwriting was perfectly formed and neat, very neat.

Monday.
I'm happy you came to see me. I hoped you would.
Ring me on 07972 147738 whenever you finish work
and I'll come and see you.

S.

CHAPTER THIRTEEN

Maggie Littlewood's eyes literally sparkled and shone through her sadness.

She greeted Irvine and Kennedy at the front door of the house she shared with her husband Roger in Well Walk, just off Hampstead Heath. From the outside, these houses had always looked to Kennedy as if they'd be tiny inside. Not so. The hundred-year-plus-old house was very cosy and cottage-like, but comfortably proportioned on the inside. Mrs Littlewood was obviously a house-proud woman. The house was very busy with antique furniture, ornaments, bric-a-brac, several photos of a much younger - and stunning in a period drama kind of way - Mrs Littlewood, and various-sized paintings absolutely everywhere. But for all the busyness of the house, there was not a speck of dust visible to the naked eye. Unlike Patrick Mylan's "show" house, Roger and Maggie's house was most certainly a home.

Maggie was dressed in her around-the-house clothes: a loose fitting, aqua training top and matching trousers. She'd big eyes in a smallish face. Her hair was white and permed, and her make-up enhanced her senior years rather than belittling them. She was immediately very mumsy and caring. She showed them straight through the house into the small back and even better groomed garden where Roger and she had obviously been enjoying afternoon tea and scones when Camden Town's finest CID officers had come calling. Maggie introduced Kennedy and Irvine to Roger and then disappeared back into the house.

"It's a sorry affair with poor Patrick, isn't it? Have you any idea what happened?" Roger asked.

"We're still looking into it," Kennedy replied, studying him.

Kennedy reckoned he was honing in on his sixtieth year, if he hadn't already recently said goodbye to it. He looked fit and slim, but the years had definitely taken their toll. His carefully combed hair was thinning and looked too reddish-black to be his natural colour. His face looked slightly drawn and pale. He was dressed in dark blue chinos, a white shirt, a red sleeveless jumper and brown moccasins. He was instantly likeable, very friendly and welcoming to Kennedy and Irvine.

"Roger, clear a bit of space for me on the table, pet," Maggie ordered as she reappeared at the back door carrying a try laden with a fresh pot of tea and some more steaming hot scones.

"I feel I should say, you shouldn't have bothered, but I'm very glad you did," Kennedy said as he and Irvine rose to help Roger and Maggie. "I have to tell you, I'm extremely fond of tea and scones."

"Aye, and you look like you could do with some fattening up. As my dear old mother would have said, you look like you enjoy your salads too much."

"Maggie!" Roger protested.

"Well, it's true, isn't it, Sergeant Irvine?" Maggie asked impishly.

"Ach sure, you know, I think a daily helping of porridge would work wonders," Irvine ventured cautiously, as they all sat down at the table and Maggie served them the tea and scones.

Roger went to help himself to a scone only to receive a slap on the back of his hand from his wife.

"Roger, don't you dare. You've already had three," Maggie scolded with a degree of seriousness Roger knew not to ignore. She sat down again and grew quiet and serious. Roger obviously knew what was troubling her because he rubbed her back without making a big fuss over it. They were quiet for quite a few seconds as Irvine and Kennedy jammed and creamed up their scones.

Roger filled the silence with, "When my wife is quiet, I always feel it would be rude to interrupt her."

"More like you're after a bit of peace and quiet yourself, no doubt," she said before returning to her thoughts again.

"These really are delicious," Irvine said, his accent helping in no small way to make them *really* sound like they were delicious.

"Patrick loved my scones too," Maggie said. "We'd often sit out here, enjoying our tea and scones, just the three of us, wouldn't we, Roger?"

"Aye, Maggie," Roger replied as he looked off to the right of the table, up at the big blue sky high above his hedge. So high up, Kennedy reckoned, that his wife wouldn't see his tears.

"When did you see him last?" Irvine asked.

"Well, let's see," Maggie began, nodding as she spoke; Kennedy wondered was she conscious she did this. "We were around at his house just over a fortnight ago, Saturday night. He'd one of his groups around for 'a wee bit of supper.' That was how he always extended his invitations."

"Who was there that night?"

"Who was there, Roger?" Maggie repeated Irvine's question.

"Oh, the usual crowd," Roger began expansively. His deep, distinctive voice would have been perfect to deliver a talking book. "The songwriter..."

"...Tim Dickens," Maggie completed her husband's sentence.

"The actress..." Roger began again.

"...lovely Nealey, Nealey Dean; she's such a nice girl."

Irvine sat up a bit in his seat at that point.

"And then Martin Friel with his wife Marianne, Tony Stevenson with his wife Valerie, and ourselves," Roger said. "Martin, Tony, Maggie, and myself have known Patrick from the time we all worked together at Credit Suisse."

"Patrick didn't have a partner then?" Kennedy asked diplomatically.

"Please don't get her started," Roger said as Maggie tutted to the high blue sky.

"Oh, come on, pet, you wanted him to settle down with someone as well," Maggie retorted.

"Well, Patrick was very generous to his friends, we all loved him, but I suppose the bottom line just was that he'd never met the right..."

"Roger, Patrick wasn't really ready to settle down and you know it. As we all kept saying, you really have to want to meet someone before you do meet someone. He wasn't at the right stage in his life for love. I think he'd really have preferred to wipe his bum with a brick than settle down."

"Maggie!" Roger blurted in a half laugh. "We're in mixed company - civilians and police officers."

"Oh they're all right. They know what I'm trying to say, don't you,

Inspector Kennedy?" Maggie asked, her head nodding slowly.

"I think I know what you're saying; you're saying he wasn't really up for meeting anyone."

"No, not quite," Roger offered; "she was trying to say, Patrick would have run a million miles before getting involved in a serious relationship."

"Right," Kennedy and Irvine said simultaneously.

"Would you mind telling us how you all met?" Kennedy asked.

"We all joined Credit Suisse on the same day," Roger said with a smile.

"That's Tony, Martin, Patrick, Roger, and myself," Maggie said, and added in a sweeter voice, "That was also the first time Roger and I met."

"Actually, Martin came a bit later, didn't he? He started off as a teacher."

"Yes, of course, you're right," Maggie said as if she hadn't realised this fact for years.

"How long ago was that?" Kennedy asked.

"Twenty-three years ago in September," Roger answered.

"That's a long time," Kennedy said.

"Don't remind us," Roger laughed.

"So when did youse leave?" Irvine asked.

"I left first," Maggie volunteered. "Roger and I got together after three years."

"I was already married," Roger offered. "It was a bit difficult for a while."

"He separated from his first wife in 1990. We married in 1991, and John, our first son, was born in 1992. I was pregnant with John when I left Credit Suisse. Patrick left the following year. Tony and Martin left somewhere around 1999, and Roger stayed on until he retired three years ago."

"I admired Patrick, Tony, and Martin for going it alone, but I've always been a company man..."

"Please don't say you had to stay because you had a family," Maggie said, without a hint of bitterness.

"No, no, never," Roger laughed. "I've always admitted I thrive best as a company man."

"Yes, pet, you have, and we've had a great life because of it," Maggie said, looking back at their lovely house. "Goodness, can you imagine what they must all have been going through this year though?"

"Ah, it had to happen; the whole thing got out of control," Roger said, "but not before they took good care of themselves though."

"Where had Patrick come from?" Kennedy asked, looking at Maggie.

"You mean his family? They've all been dead since before we met him. His mother died when he was young. His father might have left, it's all a bit confusing, and Patrick didn't like talking about it. They were from a place called Sligo in the west of Ireland," Maggie replied. "He was brought up by an aunt and uncle on his mother's side."

"Right," Kennedy said, encouraging more.

"Patrick finished school when he was fifteen and came straight over to London. He worked on the roads. Then he got a job in a hotel down in Bayswater. He did very well there. Put himself through night classes, studied to become an accountant. Worked for NatWest for a few years, didn't like it, left, and joined Credit Suisse which, as I say, is how we all met up."

"His aunt and uncle?" Kennedy asked.

"They were very old when he left Ireland," Maggie continued. "They died a few years later. The only reason he even found out is that he'd send them regular letters with cheques, and then one day he received a pile of unopened return-to-sender letters with his cheques uncashed. Apparently his own parents were very old when they had him. He was an only child. He did a bit of research on his family a good few years back but couldn't turn up anything beyond what he already knew."

"It's a very sad story, isn't it?" Roger said.

"I think that's been his big problem," Maggie started back up again. "He'd really never known the love of a parent, of a brother, a sister. He told me his uncle really just treated him the same way he treated the other farm hands. If you've never been loved as a child, how could you possibly know how to love someone in your adult years?"

"Well…" Roger started, drawing the word out.

"I know you think it poppycock, pet," Maggie said, putting her hand on his arm as a signal to stop, "but it makes sense to me. I think Patrick was a perfect example of what lack of love has done."

"Were there any disastrous relationships?" Kennedy asked.

"No, I don't believe so. Oh, of course he'd enjoy female companionship," Maggie said, looking more at her husband than Kennedy. "Look, pet, be a love and take the stuff from the table in to the kitchen;

I fear rain isn't too far away. Maybe the nice sergeant here would help you in with it?"

Both did as they were bid, and when they'd gone indoors with their first load, she continued to Kennedy, "Let me show you around the garden." When Kennedy didn't show much enthusiasm about leaving his teacup and final untouched scone behind, she continued, "I need to be out of earshot of Roger. He thinks I have a blind spot when it comes to Patrick.

"You see, Inspector Kennedy, Patrick used to pay for the company of his ladies, if you see what I mean," she continued as they sauntered around her small garden.

"You mean call girls?" Kennedy asked, thinking it sounded nicer than hookers or prostitutes.

"In a way, but not really. He was too careful for that. Look, I know I'm not making much sense, but Patrick was a dear friend to Roger and me. I'm having a difficult time believing he committed suicide. So I'm treading a difficult line here because, on the one hand I don't want to speak ill of the dead, but at the same time, I'm trying to be helpful to you in your investigation so you can find out what happened to our dear friend."

"That makes perfect sense, Mrs Littlewood."

"Oh, Maggie. We're Maggie and Roger to everyone."

"Of course, Maggie, and any information you give me will be very helpful, no matter how small or unimportant you think it might be, and I promise I'll be as discreet as possible with the information you give me."

"Thank you, Inspector," she said and squeezed his arm as she continued. "Patrick spoke to me about this a couple of times, mostly when I'd tried to fix him up on a blind date, and usually when he'd a few drinks. He told me he wasn't comfortable with women in that way. When Nealey came on the scene, I started to get my hopes up. He genuinely seemed to like her, and she's such a beautiful girl, so wholesome, I thought it was a match. But he claimed he couldn't make that natural connection with Nealey or 'anyone for that matter,' he said. He told me he had women he enjoyed a physical relationship with when he needed it. The way he described it to me, it was more like a business arrangement. He wouldn't say any more. I told him to be very careful.

He told me not to worry; it wasn't like that. He said, 'We're not talking about ladies of the night.' I told him, 'Just because it isn't dark doesn't mean they won't rob you blind.' He got a fit of the giggles at that and changed the subject."

"Could you tell me what you were doing between the hours of four o'clock and eight o'clock on Saturday last?" Kennedy asked.

"Oh my goodness, it sounds so much like police-speak from the telly. Is that the time of the poor boy's demise?"

Kennedy quickly pulled himself up. "If we can rule people out, it allows us to concentrate on people we can't rule out."

"I understand," she said, nodding along to the beat of her reply. "On Saturday afternoon I always go down the West End. I have this circuit of shops I do, including a few pit stops for liquid refreshments like espressos and maybe even a sherry as a little treat for myself. I usually get back here just before eight o'clock, by which time Roger has dinner ready for us. He does all the cooking in this house. He's very good, you know. He's got his wee vegetable patch over there behind his shed."

"Do you have a few pals you do your shopping run with?" Kennedy asked.

"No, I'm very selfish in my shopping; I hate hanging out with people who only want you there as a back-up opinion on their purchases. I find that such a bore. I'd rather put on my lipstick with a paintbrush than be all girly. I see something I like, I buy it."

Kennedy considered this and tried to shake the image out of his mind as she showed him some blood-red roses.

"Do you think maybe one of these girls, you know… maybe?" Maggie said nervously, returning to her earlier thread and nodding her head furiously.

"You never met any of them?" Kennedy asked ignoring her question.

"No, never," she said, dropping her voice considerably as Roger and Irvine crossed the perfectly manicured lawn towards them. "Not a word to Roger now, Inspector, you promised."

Kennedy didn't remember that particular promise, but neither did he have a problem keeping it. What he was having a problem with was Maggie's claim.

Kennedy and Irvine left Roger and Maggie to their memories and to their garden. Irvine advised Kennedy that he was a bit uncertain about Roger's alibi. Roger claimed that he spent all of Saturday in the garden by himself.

CHAPTER FOURTEEN

After a few phone calls, DC Dot King discovered that Tony Stevenson was self-employed and worked from home. In fact, Mr Stevenson was at home at that very moment and was happy for her to come around to ask him a few questions about his recently departed friend Mr Patrick Mylan. She wasn't expecting him to be exactly slumming it, but she half expected him to be living on the Islington side of Camden Town, where house and garden space was as rare as tattoo-free Camden Marketeers. To her and Allaway's surprise, he lived in a grand house up on leafy Chalcot Square.

Tony wasn't exactly overweight, but he looked as if he enjoyed his food and might even possess a bit of a sweet tooth. He was dressed in brown cords, a light blue Ralph Lauren traditional shirt, black socks (no shoes), and he favoured his black hair short but not so short you could see the skin. He had tortoiseshell Harry Potter glasses which magnified his brown eyes, a pleasant ever-ready smile and red flushed cheeks.

"Come on in, will you?" he said, shaking their hands in turn.

He showed them through to his house office, which King reckoned just might be bigger than the entire flat she shared with "my Ashley." The office was sparsely furnished and extremely tidy, so it appeared to be even bigger than it was. He had a fine Nick Botting self-portrait above his fireplace and a large map of the world centred on the wall behind his black shiny desk. On his desk he had two Apple computer screens, which pulsed continuously and beeped a wee electronic attempt at two notes every time a message came in on one of the screens. The other screen was filled with ever-changing, non-stop, stock market information. Stevenson put both screens to sleep and invited King and Allaway to join him on Perspex bucket seats around a circular glass table. They each had a spare seat on either side.

"Have you worked out what happened yet?" Stevenson asked in a faint Mancunian accent, which King immediately tied in with the Man U scarf hanging on the back of the office door.

"No, we're still carrying out our investigation," King replied as she pulled out her notebook.

"When was the last time you saw him?" Allaway asked.

"Saw him or spoke to him?" Stevenson asked, drumming all eight fingers and occasionally the thumb of his right hand on the table.

"Both," Allaway said.

"Okay," Stevenson said expansively, "I spoke to him last on Saturday morning, and I saw him last two Saturdays before for dinner at his house."

King wrote in her book for longer than she needed. She was trying to signal to Allaway that she wanted him to keep asking the questions. She liked to watch people when they were answering questions. People gave a lot away to a third person they weren't directly engaged with. She wasn't yet sure what all the signs were, but she was sure they were there; she just had to figure out how to interpret them.

"What did you speak to him about when you rang on Saturday?" Allaway asked.

"I was returning a call of his I'd missed on Friday."

King sighed impatiently.

"Okay, look, we were involved in some shares together with another friend of ours called Martin Friel, and with what's going on at the minute in the marketplace, we have to watch everything like hawks. Right? If we hold our nerve, we could make a killing, but if we're careless, we could suffer a severe hit overnight."

"On that particular share," King asked, "or on everything?"

Stevenson smiled. "It's only a fool who puts all his eggs in one basket these days. What I like to try to do is hedge my bets. Right? I work on something, and I'll put say ten grand in, and then if and when that share takes off and starts to produce dividends, I'll take 150 per cent of my original investment back out. The additional 50 per cent is to cover my bad investments, and then I'll let whatever is left stay in for the ride. Right? You obviously still have to monitor it closely, but you're never scared of losing it because you can afford to lose it all."

"Do you have many losses?" Allaway asked.

Stevenson smiled before replying.

"I was just thinking, most gamblers I know would always say, 'Over the year I'm up.' But if that's the case, how come the bookies smile so much? Right? But if you do your homework, pay attention and you are not greedy, you can do well out of this."

"How do you know what to invest in?" Allaway asked in a way that suggested he might fancy his chances.

"Well, there's the blue chip stuff, right? It's expensive to buy any volume of it, and you're rarely going to make a lot on that, but it's usually solid and stable and gives you a bit of a foundation."

Allaway looked to King. He seemed to be glaring at her notes, as if he were checking to see she was getting all the relevant details down.

"Did you, Martin Friel, and Patrick Mylan invest together on everything?" King asked.

"No, Patrick was fearless. He..." Stevenson paused, collecting his thoughts; "I need you to know that I'm not speaking ill of him when I say this, but *he* was a lot like a gambler. He loved to gamble; he loved the risk, well maybe more pitting himself against the risk."

"Are you talking about instances of him buying into things other than shares here?" King asked.

"Well, of course."

"For instance?" King pushed.

"Buildings, houses, vintage cars - you know."

"Do you invest in other areas yourself?" Allaway asked as King slumped slightly in her seat.

"No, not like that," Stevenson replied, seeming to King to be a little relieved, but she couldn't be sure. "I like to put money into business and then spend time helping to make the business work."

"For instance?"

"For instance," Stevenson replied, and then obviously started to think what business he was going to reveal his interest in. "Right. This man I know, an ex-copper as it happens. He and his younger girlfriend were making quite a good living out of manufacturing candles and selling them down Camden Market. One thing led to another; a couple of Americans, a German, and someone from Scandinavia picked up on how special the candles were, and they start ordering more and more. Now it turns out that Noreen, my daughter, had gone to school with the girlfriend's younger sister, and the girls, both of whom were waiting to go to university, were roped in at the weekends to help out. I go over to pick up our Noreen one Saturday. They're all buzzing away. I had a chat with the ex-copper, right? He filled me in, told me he couldn't cope. Over a glass of wine, he and his girlfriend showed me their books. It was all very solid, but there was no planning, right?

That's what I'm good at. I'm good at organising and getting systems together.

"I bought into the company, but I also provided expertise. I went down there, rolled up my sleeves and got my hands dirty, no bother to me. I raised the money for us to buy premises, so we were no longer throwing away money on rent. I helped them find more staff, and now they're not having to work anywhere near as hard and are making more money. So now it's working well. I've made back my investment and am making good money out of it. I reckon in another year or so we'll be able to sell the entire operation to the Americans, and if and when we do, I'll feel fine over what I take out of if because I've made myself part of it. And as Noreen is really the reason I found this, I've told her that, as a reward, I'll pay the deposit and help her with the mortgage when she wants to buy her own flat. Obviously I could buy her a flat outright, but that's not the point is it. Right? We're all the same, aren't we? We all really only appreciate things when we have to work for them."

"Did Patrick Mylan have any similar projects?" King asked.

"No, he always put distance between money and the product. Which is surprising really, because he used to tell us about how when he was growing up and working on his uncle's farm, he'd have to work all the hours of the day, so he couldn't have been scared of work, could he?"

"Was he forced to do the farm work?" Allaway asked, jumping to the obvious conclusion.

"He never said as much. I think his parents died when he was young, and he went to live with his aunt and uncle on their farm, somewhere in the west of Ireland. I suppose he had to muck in."

"Did he have cousins?" King asked.

"No. When his aunt and uncle died, he said it was the end of the line."

"When did his aunt and uncle die?"

"A good few years ago. He only told us this story about his family after his aunt and uncle died."

"You never met them?" King pushed.

"No."

"Did any of the group get to meet them?" King asked.

"Nope."

"Out of your group, who would you say was closest with Mr Mylan?" This time Allaway asked the question.

"Oh, probably Maggie Littlewood. Maybe Roger as well."

"When you spoke to him on the phone that day, how did he sound?"

"How did he sound?" Stevenson asked. "He sounded like he wanted to get back to his lazy solo Saturday morning. He didn't like to do business at the weekend. He didn't have Jean Claude or Cynthia Cox come around on Saturdays; he kept Saturdays to himself. I think he'd just read the papers, potter around, and unwind, right? Most Saturday nights he'd do something though."

"Was his girlfriend around much do you know?" King asked.

"He didn't have a girlfriend."

"Was he gay?" Allaway asked.

"Ah, no, he wasn't gay."

"You say that like you know it for definite?"

"I mean I know he had an eye for girls. I'd catch him looking at our Noreen sometimes. She's at that stage where she turns heads."

"There was nothing…" King asked gently.

"No, no, no. Patrick knew better than trying any of that auld carry-on with our Noreen."

"Was everything all right between you and Mr Mylan during your telephone chat?"

"Yeah, perfect. We both agreed that we should stay with the Villa Bridgen wine shares."

"French?" King asked.

"Nappa Valley, and we'd heard they were very excited about this year's crop. Patrick asked, as he always asked, when were the bastards going to send us over a case so we could taste it for ourselves. We've been in there for four years, bailed them out, and we still hadn't even tasted it. We had our usual chuckle at that, and that's how we ended the call."

"But he didn't seem depressed to you? He didn't tell you about anything or anyone who might have been bothering him?"

"As I say, the last I heard of him, he was chuckling away to himself as he set the phone down."

"Could you tell me please what you were doing between four o'clock and eight o'clock last Saturday?" King asked.

"That's easy. I took my wife and kids on a day trip to Paris by Eurostar. We left at eight o'clock in the morning and got home just after ten o'clock that evening. I know that because the news had just started as we got in."

"But," King said, "you've just said you were on the phone to him at the same time you were on the Eurostar?"

A nod in the direction of his iPhone from Stevenson was all it took for King to realise she hadn't stumbled upon anything of importance.

Chapter Fifteen

The interview Irvine and Alloway conducted with Cynthia Cox did not work out the way that DC Dot King had planned. In fact, it was quite a disaster.

The gossip King had felt was there to be had, hadn't exactly flowed freely for Irvine either. She insisted that JCB - as she referred to Jean Claude Banks in the third person - remain around and accompany her for the interview. Once more, the interview had to be conducted in the small back garden so that Mrs Cox could continue her chain smoking.

Irvine, working on King's tip-off, knew of course that he should have separated JCB and Cox, but to do so would have antagonised her and risked shutting her down. Irvine was determined to remain civil with this woman, but some people reminded him how far down the social scale of respect the police had slipped. There was a time - and a time, Irvine would agree, when maybe some members of the police had abused their position - when being a policeman was enough to warrant respect from the general public. But Cox was making it clear that she had no time for Camden's finest. She "knew her rights" and would tolerate being involved only on her terms. Even if he'd asked for Jean Claude to leave them alone for the interview, Irvine sussed she would have insisted on the presence of her solicitor.

"Well, what have you discovered then?" she asked impatiently, before either police officer had the chance to commence proceedings.

"We're still working on our investigation," Alloway offered.

"I'll take that as nothing then," she replied, smiling insincerely for Alloway.

"If you ask me," she volunteered, as Irvine's hopes for the interview clicked up a few notches, "Paddy needed a proper job. He had too much time on his hands. Isn't that right, Jean Claude?"

"Yes, that is right, Cynthia."

"When you've too much time to do nothing, that's when the auld idle mind clicks in. Now my father, he'd never have been found hanging around on the back of a door." She stopped talking briefly to acknowledge Irvine's wincing. "What? That offends you? Oh please, let's call a spade a spade. As I was saying, my father would never have been found doing that, and the reason is that he had to work every hour God sent him to feed and clothe his family: my mother, my six sisters, and my brother. He had no time for tennis or grand dinner parties or sitting on his arse looking at a fecking computer screen for hours on end. For all we know, Mr Patrick Mylan could have been up there playing computer games or… well, we all know what you can find on the internet. Isn't that right Jean Claude?"

"Yes, that's right, Cynthia."

"Did you ever see him have an argument with anyone?" Irvine asked.

"He wouldn't have had the bottle for an argument. He'd have done his arguments through solicitors. Isn't that right, Jean Claude?"

"I do not know of his private business, Cynthia."

"No, Jean Claude, I didn't mean you knew of actual arguments he had through his solicitors; I meant generally speaking…"

For one split second, Irvine felt she was going to add, "Isn't that right, Jean Claude?"

"Did you ever discuss your families or your times in Ireland?"

"No, he was a Johnny-come-lately type. I imagine if you traced both our roots, we'd be from similar working-class families, but I think because technically he was my employer, he felt that made him a better person than me."

"You mean as in a snob?" Allaway asked.

"Don't get me wrong. To my face he was always pleasant enough, isn't that right, Jean Claude?"

"That's right, Cynthia," came the reply right on queue. The Frenchman looked happier now they weren't speaking ill of the dead.

"But I know the look. I know inside he felt he was better than me. He might never have said it, but he felt it. Mind you, it's my own fault; I shouldn't have been cleaning for him."

"Why do you say that, Mrs Cox?" Allaway asked.

"It is very difficult to explain. I'm not very good at putting these things into words. Isn't that right, Jean Claude?" she said as she stubbed out her butt on the sole of her shoe and flicked it into the garden.

"That's right, Cynthia," Jean Claude replied as he went off to fetch the butt.

"Oh, leave it, Jean Claude," Mrs Cox said dismissively. "Paddy's not here to complain about it now, is he?"

"What would he have complained about, Mrs Cox?" Irvine asked.

Cynthia Cox studied Irvine.

Irvine wondered what she saw. Of course, he knew what *he* saw when he looked in the mirror at himself, but he knew she wasn't seeing the same thing. Would she favour his qualities over his flaws, or vice versa? Was that how the laws of attraction worked? When you look at someone and their qualities - visual, physical and (eventually) spiritual - outweighed their faults, were you attracted to them? And if you saw mostly faults and flaws, were you not attracted to them? If you see someone's qualities does that mean that you ignore their faults and again vice versa?

In that moment he studied Cynthia just as much as she studied him. What did *he* see? He saw a woman who dressed more glamorously than her work suggested she could. She was well presented. From what he could tell, she seemed to have a fine figure, but middle-aged women, whom he was quite attracted to, rarely allowed their clothes to go with the flow of their bodies. Irvine often imagined what women he'd just met would look like in the heat of passion. To him this was the moment, the moment when women were totally lost in their pleasure, when they looked their most beautiful. He wasn't getting a good vibe in this department from Cynthia Cox. Perhaps if he'd met her and she hadn't betrayed a little of herself from the conversation they'd just had, he might have had a different, more appealing vision.

Her eyes flickered a few times as she broke off their mutual stare. The look in her eye suggested she knew exactly what Irvine had been thinking for those few brief seconds. Perhaps *she'd* been thinking the same? To Irvine, it looked as if she had seen something that attracted her. He didn't know what made him think this, maybe it was the fact that she looked like she had a marginally gentler smile for him than previously. More likely he reckoned, it was his ego getting the better of him.

"What would he have complained about?" she repeated still

looking at Irvine. "What do men always complain about? It's simple: men only really complain about how much they feel short-changed in their life, while not accepting that they've been short-changed due entirely to their own inabilities. Men only complain about what they think they should have as their God-given right, but they haven't had the knowledge or suss to get." She smiled, and while she continued staring at Irvine, she concluded with, "Isn't that right, Jean Claude?"

PART TWO

CAMDEN TOWN

Chapter Sixteen

Kennedy wandered into the reception area of North Bridge house late in the afternoon. His mind was miles away as he tried his hardest to imagine what Patrick Mylan's voice might have sounded like.

"Can you at least tell me which detective is working on the case?"

Involuntarily, Kennedy took an extremely deep breath. His brain seemed to be having great difficulty getting the oxygen pumped through his body, to a body in need.

Tim Flynn, the efficient and diplomatic desk sergeant, clocked Kennedy's discomfort, but outwardly ignored him, thereby allowing him the time to step through the side door unrecognised. Neither policeman, however, had allowed for the intuition of the speaker, who immediately raised her head, like a deer magnetised by a familiar scent.

As the Beatle bob (circa 1966's *Rubber Soul* album sleeve shot) swung around, canopying her hair in a movement the Fab Four would have been proud of, ann rea said his name before her eyes had a chance to make contact with him.

"Ms rea has been asking if there are any developments with the death in the swimming pool," Flynn said slowly and deliberately, giving them both a chance to compose themselves.

Kennedy still hadn't said her name. He found himself unable to do so.

ann rea looked around the reception area. There was a woman in advanced stages of desperation because she'd managed to lose her small daughter in Camden. If the mother had lost the daughter, the daughter certainly hadn't lost the mother, because at that moment, the cute-as-a-wee-dote, more than slightly precocious and no more than six-year-old daughter waltzed in and said to her mother, "Mum, whatever am I going to do with you? I hadn't even finished my hot chocolate. Now come back with me to the York & Albany before the nice waitress takes my cup away. You know how much I love to get my finger in the frothy bits at the bottom of the cup."

There was a bloodstained fifty-year-old man, in a thirty-year-old body, who looked as if he'd slept in his Paul Smith suit - or had the suit in question been specifically designed to look like that? This character with the black, curly hair was showing his licence and insurance details to Flynn.

Behind them a woman, perhaps in her mid-fifties and impressively dressed, waited patiently. Sgt Flynn kept glaring at her; it came as a surprise to Kennedy that there was a familiarity in both Flynn and her eyes - a familiarity that intrigued Kennedy.

Although not technically really in the queue, a woman with two children was next in line for attention. She was small, about five feet four, a bit overweight. The youngest child was still a baby and sat astride the side of her mother's tilted waist, secured only by her mum's left arm, while the other hand was locked in a vice-like grip on the left arm of a grossly embarrassed boy who, if the stubble on his upper lip was anything to go by, was perhaps sixteen. The mother kept saying in a hoarse voice, a little above a whisper, "I'm at my wits end with you, Ryan. I can't do anything else with you; the police are going to have to help me with you."

All of this was going on around Kennedy as he drank in the vision that was ann rea.

"I'm sorry, Kennedy. I didn't want to do this. But there was quite simply nobody else in the office, and my editor insisted that I cover this case."

She looked absolutely drained, perhaps even a little thinner than at their last meeting, Kennedy thought. Did this have something to do with their breaking up? Was that a good sign? Was he a bad person for considering, not to mention hoping, this was a good sign?

ann rea looked at the mother with two kids, and then back at Kennedy. He nodded to ann rea and raised a single index finger to signal the single minute he needed. He took the little woman and her two kids through to one of the interview rooms, begged forgiveness for one minute's delay, then returned immediately to the reception area, took ann rea by the arm and led her to the front door.

"Let's not have this chat here. We both have work to do. Are you okay if we meet in the York & Albany for a coffee in, say, one hour?"

"Okay, Christy," she mouthed silently to him, giving him a weak but patient smile and disappearing to join the heavily peopled Parkway.

Her scent was still intoxicating him when he sat down in the interview room with the mother and her two kids. The elder boy was now ghostly white.

"Okay," Kennedy began, "what seems to be the problem here?"

"It's just, sir, that I'm at my wit's end with Ryan. His father left me just before the baby was born, and I just can't do this any more by myself."

Kennedy waited.

"It's the crowd he's running around with, all their swearing and their slang. When they come around to see him, I haven't a clue about a single word they are saying. They're doing drugs, aren't they, Ryan?"

Kennedy looked into Ryan's eyes. He was certainly having a bad hair day and trying just a wee bit too hard to make a statement with his Mohawk, but the whites of his eyes were pure white. Even though his body was slumped by the uncertainty of youth, he was not under the influence of anything other than wanting to fit in; to impress.

"Ma! I keep telling you, I don't do chemicals," he said in a Simpson's voice mixed with the Queen's English.

"Tell you what," Kennedy said, standing up, "why don't Ryan and I have a wee chat in here by ourselves, eh?"

The mother sat in open-mouthed shock, looking as if she were now regretting the whole idea.

"I mean ... oh shit, I mean, I'm sorry ... you're not going to arrest him for doing drugs? I thought you'd just have a chat with him, and talk some sense into him for me. He's not a bad boy really ..."

"It's okay. No one is going to be arrested," Kennedy said as he showed the mother and baby back through the reception area. "Wait here, please, and we'll be back shortly.

"Ryan, you'll have your mum worried into an early grave if you're not careful," Kennedy began as he sat back down with a boy again. "Where do you live?"

"Up by Chalk Farm tube," Ryan started, and then added, "sir," as an obvious afterthought.

"You're not in the gang, are you?"

"No!" He protested, as wooden and stiff as Pinocchio.

"Ryan, I know it's not cool to be seen to like your parents."

"Mother," Ryan said, correcting the detective. "I only have a mother, and I *do* like her. At least she stuck with us."

"Well, then for goodness sake, lad, just make sure you show her you care. You don't need to embarrass yourself by being overly affectionate in front of your friends. But at least let her know what you just told me."

Kennedy studied Ryan squirming in the chair as if someone had just spilled boiling water in his red plastic bucket seat.

"What are you interested in? Sports?" Kennedy asked.

"Nah, wasting all that energy, only for losers."

"Music?"

"No way, I can't waste money on all those posers."

"You must listen to some music?"

"I don't mind Dylan..."

"Great!" Kennedy said, visibly relieved.

"But I mean to say, it's all just business now isn't it? But back in your day there was some great music being made."

"Back in my day, you cheeky little sod. Do I really look that old?"

"Well, your style is still pretty cool, if a bit out there for a cop."

Maybe all of ann rea's bugging him to grow his middle parted hair over his ears had hit the mark with at least one person, if not his boss.

"Okay," Kennedy said, "no sport, no music except Dylan, what about the movies?"

"Yeah, I enjoy films, I always have."

"Who do you like?"

"Clint Eastwood."

"As an actor or director?" Kennedy continued with a smile crossing his face.

"As both actually," Ryan said, allowing himself to break into a smile for the first time, "It's the writing side that I'm interested in. Eastwood *is* a great director, but I think a big part of his secret as both an actor and a director is that, he always uses great writers."

"So, you and your mates are into movies then?"

"Nah my mates aren't. My mom has always been into films though."

"So who would you discuss this stuff with?"

"My notebook," Ryan admitted. "Sad or what?"

"No, not at all," Kennedy said immediately. "You get a buzz from writing it all down?"

"Yes, I love writing."

"Then that's what you should do?"

"Not going to happen."

"Why not?" Kennedy pushed.

"'Cause it's me, Ryan Speys from Chalk Farm."

"Oh don't be so stupid," Kennedy said harshly.

Ryan shook his head furiously in surprise, but he seemed pleased not to be humoured.

"Look Ryan, sorry, but everything is there waiting for you. Listen to me now: no one, but no one, is going to put it on a plate for you. I'm not going to patronise you by saying you're not like the rest of your peers or any of that old baloney, but if I can tell you one thing, I'd tell you this. If you have a passion for something, a passion for anything, well then that immediately sets you apart from the pack. On top of which, if you're prepared to work at it, that puts you in a different league altogether. And then…"

"Who knows?" Ryan added sarcastically.

"No Ryan, not, 'who knows,' but more… then you'll at least have a chance of enjoying your life."

"But all the websites say there are too many writers. They say that the publishers are either closing down or have slush piles of manuscripts bigger than our tower block."

"Hey, slow down Ryan, slow way down. We all have to crawl before we can walk."

"Sorry?"

"Okay Ryan. I'll do something for you, if you do something for me. Okay?"

They both looked at each other for a few seconds.

"Deal?" Kennedy eventually asked, sticking out his hand towards Ryan.

Ryan met Kennedy's hand with his own mid-table and shook it furiously. "Deal!"

"Okay, I've a mate, a friend who is a journalist for the *Camden News Journal*. I'll talk to her about getting you part-time work around their office, and in return I want you to become a better son to your mother."

Ryan studied Kennedy carefully for a considerable time.

"Thank you, sir," he eventually said. "But what's in it for you?"

"Sorry?"

"Well, you said you'd do something for me if I did something for you. But it appears to me that both parts of the deal are to my advantage."

Kennedy nodded to himself slowly. He thought Ryan Speys, of Chalk Farm, with that attitude, at least must have a chance in the world.

"Oh, my friend, the journalist, will think that I have some very cool friends. That will be more than enough for me," he said.

CHAPTER SEVENTEEN

Ryan Speys' situation and Kennedy's promise meant that at the very least the first part of his meeting with ann rea over their coffee in the York & Albany turned out to be a whole lot easier than either had expected.

"Of course I can do that. I'd be happy to, Christy," she said.

"Thanks a million," Kennedy said, fearing they'd immediately run out of safe ground conversational steam.

It took seventeen minutes of their conversion until either of them was brave enough to open up the recent wound.

"I'm sorry."

There it was; she'd said it.

"I know you don't love me. I know it's over," he said quietly, steadying himself by lifting his glass of cold, crisp white wine. The words sounded much gentler now than how he'd heard his voice say them when he'd imagined this meeting. Still, it was devastating for him to have to admit.

He and ann rea were sitting at one of the tables outside the York & Albany. It was early evening and the office crowds had disappeared as the restaurant-cum-bar was getting ready for its diners. Straight across the road was North Bridge House, and Kennedy was aware that anyone over there could look out of their windows and see him and ann rea. To the outside world, to all his colleagues, it might look like they were having a cosy wee chat.

"Oh, Christy," she sobbed, and then made a fuss over searching for a Kleenex in her bag. As usual for ann rea, she had to remove every single item before she found the thing she was looking for. Some of them were presents Kennedy had bought for her: there was the tan leather wallet; there was her small pink Sony tape recorder for her interviews; her Beatle key ring; there was the last book he had bought her, a paperback. She fanned through the well-thumbed pages of *One Day* by David Nicholls.

"I love this," she said, stopping her unpacking routine for a few moments as she considered the book. "I'm savouring it, allowing myself only a few pages at a time. It's so sad; please don't tell me if they get back together again. I suppose for the book to work they have to, but I'm nervous." And then she dug back into her bag and hoaked around a bit more, producing her notebook with telephone numbers scribbled on the front page, a few pens and more pencils, her indispensable jar of Clarins Cream, some Night Nurse capsules, perhaps their presence betraying another reason for the running nose. Then she got frustrated because her tears were dropping from her almond shaped eyes into her bag.

Something strange had happened to Kennedy when he'd said to ann rea, "I know you don't love me. I know it's over." Up until that point, up until he'd vocally confirmed his worst fear, there had still been a chance something would happen to make it all right again. Now that he'd actually said the words to her, he shivered down to the toes of his blue and pink socks, realising that he'd made it real. Well, it wasn't that it wasn't real up to that point. By her lack of attention and no contact, she'd already proved that point, but now he knew he'd stopped hoping for something he just couldn't have. Of course, it didn't mean he had finished his walk in the dark forest; it didn't mean that his pain was over. It did, however, mean that the pain wasn't going to get any worse. Kennedy imagined that life would never ever feel as bad as this again.

"Christy," she started as she dried her nose and tried to laugh through the end of her tears, "I'm sorry about this. I know how much you hate public displays of emotion, but I couldn't really get through this if we weren't out here. I've thought a lot about this, and I suppose the thing I keep coming back to is: if I have to think so much about whether or not I love you, then I obviously…"

"I get the picture," he said, trying hard not to sound bitter.

"Oh, Christy, you don't do sarcasm very well," she said fondly, but, Kennedy felt, with just the slightest hint of sarcasm. "I've realised that what most of us do is sit around waiting for things to go wrong with our lives when what we really should be doing is getting on with our lives and enjoying them. And I keep trying to do that. But it won't work for me. I'm stuck in something and I need to get out of it. I want,

I really *need* to spend part of my life, at least, living my life rather than waiting for something to go wrong."

Kennedy wondered if that was a variation of, "This is not about you, it's about me." Could she really be trying to say to him, "This is not your fault?" Of course it was, at the very least, half of his fault.

"Christy, I won't say, 'I really do love you, but not in the way you want me to.' But I will say: I do feel we shared something very special. We've been closer than most married couples ever will be in their lives, and maybe I can't help crying now because, sadly, I feel with all that's happening to us, we'll probably lose our friendship as well as everything else. I don't think I've ever talked so much to anyone in my whole life. You know what; we talked so much I no longer heard your accent.

"Look, I'm really sorry I behaved the way I did around the time of the Willie Henderson incident, but I needed to do *something*, Kennedy, and you handed me the perfect excuse on a plate. I thought it would make me feel better. But since then I wake up in the mornings and I feel good, and I feel strange about feeling good, and then I realise how bad I really feel, and it all comes flooding back to me about how messed up my life is. I imagine that must be what it's like when someone close to you dies: when you first wake each morning, you feel okay, but then as your mind clicks into gear, you start to remember all the black clouds that hang around your shoulder and just won't go away. Christy, I need to make them go away.

"Oh God, if you weren't someone I cared so much about, it might be easier…"

"You really think that makes me feel better?"

"No, no, I didn't mean that the way it sounded," she pleaded, "but I was feeling so shit every day that passed when I wasn't dealing with this."

She took his hand.

"We had to deal with it, Christy. I don't want to lose you as a friend, and my biggest fear is that I might have already jeopardised our friendship by my inability to deal with this…" she said breaking down into an uncontrollable fit of sobbing.

"Oh, ann rea, it'll be okay," Kennedy said, reaching across to take her hand.

"Kennedy, don't be nice to me at a time like this. I couldn't stand it. Please, just leave me, now, this moment, *please.*"

"ann rea, I can't leave you like this."

"Please, Kennedy, if you stay I'll only get worse, and I'll never get away from here."

Kennedy rose and kissed her on the top of her mop-top, ruffled her hair, and barely managed to get the word "goodbye" pronounced in a decipherable state.

Kennedy could never work out why it was girls were usually so cut up when they dropped you. In his limited romantic history, this had always been the case.

First off there had been Betty Booth. She was such a good pre-teen friend she'd even put a pair of the US Cavalry gloves he'd seen James Stewart wear on to her Santa Claus list. By the time Christmas arrived, she'd dropped him for an older man - Kennedy's then best friend, Gerald Kelly, who was all of ten years old. Next came Margaret Hutchinson. Well, he had to admit that was more him admiring her from afar, so technically she'd never really dumped him. But the realisation that nothing was ever going to happen between them was just as big a gunk to his system.

Next came his first *real* girlfriend. She actually came up to him at college and asked him if he'd go out with her best friend. He said, "I'd prefer to go out with you."

"Okay, yes, that would be nice," she said sweetly, "but can you wait for a fortnight so I can either find a new boyfriend for my best friend, or at the very least by that point she'll have gotten over you?"

So, in the middle of the second week, Adel officially became his girlfriend. "Friend" as in they got on well with each other and "girlfriend" as in they kissed; in fact Kennedy seemed to remember they kissed a lot. They even enjoyed an arousing snogging session on a certain Saturday afternoon at the matinee. The same Saturday and the same cinema where she said, in a cinema whisper, "We're too young to be going steady. We've hardly lived. We shouldn't be exclusive. We should also see other people." Which was code, and not a very subtle code, for "There is someone else I want to go out with."

Kennedy dealt with it as maturely as he could; he refused to ever speak to her again, but he'd heard from her best friend - yes, the same best friend who'd indirectly started the whole affair - that Adel couldn't come to college that week because she was at home crying all the time.

Then came his first English girlfriend, Budgie. He could still see her, a cigarette in one hand, using the other to rub cigarette ash into her denim jeans to try and age them. She broke up with him by letter, then made up with him by phone, and then, after a few more rocky blips, dumped him for the third and final time in person, in her beautiful English voice, at eight forty-five on a Wednesday night in Wimbledon; the time, the day, and the place, if not the date, etched into his memory for ever. Kennedy took a long time to get over her, which he eventually did, but he never forgot her. She'd told him, "You never ever forget the first person you make love to." But she cried a lot on the three times she dumped him.

Then there were the lean times on the female front, several relationships but none that hurt when they broke up, so, no more tears were shed in the wilderness years. Then from, out of the blue, ann rea, and now she was starting to cry, so Kennedy accepted that the signs weren't great.

He wondered if any of the girls had been aware there was a simple way for them to make themselves feel better. Easy, don't dump him! Really, it was that simple!

***

Kennedy did what he always did when he wanted to clear his head; he went for a long walk. When he was young, it would be along the beach in Portrush, but since he moved to NW1, he'd taken a shine to Regent's Park. He tried to figure out exactly what was happening to him. He didn't feel as bad as he thought he would. Maybe it was just that he'd been living with this for so long, and now that it was definitely really over, it wasn't really such a big shock to the system as he felt it might have been. Perhaps he'd been in training for the last couple of months for this exact moment. However, what ann rea had said was spot on; like her, he'd wake up the following morning feeling okay, but then as the realisation of what had happened the day before came to light, he'd hurt again.

How do you avoid the hurt? he wondered, as he passed the boating pond over on the Mosque side of the park. The bottom line was that to him ann rea was the perfect woman, but the fact of the matter was that things between them definitely were not going to work out.

It was another major gunk to him, perhaps the biggest of his life, and he accepted this was simply because he was realising how special a person he'd just let slip through his fingers.

About thirty minutes later, towards the end of his walk, Kennedy reached the two telephone boxes standing proudly like faithful and trusted guards at the foot of St George's Terrace, just opposite Primrose Hill. They were two of the few vintage telephone kiosks in London to have survived Red Ken's 1990s modernisation. It was eight-forty. Even though he was, at the most, a hundred feet from his house, he entered the telephone box on the left, took out the piece of paper Miss Chada had palmed to him earlier and made the call he always knew he would. Twenty minutes later he answered the ring on his doorbell and he admired the perfect-bodied woman as she whished past him into his house.

Kennedy thought Miss Chada was so beautiful that when she walked into a room people would stop whatever they were doing and be helplessly drawn to her earthy, undisputable beauty. Just like the way bees are drawn to flowers, Kennedy figured, but unlike the bees who have no inhibitions whatsoever in their overtures to the roses, Miss Chada, nine times out of ten, would remain unattended, and that's because the boys would be scared of her and the girls jealous of her.

For some reason though, Sharenna Chada had picked Kennedy. She wasn't offering to give, or take, love, but what she was offering, and what he greedily accepted, sent him to an exhausted and contented sleep ninety minutes later.

CHAPTER EIGHTEEN

Tuesday came slowly and sluggishly for Kennedy. He remembered getting up at three-thirty in the morning to make Miss Chada - he wondered why did he keep thinking of her as Miss Chada and not Sharenna - a cup of tea and some toast. Although she said she didn't need it, she smiled as he made it, watching his every move intently. She said she had never seen anyone make such a fuss about preparing tea and toast; she also said it was very nice of him to do this for her. She seemed to enjoy her tea and toast immensely. Kennedy had the feeling that she was not used to having people do things for her. Without commenting on it, she immediately washed the dishes in the sink and cleared away the crumbs by the toaster. He'd walked her to her car, again something she seemed to take a certain pride from. She seemed in no hurry to rush the journey. They said goodnight. There was one awkward moment when Kennedy considered if he perhaps should kiss her.

She seemed to read his mind, because she rubbed his arm gently and then said in a whisper, "It is enough for me to tell you that I would like to return to your bed. I know that you would like me to return there too." She moved her hand from his arm to the side of his face. "For as long as we can retain this need and this honesty, I promise you I will return to your bed." She smiled her sad smile. Her smile suggested that she knew more about them and what they would do than he did.

As she drove away, leaving Kennedy standing in the middle of his road with his hands deep in his pockets, the thought running around his head was that the first time he'd been with Miss Chada, it had been like a master class in the art of lovemaking; she knew exactly what to do, and when, to pleasure them both. But a few hours ago, during their third session, their mating had been more natural, relaxed, and consequently all the more enjoyable.

***

"You've changed," Nealey Dean said to Kennedy the minute she opened the door to her apartment some six hours later. "Something has happened to you."

Kennedy blushed as he recalled standing outside his house in the middle of the night watching Miss Chada drive away. He'd slept well, as well as any night during recent months, but the morning had arrived too soon.

"Good morning, Miss Dean," Kennedy said as she took the hand he'd offered and used it to pull him towards her for a peck on each cheek. He hoped she didn't notice his blush.

"I don't know what it is; you look taller, more confident," she continued, seeming genuinely intrigued by Kennedy's aura. She completely ignored Dot King.

Kennedy shrugged his shoulders. Happily, Nealey let it go.

"Oh my goodness, Christy," she said, taking him by the arm and walking him through to her sitting room, "I'm so glad you didn't bring James with you. That was very awkward last time."

"Yes, I'm sorry to have put you through that," Kennedy replied.

"Not for me," she laughed. "I meant for James. I was perfectly fine, but the poor man was as nervous as an agent at a showcase performance."

"Oh," Kennedy said, breaking into an involuntary smile.

"Okay, here's what I'd like to do," Nealey said, still clinging to Kennedy's arm like a bride to her reluctant father, "Christy and I will make coffee, and of course tea for the inspector here, if you," here she looked directly at Dot King, "will nip out and get some croissants, please?"

"We're not supposed to leave a male officer alone with a female…"

"Oh my goodness," Nealey guffawed, "I promise you I won't attack him. He'll be safe with me."

"Actually, I think the rule is more to protect you," King persisted.

"Well, here's the thing," Nealey continued, impishly hugging Kennedy's arm even tighter, "I can go down and fetch them, but then you're going to have to wait until I come back before we start our interview. Or Christy here can go down, and again we're going to have to wait until he comes back. *Or* you can go down, and Christy and I can start right away."

"*Or* we could just forget the croissants," King suggested, looking beseechingly at Kennedy.

"You're not suggesting that you want to deprive me of my early morning ritual," Nealey stated firmly.

"It's fine…" Kennedy started.

"Yes, it's fine, Constable King," Nealey continued, jumping in very quickly, dropping Kennedy's arm, nipping over to the sofa and searching behind the cushions until she found a ten pound note, "and I'll tell you what, we'll leave the door of the apartment open."

King looked to Kennedy. Kennedy nodded agreement to King.

Nealey made a fuss of closing the door after King. She returned to Kennedy on route to her small kitchen area. "Sorry about that," she apologised, "but there is nothing that brings out the bossy boots in me more than another bossy woman!"

Kennedy accompanied Nealey Dean into the kitchen area and pulled out one of her two high stools.

"I know what's happened," she declared as she went through her cupboards. "You're back with ann rea."

"Ah, sadly not; that's not going to happen," Kennedy admitted honestly, thinking it was a little strange that Nealey Dean was the first person he should make such a declaration to.

"Really?"

"Yes," Kennedy replied quietly.

"How do you feel about that?"

"Well, not as bad as I thought I would. I mean I've… we've been trying to deal with this from shortly after we met."

"You mean your work?"

"No, not at all. ann rea was totally fine about that," Kennedy replied, wondering if he really wanted to talk about this. "When we met she had just broken up with a guy she was in love with. He left her and got married shortly thereafter, so her point was, 'I don't really know what my feelings are, and if I don't, well then, surely I can't trust them with you either.'"

"And the fact that you were so convinced about your feelings freaked her even more." she offered sympathetically. "Yep, been there, done that, bought the T-shirt. How long were you dating?"

"A bit over four years."

"And you've been going through this for that long?"

"For a lot of the time we were enjoying ourselves," Kennedy said, genuinely smiling.

"I must say you seem okay about the break up... there is something about you... something is going on. OH-MI-GOD, I've got it," she said, stopping her preparation and dropping her arms to her side and bending over towards Kennedy slightly. *"You've met someone else."*

Nealey Dean's words were not a question; they were a statement of fact. Kennedy was impressed and embarrassed.

"Well, it's early days..."

"*Obviously,*" she added, raising her dark eyebrows so Kennedy could see them through her blonde fringe.

"And... it's different," was all Kennedy could think to say.

"Let's see," she continued expansively as she started back into her coffee and tea preparation routine, "what's the quickest I've ever started up a new relationship? I've never cheated, so there's never been an overlap. I don't think you've ever cheated either, Christy."

Christy nodded agreement.

"You see. You've just proved my point. Some men would feel that it was a flaw not to be considered a rake, you know, and even if they hadn't admitted it or denied it there, their body language would have been, at the least, just a tad indignant."

"You were going to tell me about your quickest new boyfriend."

"Ah, that would have been Usain Bolt."

Now it was the turn of Kennedy's eyebrows to rise involuntary.

"Not the quickest runner but the..."

"Got you," she laughed. Nealey Dean had a brilliant laugh. Not all beautiful women look beautiful when they laugh, but Nealey Dean's laugh lit up not just her entire body, but the whole room as well. "Oh yes, I remember. If you dare tell James, I'll kill you myself, and then I'll get my vengeance on both of you by turning myself in to Constable King so she can get the credit for solving the case."

"I wouldn't be around to worry," Kennedy commented, deadpan.

"Oh yes... you're right, of course," she said through a patient smile, "so I was with this boy, we're talking late teens, and I was so into him, even to the point that I was considering turning down acting jobs just so we could be together, and then he cheated on me. He didn't even think it mattered; he said it didn't mean anything. 'It was just sex,' he claimed. So I dumped him on a Saturday over lunch and went out with his best friend that same night. I quite liked the replacement anyway; we'd all been friends before I started dating God's gift to women.

"I'll tell you, Christy, there's no lust like vengeful lust," Nealey Dean said impishly, and added, "Now, help me take this through to the living room and tell me how you're getting on with finding out what happened to Patrick."

"We need to find out more about him." Kennedy was extremely happy to be switching gears. "The last time we met, you were telling me a little about Mr Mylan's love life with Chloe Simmons."

"Yes?"

"Have you met her since?" Kennedy asked.

"Sadly not," she replied. "I mean, I really would have loved to. For research purposes only, of course," she added quickly.

"Why of course."

"I really would love to have chatted to someone who was knowingly going out with someone for sex and only sex."

"You think Mr Mylan made it that clear to her?"

"Well. I did get that feeling. But with Chloe, from our brief conversation, I didn't get the impression she felt she was a victim."

"And what about any of Chloe's predecessors; did Mr Mylan ever mention any of them?" Kennedy asked.

"No. I did ask Tim if he knew anything about them. I mean, I never took him into my confidence about what Patrick had told me; I just asked him about Patrick's earlier girlfriends," she paused as she went to open the door and let DC King in and then continued her conversation with Kennedy, "but the surprising thing for me was not that he didn't know but that he didn't even seem interested."

"Wouldn't that have suggested that maybe Mr Dickens knew something about Mr Mylan but didn't want to betray a confidence?" Kennedy asked as King dished out several calorie enemies.

"As in Patrick was gay?" Nealey replied.

"Perhaps," Kennedy said.

"Not possible, Christy. Girls can tell the gay men, can't we, Constable King?"

"Maybe only when they want us to," King replied, accepting the olive branch.

"Oh I don't know," Nealey said. "I'd say my own radar hasn't let me down yet."

"But would it be fair to say that you feel Tim Dickens felt Mr Mylan might be?" Kennedy asked, giving up on his tea. They'd been so involved in their earlier conversation that she'd committed the mortal sin of stewing his tea. Both King and Dean seemed to be enjoying the coffee though.

"Okay, Christy, I'll give you that." Nealey conceded.

"Who would you say was closest to Mr Mylan?"

"I'd say Roger and Maggie Littlewood, especially Maggie; she seemed genuinely fond of Patrick and was always looking out for him. They'd often be off in the corner by themselves rabbiting away."

"And there was nothing…" King started.

"Oh no. Roger and Maggie were the perfect couple, tight as tiger cubs," Nealey interrupted quickly. She looked as if she might be still considering the possibility of such a relationship. She then stared at Kennedy as she said, "Maggie is very comfortable with all her friends, male and female. I agree with her; you can't let any of that kind of green-eyed baggage get in the way of a potentially great friendship. My father doesn't have any female friends who are not friends of my mother. All his real friends, all his mates, are male. But that's a generation thing, I suppose."

"Did Mr Mylan ever give you any of his stock market tips?" Kennedy asked.

"Oh, he talked about them briefly the first time we met, but I can't be bothered with all of that, I really can't. I'm an actress. I make money acting, and I don't want to be distracting myself worrying each morning about what might have happened to the few pence I've managed to put away. I much prefer to ring-fence it, stick it away somewhere safe where, although I may never make a fortune on it, I'll never lose it either."

"Did Patrick drink a lot?" Kennedy asked.

"Not as much as Roger. That sounded like I was perhaps trying to protect Patrick's name a bit when in fact I wasn't. Yes, he liked his wine, but he never got ugly, he never drank too much. Oh gosh, now I've made it sound like Roger does. Let's start from the beginning again. I'd say he and his mates liked their wine, but none of them are, or were, slaves to it."

"Tell me about Tim."

"Tim, what about Tim?"

"Is he married?"

"Oh, Christy, that was devious, very devious. We touch briefly on whether or not Patrick might be gay, and then you take the conversation well away from the topic and back via Tim. You know that Tim is not married... and..."

"And that was equally devious, wasn't it?" An admiring smile creeping over Kennedy's face.

"Sorry?"

"I ask you a question and you avoid it by turning the spotlight back on me and away from the question."

She smiled.

"Okay, I didn't believe Patrick was gay, therefore I wouldn't have suspected any such relationship."

"And Mr Dickens?"

"Surely we don't need to cast aspersions on Tim as well?"

"Nealey, I need to find out every single thing I can about Mr Mylan and his group of acquaintances. Somewhere in the middle of it all, there just might be a clue as to what happened and why it happened to him."

"You know, I've never thought about it," she said, and the three of them knew she was lying.

"I understood you felt you could always tell these things," King suggested, but cleverly restrained herself from sounding smug about it.

"All I can tell you is that he's always been a good friend to me, and neither of us has ever got into the romantic side of each other's lives. And that's positively all I have to say on the subject."

"Okay, Nealey, we respect that," Kennedy said, feeling they'd run out of steam. "These dinner parties of Mr Mylan's, do you ever remember anyone who attended them who argued with Mr Mylan?"

"No, none of that, ever. Lively yes, confrontational no," she said. "I've been thinking about nothing else recently, to be honest, and I haven't as yet turned up one piece of information that might be helpful."

The ensuing silence was broken with, "Tell me, Constable King, have you always wanted to be in the police force, or was it a career choice you made later in life?"

"I always wanted to be a detective," King replied quickly.

"Was your father in the police?" Nealey Dean probed, obviously doing some research for her own career of choice.

"No, and no relations," King offered. "I considered a few things, but there was never anything else that interested me as much as this."

"What, catching the criminals or solving the crime?"

"Well, they're obviously connected at the hip, but I'd have to say my priority has always been the need to solve the crime."

"And yourself, Christy?" Nealey asked in a gentler voice.

"Solving the puzzle of the crime," Kennedy replied, "which reminds me, we need to…"

"Yes, of course, sorry," Nealey said, standing up. "I'm always doing that, trying to get a fix on people. Invaluable for my work as you can imagine."

As the detectives were leaving the flat, Nealey Dean hung back with Kennedy, encouraging King to lead the way. By the time King had opened the door and was in the corridor of the mansion block, she realised that Kennedy and Dean were still in the flat.

"Maybe James and I," Dean said in a quiet voice, "and you and your new lady could go out some time together for dinner or drinks?"

"I don't think it's that kind of a relationship," Kennedy replied honestly.

"Right," she said, looking bemused. "Okay," she continued, nodding her head very slowly. "I see. I get it now."

CHAPTER NINETEEN

At the same time, on that particular summer Tuesday morning, DS Irvine and DS Allaway were in Martin Friel's office. Friel & Associates was based on the first and second floors on Parkway just above the sadly missed Regent's Book Shop, not a million miles from North Bridge House. The offices were small but cleverly decorated with lots of mirrors and were tidy, very tidy. Friel was friendly immediately, and with generous handshakes all around, he invited them up to the second floor to his meeting room while his secretary nipped out to fetch them each a cappuccino and, in Friel's words, "a nibble or two."

"I'm still waiting for my associates to come in," Friel deadpanned in an accent halfway between the Black Country and America, "but they haven't come in once so far." He chuckled heartily. "Oh well, at least I don't have to share my profits with anyone."

This time he laughed longer and louder. Irvine reckoned it must have been one of his regular routines, but he still genuinely seemed to get a great amusement out of it. He was dressed in a pair of tan Camper trainers, tan cords, and a multi-coloured knitted jumper, which looked very expensive and best suited for a golf course. He was fresh faced and recently shaved, so that his skin positively glowed. His hair was thick, black, and cut to about half an inch all over.

"But seriously, I was a teacher for years while working part-time on investments. I started to make more on investments, so I switched careers and eventually ended up at Credit Suisse where I met the crew. When I started up here by myself, I thought Friel & Associates sounded better, grander if you will, than a plain, simple 'Martin Friel.'"

"What did you teach?" Irvine asked. "Economics?"

"No, physical education actually, in Wolverhampton," Friel replied. "I've found it very handy in this business."

When Irvine and Allaway stared at him blankly, he added, "I was in great shape to run away from my creditors," breaking into his infectious laugh again. "No, seriously," he said, turning moods on a six-pence, "I know you've come here to talk to me about Patrick; I'm just trying to break the ice. Apart from which, I'm as nervous as a judge on court with John McEnroe."

By which point the cappuccinos and muffins arrived. Allaway took out his notebook and set it down on the table by his untouched muffin, to show that it was time to get on with the proceedings.

The room was expensively decorated. With the double-glazed windows and thick linen shutter blinds, the occupants could imagine they were three miles away in the City, should they so wish. The walls were an off-white, the thick carpet a deep blue, and the two sofas and two matching chairs placed around a large stained-glass coffee table were black leather. The original fireplace had been replaced with a bookshelf crammed with books by and about various famous business people. Above the built-in bookshelf was a large framed poster of Manchester United's 2008/2009 League-winning side. On the other walls were framed Man United shirts signed, Irvine reckoned, by the players who had owned them.

Friel obviously noticed Irvine clocking his book collection. He walked across to his books and took out a Branson edition, *Business Stripped Bare: Adventures of a Global Entrepreneur*, and fast-flicked through it a few times.

"What Richard forgets to reveal here, and in his other books, is that the real key to his success is, and has always been, his ability in picking great lieutenants. And there's nothing wrong with that. It's certainly worked well for him, not to mention Churchill, Napoleon, and John F. Kennedy."

"Right," Irvine said. Allaway jumped in.

"So, do you make a good living doing this, you know, investing?"

"I could show you a method, which is based on analysing shares closely for two hours, each and every day. You study a screen two hours a day, watching for candlesticks, falls and rises. You simply clock the movements, and within a month you could be making a living out of it. But," Friel held out the "But" the way Chris Tarrant held it out while showing the cheque on the current state of play before withdrawing it again, "within a month you'd be bored to tears."

"But isn't it just like gambling?" Allaway suggested, carrying on his new interest from the recent Tony Stevenson interview.

"Not even a little," Friel tutted. "In horse racing you have a horse and you have ten minutes, and at the end of the ten minutes there is a very good chance the bookie is going to be taking your hard-earned cash home to his magnificent country house. But with shares, you will get a certificate, and that certificate will have a life of several years; in those years you could be earning from it annually while still awaiting your big winnings - you know, when you eventually sell."

"Right," Allaway replied, seeming to take the point on board.

Irvine knew that if they stood any chance of solving this case, then they needed to have at least some sense of the workings and dealings of this world.

"How do you know which shares to go with?" he asked, thinking it was as good a place as any to start.

"You know, the honest answer to that is that you just follow your nose and don't be scared of being wrong. If you don't want to lose, then don't buy shares."

Irvine looked as if he'd been expecting more.

"Okay, two fellows we knew, David Bramhill and Joe O'Farrell. They've been good to us, we'd invested in a few of their projects in the past, things like Cambridge Mineral and Encore Oil, and they'd done well for us..."

"When you say us, you mean you and Patrick Mylan and Tony Stevenson?"

"Yes, Patrick, Tony, and myself: Toblerone..."

Irvine arched his eyebrows into a transparent question mark.

"Okay, we, all three, came from Credit Suisse, Toblerone is Swiss and has three sides."

"Right," Irvine said, forcing a smile.

"Anyway, Bramhill and O'Farrell rang up once, like they'd do from time to time, and said they were starting up a new project called Nighthawk Energy. This was about four years ago. Now Warren Buffett claims that he usually prefers to invest more in the people running the company than in the company's product. I've always found this to be solid advice. Bramhill and O'Farrell are always on the case. You know, in contrast to where you've got a chairman who believes the company is there purely as his own personal plaything and primarily to finance his lifestyle. We've always respected David and Joe and their approach.

I believe they put £56,000 of their own money into Nighthawk Energy, creating, at a quarter pence per share, something like 22.4 million shares. They were selling some of the Hawk shares to people like us, people they'd used before, to raise funds. We bought in at 2p a share, which meant their shares were immediately worth eight times the original value. They even sold some to Credit Suisse who bought in at 4p, 8p, and 12p. Credit Suisse sold their shares at 25p and then bought back in again later. Once Nighthawk Energy, or Hawk as the company came to be referred to, came on to people's radar, the brokers, bankers, and hedge fund managers, who are out there all the time looking for stuff to buy, became interested. I believe a lot of those came in at around the 8p stage. So, all the time the value of our shares was increasing, but obviously we couldn't sell at that stage because it wasn't, as then, listed as a share. Of course, it's currently listed, and to cut a long story very short, the shares are currently around the 42p mark. Okay, and here's where it gets interesting. On top of the increase of the share price, Hawk is involved, on a 50/50 basis, with Running Foxes, on the Jolly Farm project, where they've just discovered an extremely large reserve of oil. Word has it they'd hit around 1.6 billion barrels of oil. *So* they expect the shares to triple in the next few months."

No wonder Martin Friel has such a great sense of humour, Irvine thought, as Allaway voiced it even more succinctly, "So, you'll make sixty times your original investment?"

"Yes, but I did buy the muffins," Friel said, guffawing. "Sorry. Seriously, we did - well pretty close. We bought only the original chunk of Hawk shares at 2p, but by the time we bought more shares, we had to pay 4p and 6p."

"So how much have you invested in this?" Irvine asked.

"Well, I'd prefer not to say," Friel replied coyly.

"But surely all of this is above board?" Irvine said quickly.

"Of course. It's just that I don't like to boast."

"But this must all be public record, Mr Friel. We really do need to know."

"Okay, £100,000."

"What? You're going to make a £100,000?" Allaway said, clearly mentally dividing it by his annual salary.

"Ah, no, that was the original investment," Friel replied humbly.

"But split between the three of you?" Allaway continued, now clearly in shock.

"Ah no, that would be £100,000 each."

"So you stand to make six million quid each on this one deal?" Allaway squeaked.

"Closer to four mil, actually."

"How many people would have known that Patrick Mylan had such holdings?" Irvine asked.

"We're not the Flaming Ferraris; we're very discreet," Friel claimed, "Really just the three of us, our accountants - a few people like that."

"Did you, Toblerone, did you all get on well with each other?" Irvine asked.

"Yes, we were a good team, and we really got on extremely well with each other socially."

"And you're all on the same share?"

"If we go in to a project as Toblerone, we go in as equal partners. If one of us is not as fussed on a project as the others, we'll do it ourselves individually."

"Are there any projects you can think of where only one of you went into it, as an individual, and the others didn't and..." Irvine said leaving the important bit unsaid.

"And the others felt bad about it?"

"Well, yes, I suppose."

"I mean, not everyone thinks the same way," Friel started, and then looking like he was searching through his mind for an example. "Yes, Donegal Creameries. That would be a good example. I'd a wee bit of local knowledge on this one. Around the early nineties, I was having a wee look at them, and the shares were floating anywhere between 1.20 euro and, say, 1.60 euro per share, and they were pretty static. But I discovered that their property portfolio hadn't been valued for... I forget, it was either eight years or twelve years, and so I bought in, against the advice of everyone. The property boom happened, Donegal Creameries subsequently revalued their properties, and the share shot up to 5.00 euro, and I, well I did very well out of it."

"How much did you have on that one?" Allaway asked.

"There you go again, Constable; you're making it sound like I was backing a horse. Again the shares had been pretty static for a good while;

they were going about their core business, and I had certificates, which never ran out, showing that I had a share of the profit of the company. So in my mind I wasn't gambling."

Friel stopped his narrative and looked at both the Camden Town policemen. His eyes lingered on Allaway a bit longer.

Before they'd a chance to ask another question, Friel volunteered, "Look, if you feel it is relevant, I will obviously provide you with exact figures on all of these deals. It's just…" Friel paused looking like he was having difficultly picking his words, "well, let's say I've found that people, no matter how much they are intrigued, they don't always *really* want to hear about other people doing fabulously. There's a bit of, 'Haven't you had enough good luck already?'"

"Okay, that makes sense, Mr Friel," Irvine said, "and did either Mr Stevenson or Mr Mylan feel upset that the shares had done so well for you?"

"Nope. As I said, that wasn't the way we worked. We all had our individual successes *and* failures," Friel replied, looking at Allaway again. "I'm always happy to talk about my failures."

"What about the other way around; was there a share Mr Mylan was involved in that you weren't?" Irvine continued, knowing that he'd left Allaway far behind, diligently trying to work out how many years he'd have to work as a detective sergeant to collect four million pounds.

"Oh, yes, there was one," Martin Friel declared. "You see, I'm not a big man for futures. Can't abide them. I think that not only are they destroying our banking business, they're also destroying entire countries. You know, you make a jumper, like this one for example, and you sell it for say £100. Great deal, everyone is happy. But if I come along and want to gamble on what it will cost you to make this jumper in five years time and what you'll be able to sell it for at that point, well that's just crap, isn't it? Someone's trying too hard to be too darn clever."

"Okay, and?"

"Sorry, I got carried away in a soapbox moment there. Patrick wanted us, Toblerone, to buy into the future sales of Tim Dickens' CDs. He'd read somewhere that David Bowie sold the rights to his future CD sales to a bank; Bowie was happy, he got millions of pounds up front, and the bank had some genuine assets to hold on to."

"But surely if record sales were going to be worth anything, then Bowie would have held on to them?" Allaway asked.

"Exactly the point I made to Patrick and Tony. I told them I didn't want to be in on this one."

"I suppose though, if you were the bank who'd bought into Michael Jackson's future sales before he died, you'd be quite happy now, wouldn't you?" Allaway offered. "Apparently in the weeks after his death, he was selling a million albums a week, worldwide."

"Good point, but Tim Dickens is a friend of ours and I wouldn't particularly want to be involved in profiting from his death. Tim wasn't really keen on the project; it was Patrick who kept pushing it. Tim was happy the way things were. He did okay on his publishing. His records and CDs weren't selling great, but he was happy not to be in the front line any more and was feeling comfortable and content with his life. Then one night, after one of his dinner parties, Patrick declared he'd been doing a bit of research, and he figured that he could offer five million pounds to Tim for a 50 per cent stake in his future royalties from songs and records. Tony and I thought the subject had been dropped when we both declared ourselves out of the deal, but Patrick was convinced and put his offer on the table."

"The five million pounds made Tim sit up and take notice, I bet," Allaway ventured.

"You're not wrong, Constable; you're not wrong. Tim nearly bit his hand off."

"How long ago what this?" Irvine asked.

"About six years ago," Friel replied.

"Which would have been before the X Factor girl, Pricilla White, had the number one Christmas single with *No More Sad Lonely City Streets*, one of Tim Dickens' famous songs," Allaway said.

"Correct, which was right before the same version of the same song appeared in a certain USA diva's comeback movie. The sound track album was a multi million seller, and the diva in question also covered *No More Sad Lonely City Streets* on her comeback album, which has, I believe, sold over twelve million copies to date. Which was also before Tim Dickens' own *Best of* CD was released and sold well all over the world; it sold six point three million copies in fact. I know all of this only because Patrick liked to remind Tony and myself about it at every available opportunity."

"So, what you're saying is that Patrick Mylan was doing well, thank you very much?"

"Yes, indeed. Not many were doing better," was Friel's reply, which coming from a man in the process of picking up a £4 million windfall was quite a nod.

"And would you mind telling me what you were doing on Saturday between the hours of four o'clock in the afternoon and eight o'clock in the evening?" Irvine asked.

"Dead easy. Some Saturdays I get to overdose in my favourite pastimes."

"Football?" Irvine promoted.

"No, my other hobby - watching movies."

"Okay, what did you go and see?"

"*Crazy Heart* with Jeff Bridges, which was just incredible, and then *The Road*, hard work but worth sticking with, and then I'd a pint and a pie at my local."

"Did you go to the movies with anyone?"

"No, 'fraid not. I prefer to go by myself. I go into the zone when I'm in the cinema, which makes me very boring company."

CHAPTER TWENTY

Irvine very quickly got the message to Kennedy, via Desk Sgt Tim Flynn, about Mylan's investing in Dickens' career.

Having returned to North Bridge House from interviewing Nealey Dean, Kennedy requested Irvine to pick him up there. At ten forty-five that Tuesday morning, they both came knocking on the door of Rodney Stuart in Camden Town Mews.

Rodney Stuart was a man reluctantly approaching his fifties. He was slim (ish), but not in a fit kind of way. He'd obviously lost weight but hadn't bothered to do the necessary exercise, so the skin kind of hung off him like a corpse. His jowls were more Sigmund Freud's chow, Lun, than Dr Freud himself. He'd obviously tuned into MTV at least once, because his dyed blonde, three-quarters of an inch long hair was oiled and spiked upwards and outwards, so that his scalp and all its blemishes were clearly visible. His red blotched face gleamed as if someone had shined it with cooking oil. His brown, bloodshot eyes moved in a slow, uninterested way. Mr Stuart's nod to his nationality was a Stuart's tartan tie, undone in a permanent kind of way, and adding a bit of colour to his flawless starched white shirt. He wore severely creased black chinos and a very, very expensive looking pair of trainers.

Just one look was all it took for Kennedy to reckon that the first quality Stuart looked for in a girlfriend was bad eyesight. Kennedy imagined someone like ann rea giving him a severe "You're not going out dressed like that, Rodney" talking to, and never ever, for one second, making it sound like a question. Kennedy wondered if he was doomed forever to these ann rea lapses. As he sat down in Stuart's packed office, he noticed that recalling her didn't give him the pangs of regret they had done as close as just over a week ago.

For all of Stuart's physical and dress presentation, he immediately came across as very friendly and approachable, and his soft accent sounded more mid-Atlantic than Mid Lothian.

"Sorry business this, isn't it, man?" Rodney started off the proceedings, slipping into pure Scottish for the word "sorry."

"Aye, rum do, a rum do," Irvine said, sounding even more Sean Connery than normal.

"How long had you worked with Mr Mylan?" Kennedy asked, slightly distracted by how chock-a-block Stuart's generously sized office was. There were files packed in every available shelf space and some even in neat piles on the floor, covering his old subtly patterned red and orange carpet, which was threadbare in a couple of noticeable, obviously busy, spots in the room.

"Oh Paddy and I go way back," Stuart replied. When it became clear that Kennedy was seeking more specific details, he continued, "I think I've known him just over fourteen years. I was first introduced to him when I worked for Pat Savage at O.J. Kilkenny and Co., a firm of accountants over in Holland Park. Then, when I left there a couple of years later to set up on my own, Paddy came with me as one of my first clients. O.J. Kilkenny and Co. specialises in music business clients, and they're one of the best in that field, but I wanted my client list to be broader than that.

Kennedy could see Irvine noting down the names Pat Savage and O.J. Kilkenny.

"So you'd know the ins and outs of Mr Mylan's business?" Kennedy continued.

"Oh, I'll say," Stuart offered in a bizarre Monty Python, 'nudge, nudge, wink, wink' moment.

"Okay," Kennedy sighed, hoping he was drawing a line under such behaviour, "is there anything obvious in his business dealings that we should be paying attention to?"

"I believe as this is a murder investigation and the client in question is deceased, then all client confidentiality goes out the window," Rodney Stuart said.

"We are investigating the death of Mr Patrick Mylan, so every single bit of information we can get at this stage will be extremely helpful."

"So you're saying that it could have been a suicide, man?" Stuart replied, immediately picking up on the wording of Kennedy's statement.

"What do *you* think?" Irvine asked, pushing it back again.

"Or an accident?" Stuart countered once again.

"Were you aware by any chance that Mr Mylan practised…" Kennedy said trying to put the interview back on track again but stalling.

"Autoerotic asphyxiation?" Stuart completed the Ulster detective's sentence, proving once again that the Camden Town bush telegraph was second to none.

"Yes," Kennedy said.

"Look, Paddy wasn't like you and me. When you make that much money at a relatively young age, four important things happen to you. One, you start to trust no one - particularly when you've been burned once. Two, it gets harder and harder to find the buzz. That's why some people turn to drugs at that stage. Paddy didn't; it would appear he sought his major hits elsewhere, man. And three and four are linked. All of a sudden you grow more attractive to the opposite sex, and, four, as far as they're concerned, you become very funny."

Irvine started to say something. Stuart cut him off with, "I know, I know, how does one so young become so cynical?"

"So you're saying that Mr Mylan got his kicks from kinky sex?" Irvine asked.

"All I can tell you is this: Paddy was no longer looking for love. I don't know the reason why. Maybe some of his older friends can tell you, Roger and Maggie Littlewood for instance. But I can tell you this: his relationships with women were limited to when he occasionally wanted to enjoy some intimate female company. Now he clearly didn't want to be compromised by seeking out hookers, so he found women who … well, let's just say, women who for one reason or other were not seeking any emotional connection either."

"Are we talking about several women here?" Irvine asked.

"No, not at the same time, man. He believed in monogamy - probably for hygienic reasons. I don't know; I never asked him. We never discussed it, but he needed his woman on call, as it were, and he looked after them very well."

"And that's where you came in?"

"Oh, that hurt," he stage grimaced. "You just made me sound like a pimp, Sergeant. But yes, I was the one who paid the bills, man, but then again I paid all his bills. I can tell you this for nothing, though,"

he added, just a wee bit too camp, "I certainly never *found* him any of his women."

"How did he find these women?" Kennedy asked as he considered this non-emotional approach to dating.

"I never knew. It was none of my business. My business was looking after his financial affairs, and I don't mind admitting he was my biggest client, so I was certainly never going to overstep the mark."

"And would you have a list of these women?"

"Well, I do have the current one's details, a Miss Chloe Simmons. She's been around for a few years now. She's a bit of a sweetheart. I mean, in Paddy's defence, he wasn't changing them like he changed his socks. It wasn't anything like that."

"We seem to be having trouble tracking her down," Irvine said, back-tracking just a little.

"Oh, she lives in Wimbledon, man," he replied. Swinging around to his desk, taking a telephone book out of his top drawer and lifting a pen out of a Ben and Jerry's Ice Cream ceramic pot, he scribbled down a name, address, and telephone number on a piece of paper. He made to hand it to Irvine, but at the last possible moment switched direction and passed it to Kennedy.

Stuart's script was incredibly neat, tidy, and completed with a very stylish flourish.

"So Miss Simmons is Mr Mylan's current partner?"

"Was," Stuart corrected Irvine; "*was* Mr Mylan's *last* partner. Nice girl."

"You met her?" Kennedy asked.

"Yes, of course. I had dealings with her on Paddy's behalf."

"And… er, was there any conflict between the two of them?" Irvine asked.

"No, no, no," Stuart protested, "too nice a girl. If you were looking for conflict, you only needed to ask."

"Oh?" Irvine said.

"Again, it's all going to come out and I… well look, here's the thing, man, if you're looking for someone who wanted to break a deal with Paddy, then look no further than Tim Dickens."

"You're talking about the deal where Mr Mylan bought up a share of Mr Dickens' songwriting, publishing, and CD royalties?"

"I am actually," Stuart replied, seeming very impressed with Irvine's inside knowledge.

"Yes, we know Mr Mylan paid Tim Dickens five million pounds sterling for a 50 per cent share of his future earnings," Irvine continued.

"But did you know that unlike the majority of record and publishing deals, it was open-ended?"

"Ah no," Irvine admitted, committing the fact to his notebook.

"And did you know that unlike the majority of publishing deals, the contracting partner, this time Mr Patrick Mylan, was taking 50 per cent and not the usual 10 per cent or 15 per cent publishers usually take?"

"No, we... I didn't know that."

"And did you know that after the CD distributors took their normal cut, Mr Mylan got 50 per cent of the balance. A manager, say for instance, would have normally take 15 per cent to 20 per cent."

"But surely Mr Mylan wasn't a manager?" Kennedy asked.

"Quite, and he wasn't even doing a manager's job, yet he was taking two and a half times what a manager would take," Stuart said.

"Can we just go back here a little? Could you clarify the ramifications of this deal for us?" Kennedy asked.

"Happy to, man." Rodney Stuart's glee was noticeable. "You see, I learned all about this when I was at O.J. Kilkenny's. When you do a deal with a manager, you do it for a limited period of time, and then, of course, there will be a spin-off time where that manager will continue to earn royalties on the material he worked on. Usually this is for three to five years after the contract ends and at a lower rate, usually, say, for half commission. Same with a publisher. The artist signs with a publisher for, say, five to seven years, and these days most of the better deals are written where the artist retains the rights to his songwriting catalogue at the end of the deal. Lesser so, but some of the record deals now have similar provision where if the artist is re-couped at the end of the deal - sold enough records to wipe the slate clean from all and any advance the record company has paid the artist.

"Now at the time we did the deal with Tim Dickens..." Stuart continued, but was interrupted by Kennedy.

"You did the actual deal for Mr Mylan?" Kennedy asked.

"Yes! As I mentioned, through my time at Kilkenny's, Pat Savage was a good mentor, so I had the knowledge, and I knew a little about the David Bowie model. Paddy didn't."

"Sorry, you were saying?" Kennedy prompted.

"Tim Dickens was in pretty good shape, financially speaking. I mean, he hadn't sold a ticket or a CD in anger for a good few years. I think he actually used the term 'record' with us in the early talks. But he had taken care of his money, so he wasn't hurting. Paddy had made him a few offers, but he wasn't really interested. I did a bit of research and discovered that Tim Dickens owned all his own masters and all his publishing. I also discovered that he had around five mil stashed away, so I told Paddy that, in my opinion, it was going to take a similar amount to move him. I also advised Paddy that these days, all it needed with a heritage act like Tim Dickens was for a cover version of one of his songs, or a movie or an advert to materialise, and the back catalogue would shift the proverbial truckload. I also told him that from the little I knew of artists, if the deal did work out and he started to sell records again, Tim Dickens would resent Paddy for the amount of money he was making off him. He would suddenly forget the fact that Paddy put five million quid on the table and would look at it like Paddy was stealing half of his income and - here's the big thing - FOR EVER! Paddy was desperate to get into show business, so he was happy to make the offer. However, against my advice, he insisted that if he was going to invest five million it was going to have to be for 50 per cent of everything and forever. Or as Paddy put it, 'For as long as he's making a buck from his songs and CDs, then I want to make one too."

"Tell me this," Kennedy asked, "the original five million pounds Mr Mylan invested, was he to get that back first before they split, or was it just recouped out of Mr Mylan's share?"

"Oh no, that had to come out of the overall income pot first, otherwise Paddy had a great chance of never recouping. I mean, at five million he was in with a good chance of recouping that amount over the years, even if nothing had happened to kick-start the catalogue sales again. There's always pipeline money on CD royalties, publishing, collection societies, etc. That takes for ever and a day to come in. As I say, man, it might have taken him a while, but I'm sure eventually he'd have got his money back. That was the main reason I recommended Paddy do the deal."

Here he stopped to catch his breath, and just as Irvine was about to ask something, Rodney Stuart started back up again.

"But none of us had the faintest clue how much it was going to explode. I mean, in twelve months Paddy had turned his five million quid investment into a clear million pound profit and extended Tim Dickens' career (and Paddy's joint income) by at least ten good years."

"When did Tim Dickens start to feel resentful about the deal?" Kennedy asked.

"At the end of that first glorious year," Stuart replied. "I mean, you could have set your watch to it. His accountant or lawyer or whoever was advising him looked at the figures and saw only what they were giving away, not what they'd made out of the deal."

"Did he speak to Mr Mylan about it?" Irvine asked.

"Well, not at first. That's not Tim Dickens' style. He had his people do it while all the time keeping up this pleasant non-confrontational façade when he personally met up with Paddy. Tim Dickens' lawyer wrote to me, politely enough, saying the deal had worked out great for all parties, and now that Mr Mylan had his investment repaid perhaps it was time to renegotiate."

"Then what happened?"

"Paddy replied, through me, saying he'd be more than happy to renegotiate and suggested that perhaps Tim Dickens could take 40 per cent, in which case he would be more than happy with the balance of 60 per cent!"

Kennedy and Irvine laughed heartily. Rodney Stuart joined in.

"I imagine Tim Dickens would have gone absolutely ballistic at that. A joke was a joke, and I counselled Paddy that perhaps we should throw them back ten points. My point was that the deal had turned out marvellously well for us, and so it would be good vibes for us to keep them sweet this early in the relationship. Paddy's point... and on reflection he wasn't wrong... He was cute enough in business.

"He may not have known the ins and outs of a music business deal like I did, but he did know people. Anyway, he maintained that if we gave them back ten points, they'd be back the following year looking for another ten points, and they'd never stop until they'd got it all back again. In his world, a deal was a deal. He'd put his hand in his pocket for five big ones when no one cared about Tim Dickens or his songs. His money had bought him into the deal, and he wasn't about to just hand it back again. Equally we should all remember that if the deal had gone wrong Paddy could have lost his five million. It was a non-returnable advance."

"What happened next?" Irvine asked.

"Tim Dickens rang me up about it. He was very patient and patronising with me. He said, 'Look, you know I thought we'd left all this slavery in the music business behind us.' I told him that he was insulting to slaves; slaves didn't have five million quid cash paid to them in advance and didn't get a chance to sign a contract agreeing all the terms. He said it wasn't fair. I told him it was very fair. I told him that as far as I was concerned his career had been, to all intents and purposes, over. I told him my view was when an investor matched his current wealth in exchange for a share of any future earnings, he'd secured a very fair deal. He said, 'So that means you won't recommend to your client that he change the deal to one that is more favourable to me as the artist?' I told him to dream on. I also advised him that the reality was it really didn't matter what I said. I told him Mr Mylan was the principal in the deal, and he most certainly would never change the terms of their agreement. Dickens terminated the call, man, without even saying goodbye."

"Then what happened?" Kennedy asked.

"Then they tried the Don Arden approach."

"Sorry?"

"Mr Arden used to be this sixties pop group manager, and when he couldn't get what he needed through negotiation, he would allegedly try to persuade the artist, or current manager he wanted to replace, to his way of thinking."

"Oh, was he the guy who used to hang people outside windows by their ankles until they signed on the dotted line?" Irvine asked.

"I couldn't possibly say," Stuart said, through a smirk that suggested he'd just love to spend a few hours saying everything, "but the fact that people *thought* that Mr Arden might have resorted to such tactics always worked in Mr Arden's favour."

"So Tim Dickens did this to Mr Mylan?" Kennedy asked.

"Well no, not exactly. As I said, he has people to do things for him. With this particular approach, I believe he sent the puissant Mr Marcus Urry to have words with Paddy."

"And who would Mr Marcus Urry be when he's at home?" Irvine asked.

"I'm sure if you check you'll find he's already on your radar. He's been in Tim Dickens' employ for getting on to twenty years now. He's his fixer, security officer, and head roadie. In other words, any time Tim Dickens needs to not get his hands dirty…"

"He uses Mr Urry's hands?" Irvine suggested.

"In a word, yes."

"So Marcus Urry went to see Mr Mylan?" Kennedy prompted.

"Yes. Barged his way into the house past Jean Claude and demanded to have a private audience with Paddy. Paddy was no fool, and he didn't scare easily. I've seen him in a few tricky situations; believe me, he could handle himself. Marcus barged around Paddy's office, banging doors and desks and tabletops, shouting and screaming that he wasn't going to leave until he'd a new, signed agreement. Paddy said, 'Do your worst, son. There's not going to be a new deal - not today, not any day!'"

"Then what happened?" Irvine asked.

"Well, as Paddy tells it, Marcus throws everything from Paddy's desk and starts to come around to Paddy's side of the desk. He sides up to Paddy, trying to give the impression of someone who could be breathing flames if he wanted to, telling Paddy that he was running out of time. Paddy grabbed a large volume of Shakespeare from the shelf behind him, bopped Urry over the head. Urry fell in a pile on the floor. I asked Paddy how everything turned out, and he said, 'Oh not too bad Rodney, the book wasn't too badly damaged; I don't think I'll have to reduce the price if I ever need to sell it."

"Okay, final question, Mr Stuart…"

"Oops, this sounds official," Rodney interrupted nervously.

"Can you tell me what you were doing between sixteen hundred hours and twenty hundred hours on Saturday?"

"You don't think I murdered Paddy Mylan, do you? You couldn't possibly."

"We'd like to eliminate you from our investigation," Irvine continued, a little surprised by the accountant's reaction, "so could you please tell me what you were doing between sixteen hundred hours and twenty hundred hours on Saturday?"

"I really can't," Stuart replied, grimacing slightly.

"Why not?"

"I'm afraid I missed that particular lesson at school, but if you convert your hundred hour clock into English for me, I'll be happy to help."

"Four and eight o'clock," Irvine sighed.

"In the afternoon?"

"Yes."

"That's easy. I was in my office. I sometimes steal a full day here on Saturday. I find I can get so much more work done because the phones never ring."

"Anyone in the office with you?"

"Nope. I was here all on my lonesome."

CHAPTER TWENTY-ONE

Kennedy was obviously very keen to interview Tim Dickens, and Irvine filled him in on their earlier interview on their way over to Marylebone. On route Kennedy asked Desk Sgt Tim Flynn to contact his counterpart in Wimbledon and have them track down Chloe Simmons at the address supplied by Rodney Stuart.

When Kennedy and Irvine arrived at Leinster Mews, Tim Dickens and his PA, Alice, were locking the door. As the police walked down the mews towards Dickens' double-fronted property, Kennedy couldn't help wondering exactly what details the PA might have on Dickens that she could be persuaded to surrender. The closer he got, the more he could see - from the look in her eye when she clocked exactly who it was who was returning to interview her boss - she was transparently, fiercely loyal and most likely wouldn't give up anything easily. As Dickens and Robbins were both dressed head-to-toe in black, just this side of looking like Goth twins, they looked more like a romantic couple than business acquaintances.

It was Alice who forced a smile for Kennedy and Irvine as she said, "Now is not a good time. We're on our way to an important meeting."

"Going to see your lawyers," Kennedy replied, addressing Dickens directly, "to see if it's going to be easier now to get extracted from the deal you did with Patrick Mylan?"

"Or were you planning on sending Marcus Urry over again to soften up Rodney Stuart before you sent in the legal team?" Irvine added as they arrived at the doorstep.

Dickens stretched out both his arms out and turned his open palms to the heavens in a 'who me?' gesture. In the process, he offered a duplicitous smile, so successfully Hughie Green in his prime would have been proud of it.

The PA attempted to intervene once more, but Tim Dickens put his hand softly on her shoulder and said, "Let's open up again, Alice, and get the tea and coffee pots fired up again. I have a feeling we're all going to need some caffeine for this."

She looked totally exasperated and wasn't shy of showing it.

"So you've obviously been talking to Rodney Stuart," Tim Dickens continued as he showed them into his office beyond the reception room, the walls of which were decorated completely with the obligatorily gold, silver, and platinum discs. Try though he did, Kennedy, couldn't spot any rhodium awards, like the one made by the *Guinness Book of Records* to celebrate Paul McCartney's status as the most successful recording artist in the history of the world, ever!

Before Kennedy or Irvine had a chance to respond, Tim Dickens said, "I wonder how a man as apparently indiscreet as Rodney ever managed to succeed in this business."

"So you didn't actually do a deal with Mr Mylan then?" Irvine asked.

"Yes, I did do a deal with Mr Mylan, but surely that's no one's business but mine and Mr Mylan's?"

"That's not strictly the case, you see," Kennedy started. "If your business partner dies in mysterious circumstances, as Mr Mylan did, and before he died you were in dispute with him, as you were, and if one of your representatives physically threatened Mr Mylan, as Mr Urry did, well, then I'm afraid to have to say that it does become very much our business."

"Don't hold the actions of a keen, over protective employee against me."

"So, you didn't ask him to pay Mr Mylan a visit?" Kennedy asked, looking directly into Tim Dickens' eyes.

Tim Dickens was favoured by the distraction of his PA arriving back with teas and coffees at that point. Everyone helped themselves to milk, sugar, and Penguin bars. Tim Dickens made a bit of a fuss over slicing his bar in half, claiming that was the only treat he allowed himself, half a chocolate Penguin biscuit, each day.

Eventually, Alice left to reschedule the meetings they'd been leaving to attend.

Kennedy repeated his question.

"Look, Inspector, that just got out of hand. Marcus has been with me a long while. He's been through the good and bad with me over the years. He's been very supportive. Did he go and see Patrick on my behalf? Yes. We'd frustrated all options through the normal legal routes. Did he over-step the mark? Quite possibly, but as I say, you have to realise that he was coming from a good place and he had my interest at heart."

"Just so I'm clear about this, exactly what problem did you have with the deal?" Kennedy asked.

Tim Dickens burst into laughter. It was a smug "you couldn't possibly understand what we're talking about here" kind of laugh.

"Look, he was after 50 per cent of my total income *for ever!*" Dickens snarled.

"But, correct me if I'm wrong, that was the deal you agreed, was it not?"

"Yes, but it doesn't mean it was a fair deal, Inspector."

"But surely it's the agreement you signed up to?" Kennedy asked.

"Look, in the music business, a deal is only a deal until such times as you are in a position to renegotiate the deal. When you start off your career, all the deals are top-heavy in favour of your management company, your record company, your publishing company, and your merchandising company. That's because all of the aforementioned companies are speculating on your career, on the *chance* that it, your career, will happen. Then, one of two things happens: either you flop and the companies drop you, or you break - you start to become successful and sell records, tickets, and T-shirts. Now if you are lucky enough for the latter to happen, then when some time has passed and the companies have recouped their initial investments and made a few bob on top, then it's standard music business practice to have your lawyer go back in to said companies and renegotiate your deals, biasing them more in your favour."

"Yes, but again, correct me if I'm wrong, this wasn't that kind of a deal," Kennedy replied. "This was more like an investment bank transaction. This was where a company, or in this case a private individual, goes to you when your sales have all but disappeared and says, 'Okay, I want to gamble on your future.' In other words, they invest a good chuck of change in order to receive a piece of your future earnings."

"But *half* of my earnings?" Tim Dickens said, his voice uncharacteristically hitting the higher register.

Kennedy tried a different approach. "Would there ever have been an instance where *Mr Mylan* would have come back to *you* during the deal and said, 'Okay, look, I know I've already paid you your five million pounds, but this deal is not turning out as good for me as I expected, so what I'd like to do is for you to give me back a couple of million pounds of my money and change the percentage so that 60 per cent comes to me and you can keep 40 per cent?'"

"Why no, of course not," Tim Dickens laughed at Kennedy as though he were a five-year-old wanting to go into a pub and have a drink with his father. "Look, Inspector, what you have to realise is, the music business is different. Historically speaking, artists have been ripped off by the big companies. The artist pays for the recording of their albums; yet the record company, for some bizarre reason, known only to themselves, own the masters. The record company and publishing houses keep a large percentage of the artist's royalties on reserve as an accounting procedure. The publishing houses all share in the black box fund - a fund of unclaimed or undistributed royalties. They do not, to my knowledge, share any of these funds with the artist. The record companies charge the artists for videos, which the companies claim and use as their own, doing separate deals with the likes of MTV. The record company can be earning profits on an album at the same time as the artist—due to accounting procedures—are unrecouped and still in debt. I mean, it just goes on and on," Tim Dickens ranted, now seeming to loose the point he was trying to make.

"Yes," Kennedy said, pulling it back on track again, "but again, I repeat: the main difference to me seems to be that Patrick Mylan was neither a publisher nor a record company. He was an investor. From my understanding, he was very up front with you. He gambled five million pounds on you, which, at the time of the deal, was reportedly equal to your total wealth."

"According to Rodney Stuart, I suppose," Tim Dickens grimaced.

"Reportedly, he wasn't ripping you off…"

"According to Rodney bloody Stuart, no less…"

"Do you have any reason to believe Mr Mylan *was* trying to rip you off?" Kennedy asked, sensing something.

Tim Dickens stopped in his tracks, considering both members of Camden Town CID for a few seconds.

"Well?" Kennedy pushed.

"He had no need to, did he? His deal with me was pure highway robbery," was all Tim Dickens managed to come up with. His PA returned to the room, nodding at Dickens and tapping her Gucci watch.

"Look, if there's nothing else," Tim Dickens began, "I really do have a busy day."

"We're not quite finished yet," Kennedy said firmly.

"I know where this is going," Tim Dickens declared with a large sigh, his frustration obvious. "You think I couldn't get the deal I was after with Patrick, so I topped him? You really think I, a songwriter with my reputation, would murder him... *pleeeeeease.*"

"We have to investigate all avenues, sir," Irvine offered diplomatically.

"But if that was the case, the London record companies would have been littered with corpses years ago, and from what I've been told about Patrick's demise, none of them would have had as big a smile on their face as Patrick did."

"Tell me, sir," Kennedy began, not entirely happy with the proceedings, "what were you doing between the hours of four o'clock on Saturday afternoon and eight o'clock on Saturday evening?"

"But I've already answered that," Dickens protested.

"Yes, it seems our colleague DC King asked you about the incorrect day," Kennedy apologised as he checked his notes. "She asked you what you were doing on Sunday. You replied that you were writing a song and were alone. What we need to know is what you were doing the day before; that's Saturday last, between the hours of four o'clock and eight o'clock, please?"

The question seemed to pull the rug out from under Tim Dickens' feet. To be honest, the songwriter's reaction took Kennedy totally by surprise too. Kennedy, Irvine, and Tim Dickens seemed to be locked in this moment when they were all disturbed again by Alice.

"Oh, that's easy to clear up," she said sweetly, in a voice a lot less businesslike than she'd been using thus far, "Timothy was with me all day Saturday."

CHAPTER TWENTY-TWO

"Okay," Kennedy said, starting the proceedings by clapping his hands together loudly three times, "where exactly are we on this?"

He and his team were gathered around the twelve by four foot Perspex sheet (which had replaced the traditional blackboard) in the basement of North Bridge House. The magic of the Perspex sheet was it was easier to attach photos to, easier to write on, and you could use various coloured pens to clearly show the different lines of your investigation.

It was just after lunchtime, and they still had a lot more interviews to do, but Kennedy felt they should regroup and catch up before proceeding any further.

"Slim pickings so far," Irvine offered, as he studied the names on the board and the notes and connecting lines.

Irvine was, as usual, spot on. They had a lot, but not anything meaningful. Kennedy had a sense of the investigation slipping away from him. Was it really a murder investigation or had he been hoping for something more serious than a suicide to get his teeth stuck into as a way of putting his illness behind him? Or was he allowing the case to slip away from him by being distracted by Miss Sharenna Chada? No, he refused to accept that. His dallying with Miss Chada, pleasant though it was, wasn't preoccupying him. So what was?

Kennedy knew from experience that he needed to have a session with his team as a way of focusing everyone, including himself, on the case. These meetings served to put a shape on the case; people could see and discuss the threads. They could talk over the frustrations of a lack of progress or leads and go away feeling they knew what they needed to do. They would know whom they needed to talk to; they would know which facts they would need to check or recheck. They knew that removing people from the suspect list was sometimes even more productive in solving the case than adding suspects.

Kennedy also knew that this case could be as simple as a rich man - a man with more money than he'd ever spend - taking his own life. A man disappointed by an artist he'd respected turning on him just because he'd been in some way responsible for the artist becoming successful again, So, rather than being allowed to feel a sense of achievement and shared responsibility for the new resurgent success, he was made to feel guilty. A man who, if his acquaintances were correct, had no love in his life and surprisingly few interests apart from tennis and the stock market. A man who just maybe woke up one day, like last Saturday for instance, and decided that, all things considered, he would rather not go on. Kennedy knew that this was never a route he would have chosen - *even* in the worst days with his back. However, there was still something in the way Mylan was found that troubled Kennedy. Could this perhaps be a statement of some kind, of an intended final humiliation for Mylan? Suicide could be the answer to the question: "What happened to this man?" And if that was the solution to his case, then so be it, he didn't need more. It was still a puzzle to solve, and solving such puzzles was Kennedy's one and only drug.

"Who are our suspects so far?" he asked, as he took a green marker and started to write on the Perspex screen.

Kennedy didn't even think about it, and before he knew it, his hand had produced the first name on the list.

Tim Dickens

He looked at the name for a little time, and then wrote underneath, but joined by a seagull:

Marcus Urry

With a blue marker and at the other side of the board, he wrote down the names:

Jean Claude Banks
Cynthia Cox
Roger and Maggie Littlewood
Martin Friel
Tony Stevenson
Rodney Stuart
Chloe Simmons
Nealey Dean

Kennedy then linked Roger and Maggie, Friel and Stevenson with lines - broken in the middle with the note Credit Suisse - to the name at the top of the board: *PATRICK MYLAN*, in thick black lettering and capitals.

"Has anyone studied the autopsy report?" DC Dot King asked.

"Yes," Allaway replied. Everyone knew Allaway read everything available on each of the cases. Since he'd been promoted to DS, he'd also shown that he had an ability to recall most of the information he read.

"And was Mr Mylan physically healthy when he died?" King continued.

"Yes. According to Taylor, he was in remarkably good shape. The only evident medical intervention - apparent from several old scars - was having his appendix removed."

"So we can scrap a terminal illness from his motivation to commit suicide then," King surmised, scoring through some lettering in her notebook several times.

"Also," Allaway continued, checking his notes, "Dr Taylor discovered there was an extremely high level of alcohol present in Mylan's bloodstream at the time of his death."

"None of his acquaintances claimed he was a big drinker, did they?" King asked.

"None so far," Irvine agreed.

"Okay," Kennedy said, gathering up the momentum again, "let's check Tim Dickens' PA's alibi for her boss. She said she was with him *all* day Saturday."

"Really?" King asked.

"Don't get too excited, like I did," Irvine said; "no dirt is about to be spilt. She claimed they spent Saturday locked up in the office, phones off, going through the royalty statements they'd just received from his publishing company for songwriting income and from the record company for CD sales income. Accordingly to Alice Robbins, the statements together are larger than a bound edition of the complete works of Charles Dickens, and if they didn't take time to analyse them properly, then 'Timothy,'" and Irvine paused to make air quotes around Timothy, "could have substantial amounts of money slip away from him."

"How much money does the man need?" Allaway asked, voicing his own recent preoccupation with money.

"Before I could ask her that question, which she obviously saw in my eyes, she said, 'All Mr Dickens needs is that which is his.'"

"No witnesses to the accounting session incarceration then?" King asked.

"No. She said it was a lockout: no phones, no visitors. She said it's the only way they can get through it," Irvine replied.

"Okay," Kennedy said, "let's check with the neighbours. Maybe someone saw them coming or going. Saw some lights on at the weekend. Did they send out for food? Did he take her to a restaurant afterwards?"

"Are they having a relationship?" King asked.

"I'd say not," Irvine replied.

"Why?" King pushed.

"She seems very professional. She doesn't look at him that way, and..." Irvine paused for quite a long period of time.

"Yeah, and?" King asked, more forcefully this time.

"And I think he doesn't give off that vibe..."

"Doesn't give off what vibe?" King repeated incredulously. "Which police manual did you find that approach in?"

"Yeah, it's just a feeling. He seemed content, happy as he was. Like earlier today when we were questioning him about his deal with Mylan, yes, he got a bit loud about it, but he never really seemed to... you know... boil over about it."

"I'd be more nervous of someone who keeps it in check all the time. When they eventually lose it, there could be hell to pay," King argued.

"Let's check it anyway. Someone must have seen them. And if they weren't there, where were they? He's a public figure; someone would have spotted him near Mylan's, if that's where he was. Let's dig further into this Patrick Mylan/Tim Dickens deal. Have the SOCO gang anything yet?"

"I just checked on the way in, sir," Allaway replied, "and nothing so far."

"Okay, let's get back to talking to people. We need a better picture of Patrick Mylan. We need to track this Marcus Urry roadie chap. We need ..." Kennedy faltered.

"*Some*thing," King offered.

"*Some*thing would do great," Kennedy replied with a generous smile.

CHAPTER TWENTY-THREE

Kennedy wasn't entirely sure of the reason, but the meeting ended on a bit of an up. When Sgt Tim Flynn came to find Kennedy as he was exiting the basement chatting with Irvine, he said he'd contacted Wimbledon CID, as requested, and handed Kennedy a name and a number on a piece of paper.

Kennedy returned to his office as his team drifted off to attend to their own chores. He absentmindedly dialled the unique collection of numbers which, thanks to Alexander Graham Bell, amongst others, resulted in a telephone ringing on the desk of a police officer less than a dozen miles away in Wimbledon.

"Hello, Detective Inspector Anne Coles here; how can I help you?" announced the chipper voice on the other end of Kennedy's line.

Kennedy nearly dropped the phone in shock. In fact, for a microsecond, he considered setting the phone down again without saying a word. In that same microsecond he considered Tim Flynn's message for a second time: "Ring D.I. A. Coles Wimbledon CID Re: interview subject." He hadn't twigged the "A" as being for Anne, probably because the last time they'd come into contact was just over four years ago when she was a DC.

"My goodness, DC to DI in four years, that's quite an achievement," Kennedy said, finding something neutral to say at last.

"I wondered if you'd ring yourself," Coles replied, sounding every ounce like the English rose Kennedy remembered. "To be honest, south of the river, four years is considered quite a slow rise."

"Goodness, it's great to hear your voice again," he said, stopping worrying about the weight and content of his words.

"How are you, sir? I mean after your…"

"Never felt better," Kennedy interrupted, jumping in immediately, hoping to prevent her feeling guilty about their history.

Just before Kennedy had very nearly met his maker in the tumbled-down version of the York & Albany, Anne Coles had declared her romantic interest in him. She'd invited him out on a date. He and ann rea were in one of their "this just isn't going to work out" phases, so Kennedy had accepted her invitation. However, before the date could take place, Kennedy had been stabbed while on duty in the York & Albany, and because she'd let her personal feelings rule her head, she'd panicked in helplessness. If it hadn't been for ann rea's instincts that Kennedy was in some kind of danger, and if she hadn't gone to seek him out, Kennedy could have bled to death. Superintendent Thomas Castle felt it was better for all concerned if DC Coles were transferred out of Camden Town; and that is how she ended up in Wimbledon CID four years later, talking on the telephone to DI Christy Kennedy.

"So this Chloe Simmons, what kind of bother is she involved in?" Coles asked, changing the subject so quickly he felt there must have been other people able to tune into her conversation.

"Difficult to know. We found this man dead in a… well, shall we just say a compromising position. Maybe an accident, maybe he committed suicide, and maybe he didn't. Miss Simmons had a relationship of sorts with him, and I need to chat with her."

"That's what I'm here to help you with," she said, then paused. "I suppose you still don't drive?"

"Correct."

"How's about you get the tube over here. It'll be much quicker than driving anyway, and I'll pick you up at the station."

"Sounds like an idea," Kennedy replied.

The thing about four years is it's either miraculous or totally destructive in what it can do to a person. In Anne Coles' case, it wasn't that a miracle had ever been needed, but the ageing process had delivered her to a perfect thirty-two-year-old woman. She had a few more lines around her eyes, she was slightly more drawn than before, and she displayed, without being particularly cocky, an air of confidence that had been absent when she was stationed at North Bridge House.

When he met her at the entrance to the busy joint underground and mail line station, she immediately kissed him briefly on both cheeks. He wondered whether her newfound confidence came from age or promotion.

"You're thinner," she said, looking a little shocked.

"And you're stunning," he replied, still taking in the vision before him.

She was full figured, but more Scarlett Johansson than Ma Larkin, and her long luscious blonde hair was no longer restrained under her uniform cap the way it had been the last time Kennedy saw her. She looked simply beautiful. Kennedy thought she'd put considerable effort into looking stunning, but such efforts made her none the less attractive. When she'd kissed him briefly, he'd immediately recognised her distinctive scent.

"So we're off to see Miss Simmons," Coles said, reminding Kennedy that the reason for the visit wasn't a trip down memory lane.

"Yes," Kennedy replied, nudging himself back to the professional he hoped he was.

"Tell me more."

"Okay. We found this man, a Mr Patrick Mylan. It would appear, or it was made to appear, that he died while in the throes of a solo sexual act."

Coles wriggled her nose in confusion the way she had sometimes done before.

"Oooo- k-a-y," she said, "I get it. Very discreetly put, sir."

"As a detective inspector, I don't believe it's necessary for you to call me sir, or else I'll have to start calling you ma'am. Christy, okay?"

"Okay, Christy and Anne it is then," she replied as they reached her car, a VW Polo. *So obviously not from the Wimbledon CID car pool,* Kennedy thought as she continued, "So why are you suspicious about it?"

"Mainly because, at the time of his death, Mr Mylan was wearing suspenders…"

"A woman's suspender belt?" Coles asked.

"No, a man's. I believe is the exact term used to describe them are sock garters."

"Men's? Do such items exist?" she asked.

"Yes, but not for quite some time, or so I thought. They go on just below each knee and are used to hold up your socks."

"So maybe your Mr Mylan was just a wee bit old-fashioned. There's nothing wrong with that."

"Well, there were no signs on his legs that indicated continued use of elastic. It just looked like someone had wanted to humiliate him in public."

For the rest of the journey up along Worple Road to midway between Wimbledon and Raynes Park, Kennedy talked her through the
investigation so far. Luckily enough, the journey was a short one, so he
didn't run out of facts to tell her, but it was close, very close.

Miss Chloe Simmons' address was a new build and not the standard older houses both Worple Road and Kennedy favoured. The common parts of the six spacious flats on three floors were very clean and
well stocked with fresh flowers. A smartly dressed doorman held the
door open for them and advised them to go straight up to apartment six
on the top floor. Coles had already checked, and Miss Simmons was in
residence waiting for them.

As they rode up in the lift, Kennedy once again had the opportunity
to experience Coles' combination of intoxicating fragrances. Kennedy
remembered something else he'd thought about Anne Coles: she always looked so incredibly kissable. It wasn't that she was sad or had
that air, because she frequently broke into a smile and enjoyed a good
laugh, but she always looked like her full lips would be responsive to a
great kissing session. He wondered if that had been the reason why
he'd accepted her original invitation to go on a date.

Just then the lift wheezed to a stop and the doors slid open silently.
Chloe Simmons was waiting for them in the hallway, and she went first
to DI Anne Coles with her hand outstretched. "Are you the police officer I spoke to on the phone?"

"Yes," Coles replied, presenting her warrant card, "and this is Detective Inspector Christy Kennedy."

Kennedy also flashed his card, and they moved into her apartment.

Miss Simmons would have been in a position to enjoy great views…
if only there had been great views to enjoy. All they could see out of
every window of the spacious and modern apartment was suburbia at
its most suburban.

Chloe looked as if she'd just turned twenty, but Kennedy was sure
she must be older. She was slim, naturally beautiful, very English - but
in a different way from Coles' rose of England look. She had a pale
complexion, long, lush, straight, dark brown hair, and not a speck of
make-up. She was in her bare feet, yet still taller than Coles and just as
tall as Kennedy. She was wearing thick black tights or body hugging
trousers (Kennedy could never figure out which of the two this item

was meant to be), and she wore a very short and very tight, black mini-skirt. An extremely expensive looking black shirt subtly accentuated her magnificent breasts.

Miss Simmons was aware of what had happened to Patrick Mylan. "The nice" Rodney Stuart had advised her on the previous day (Monday). She seemed concerned in the way one was concerned when a non-blood relative died, as opposed to someone close to you dying. She was very respectful, but not unduly upset.

She offered Kennedy and Coles a glass of the red wine she was drinking. They both opted for glasses of water, the only alternate offered.

"You look gorgeous," she said to Coles, when they'd settled down. "I mean, when I saw you first coming out of the lift, I immediately thought, *She looks so stunning she can't be a policewoman.* I mean, no disrespect to the Met or anything, but you give a new meaning to the saying, 'May the force be with you.'"

"Why, thank you," Coles replied, accepting the compliment graciously and with poise, "that's very nice of you to say. I will admit I'm seeing someone special later." Coles flashed Kennedy a look at this stage. Kennedy *thought* he could read the look, but at the same time he didn't want to read something into the look that wasn't there - or be distracted from the reason for his rare visit south of the river.

"We believe you had a relationship with Mr Patrick Mylan."

Chloe Simmons studied Kennedy for a few moments, looked at Coles again, back to Kennedy and started to smile.

"This feels weird. Neither of you looks like a police officer. I get a good feeling from both of you though, and I go on my feelings a lot. Also, I'm halfway through my bottle of 2005 Napa Valley Cabernet Sauvignon, which I've been saving for a while, so I'm happy to be candid with you. However, I would plead with you to be discreet with the information I'm about to give you."

Without awaiting confirmation, she ploughed on, "I was Patrick's…for want of a better word, I was his concubine. I was Patrick Mylan's concubine."

The hint of bass in her voice combined with her perfect diction made this sound very earthly, sexual, and extremely pleasing to listen to.

"That must be brilliant Cabernet Sauvignon," Coles said, and then looked as if she regretted it the moment the words had left her lips.

"Yes," Chloe laughed, "I'm probably a bit squiffy at this stage all right."

"Let me get this correct: you're saying you were Mr Mylan's lover?"

"No, no, no," Chloe said quietly, as if there were someone in one of the rooms listening to them, "I was his concubine. Concubine as in a Latin word, by way of France - the French are so civil in matters of the heart, aren't they? They never mistake lust for love. Where was I? Oh yes, it means to lie down with, be a bed-mate, as it were. Lover implies a love affair, where love is involved. We were not lovers. I lay with him. Infrequently, but regularly, I lay with him. Can you be infrequent and regular? Infrequently regular - does that work for you, Inspector?" she was now looking at Kennedy.

"Yes, I think that works," Kennedy replied.

Chloe's clear honest eyes willed you on when you spoke to her. It was as though she were encouraging the words from you.

"Anyway, I'm sure you get the picture," she continued, sparing Houdini the trouble of having to come back from the grave to figure out how to make the wine disappear from the glass.

"Okay," Kennedy sighed, trying to get a fix on where best to take the questioning. He knew what he wanted to ask, but he wasn't sure Chloe would cooperate, and even if she did, that DI Anne Coles would encourage her. "When did you first meet Patrick Mylan?"

"I met Patrick - you know he hated to be called Paddy? - in the spring of ninety-five, and way back then I was scared to look people in the eye, but I loved to dance. I loved to dance in front of the fire…"

"But way back then you would only have been…" Coles started in genuine shock.

"Ten, I was ten, way back then," Chloe said with a big smile, "but don't fret about my welfare. He wasn't a perv. I promise you nothing happened until my twenty-second birthday. He was a friend of my father's. Patrick didn't really ever become a friend of my mum. I've two other sisters, six and seven years older, so I suppose that made us a certain type of family. Patrick would come around from time to time to collect my dad, and I always imagined they'd head off somewhere quite exotic. My mum always thought they were out with women, but Patrick later told me he'd never once witnessed my father being unfaithful to my mum.

"I grew older; Patrick would always ask me to dance when he came around for my dad, and even as a teenager I was quite happy to, because he'd always give me a twenty pound note. Then I reached the age where I started to think he *might* be a bit of a perv; so I would make sure I stayed up in my room or was out when he came around.

"I was eighteen when I started to get comfortable with him again. I suppose I'd had enough of spotty boys by then. Sadly, my dad died when I was nineteen. From the earliest I can remember, my dad was always going away on trips. He did something in banking - I could never figure out what, but he travelled a lot. When I was young, I remember when he'd get back from a trip I'd shy away from him. My mum says I always said, 'You go away,' and I'd push him away from me and hide behind my mother's skirt. I mean, after a few hours I'd be fine. But I always remember this sense of loss, betrayal, whatever, whenever he went away. It would always take me some time to forgive him for having left me. And then, just when we were getting on great, he went and died on me; he went away for good.

"Patrick turned up at the funeral. I went up to him and reintroduced myself; he said he didn't recognise me. He didn't flirt or anything crass. He never did; it just wasn't his style. I was clearly upset, so he offered me a lift back to the house. I persuaded him to take me for a drink on the way. Patrick introduced me to good wine. He was a great talker. Oh God, he had such a beautiful soft Irish voice, a different Irish lilt from yours. You could hear inside his head through his voice. He'd talk and I'd just melt."

Here Chloe stopped, cradling her arms across her bosom, lost in the memory. She rose from the sofa where she'd her long legs curled up under her, and she seemed to float her way across the bleached wooden floor. She tipped the remains of the wine from her glass and then refilled it, only this time with the mineral water.

"Patrick taught me never to drink wine to get drunk. He said you should only drink wine where you're prepared to savour it with good food."

Kennedy hoped that her uninhibited, free-flow description of her time with Mylan wouldn't become more stifled with the mineral water. For the first time since this investigation had started, Kennedy was getting a sense of the victim. Just little hints, but nonetheless, thanks to this young woman, something was starting to come through.

"We had a very, very slow start. Four whole years, for heaven's sake, but in those four years I always had the impression he was grooming me. He never said anything blatant, but there were subtle things. He'd educate me in food and wine; he'd take me to the theatre, to films, to the opera. He'd buy me books, books about the art of lovemaking, about concubines, about erotic art, about *all* the beauties of foreign countries. When I was twenty-one, I think the penny finally dropped for me. Up until then, he'd never been anything but the prefect gentleman. Never even the slight hint of innuendo. But for my twenty-first birthday, he took me out for a beautiful meal at the Ivy, and before we left he gave me a present which he said I wasn't allowed to open until I was back in the privacy of my home."

Chloe took a slow sip of her mineral water.

"Oh my goodness, when I got home, I was up the stairs like a bat out of hell, but then I forced myself to sit down slowly and unwrap the present like the lady I knew Patrick would want me to be, rather than the frustrated teenager I was acting like."

Again she stopped. Coles couldn't resist.

"What had he bought you?" she whispered.

"It wasn't so much what he bought me as what the present told me," Chloe whispered back. "He'd bought me the most beautiful pair of silk stockings I'd ever seen. I couldn't wait to try them on, but again I asked myself what would Patrick want me to do? So I went and had a long bath, soaked in the scents and oils he'd already bought me. I knew from that point on, both of us were preparing myself for him. I got out of the bath, slowly towelled myself down, put on my silk Chinese dressing gown and then and only then allowed myself to put my stockings on. Oh my God, what bliss. Have you ever…no, probably inappropriate to ask while on duty, I mean with your colleague here and all."

"I know exactly the feeling you describe," Coles said proudly, still in a whisper.

Kennedy felt his cheeks flush.

"So for the following two years I prepared myself for Patrick. Nothing was ever said, it wasn't as obvious as that, but through his presents he offered me more and more knowledge and instruction in to what was to be my role in his life. He taught me to love the scents and taste of a man. He taught me all about how important the preparation was. One night in the grooming years, we were out to dinner, and he asked me if I remembered, as a child growing up, which I preferred, Christmas Eve or Christmas Day. I immediately went to say, 'Christmas Day, of course,' but then on reflection I started to remember how sometimes, quite a few times in fact, Christmas Day was a disappointment. He said this was because in a lot of instances, including making love, anticipation was better than participation. So he said, 'You have to learn to take full joy from the anticipation as well.' Then when it appeared that I might just be taking too much enjoyment out of the Christmas Eves, he instructed me to remember that there also has to be participation at some point so that the anticipation process can exist."

The three all laughed their different laughs. Simmons had a reflective laugh. Coles - well, to Kennedy, Coles' laugh looked like a laugh of envy; every time she caught his eye, she gave him a private discreet acknowledgement. And Kennedy's laugh - well, he figured his laugh probably sounded guilty, for he was certainly feeling guilty being party to this amazing young woman's intimate confessions.

"Before you and Mr Mylan got together, did you have, you know, any reservations?" Coles asked, sounding as thought she were voicing what would have been her own concerns.

"Only a few at the Ivy," Simmons said, and then broke into another hearty chuckle. She had a very sexy, throaty laugh. "Sorry, I couldn't resist, but all joking aside, no, absolutely not. If, for one moment, I had any doubt about my choice, I only had to look at my sister. Everyone said she was the most beautiful girl in her year at school and college, and she was voted the girl most likely to succeed. The mistake she made was she believed them and thought her looks were her passport to an easy life. Wrong! At the time Patrick was grooming me, my sister had two young babies screaming at her for attention and a husband who didn't love her any more and was off cheating on her. She eventually dumped him, but her life was a mess by that stage, ruined by her looks. At least that's what my eldest sister said, and I think she hit the nail right on the head."

"Was there a chance Mr Mylan might have been grooming someone to replace you?" Christy asked.

"Oh, as in, I'm the creator of The Concubine's Revenge?"

"Perhaps," Kennedy admitted.

"Christy, can I call you Christy?" she asked, and then proceeded as though he'd agreed, "What you have to realise is that all men always want something, maybe even someone, new — so you have to ensure that they don't ever get to know the real you. You have to ensure you're always revealing a new 'you' or at least a new part of yourself. You always have to be a sexual mystery to them.

"What most beautiful girls don't realise is that most men prefer them to remain enigmatic. Men like to imagine what mysteries we just might be hiding. How the troubled dark souls lurking beneath our surface will explode in sexual passion the second they bed us. What all us girls have to realise is that the mystery, and consequently the majority of the attraction, disappears the very second we open our mouths and mention something revolutionary like how expensive the price of fish is or what a pain it is to need a parking permit for someone who comes around to see you or how important it is we all do something about our green footprint.

"No, what most men want beautiful women to do is shut up, look stunning, appear deep and entertain that week's fantasy.

"I didn't ever live with Patrick. But, as I mentioned, our relationship changed on the night of my twenty-second birthday. I stopped being his … student, and I became his concubine. I pleasured him when he needed me to pleasure him. It's really as simple as that. Was I hooker? I will admit that I was exclusively his and that he paid for my lifestyle, my education, and everything you see around you. But I cared about him, and he cared about me. You don't spend all those years teaching someone the art of loving and then not, in turn, care for them even just a little. And really, we did know each other for many years before anything happened.

"God knows when he made his decision about me. He would never admit it to me. The only thing I can tell you for definite is that he never ever forced me to do anything I didn't want to do. It wasn't even as if being with him was my life. I never once thought I had to sit around looking pretty and available, waiting for the phone to ring. My life is much too important to me for that. And in fairness to Patrick, and his relationship with my father, if that was what *he'd* wanted then he wouldn't have picked me. I'll tell you this: yes, I felt that he had groomed me, but he did it in such a way that it was me and me alone who… what's the best way to put this? Well, I definitely was the one who made the first move."

Kennedy, and probably Coles as well, figured that she was about to tell them how she had made the first move. Neither showed their disappointment when she continued:

"We had dates, yes; that's the way I like to look at it. We had regular dates together. And I swear to you, in the time I was his woman, I know he was with no other."

"Miss Simmons," Kennedy started.

"You must call me Chloe, you simply must. I feel you know me better than my mother does at this stage."

"Okay, Chloe; when you were going through this grooming process, was there… would there have been…" Kennedy struggled to find a way to raise his question.

"You mean would there have been another concubine, his current concubine, my predecessor?" Chloe came to Kennedy's rescue.

"Yes, thank you, Chloe. That's the question I was trying to ask."

"Most definitely," she confirmed immediately. "It was the way he led his life. I use the word concubine only because that's the word Patrick used. I believe Patrick introduced the word so he was making clear the parameters of our relationship. He was making it clear there would be no love, even though love to some degree surely existed. He was letting me know there would be no marriage, no children. He was confirming to me our relationship was to be built on mutual pleasure. I will happily admit to you it was most certainly a mutual pleasure. But, perhaps most importantly, he was admitting to me that there would be a successor."

"So do you think he might have already been grooming your successor?" Kennedy asked.

"I most definitely believe so."

"Do you know who that might have been?" Coles asked, in clear disbelief.

"No, I don't. But remember, I told you how long he'd known me, and certainly for a good percentage of that time he was cultivating me, so I have to assume he was already working on my successor."

"And you have no clues?" Kennedy asked.

Chloe took another sip of her water. She looked as if there were something on her mind. She held the glass to her lips and took another sip, perhaps to give her more time to formulate her answer.

"I suppose if I'm honest, recently when we were together, he wasn't always in my arms, if you know what I mean."

"And what about the lady you succeeded?" Kennedy asked, feeling not entirely comfortable asking these necessary questions.

"Patrick always said, 'Never betray your partner, because all you're really doing is betraying yourself.' He also said, 'Take joy not from what you seek, but from what you already have.' Sometimes I felt he was trying a wee bit too hard with these sayings of his. Maybe they even bordered on pompous, but at the core of most of them there was something important he felt he needed to share with me. He believed most of it. He believed we'd both eventually have other partners, but during the time we were sharing, this was not important, and he didn't want it to become a preoccupation. At the time he and I were together, the partner he had before me wasn't important, and that wasn't him disrespecting her."

"You never asked him about her?" Kennedy asked.

"Of course I did," she replied, laughing heartily. "When I wasn't being as spiritual or as Zen as he'd like me to be, I most certainly quizzed him."

"And?"

"And he'd say something Zen like, 'I am always only with one.'"

"Did you meet any of his friends?" Coles asked.

"Rarely, but when we did he would never be disrespectful and try to hide me. He was always the perfect gentleman. He took pride in treating people the way he wanted to be treated himself."

"But you met some of his friends?" Kennedy continued.

"Occasionally, as I said, very occasionally."

"Did you ever get to know them?"

"Not really," she said, smiling again at Kennedy.

"Which implies that maybe you might have?" he pushed gently.

"I was smiling because when I heard from Rodney about Patrick, I was aware this was all going to come out. I imagined sitting down with a couple of cynical coppers like those on *The Bill* and trying to get through this with them smirking and being rude and crude … ohhhh," she said as a shiver worked its way through her entire body. "But then I got you two, and it's really been like sharing a glass of wine with a couple of friends and talking as mates. The couple of glasses I had before you got here also helped immensely, of course. Are you married?" she said looking at Kennedy.

Kennedy shook his head.

"And you?"

Coles looked at Kennedy, smiled nervously, blushed slightly, looked back at Simmons and said, "No, I'm too busy with my career."

"You know," Simmons said reflectively, "I've got to start to think about all of that now. Not marriage, of course, but the dating game. It will be a new thing for me."

"Oh my goodness," Coles blurted, "can you imagine your first date? With all your knowledge, the bloke will think he's died and gone to heaven."

"I'm not sure it's a good idea to go to bed with someone on your first date. What would you say, Christy?"

"No, no, no," said Coles. "I mean, I didn't mean it like that… I meant, I suppose in a way I did, but I just meant, you know, with all of your experience."

"We get the picture, don't we, Christy?" Simmons continued, looking as if she were thoroughly enjoying herself by holding on tightly to the moral high ground.

Kennedy said nothing but did enjoy watching Coles squirm a bit. Looking as good as she did, the addition of vulnerability was starting to make Coles look irresistible to Kennedy.

"Can we backtrack a wee bit?" he said, looking to Chloe. "We were talking about Mr Mylan's friends, and you…"

"I was hoping we'd passed that moment," Simmons admitted.

"But there was one of his friends you were thinking about?" Kennedy continued.

"Yes," she replied with a tolerant sigh. "It was that actress, you know Nealey …… what's her second name?"

"Nealey Dean?"

"Yes. I met her once up at Patrick's. I think she was aware of me."

"She knew who you were?" Coles asked.

"She said she'd been dying to meet me, so Patrick must have liked her, because he never usually discussed his… his concubines. She was very, very nice, full of fire. I think we would have gotten on well; we shared a similar sense of humour. She was either dashing off genuinely or Patrick had warned her not to hang around, because she left soon after I arrived, but she acted like she didn't want to leave. I think Patrick liked her a lot. I did wonder if he was considering dating her. I knew he liked her in that way."

"How did you know?" Kennedy asked.

"That night in bed, Patrick was just *different*."

CHAPTER TWENTY-FOUR

Kennedy and Coles left Simmons to plan the remainder of her life and got into Coles' car without saying a word.

He wondered if he should offer to take her out for a meal. She had implied to Chloe Simmons that she had got all dressed up to see him, but it might seem chauvinistic if he just assumed they were going to go back to her place, have a few glasses of wine... He thought that she'd probably heard from someone in North Bridge House that he'd split up with ann rea. She couldn't be aware of Sharenna Chada, for no one was aware of her. He chastised himself when he thought of Miss Chada and how good she'd been for him in more ways than one. But they weren't exactly dating in the old-fashioned meaning of the word. In fact they weren't dating under any interpretation of the word.

DI Anne Coles made the decision for him.

"I was thinking we should go for a drink."

"That sounds great," Kennedy agreed quickly.

It was 18.40 when they reached the Prince of Wales, which was quite close to the station where she'd picked him up. He wondered if it was either the local police hang-out or, perhaps, close to her home.

Kennedy went to the bar to get their drinks and Coles went off, "to find a quiet corner."

She didn't want to kiss in a public place, did she? As he looked over he saw she was touching up her make-up. He was feeling about ten feet tall. He felt slightly guilty for not having thought much about Coles after she'd left North Bridge House, but since then she had blossomed into this amazing woman and... and she still seemed interested in him and... he was single - well, apart from the potentially complicated re-lationship with Sharenna. As the barman poured two glasses of Chardonnay, Kennedy wondered again what exactly his relationship with Sharenna Chada was. After tonight, would he need to stop seeing her socially? He knew he didn't want to stop seeing her professionally, so effective was her work as a osteopath. He didn't really want to stop seeing her socially either. Kennedy wondered if he should try and continue to see both. He'd never ever cheated on a girl or woman in his life…but …he'd just been dumped… and…

The barman put the two glasses of wine on the counter. Kennedy turned and started to walk over to Coles. He suddenly realised that, in all of the scenarios, he'd been considering her as a sex object, and he realised they were going to talk about… What were they going to talk about?

She was looking at him now as he crossed the room. She was smiling her vulnerable smile. She looked so beautiful. Her hair was puffed up in a Farrah Fawcet type of healthy wild mane. She'd found them a corner booth, and she uncrossed her legs and moved them to one side to make room for him to take the seat beside her. As she did so, she unintentionally flashed a bit of leg and, in that one split second, Kennedy realised exactly why Coles had whispered to Simmons that she was aware of the joys of wearing silk stockings. Now it was Kennedy's turn to feel a shudder go through his entire body.

He chastised himself for not being considerate enough to check if Anne Coles had wanted some bar food. Was he in too big a hurry? Was his haste shared by Anne Coles?

Then circumstances took over, and events unfolded much hastier than Kennedy had ever dreamt possible.

CHAPTER TWENTY-FIVE

They'd no sooner clinked glasses than she said, "Ah, here he is, a bit earlier than I expected. Christy, I'd like to introduce you to my boyfriend, William Campbell. Bill, this is a former colleague of mine, Christy Kennedy."

Kennedy turned to see a mountain of a man, "her Gentle Giant" is actually what she called him. And wasn't the Gentle Giant just as keen to impart news? He was "bursting to tell anyone who'd listen."

"Has she told you yet?" he said, with all the enthusiasm Kennedy had being experiencing up a minute ago. "She's agreed to do me the honour of becoming my wife."

She protested that she and Kennedy hadn't had time to discuss anything yet, least of all her wedding news.

It just makes you sick, doesn't it? Kennedy thought to himself. It all went downhill very quickly from there. Her Gentle Giant hadn't time for a drink; they *needed* to go; *he'd* booked them in for a celebratory engagement dinner over in Kingston, "and we had *better* get our skates on."

"That's why I thought it was best we had our drink in here," she said to Kennedy, ninety-three seconds later, as she and the Gentle Giant speedily departed the Prince of Wales. "It's closer to the station, and of course you still don't drive. Must rush, byeeeeeeeeeeeeeeeeee."

Chapter Twenty-Six

On the slow train back to Camden via Waterloo, Kennedy reflected on happier times. Times like just over an hour ago, when he and Chloe Simmons, looking like a mysterious exotic goddess, and DI Anne Coles, looking like a dead ringer for Scarlett Johansson, were sitting together, chatting happily away about Simmons' willingness to be groomed as a sex slave for the recently departed Patrick Mylan.

To look at, Anne Coles and Chloe Simmons, while totally different, were to Kennedy both ten out of ten. Kennedy wondered if someone were only a true ten if you never experienced her fully. As Kennedy recalled the attractiveness and charm that were Coles and Simmons, he thought about what attracts a man to a woman. Perhaps the sexual act is not the most important part of the captivating dance. What then was? Surely it couldn't be something so fickle as love? Equally he knew he had been severely prejudiced by ann rea's (another, but again different ten) dumping him.

Even if he could ever figure out the most important part of the dance, then came the *really* big question: what was the most important part of the dance from the woman's side? He knew how much he'd been attracted to ann rea and how important she had felt it was to keep the air of mystery alive in their relationship by not taking each other for granted, physically speaking. But could that really just have been her knowing he wasn't really the man for her, while, at the same time, wanting to prolong the relationship for as long as possible because she "liked" him or was "fond" of him? He wondered what it meant for a female to acknowledge to herself that her partner had less than the perfect body, and to accept that her partner was not, in fact, her ideal lover.

Men made such a fuss over the look of a woman. And why wouldn't they? Kennedy believed there was nothing finer to behold. But what truly defines the perfect body for someone? Has it anything to do with the age of the person who is observing? Or could it have more to do with the person who is being observed? Kennedy would admit to preferring his lover to look like all their bits - legs, arms, neck (he did love an elegant décolleté), bum, breasts, etc - are all separate, rather than part of a single body mass. But what must it feel like, to have to admit to yourself that your partner has less than the perfect body? Could that have been the deciding factor for ann rea? Had she ever, he wondered, though, *Yep, I quite like Kennedy; yes I think he's an okay guy, but the bottom line is that he just doesn't turn me on any more.* Kennedy comforted himself that ann rea had never even hinted at that. While making love, ann rea looked like the most beautiful animal in the world, *but* she always looked like she was totally lost in her own pleasure. Miss Chada, on the other hand, looked as if she were somewhat conscious of his pleasure while, at the same time, she also looked as if she were never really there.

His vanity had led him to assume Anne Coles was still attracted to him, that he was "the special one" she had told Simmons she was meeting later - the one she had taken care and attention over her dress for. But then the Gentle Giant had showed up.

Kennedy was convinced there was some kind of magic in the air as they left Simmons' apartment, and there had been. The only problem was that the magic just hadn't been for him.

***

By the time he got back to Primrose Hill, it had just turned nine o'clock. For the first time since he left Wimbledon, he didn't regret not being detained there, because there sitting waiting for him in her car outside his house in Rothwell Street was Sharenna Chada. She seemed happy to see him, although it was hard to tell because she never smiled a lot.

He went to the car, opened the door, sat in beside her and said, "Brilliant to see you."

"You're not cross I just turned up?" she said tentatively.

"The opposite in fact."

"But you don't want me to come into your house?" she said, nodding in the direction of his door.

"Sorry?" he replied a little confused. "Oh, me sitting here… no, I though it might be nice if I took you *out* for dinner. Maybe you could show me that amazing Indian restaurant our food came from last Saturday… only if you want to, of course."

"I would like nothing more… well maybe that's not quite true but perhaps we can discuss that later."

CHAPTER TWENTY-SEVEN

At the same time Christy Kennedy and Sharenna Chada were starting into their first course in the Bombay Bicycle Club in Hampstead, DS James Irvine and DC Dot King had tracked Marcus Urry down to a suite of rehearsal rooms in Islington.

It appeared to Irvine that Urry was just hanging out at the Once Moore with Feeling complex. He was a friend, he would later claim, of the owner, Ivan Moore, and seemed to be happy holding court with some of the younger roadies, regaling them with stories of what it was like on the road in the good old glory days with his governor, Tim Dickens.

Urry obviously considered himself to be an armchair philosopher and, it appeared, had an opinion on absolutely everything inside and outside of the music business. These days, with Tim Dickens off the road, he claimed he was spending the most of his time on a course - a golf course, practising his swing. He demonstrated accordingly with his air golf club.

Irvine knew all of this only because Urry kept the two members of Camden Town CID waiting until he'd finished holding court with his fellow roadies. There seemed to be lots of Quo stories and Van the Man stories in his repertoire. Irvine started the interview off by playing up to the man's obvious ego.

"Did you work with Van Morrison then?"

Marcus Urry refused point blank to ever look the person he was talking to in the eye. Irvine found this surprising, because physically and by his dress sense Urry screamed out, "Look at me! Look at me!" He had long, unnaturally dark brown hair, which fell in a fan close to his waist. The unhealthy looking hair was receding high on his crown and preened out high on his head like tuft on a peacock. He had a long, thick handlebar moustache, which merged with his even longer and thicker sideburns. He looked like someone who (rarely) cut his own hair.

Piss holes in the snow for eyes completed his facial appearance. Irvine thought he looked like a mass murderer.

He was quite stout but tried to hide his weight under a pair of dark blue dungarees, and as he was holding court, he liked to have his arms folded and resting behind the bib of the trousers. A red plaid lumberjack shirt completed his uniform.

"I'll tell you a great Van story," Urry started, avoiding Irvine's question. "He'd turned up, not far from here actually, to rehearse some new musicians. He'd hired a complete new road crew. Band and crew arrived first and were working away at their stuff. Then this wee man in a long Crombie turns up. The sound engineer takes one look at him, sizes him up and shouts to the rest of the band and crew, 'Did anyone order a taxi?' Van gets rattled about being mistaken for a taxi driver and mumbles something to the sound engineer. The sound engineer understands only the word 'van.' 'Sorry, mate,' he apologises to Van, and turns back to the band and crew and shouts, 'Sorry, make that, did anyone order a van?'"

Irvine could hear a few sniggers from the crew behind them and, working on the theory of divide and conquer, he asked Urry to accompany them to the smallish but quiet canteen where Urry directed King, "Be a doll and get me a mug of tea and a bacon buttie; bacon well done. Tell them it's for Marcus. They know how I like my tea and buttie done here."

Irvine diffuses the situation, saying, "It's my turn, *Detective* Constable King. I'll get them in."

Irvine placed the order at the counter with a young girl, who immediately said, "Where ye from?"

"Paisley," Irvine admitted, "and you?"

"Aberdeen. Aye, well someone has to."

"You're not wrong."

"Is this for Hurry Urry?" she asked.

"Aye. He says you know how he likes it."

"Aye, we do," she whispered. "He just loves it with spit in the tea, and he likes the bacon slapped around the floors a bit as well."

"Right," Irvine laughed. "Does he work in here a lot?"

"Chauvinist prat. He hasn't worked a day since his boss went off the road in the eighties. But he knows it all," she replied, continuing to examine Irvine, all the time working on the sandwiches, mug of tea, and cappuccino for King. We don't get many suits or tweeds in here, pet. Are you from a record company?"

"No, actually I'm from Camden Town CID."

"Oh shit, oh damn, blast," she hissed. "Look, I was just kidding about the prat."

"So he's not a prat then?" Irvine smiled, showing he was fine with her indiscretion.

She relaxed again. "Oh, he's a prat all right," she said, confirming that no one can make the word prat sound as big an insult as the Scottish. "No, I was just kidding about spitting in his tea and slapping the bacon around the floor."

"Oh good, I'm not going to have to take you in then." Irvine smiled again as he paid for the tray full.

"No, we'd never do that. We might use toilet water for his tea, but we'd never ever spit in it; and we might clean our shoes with his bacon, but we'd never ever, well hardly ever, slap it around the floors."

By the time Irvine reached the table, Hurry Urry was holding forth, and King was now his captive audience.

"... and I'll tell you this for nothing, that one, well she was always absolutely gagging for it," Urry was saying, leaning his head backwards to shake his long hair from side to side.

"Marcus here was telling me about this famous female singer who liked to take her road crew to bed. What was her name, Marcus?" King asked.

"Rule number one," Urry lectured, raising his hand in a stop sign, "you never discuss libellous issues when there are three or more people present. There's always one (or more) to collaborate what was said and by whom. Do you get my drift?"

"I do," King said, now happy to be distracted with her drink as Urry tore into his sandwich.

"The wee shite," Urry snarled. "She knows I don't like this much butter in my buttie, and she's meant to cut off the fat from my bacon. And the tea tastes vile. How many fecking times...?" And he stomped off in the direction of the counter.

The Scottish waitress was sweet as pumpkin pie with Urry and persuaded him to return to the table; she would make a new sandwich and bring it over herself.

Urry was just concluding another Van the Man story when the waitress returned.

Urry quickly took a large bite of his sandwich.

"Now this is perfect" he said through a mouthful of sandwich (not a pretty sight) as he turned his back immediately on the waitress. "Why couldn't you have done this the first time around?"

"Oh, I think I must have been distracted by Sean Connery here," she said from behind Urry's shoulder. She winked at Irvine, mimicked someone pulling a toilet chain and winked at Irvine once again.

King was confused by the waitress' pantomime but she kept stum.

"Okay, guys, I've got things to do, people to see, or should that be people to do? Whatever. Let's cut to the chase here," Urry said as he washed down his second bite of sandwich with a mouthful of tea, once again speaking with his mouth full. "You guys want to speak to me about Paddy Mylan and my part in his downfall?"

The only one laughing was Marcus Urry.

"Look, I speak my mind. I always speak my mind; there's no other way to live your life, get my drift? I can't be arsed with all the politically correct shite. Paddy was seriously taking the piss with my boss' income. He tried to be cool and had all these illusions of grandeur, but behind it all he was only a dumb-fecked paddy…"

"Steady on," Irvine said.

"Do you want me to tell you my side or do you want to waste my time with your polite interruptions about your perceptions about my manners? I'm not saying you should think that Mr Patrick Mylan was a dumb-fecked paddy, but I'm saying *I* do. I'm not so insecure that I need you to think the same as I do. Sorry? No, I'm most certainly not sorry. That's what I believe. This is still England, and so that will be my privilege, to speak my mind. End of. Get my drift?"

"Yes, but surely you can also see that, socially speaking, it's just as easy to be well mannered?" King offered.

"I don't give a feck what you think. It's of no importance to me. End of."

"Okay, can we get back to Mr Mylan?" Irvine suggested, trying to drag at least something from this interview.

"At last, the penny has dropped. Proceed," Urry ordered.

"This is excellent coffee," Irvine said, refusing to rise to the bait.

"Yeah, I know what you mean," King said, picking up on Irvine's lead. "It's very light and frothy, just how I love it."

"Is this a fecking Once Moore with Feelings coffee love fest or what?" Urry grunted. "American shit, rotting your guts. You should be drinking good old English tea. If it's good enough for the Queen, then it's good enough for me,"

"I thought coffee came from Brazil," Irvine said deadpan,

"And surely tea's from India," King added, keeping up her side of the banter.

"Right, that's it, I'm fecked if I'm going to stay here and listen to the Met's answer to Ant and Dec. I've stuff to do…"

"People to threaten?" Irvine continued seamlessly, catching Urry in a rare eyeball stare that just dared him to try and leave the table.

"Okay, bring it on; here we go," Urry said triumphantly. "At long last we've reached the topic you're here to discuss."

King took out her notebook.

"Yes, love, write this down, because I'm only going to say it once. I've worked with Tim Dickens for a long time. He's a mate, been a good mate, and you know what? He looks after his crew really well, and in my book you can't do better than that. I mean, he's never done a Pete Townsend and given his crew the entire proceeds from a big US show to split between them as a tour bonus. But nonetheless, Tim Dickens has always looked after the crew well, and he's always looked after me *particularly* well. Hell, I'm still on a retainer, and it's over seven years since my boss even dreamt of treading the boards again.

"So, to me it's very simple. Someone threatens my boss' livelihood, they're in effect threatening my livelihood. It's not going to happen. End of. I heard through the grapevine what was going on…"

"What exactly was going on?" Irvine interrupted, wondering exactly how much Marcus Urry knew.

"*What was going on* was Paddy fecking Mylan had my boss by the balls and wasn't prepared to let them go. And, you know, when someone has my boss by the balls, then…"

"Then they'd got you by the balls… yeah, we know," Irvine said, considering the degrees of hygiene of the two gentlemen in question.

"Exactly!" Urry said proudly.

"But let's assume you're using balls as a metaphor…" Irvine started.

"No, Sergeant, the actual metaphor is the holding of the balls," Urry said. He held his strenuously toned arm into the middle of the table and slowly opened his hand palm up, and then slowly and with great menace in his eyes, he closed his hairy fingers tighter and tighter into a fist until Irvine felt his own eyes about to water.

"We get all of that, Marcus. We know you can probably rip the heads off chickens with your teeth and you can frighten babies, but what I'm trying to find out is how much in the know you were about your bosses' business dealings."

"Tim Dickens got greedy. Paddy Mylan wanted a bit of rock 'n' roll glamour. They both tangoed. For a while Paddy led the dance; then Dickens took over. Soon Dickens discovered that even though he was leading the dance, he was still getting shafted. I was called in to disentangle the dancers and clean up the mess. End of."

"So you got Tim Dickens out of the deal?" King asked.

"Well, Paddy's D for dead, so the deal is D for dead as well."

"So you're admitting you killed him?" Irvine asked, in disbelief.

"No, dick-head, but maybe I scared him into taking his own life. Do I need to draw pictures for you? Bring back Morse, for heaven's sake!" Urry said to an imaginary audience.

"So you're claiming you scared him into committing suicide?" Irvine continued, still not quite believing what he had just heard.

"Listen, I'm only going to say this once, so jot it down, sweetie," Urry said, pausing to wink at King. "You more than most must realise how pathetically stupid most murderers are. If I ever committed a crime, I can absolutely guarantee neither you, nor any of your mob, would ever have a hope in hell's chance of catching me. Get my drift?"

"Yeah, Marcus, we get it. You're a clever barsteward, but can we just go back a teeny wee bit here and tidy up this 'scaring' Mr Patrick Mylan issue?"

Another extended sigh from Urry.

"Okay, time out here," Urry announced. "Can I just say, were I to have had a chat with Mr Mylan and, as a result of that chat, he realised the error of his ways and found a convenient, if sordid, way to end his life, then I can't be held accountable for his actions, now can I?"

Irvine blew through his closed lips slowly, counted to ten and said, "Okay, Marcus, why don't you tell us *exactly* what happened?"

"Well, I rang up to fix an appointment to see Patrick 'I'm so grand these days you can't call me Paddy' Mylan. He wouldn't agree. I told his Frenchman I was going to turn up anyway. He told me I wouldn't be let in. I reminded him of England's victory at Waterloo, and I advised him in no uncertain terms that he'd be just as foolish to try to resist."

"I believe you'll find that the English were assisted by the Dutch, the Germans, and the Belgians at that particular battle," King offered.

"Whatever," Urry grunted. "We led the charge, and we certainly kicked Napoleon's ass. So I show up, I had a very large roll of plastic under my arm, and Jean Michel…"

"Jean Claude?" King offered.

"No, there was just one of them there," Urry replied impatiently.

"Mr Mylan's assistant is called Jean Claude, not Jean Michel."

"And the difference is?" Urry snarled. "So, Jean Michel, Jean Claude, whoever, puts up little or no resistance. Mylan had more bottles, I'll grant him that. He brings me through to his office. I sit down and I start to tell him a few stories from the good old days of rock 'n' roll, the days when you had the likes of Peter Grant standing up to the music business tossers in order to protect his charges, the Zep. I went to great length to advise Paddy exactly what happened to those who'd fallen by the wayside, if you get my drift. Anyway, long story short, I'm telling him all these tales. It's all very civilised.

"Eventually he asks me what the large roll of plastic is for. So I get up," Urry continued, bursting to get the next part of his story out, "I start to unroll the plastic, and I take a pair of scissors from my pocket, and I cut the plastic up into pieces, and as I do so, I put one piece over the sofa, another over the chair, another over a rug. All the time he's looking at me and he's getting more and more scared, and then, when I'd enough pieces of the furniture covered to make my point, I say, 'Ah this? This is just a trick I learned from a New York manager who in turn allegedly learned it from the Mafia. We find when we do it this way, the blood causes less damage to the furniture."

"And what happened?" Irvine asked.

"I believe he was in need of his brown trousers," Urry spat out, just about containing himself until he managed to get his punch line out.

"I'd heard somewhere that you beat a hasty retreat after he'd threatened you with a very large volume of Shakespeare's works."

Urry slowed up his chortling to boast, "Listen, Sergeant, when you're behind enemy lines, you need to be resourceful to escape with your information. Tactics, Sergeant. It pays to be a master tactician. I *allowed* him to think he was scaring me off with the book. But look at the facts: I managed to infiltrate his mind, show him the error of his ways and plant the seeds of destruction, which clearly sprouted forth a week or so later when he topped himself. End of."

Irvine was trying to work out if Urry was a dangerous thug or simply a buffoon.

"Tell me this, sir," he said, taking his jacket from the back of his chair and standing up to put it on again, "can you tell me what you were doing between the hours of four o'clock and eight o'clock last Saturday afternoon?"

"Yes, I'd be happy to, or would you prefer to, miss," he said looking at King.

"Sorry?" King asked, slightly stunned.

"You know, tell the good sergeant here what we were up to last Saturday afternoon." He then stopped talking, opened his mouth, slid and furiously wagged his tongue from side to side. "You should have seen your innocent constable here, sergeant. She was absolutely gagging for it. You get my drift?"

Then he roared with laughter, cleaning away the resultant spittle with the back of his hand.

King held her composure, "I do believe, sir, you're mistaking me for your regular girlfriend."

"What?" Urry grunted, looking really pissed off that he hadn't managed to get the constable to rise to his bait.

"Yes, she's a real doll, I hear." King paused as Hurry Urry sat up again in his seat proudly and puffed his chest out. "A blow-up doll."

Before they left, King and Irvine extracted Urry's feeble alibi: supposedly he'd been around at his mum's in the Elephant and Castle for lunch and had fallen asleep on the sofa.

Just as King was about to turn the key in the ignition, Irvine, claiming he'd forgotten something, ran back into the rehearsal rooms. He met Urry in the stairwell. He stood in front of Urry, and Urry stopped in his tracks. He took a step towards Urry, and Urry took a step back. Irvine slowly took another step. This time Urry's step took his back to the wall, and Irvine leaned in so close that their noses were less than half an inch apart.

"What you need to realise, Marcus," Irvine whispered in a hiss, "is that being in the right, particularly your version of right, won't always save you. For instance, if I ever hear of any more chauvinism, rudeness, or bigotry from you, I'll quite happily dump you in jail overnight; and with your long, smooth hair and your generous soft girth, I know for a fact that an inmate or two, or maybe even three, will find you extremely attractive. And yes, I will admit that after your night of hitherto unknown passion, you will be released from prison the following morning. You'll be let out because you are, as you say, a master tactician and are always in the right, but you'll still be walking funny. Get my drift?"

Chapter Twenty-Eight

Wednesday morning at five o'clock as the day began, Kennedy woke to find the other side of the bed, the side he usually slept on, empty but still warm to his touch from the body of Sharenna Chada. He thought she must have left while he was asleep, but then he noticed the light coat she wore was still carefully placed on the back of one of the two chairs in his bedroom, chairs that were never used for sitting on but as clotheshorses. His bedroom door, which he usually slept with closed, was open. He could hear no sounds coming from the bathroom half a flight up.

Maybe she'd left forgetting her coat? Kennedy was now alert. He knew he'd have trouble getting back to sleep. Once his brain clicked into gear, he could never return to dreamland. He mentally thanked Miss Chada that his back no longer troubled him as it had only four days ago. Thinking he could hear some noises down on the ground floor, Kennedy got up, slung on a puffin-emblazoned Rathlin Island T-shirt and headed out of his bedroom. Walking down the stairs without them creaking was an impossible feat, but he crept downstairs as quietly as he could.

When he reached the first floor landing, he thought he could hear something in his L-shaped lounge, book, and music room. Ever so quietly, he stuck his head through the door, and there, standing at the top of the antique stepladder reading a book, was the mostly undressed Miss Chada. He hadn't disturbed her, so he continued to stare and marvel at the flowing curves, which surely would have inspired even Michelangelo. Sharenna preferred not to fully show off her body to anyone, well at least not to Kennedy. Now he came to think about it, ann rea was similar. In her case she was always saying it was important they kept the mystery of each other's bodies alive for each other. Kennedy felt, in Sharenna's case, it had much more to do with shyness, and she never fully undressed until she was under the bed covers excepting of course that first fateful night, when aided by several glasses of wine, she'd performed an extremely sensual strip for Kennedy.

Kennedy felt guilty about the way he had crept up on her, so he took several steps backwards on to the landing and called out, "Sharenna, where are you?"

He heard her fussing around, returning books and descending the stepladder, and then she called out, "I am with your books."

Kennedy was intrigued by her charming turn of phrase.

"How long have you been up?"

"The ladder?" she asked as she very discreetly slipped into the seat by his desk. She immediately swung around so that her back was to him and her modesty sheltered.

"No," he laughed, "up out of bed?"

"Ah I must learn better how to eat," she said, obviously annoyed with herself. "Perhaps how not to eat would be more fitting. Indian food late at night always does this to me. I didn't want to disturb you so I came down. I was going to prepare some tea and toast for you like you did for me last time. That was very nice. But it was too early to wake you. So I was just wandering around your beautiful house. It's very clean."

"Thank you."

"It is too big for one person…" She stopped mid track. She mentally retreated but chose not to qualify it by saying, "Of course I wasn't suggesting that I…" Kennedy figured for Miss Chada even to say she wouldn't, wasn't, couldn't, would also have been too indiscreet. Instead she chose to move away from the subject altogether.

"So many books," she said instead, as if no other matter were crossing her mind. "Have you read them all?"

"No," Kennedy admitted. "I have an A list of 'must reads' and a B list of 'will read sometime,' but the A list never drops to a level that permits dipping into the B list."

"Perhaps when you retire you will read your books. I can see you in your books. It is so important to read."

She was looking around his desk now. She tidied it up; she opened and closed the drawer without actually looking into it. She turned on his desk lamp. The resultant glare was too cruel to the early morning light, and she killed it immediately.

"What do you read?" he asked.

"I read Dickens and Shakespeare and lots of books to help me with my work," she started.

"Really?"

"You mean I shouldn't read Dickens or Shakespeare? Maybe you mean I shouldn't try to get more knowledge to help me with my work?"

"No, no, I didn't mean either," Kennedy said, as she smiled tolerantly. "It's more I was expecting Indian writers or maybe some modern ones."

"I would prefer not to pollute my mind."

"Where did you grow up, Sharenna?" Kennedy asked. He knew little or nothing about her.

"Oh," she said, swinging in the captain's chair, still with her back to Kennedy, "it's much too early in the day for a late night conversation."

Kennedy was considering this when she continued. "But if you would like to return to your bed," she whispered, "I will join you there."

Two minutes later, under the cloak of darkness of his room, she slid under the blankets beside him. Her blemish-free skin, chilled by the cool morning air, sidled up close to him, and they continued to get to know each other better, if only in the carnal sense.

***

As Kennedy walked over Primrose Hill three hours later, he thought of Patrick Mylan and his relationship with Chloe Simmons. Both parties to the agreement seemed relatively happy with their sides of the bargain. Mylan was receiving the sex he desired without, in his book, the downside of a proper relationship. Chloe, in her own words, was happy to set herself up and put herself beyond the misery someone like her sister was subject to in the love stakes. Admittedly, she had been putting her emotional life on hold, but now those restraints had disappeared with the death of Mylan, she seemed quite excited and intrigued by what the next part of her life held in store for her.

But what about myself? Kennedy thought. What about him and the mysterious Miss Chada? Mysterious was probably too strong a word. He had known her in a professional way for over a year, although he still didn't really know a lot about her. But what about their situation? Was what they were enjoying a deal or a relationship?

They'd been together several times now, and after the initial "getting to know you" stage, physically speaking, each occasion had been very rewarding. He was still amazed that one so outwardly shy, innocent even, could give of herself so freely. There were no "buts" in Kennedy's equation. The physical side of Kennedy's relationship with ann rea, magic though it had been, had on reflection been somewhat blemished by the toil and dilemma of the emotional side. After all of that, it was altogether an extremely pleasant change to enjoy the honesty of his relationship with Miss Chada.

Walking up the steps of North Bridge House, Kennedy wondered if what he had with Miss Chada was enough to enjoy a continued and deepening relationship, or did one in fact need the emotionally charged side to click in before that could become a reality?

The Ulster detective updated his noticeboard, and triggered by his memory of Miss Chada's journey of discovery as she wandered around his house in the early morning, he decided he needed to go and have another look around the house of Mr Patrick Mylan.

A very subdued Jean Claude Banks greeted him at the front door. The house felt very lonely and very sad. Jean Claude Banks seemed very happy when Kennedy said his preference was to look around the house on his own.

"All zee chambers are open," Jean Claude said to Kennedy as he wandered up the stairs.

Houses. Kennedy thought about houses a lot. He thought about what houses could tell you about their owners. What people thought about their houses could tell you even more about the people in question.

Some people, Kennedy felt, lived their lives in houses without ever being aware about the fabric of the building, without ever thinking about the history of their houses. Such people, Kennedy reckoned, rarely succeeded in making their houses into homes. As he continued to look around Mylan's house, he couldn't help but feel that this man had lived a life and died without leaving a lasting stamp or mark of any kind on his living accommodation.

Kennedy focused in on Patrick Mylan. He wondered about his parents who had died when Patrick was very young. He wondered about his siblings. The word from Mylan's friends was that there weren't any, but they were dealing with the truth as supplied to them by Patrick Mylan. Was that what he'd wanted them to believe? Kennedy tried to imagine the place Mylan must have grown up in. What would the change from his parents' home to his uncle's farm have done to Mylan while he was at such an impressionable age? Not for the first time, Kennedy wondered what Mylan's voice sounded like, how his phrasing reflected his personality or vice versa. He'd started to pick up some hints while interviewing Chloe Simmons with DI Coles. (He felt very embarrassed when he recalled his near major faux pas with Coles.)

What he needed most was to find out what Mylan's friends really thought of him, not what they were now graciously saying about him a few days after his death. "Never to speak ill of the dead." Death, or maybe it was the fear of death, did tend to make people try not to cross this line. Cynthia Cox was the only one acting as if she'd never been imparted with these words of wisdom. Yet Kennedy wasn't sure how much store he could set by her words. She was much too chippy, he felt, to give a true reflection.

As he wandered around the house by himself, he felt as if he were walking around a hotel suite that was spotlessly clean and awaiting its next guest. Mrs Cox had that, at least, to take credit for.

Not getting anything inside the house, the detective left Jean Claude at the front door, saying he had all he needed for now. He was going to have a walk around the garden and then leave. When he was in the middle of the smallish back garden, he looked to the row of terraced houses at the foot of it. Their owners, with their Victorian looking balconies, hadn't spotted any untoward goings-on the previous Saturday. Kennedy noticed the bridge to his left of the houses. From there he could stand and look back at Mylan's house. He passed the church en route, but the view from the bridge did not produce anything apart from the knowledge that there was a nursery school in the back of St Mark's Church.

He wandered across the road on the crown of the bridge and walked into Princess Road and down to the Albert pub. Would the Albert have been Mylan's regular? It certainly was the closest to his house. Kennedy wondered if any of his team had checked with the pub to see if the owner or staff had any memories of Mylan? The pub wasn't open, otherwise he'd have checked himself. He walked back towards the church. St Mark's square was busy as usual, acting as a gateway to Regent's Park, with St Mark's Bridge (for pedestrians only) taking those keen for the sad zoo; or those in need of sports of some kind; or those needing to feed the over ninety species of ducks, swans, and geese; or those who wished to use the joyous four hundred and seventy-two acreage for nothing more than a stroll.

Kennedy walked on to St Mark's Bridge, stopped midway, leaned against the black iron railing and looked back towards Mylan's house. He had felt that he was missing something, and now, as he fixed his eyes on the house for a split second, it was so obvious that he felt like kicking himself.

CHAPTER TWENTY-NINE

Kennedy rushed back to Mylan's house, banged on the door, rushed past a startled Jean Claude Banks and took the stairs two at a time. He reached the top landing in good breath and clicked open the semi-secret door to the roof space. Somewhere beneath him, he could hear the steps as the Frenchman ascended the stairs at a more leisurely pace. Kennedy stepped into the roof space and walked into the middle of the floor, pausing to get his bearings on the house. He moved to the front bay window cut into the slope of the roof. With the majestic red brick chimney stack to his left, he turned to his right and walked to where the front slope met the gable slope. He pushed each section of the wood until, five boards in, he felt it give slightly. Because his neck had to be tilted back at a sixty-degree angle to be parallel with the slope of the roof, he awkwardly used both hands to put pressure on the wood. Eventually, a section consisting of eight pieces of the tongued and grooved wood lifted up. When this section had moved through an arc of about ninety degrees, he heard it click into something and stop. He tested it; it remained securely in place.

Kennedy walked into the space that, as suggested with the slope of the boards, shouldn't have been there. When his eyes acclimatised to the darkness, he noticed a luminous light switch at eye level about six feet away. He gingerly walked across in the direction of it and flicked the switch. It had no impact. He searched to the right of the switch, running his hand up and down the wall to no avail. Jean Claude Banks, standing behind him, looked bemused by Kennedy's discovery. Kennedy sent the Frenchman off to find a torch, and in the meantime he continued to check around in the dark space. A couple of minutes later, he discovered what he'd been looking for. About two and a half feet across from the switch and about two feet below it, he found a door handle sunk into the wooden door. The door opened easily. Mylan had obviously gone to all this trouble to hide this space from the naked eye, and yet he hadn't even bothered to lock the door.

The detective resisted fully opening the door, waiting until Jean Claude returned with a torch. Taking the already lit torch, Kennedy instructed the Frenchman to wait for him downstairs. Kennedy shone the torch around the area and discovered nothing apart from the fact that it was all painted black.

He went back to the door and opened it fully. The space inside the door was already fully lit, obviously from the luminous switch by the side of the door. He then stepped into the sixteen feet by twelve feet room he'd spotted from St Mark's Bridge several minutes earlier. The room and its entrance were *so* well concealed Kennedy reckoned Mylan had never shared this space.

The matte-black walled room was equipped with a bank of lifeless hi-tech monitors, which looked like three large sets of sunglasses. The original windows were now decked out in shelves and neatly packed with DVDs. There was a napping Apple computer set up. Centred in the room was a very elaborate chair, which seemed, from the number of levers, switches, buttons, etc., to cater for every solo whim a man could ever have, including, when fully extended, the best night sleep anyone ever enjoyed. In the middle of the twelve-foot wall opposite the door, there was the biggest flat screen Kennedy had ever seen, but it was the massive poster on the larger wall that stopped Kennedy in his tracks. The poster, which was maybe just a wee bit too blurred to be an official poster, contained a near life-size photo of Nealey Dean in a very advanced stage of undress. Miss Dean, in not much more than a Marilyn Monroe type wig, looked as if she'd been caught unawares, but she still retained her composure and her modesty.

Kennedy carefully sat in the chair and swung around towards the Nealey Dean poster. Pretty soon he was going to have to have the SOCO boys and girls around here again to go through the computers and DVDs. Should he leave the poster up? If it had been of ann rea, what would he have expected Irvine to do? What would ann rea have expected him to do? He swivelled around three hundred and sixty degree in the chair and again tried to figure out what to do.

Then he noticed another door on the same wall as the entrance door. He opened it, tugged on the string inside the door and stood

staring as the light burst in on this all-white tiled, four-foot square immaculate bathroom with miniature shower, toilet, and sink.

His first thought was of Patrick Mylan dying on the back of the door
of the swimming pool bathroom, and again he wondered if Mylan's
demise was by accident or by design. Here was all the evidence that
Kennedy needed that Mylan had taken much of his pleasure alone.

But his second thought was that if Mylan had wanted to indulge in
autoerotic asphyxiation, then surely he would have done it up here
with all his pictures (moving and still), aides, and devices literally at his
fingertips. He had gone to great trouble and expense to create this very
private room. So why would he risk public humiliation in his AEA endeavours by conducting them in a location so public?

Kennedy had had enough of this room and cubbyhole. He walked
back out into the main room and stood staring at the erotic image of
Nealey Dean. She caught your eye from every single position in the
room. The poster wasn't framed; it was dry mounted. It didn't look
heavy. Did he want to be guilty of removing evidence from the scene?
No, he couldn't do that. He could never do that, but what about Irvine
and Dean?

He took the poster down from the wall, turned it around and put it
back so that Miss Dean's image was facing the wall. Now, from where
he stood, it just looked like a piece of very expensive art. An eight-foot
by four-foot white piece, which when considered against the dense
black background of the walls looked very J. Lennon *circa* 1972. In the
bottom right hand corner of the virgin white space, Kennedy did a
small pen and ink, long hair, beard, and glasses logo that Lennon always did with his signature in the post-Beatle, pre-NYC years.

Kennedy hadn't broken the habit of a lifetime; he hadn't removed
evidence from the scene of a crime. He was able to walk back to North
Bridge House with an almost clear conscience.

CHAPTER THIRTY

Kennedy summoned his team for a pep talk. He'd already started to hear the mutterings of suicide, and there's nothing that can derail an investigation more quickly than even one member of the team not having the stomach for it - or openly thinking they're on the wrong track.

He advised his team about what he'd discovered (minus details of the Nealey Dean poster) and told them why he felt this now proved Patrick Mylan had actually been murdered.

Next he focused them in on the current list of people being questioned. It was not exactly a suspect list, but more of a target list.

The list read:

Maggie Littlewood
Roger Littlewood
Marcus Urry
Cynthia Cox
Jean Claude Banks
Tony Stevenson
Martin Friel
Chloe Simmons
Rodney Stuart
Nealey Dean
Tim Dickens
Alice Robbins
POP U

POP U had been a DC Dot King innovation. It stood for Person Or Persons Unknown. She felt it ensured people always consider another option until a case has been successfully solved.

"Okay," Kennedy said, looking at the list himself, "how do we feel about the alibis we've documented so far?"

"I think it's amusing that it turns out that Jean Claude's and Cynthia Cox's alibis are identical," Allaway said, starting off the proceedings. "Do we think there's anything going on there?"

"Oh, come on, of course they're an item. She has him wrapped around her little finger," King offered, amused no one had picked up on that.

"So they rehearsed their alibi?" Allaway asked.

"Or they were both together all day Saturday, and they were reciting exactly what they did," King said.

"Okay, let's check with the staff in the Baroque and the Belco. Neither Jean Claude nor Cynthia are exactly wallflowers, so if they were there people are going to have noticed them," Kennedy said, happy they appeared to be moving into gear. "Also, let's check with the optician she says she dropped into at five o'clock."

"Good idea," King agreed. "She seems like the kind of person who would try on every single pair of spectacles they'd have and then opt for a pair from off-the-shelf in Boots."

"Next?" Kennedy asked, looking back at the list.

"Urry's mum confirmed he was around with her on Saturday and that she left him asleep on the sofa," Allaway said.

"Where did his mum go, and what time did she go out?" Kennedy asked.

Allaway checked his notes. "She left the house just before five o'clock, and she attended a bingo session, getting back to her house at nine-thirty, by which time Wolfman Marcus was gone."

"He'd still have had the opportunity," Irvine said. "If Dr Taylor's estimate is out by even half an hour, Marcus doesn't really have an alibi for the entire window. I quite fancy him for this."

"I agree he's not a nice person," King said, "but this particular murder is much too clever for Marcus."

There, that sounds better, Kennedy thought. One of the team was at last referring to the investigation as a murder.

"Well, I still think it would be dangerous to rule him out altogether," Irvine persisted. "There's something about him - his superiority complex maybe. It wouldn't take very much to convince me that he was capable of murder."

Kennedy underlined Urry's name a couple of times and put a question mark by his alibi details. Then he turned and said, "Okay, while we're on this track, how about Tim Dickens and his PA, Alice Robbins? They shared Urry's motive."

"Alice claimed they both were together, going through his royalty statements," Irvine said, reading from the notes of the interview he and Kennedy had conducted, "but Tim Dickens seems to me to be the one who'll benefit most from Mylan's demise."

"Let's see them separately this time, and pin them both down to actual details about exactly what they were doing and when. Did she nip out for a coffee? Did they order a takeaway? Where from? When did they take a break for anything? Then we'll see how close their versions of the story are."

"Or how well rehearsed they are," King suggested, before reading off the next name on Kennedy's noticeboard: "Tony Stevenson, a member of Toblerone. He claims he was on a day trip to Paris with his wife and two daughters. He's produced their boarding cards and his credit card receipts for several purchases he made while in Paris."

"At last," Irvine sighed loudly, "someone whose alibi actually checks out. Let's remove him from our list."

"Yep," Kennedy agreed, complying with Irvine's request. "However, let's not forget him; he can still give us a lot of background on Mylan. Okay, our third Toblerone man, Martin Friel?"

"He was at the cinema. He saw two movies back to back. I still need to check that out," Allaway admitted.

"Roger Littlewood was gardening by himself. His wife Maggie was shopping down the West End," Kennedy said, continuing with his list. "We need more information on both of them."

"Rodney Stuart: again no real alibi. He claimed to have been by himself in the office all day Saturday," Irvine said, "and he wasn't backwards about putting Marcus Urry's name well and truly in the frame. How did your interview go with Chloe Simmons?" he asked, turning to his boss.

At that split second, Kennedy realised he hadn't asked the stunning Chloe Simmons what she was doing on Saturday last. Was that because he was distracted from his work by Anne Coles? Then he remembered that he also hadn't asked Miss Simmons whether or not Patrick Mylan wore sock garters.

"Well," Kennedy began expansively, "she seemed… I mean she wasn't jumping up and down with joy or anything, but I got the impression she wasn't exactly grief-stricken at Mr Mylan's death. It was more that she seemed happy to be getting on to the next part of her life."

"Enough for her to have ended his?" King asked, with genuine interest.

Kennedy just stared at her, not in a patronising manner, but she read him well.

"Yes, yes, I know," she began: "much too early to even think about."

"What we really need to know is, who Mylan's… who his girlfriend before Miss Simmons was," Kennedy said.

"What? You think she might have been jealous of Chloe?" King asked.

"Let's just put her in the POP U section for now," Kennedy smiled, adding "Mylan's ex" to his list with three question marks beside it.

"I should have asked Nealey what she was doing on Saturday," Irvine interjected out of the blue, "if only to officially remove her name from the list. I'll go and see her at the end of this meeting. Maybe she knows something about Mylan's earlier girlfriend."

"Actually, I'd prefer if you took DS Allaway and conducted the Tim Dickens and Alice Robbins interviews," Kennedy said, happy he'd been spared the embarrassment of someone inquiring about what Miss Simmons had been doing between the hours of four and eight on Saturday. "DC King and myself will drop in on Miss Dean on our way down to Wimbledon to re-interview Miss Simmons."

"Have the forensic accounting people come up with anything yet?" Kennedy asked.

"I rang them just this morning," King replied quickly.

"And?"

"They just laughed and set the phone down."

"Sounds like Superintendent Castle needs to make the next call for us," Kennedy said. "What about Patrick Mylan's mobile phone records?"

"The company promised them for after lunchtime," King replied.

"It looks like either Tim Dickens or Chloe Simmons would have the best motive; she gets her life back and her property as part of the deal," Irvine concluded, as the meeting wound down.

"Or POP U?" King offered helpfully.

CHAPTER THIRTY-ONE

When Kennedy and King came calling, the doorman at Nealey Dean's mansion block said she wasn't due back until after five o'clock. Kennedy left a message saying they'd call and see her then. He figured they'd be able to fit in their visit to Wimbledon in the meantime.

As they arrived in Wimbledon just after lunchtime, Kennedy informed King that he hadn't thought Wimbledon was so far south that they'd need a passport. From his years in Ulster watching reports about the Wimbledon tennis fortnight, when he'd moved to London first, he had really always expected people to be walking around Wimbledon in white tennis gear with rackets over their shoulder. He also remembered thinking that there must be a permanent circus at the corner of Oxford Street and Regent Street. He quickly realised that he needn't have bothered, in his pre-teen years, working out how all the animals and the audiences avoided the busy traffic of the West End of London. He also now accepted that the majority of people now walking around the streets of Wimbledon preoccupied with their lives wouldn't have a clue where the world-famous tennis tournament took place, even though it was no more than three miles away in the direction of South Fields.

Wimbledon, to Kennedy's eye, had lost the small village in a big city feel it had had when he first visited it on one of his many early voyages of discovery around the city. The reason he loved living in Primrose Hill so much was because it had been able to retain the village feel. He admitted to himself that it was probably because Primrose Hill was a heck of a lot smaller than Wimbledon.

As King drove up Worple Road in the direction of Raynes Park, drawing closer to Chloe Simmons' building, Kennedy could feel himself sinking further and further into the passenger seat, remembering how embarrassed he felt about the DI Anne Coles incident the previous evening on these very same streets.

Chloe Simmons seemed genuinely happy to see him, a fact DC Dot King was very quick to pick up on.

With pleasantries over, Simmons and King refreshed with coffee and Kennedy with tea (which Chloe insisted he make himself.) Kennedy jumped right in at the deep end.

"I've a rather delicate question to ask you, I'm afraid," Kennedy started.

"Oh, should I get the wine out again?" Chloe said, a frown crossing her youthful face. Her freshly washed hair was fuzzier than it had been the previous evening.

"No, it'll be fine. I just wanted to ask you about an item of Mr Mylan's clothing."

"Okay."

Kennedy, as much for King's benefit as his own, stopped circling, "Were you ever aware of Mr Mylan wearing garters?"

"What?" she exclaimed. "Are you kidding? Has someone been telling you Patrick was a cross dresser?"

"No, no, I don't mean a ladies' suspender belt."

"A man's? Are you kidding around with me? There's no such thing as a man's suspender belt, is there?" Chloe directed her final question to King.

"Well, when I was growing up, the older men used to wear a belt around here," Kennedy said, showing her his calf, "and then to each belt they'd attach their socks to keep them up."

"Then someone obviously invented elastic," King suggested.

"They're not something I've been aware of since I was a kid," Kennedy admitted.

"But Patrick was wearing them when he died, wasn't he?" Chloe said, as the penny dropped loudly and her full soft lips involuntarily formed a large "O."

Neither Kennedy nor King said anything.

"Never, never," Chloe said very firmly. "Patrick might have been vain, and maybe his hair implants were not the best, quite possibly he fell asleep too quickly after sex, and he might have had to work harder than he wanted to keep his waistline in check, but let me assure you, he wasn't into any of that kinky stuff with me. He never even suggested that I dress up for him in something risqué. What could he possibly be doing with male suspender belts? How would that get him off?"

"We don't know, is the honest answer, Chloe," Kennedy admitted.

"But I can't even see what would be the point of that, even if some-one else put them on him." She shuddered at the thought of it. "What would they be trying to do?"

"Humiliate him?" Kennedy said, feeling it was worth risking hon-esty.

"Ah for heavens sake, poor Patrick," she said. "What could he pos-sibly have done to someone for them to want to treat him this way. Does this mean you know who did it?"

"No, we're still working on that." Kennedy hesitated, as he was about to head off into uncharted waters again. "You know, when you visited Mr Mylan…"

"Yeah?" Chloe replied nervously, obviously picking up on Kennedy's demeanour.

"Could you tell us about it, you know the details?"

"Sorry?"

"You know, like ehm, when you'd go to see him. Would you have coffee, tea, spend an afternoon, an evening, go for a swim, talk, watch the television, go for a walk in Regent's Park…things like that?"

"Thank goodness for that. For one horrible second there, I thought you wanted to ask me details about our physical relationship."

Kennedy held the silence for one beat extra.

"And if you were, it's not going to happen this side of a half a bot-tle of Sancerre," she added, challenging Kennedy with her eye. "Okay, here's how it worked. We'd chat on the phone at least twice a week."

This took Kennedy aback, noticeably so because she continued, "Christy, our relationship wasn't, how should I put this? Let's say it wasn't clinical. We were friends. We talked. We cared about each other. We didn't always meet up *just* to relieve his physical frustration. How-ever, there is no denying that was part of the service. So I'd see him …"

"How often?" King asked.

"We didn't just meet on the first Friday of every month for a quick one. I could see him maybe as much as three times a week, and then I wouldn't see him at all for a month."

"But when you didn't see him for a month, you'd still talk on the phone?" King asked again.

"Yes, you're getting it," Chloe said, smiling warmly at King. "We'd chat about our lives, about movies, about books, about television, about how his tennis was doing, about how my studies were going."

"What are you studying?" Kennedy asked.

"Interior design," Chloe said, her eyes proudly scanning around her apartment.

"Part-time or full time?"

"I'm on an eleven-week part-time course at Merton College's adult education programme. I've got Patrick to thank for that. When he first found this place for me - my sister lives in Kingston and I didn't want to be a million miles from her - I'd a nightmare with builders and decorators. So he said, 'Just do it yourself. You know what you want; don't waste any more time.' I'd hundreds of pages I'd been tearing out of magazines for years, and I kinda knew what I wanted to do. All I really needed was a bit of confidence, and Patrick gave it to me.

"Where were we? Oh yes, so we'd talk on the phone. He'd invite me around when he wanted to see me. His rules were simple. He didn't want me turning up in slacks and an anorak with my hair stuffed up in a hat, just because we both knew I'd be taking my clothes off. He liked me to… what's the best way to put this… well, he'd say when we were *seeing* each other, he wanted me to look like the beautiful woman I was. He liked me to be classy, sensual, beautiful, but never, ever tarty."

Chloe Simmons blushed deeply at this point.

"Did he buy the flat for you?" Kennedy asked because she hadn't been clear on that point.

"Yes he did, but I wasn't to get the lease until the end of our relationship," Chloe admitted.

"Do you know if this point was covered in his will?"

"He didn't have a will."

"Are you sure?"

"Yes, we talked about it a few times. He said he'd nobody he wanted to protect and he wouldn't make a will until as such a time as he had."

As Kennedy considered this she continued, "He told me that the lease to this flat was already made out in my name."

"Last night," Kennedy started hesitantly, "we talked a little bit about the time you met Nealey Dean up at Mr Mylan's house."

"Yes?"

"And you said you talked a little with her and afterwards… Well, Mr Mylan was *different* that night was how you actually put it."

"I remember, Christy. You're not asking for me to spell it out for you in detail, are you?"

"Of course not, but do you think Mr Mylan wished that something would happen between him and Miss Dean?"

"I'd have to say yes. That would be a very definite yes."

"Did Mr Mylan ever confess to you that he was interested in Miss Dean in that way?"

"No, he didn't. It was just my intuition."

"So what did youse talk about?" Kennedy asked, drawing out the Ulster "youse."

"Oh really, Christy, nothing that would be of interest to you or your investigation. It's like probably ninety-five per cent of all our daily conversations -a total waste of time."

"So he'd never discuss any of his worries with you or anything like that?" Kennedy pressed.

"I'd surely remember that. Patrick was a great man for keeping himself to himself. I think he probably revealed a different part of himself to all of his friends. To get an accurate picture of Patrick, you'd need to chat to all of his friends, weed out the dross and the gossip, and the rest might add up to a reasonably accurate picture of the man."

"Was he a patient man?" Kennedy asked.

"Well, he was never short-tempered, but…"

"But what?" Kennedy prompted.

"Well, he was a nice, easygoing man; he was gentle, he was well mannered, and he was polite. Maybe that was the person he wanted to be, the person he wanted to come across as."

"Interesting," Kennedy said, very impressed by her observation. "What makes you say that?"

"It's like, he made his money, he was aware of his success, but it wasn't always who he'd been. The person he was, or the person I knew, might have been stepping into the shoes of the earlier man. I saw a man on one of those reality TV shows once, and he was certainly less subtle than Patrick, but he was trying really hard to come across as this cool, relaxed, intelligent type, but he wasn't quite pulling it off. He always looked like he was pretending, acting even. I don't mean to be negative about Patrick. It's just a feeling I had a few times, particularly after I watched that TV show. Maybe Patrick was a better pretender than the man on the TV show."

"Yes, I think I know what you mean," Kennedy said. "Well, we'll be out of your hair. Oh yes, do you remember what you were doing last Saturday between four o'clock in the afternoon and eight o'clock in the evening?"

"Oh that's easy. I was babysitting my two nieces for my sister. She was taking a bit of a break from the kids and having a day indulging herself. I got around there at just before noon and got back here just after midnight. I was totally wiped out and slept well into Sunday."

CHAPTER THIRTY-TWO

It took DS Allaway quite some time and some complicated negotiations to set up the meeting for an interview with Tim Dickens and Alice Robbins. In fact, as Allaway mentioned to Irvine on the way to Leinster Mews, he'd had to threaten Miss Robbins with door-stepping them if she couldn't "find them a window." Then there was a bit of a confrontation at Dickens' mews when Irvine insisted he and Allaway interview Dickens and Robbins separately.

When all of this was going on, Dickens remained aloof, happy to let his PA do what PA's do: protect her boss. Dickens only felt a need to step in when Robbins threatened to suspend the interview until Mr Dickens' lawyer could be present, "Most probably sometime early next week."

"No problem," Irvine conceded. "We'll take you and Mr Dickens in to North Bridge House, and we'll happily detain you there until your lawyer is free."

Alice Robbins looked as if she were about to blow a gasket when Dickens said, "That won't be necessary. Alice, you've work you can be doing here, and I'll take the detectives through to the studio."

Irvine was surprised by how modest the studio was. Tim Dickens clocked this immediately.

"All studios aren't like Abbey Road, you know. In fact, very few are these days," Dickens started. "I really cringe when I remember the amount of money I used to spend in the studios in the early days. You know, it was the norm for my drummer, engineer, and producer to get into the studio a week ahead of the rest of us, just to get the drum sound. And then I was still always disappointed with the end product, by how small they sounded."

He crossed the studio floor to a small drum cum percussion set-up and took the drum stool. He played a few fills.

"Do you hear how big that sounds? With all our time in the studio and all our experts, I could never get the drums to sound exactly like you've just heard them. They'd record them and put them through limiters and compressors and what have you, and all that cack was doing was making the sound smaller, tinnier, and shittier. We'd record the vocals out in the bathroom, because supposedly that was what the Beatles did. Can you imagine? We were spending, literally, thousands of pounds a day to hire these high-tech studios, and then we were recording the vocals in the khazi."

Dickens ran over to where he had his control desk and consoles. He hoaked around for a few minutes before finding a CD, which he put in the player. Pretty soon the speakers in the room were fired up with the magnificent sound of the blues.

"Muddy Waters," Dickens shouted at the top of his voice, obviously very excited. "'Baby Please Don't Go.' Just listen to the sound of that, man."

Dickens picked up a guitar and strummed along to the hypnotic track.

"You see, what I came to realise was, all the old blues records sounded the best. That was the sound we were all after. It was the pure reproduction of what they were playing. The secret was to learn the song in advance and then play it live in a room where the sound of the room and the sound of the instruments were what you got to hear. I eventually worked out - a million or so pounds of studio bills later - that we were all losing the sound of the room for the sound of the studio. But don't you see that the sound of the room is really perfect; it already has all the natural acoustics. There is little or no need for mixing. You just do it all in your set-up, your rehearsals of the song. You walk away from the mic, and your sounds get quieter; and you go closer to the mic, and it gets louder. The drums are the loudest, so you have them furthest away from the mic. You use the depth, distance, and natural echo of the real room to get the drama and fun into your music."

The singer took off the Muddy Waters CD and immediately replaced it with another CD.

A few seconds later another sound filled the same speakers with a more modern sound. Irvine recognised the catchy introduction to "No More Sad Lonely City Streets," but before he could say so, Dickens said,

"Now listen to this. You can hear where the sound very nearly strangles the song. I mean, the sound is so puny; I'm still baffled how this was ever a hit. However, this is the version I rerecorded last year. Now listen to this version," Dickens ordered as he changed the CD in his machine for another. "Man, just listen to the sound of that!"

Again Dickens started to strum along with the track and picked out a line or two to sing.

Irvine thought, but didn't admit, that he much preferred the "hit" version.

Dickens must have noted Irvine's lack of enthusiasm, because he faded the track out.

Irvine felt a little guilty. After all, here he was, in a position several hundreds, if not thousands, of Tim Dickens' fans would have given their eye teeth to have been in, and all he could do was wonder how many other artists were dissatisfied with the quality of their hits. He'd recently hear that Sir George Martin, producer of the Beatles, had reported that towards the end of the Beatles' recording career, John Lennon had told Martin he would love to be able to rerecord all of the Beatles' songs.

"What, even 'Strawberry Fields Forever'?" Martin asked, mentioning what he considered to be one of the Beatles' undisputed masterpieces.

"*Particularly* 'Strawberry Fields Forever'!" Lennon had retorted in his strongest, driest scouse.

Dickens led them through from the control room to the studio room itself and sat down at the piano stool.

Irvine studied Tim Dickens. He didn't look quite as healthy today as he had at their last meeting. His hair was slightly dishevelled, only slightly, and he didn't quite need a shave, but soon would. He was still dressed in classy, dark, lose-fitting, expensive-looking clothes, and he hooked his knee in both hands and swung around to face Irvine, as he had at their last meeting.

"Have you made any progress on the case?"

"Well, we're still gathering information," Irvine admitted.

"But you've still no clues?"

"We have lots of clues," Irvine claimed. "It's just that we don't know as yet what they are clues to."

Irvine laughed at the end of his line. Tim Dickens did not.

"Nealey says you and DI Kennedy are very good."

Did that mean he'd been boasting to Nealey? It would be fine for him to have boasted on behalf of Kennedy, because Irvine sincerely believed that, as a detective, Kennedy was one of the most gifted he'd ever met. But for him to be boasting on his own behalf, well, that just wasn't cricket, was it?

"Inspector Kennedy is very, very good." Irvine ring-fenced the subject. "I wanted to talk to you some more about your deal with Patrick Mylan."

"Yes?"

"You admitted you weren't happy with it," Irvine said, dropping an un-wormed hook into unknown waters.

"Look, this is all very difficult. I know, I mean I *really* do know, that if I'm not careful, this is going to come out, making me appear to be a greedy bastard to the man on the street. You know: 'He's already made his fortune; what does he need any more for?' And there is logic to that sentiment. When I started off first, all I was interested in was acquiring a car, a telly, and a house. That's all I wanted. No, really," the singer protested when he saw the look of disbelief on Irvine's face. "Well, maybe a girl or two thrown in as well." Dickens paused to laugh. "But you get your telly and then your car and finally you are in a position to buy your first house. But the money *continues* to come in, and you find that you've enough for another car and a second telly and maybe even a few more houses. And the money *still keeps* coming, and you realise that when you were poor and wishing for money, you felt that it would solve all of your problems. Everything would be fine if you'd just enough money to … you know… fill in whatever it is you dream for…"

"But this is different," said Allaway, attempting to cut the songwriter short.

"You start to realise," Dickens continued, ignoring him, "that money doesn't solve all of your problems. Oh, I'm not going to be a hypocrite and claim that money doesn't cushion your life, and I do mean with very deep, feathery cushions. But people start to deal with you differently. They say people change when they become successful. I'm not so sure I agree with that. I would say it's the people around famous people who change. The people you grew up with, went to school with, they think this man who's now in the charts, playing sell-out concerts, making millions - they think this man must have changed. So they behave weird around you. I'm talking about weird as in out of their own character. They can't believe that the man who can go on stage to play to thousands is still the same nerd with the same bad habits from the early days. You know, from before the success came knocking.

"So you start to make your success work for you. You teach yourself not to take it all so seriously. You have to or you'll lose your sanity."

"But Patrick Mylan wasn't trying to rip you off, was he?" Allaway interrupted. He seemed frustrated by Dickens not addressing the issues as he saw them.

On the other hand, Irvine was happy to let Dickens continue. Kennedy had a theory that if you could just find a way of getting someone to talk, of getting them started naturally into a conversation where they weren't stopping to consider the consequence of every sentence they uttered, then eventually, if they've something they were trying to hide, there was a good chance they'd reveal it.

"I'm getting to that," Dickens replied, continuing to look and talk to DS James Irvine. "When Patrick came to me, I was flattered he would consider me in the same light as someone had considered David Bowie. Of course, in Patrick's circles, he was never going to come into contact with a David Bowie. But Mylan was part of the *new* rich. He had made more money than he would ever spend, and even if the deal with me had gone pear-shaped, he was never going to miss his five million. But he was very clever. He did his research, and he worked out as near as he could what I was worth in real cash, as opposed to assets. At that point, I will admit to you that, apart from some publishing, PRS and a trickle of record royalties, my income had all but dried up."

"PRS - can you explain that to me please?" Allaway asked.

"Good question. Recording artists make their money from several sources. One is from touring. From the touring you make money from your fee, which is financed directly from ticket sales, and from merchandising (selling T-shirts etc.) at concert venues.

"As I mentioned, I'd already stopped touring, so both of these avenues had dried up for me.

"Two is from record royalties. Every time you sell an album - sorry, make that a CD - or someone downloads your music, then the person who *recorded* the album receives a payment.

"Three is from publishing royalties. Every time a CD is sold or downloaded, then the person who *wrote* the song will also receive a payment. In my case, I am the writer and the recording artist, so I get both amounts from Two and Three *and* Four, which is:

"PRS - the Performing Rights collection Society. Every time a song is played live on the radio or TV, or as part of a video, money is paid to either the writer or the performer or both. There are various collection agencies such as the PRS who will collect these funds on the artist's behalf and eventually, minus admin and collection costs, pay them on to the artist."

"So most of these funds had dried up, and then along came Patrick with his proposal," Irvine said, happy to draw a line under this part of the proceedings, although he noted how intrigued Allaway seemed to be by the information.

"Ye-s," Dickens continued, drawing it out into two syllables, "then along came Patrick who, in one single deal, offered to double my personal monetary worth."

"And then when the deal turned out so well for him, you were pissed off with him?" Allaway pushed.

"It's not as simple as that, Detective Sergeant."

"It never is," Allaway said curtly. Irvine grimaced. He'd learned from Kennedy that, until you have to, there is no reason to piss off the person you're interviewing, even if he is a suspect. Most often, naturally, if you niggled them too much, the shutters could come down.

"You see, by the time Patrick came to me," Tim Dickens continued, again totally ignoring Allaway, "I'd already invested a considerable amount of time and even more money getting back the rights to my recordings (my masters) and the copyrights of my songs (my publishing). So what I'm saying is that it wasn't just Patrick giving me a bunch of money and then me sitting on my backside and waiting for the deal to break. Yes, he'd invested in my future, but then so had I."

"How much did you pay to get your masters and publishing rights back?" Irvine asked.

"Well, that's also a difficult question to answer accurately. For a start, when I was re-signing with my record company several years back,

I didn't take anywhere near as big an advance as I could have. In order to secure the rights to my masters, I had to then lease the masters back to the record company."

Irvine guessed that Dickens felt this wasn't cutting much sympathy with the detectives, because he said, "Okay, including legal fees, payments, and time, I reckon I probably invested about one and a half million quid of my own money, and I probably lost about two million quid in advances with my record company to get my masters back."

"Three and a half million," Allaway said, after a wee bit of consideration; "that's an awful lot of change."

"So when the deal turned sweet, and Patrick was quids in, I felt - particularly in light of my investment and this new fabulous success, which was due in no small way to my songs - that maybe it was time to redress the balance of the deal."

"Okay," Irvine said, "but then why did you not put such provisions in the original deal when you and Patrick were finalising your negotiations?"

"Because I was greedy and bit his hand off when he offered me five million," Dickens admitted.

That seemed to stop Allaway in his tracks.

"Look, I really believed my career was over. And that was fine. I'd had my day, a great day, but now it's a younger person's business, although I sometimes wonder if the present day's crop will be mourned as much when they have to make way for the new wave. But the main point is, kids don't want to see people older than their parents singing about what it's like to be hurt in love. Someone my age can never make a connection with a teenager. But if the latest winner of X Factor sings one of my songs, then the penny drops big-time. I really need you to believe," Dickens said, pausing, as he stared at Irvine, "this *wasn't* about money. My point was this: I didn't need the money, I really didn't; I'll never be able to spend what I have. When I was young and people said things like that, I thought it must be an amazing position to be in, but it's not really. You lose your value for the simple things in life."

"So why chase Mr Mylan so aggressively to get more money from him?"

"Simply because they were *my* songs generating this income; I was the one who was entitled. I tried to talk to Patrick about this, and that's what annoyed me so much. It wasn't that he wouldn't give me a new deal;

it was more that he didn't care about the importance of my songs. You'll never know how much that hurt."

"Tell me this, Mr Dickens," Irvine said, "do you have any idea what happens to your songs now that Mr Mylan is no longer alive?"

"Greedy and all as I was for the advance, I still had the suss to insist on a key man clause," Dickens replied.

"Which means?" Allaway asked.

"Which basically means, no Patrick no deal."

"Which basically means, unless I'm very much mistaken, you'll be at least a few millions pounds better off now Mr Mylan is dead."

"As in I had a lot of motive?" Dickens offered, and surprisingly through a smile.

"What we'd like to do now, Mr Dickens," Irvine said, ignoring Dickens' question, "is go through your alibi in greater detail than last time."

"Okay," Dickens said, dropping his clasped hands from his knee for the first time, "fire away."

Noticing that the door to the control room of the studio was open, Irvine quietly walked across the recording room and shut the door.

"Okay, you and Miss Robbins were in here all day Saturday, analysing your royalty statements?"

"Yes, we were."

"Is that not an exercise your accountant should have been present for?" Allaway asked.

"Ah no, but it's not because he charges by the hour. I've known too many artists who get ripped off just because they haven't a clue what's going on. Some of these people really gift it to the people who rip them off. I've never allowed a lawyer or an accountant to run my life. I like to have a hands-on approach to everything concerning my finances. That's very easy for me to say *only* because Alice is my PA, and she's really on top of all of this. She insists we do our own desktop audit on the statements, and then, if we find anything, we call in the big guns."

"What time did you get here?" Irvine asked, conscious he was speaking more quietly.

"Alice picked me up at noon..."

"But I thought Miss Robbins said you were here all day?" Irvine interrupted.

"The music business, by legend, starts at the crack of lunchtime," Dickens claimed, "so a noon start was, in fact, quite industrious."

"Okay, then you got here at noon…" Irvine prompted.

"No, Miss Robbins picked me up at noon. We reached here about twelve forty-five."

"Did you stop anywhere on the way."

"Alice had already picked up two cappuccinos, so we drove straight here."

"Where did she park?"

"Just by the front door. We have a parking permit."

"What does she drive?"

"A dark blue Polo; it's nippy enough for town."

"Did you come in first or did she come in first?" Irvine asked.

"Oh, come on, does it matter who came in first? I didn't stand around taking notes," Dickens sighed.

"We're only talking about Saturday past. You'll remember if you think about it," Irvine snapped, bordering on rudeness.

"Okay, let's think… She would have parked with my side of the car to the door to here, so logically I would have come in first."

"Did you use your keys or her keys?"

"My keys," Dickens replied, sounding resigned.

"What was she wearing?"

"To be honest, I haven't a clue. Please don't tell her that though."

"Think about it. It'll still be in your memory; you just have to concentrate to recall it."

"Okay, ehm, let's see. I'm on safe ground with black: a long skirt, a black T-shirt, a black hooded fleece and a pair of those big black boots; you know, the ones with the silver clasps up the front."

"There you go," Irvine said, wondering for the first time if Dickens and his PA were lovers. "She'd be happy if she knew you noticed what she was wearing. What were you wearing?"

"Jeez, I haven't felt under this amount of pressure since I took my A Levels. Ah, Saturday… I slept in, so I wouldn't have had much chance to consider my clothes. I believe I was wearing black jeans, these Prada trainers, a dark purple v-neck cashmere jumper and my grey Armani jacket."

"So what did you do first?"

"Sorry?"

"Did you start with record royalties or the songwriting royalties?"

"The record royalties; we always start with the record statements. To be honest, we've always found there's more to be picked up there than in the publishing."

"How long did that take?"

"Maybe four hours."

"Did you pick up anything?"

"Not this time. Patrick's people had already done their audit."

"Really? Why bother then?"

"Tempting, but Alice reckons it's foolish to depend on anyone else. She says if people know we are this thorough then they're less likely to try anything on. Not only do you have to do it; you also have to be *seen* to have done it."

"Did you have a tea break before starting into the publishing statement?"

"Nah, we just had fruit and mineral water. I like such days; they clean out your system."

"Did you go out for a cigarette?"

"I don't smoke."

"Did Miss Robbins go…"

"She doesn't smoke either."

"What time did you finish?"

"About nine-thirty."

"Tell me this," Irvine asked, sounding as if he were nearly through, "in your publishing statements, how much money did you earn from 'No More Sad Lonely City Streets'?"

"Oh, that would be difficult to say. It's all in different sections for different territories and different cover versions."

"Ah, come on, Tim. You don't mean to tell me you weren't in the least bit curious to discover how much your biggest song had made for you in the previous six months?"

"Nope. That wasn't the object of the exercise."

Irvine was having trouble believing this. He was convinced this would have been the first figure Tim Dickens would have honed in on in his royalty statements.

"How did you get home afterwards?"

"Alice was off to something else, so I got a black cab out on the street."

Which was also exactly what Tim Dickens did at the end of his interview with Irvine and Allaway, leaving them in the very competent company of Miss Alice Robbins.

※※※※

Irvine thought it odd that he had never, until now, considered Miss Robbins to be her own person. He'd always looked upon her as Dickens' PA. In his mind that was her job and that was her life. As she sat down before them in the studio, however, he realised how wrong he'd been.

"Have you not yet apprehended the person who murdered Patrick Mylan?" she asked before either of them had a chance to make their pitch.

"We're still investigating exactly what happened to Mr Mylan," Allaway replied as Irvine added, "So you met Mr Dickens here on Saturday morning?"

"Actually I picked him up from his hotel."

"His hotel? I thought he *lived* in London?" Irvine was slightly taken aback.

"It's true he has a few properties here, but when in London he much prefers to stay at Blake's."

"Where do you live yourself?"

Miss Robbins was dressed head to toe in expensive black, where it was difficult to work out where one garment finished and the next one started. Her long, thick, straight, centre-parted black hair cascaded all over her upper torso. Her face seemed make-up free, but maybe her skin colour was just a wee bit too pale to be a natural skin tone. Her eyes were green, small and serious. She was thin, which made her appear even taller than her five foot six inches.

"I live in a flat in Roland Gardens."

"And that's what part of London?" Allaway asked for his notebook's benefit.

"South Ken, SW7," she replied, as though addressing a civil servant.

"How long have you worked with Mr Dickens?"

"Just over twenty-one years."

"Impossible. Sure, you're only…" Irvine started.

"I was forty-one on my last birthday."

"Sorry," Irvine apologised with sincerity, "I would never have put…"

"I started out in Tim's… in Mr Dickens' manager's office. I was the assistant to the secretary, and I dealt mostly with his fan club mail. Time passed, and eventually Tim moved me on to his payroll, still in the manager's office. Then when he split with his management, he took me on as his PA."

"What exactly do you do?" Irvine asked.

"Well, I'm involved in every aspect of his business and personal life, and I handle all of his details: make all his arrangements; organise all of his meetings; sit in on some of those (most of them these days); keep up to speed on everything for him; and I keep his diary. I suppose I'm really his organiser."

"24/7?"

"I suppose, but it never works out like that. He likes his space. I don't always know where he is, but he *always* knows where I am."

"Could that play havoc with your social life?"

"Not really, and if it does, I don't mind. He's a good boss. The work is very interesting, and the salary is excellent."

"Are you married?" Irvine asked, while Allaway took what looked like detailed notes.

"No," she said.

"A boyfriend?"

"Isn't this slightly personal for this interview?"

"No, not really. I'm just trying to ascertain your situation."

This time, the look was of someone who'd just been deeply hurt.

"Or you're trying, in your roundabout Scottish way, to *ascertain* if I'm more than a PA to Mr Dickens."

Now it was Irvine's turn for his eyes to betray him.

"Can I just say," she started more confidently, "Mr Dickens and I enjoy a very professional relationship. I admit I would count him as one of my true friends, and I would hope the same would be true for him. But we do not now, nor have we ever, had any kind of a romantic relationship."

"Okay, Miss Robbins, thank you for being so candid with us."

"Furthermore, I believe the reason our working relationship is so good is due in no small way to the fact that there has never been any mistaking the parameters of our relationship. Mind you, a lot of my friends fancy him something rotten."

"Oh, did any of them ever date him?" Irvine asked innocently.

"My goodness, no. They'd be much too immature for him," she replied, laughing for the first time.

"Can we discuss the deal Mr Dickens had with Mr Mylan?"

"Yes. Mr Dickens instructed me to be candid with you if this subject came up."

"Right. So, we know Mr Dickens was really upset by the way the deal turned out."

"Yes," she readily agreed, "but not upset enough to murder Mr Mylan."

"Mr Dickens admitted in this very room that he will be a lot better off financially now Mr Mylan is out of the picture. Alice, that's a lot of motive."

"It might be a lot of motive if you are penniless and you find a way to make a million or two overnight. Maybe, but only maybe, I would concede that in those circumstances it could be considered a motive. But please don't forget that Mr Dickens is a very wealthy and success-ful man. Surely you can see he's never going to jeopardise his liberty for financial gain. Mr Dickens is mature enough to separate his business dealing and his personal relationships with people. For instance, Mr Dickens attended a dinner party at Mr Mylan's house a week to the day before Mr Mylan died. Tim quite liked Patrick."

"What about Mr Dickens' loose cannon?"

"Marcus Urry?"

"The very same."

"He's hot-headed. He thinks he's God's gift to women; sadly he re-ally believes it. He's never going to murder someone though. He lives with his mum, for heavens sake!"

"Okay. Let's talk some more about Patrick Mylan," Irvine said. Miss Robbins looked slightly uncomfortable. "Did you know him well?"

"Do you really think I've dated every man I've come into contact with?"

"Sorry, what?" Irvine spluttered. "No, no, no, I didn't mean any-thing like that."

"Sorry, my fault. I'm just, you know, Tim under suspicion and all… sorry, what were you saying?"

"Patrick Mylan. How well did you know him?" Irvine asked again.

"Not really well. I had quite a few meetings with him about Mr Dickens. Can I be candid?"

"I wish you would."

"Patrick always seemed to me like he still hadn't found what he was looking for. Every time I hear that U2 song, I always think of Patrick. To me he was always lost. He never really got excited about anything. Personally speaking, I found he never looked at me with the hunger so evident in most men's eyes, even men you know who aren't interested in you."

"Did he have a girlfriend?"

"I don't know. I think he was quite smitten by that actress Nealey Dean."

"Did you notice that first hand, or did someone tell you that?" Irvine asked, mentally crossing his fingers.

"I believe Tim told me. That's right, Tim told me Patrick appeared to try to matchmake Tim and Miss Dean. Tim was confident Patrick knew Tim had in fact introduced Miss Dean to Patrick in the first place, and he felt that maybe he was playing some kind of game where he could set himself up. I think Tim also said Miss Dean was already dating someone."

"Does Mr Dickens have a girlfriend?"

"Luckily, that's one part of his life that I don't have to keep tabs on," she replied quickly.

"Do you have a boyfriend?"

"You've already asked me that. Anyone would think you're trying to ask me out on a date."

"But you didn't answer my question the first time either," Irvine said. "Well?"

"I was about to say, we don't have anything in common, but that's not going to work, is it?" she said, as if trying to lighten up the interview a bit - either that or trying to find a way of evading this question for some reason.

Irvine just looked at her.

"I've nothing to hide. I date men, yes. I'm currently not dating anyone in particular. I will admit that, thanks to my job, my personal life does take a bit of a hammering in the romantic stakes, but I wouldn't change it for anything."

From there they went on to discuss Miss Robbins' and Mr Dickens' shared alibi, and every single thing she said tied in exactly with what Mr Dickens had said earlier.

Maybe just a wee bit too exact, Irvine thought.

CHAPTER THIRTY-THREE

Kennedy and King took longer than they'd originally planned to travel to and from Wimbledon. By the time they got back into town, it was closing down seven o'clock, and DC Dot King was about to be late for a dinner date with "my Ashley." Kennedy had her drop him off outside the door of Nealey Dean's mansion block in Marylebone. Her protests of the wisdom of Kennedy's interviewing a female, and "a beautiful young female" at that, paled into Kennedy's, "*And she's DS Irvine's girlfriend.*"

Nealey greeted Kennedy warmly at the door to her apartment, kissing him on both cheeks and then, quite literally, pulling him into her apartment.

"We called by earlier on out way to Wimbledon," Kennedy offered by way of explanation.

"Yes, I heard," she replied, and then, as an apparent afterthought, "Is James parking the car?"

"No, I was with DC King."

"And she's prepared to leave me unchaperoned this time?"

"I assured her I'd be okay," Kennedy said, sitting down into a very comfy seat in the centre of her tidied living room.

"Correct me if I'm wrong, Christy, but isn't the rule there to protect me?" she laughed as she offered him a glass of chilled white wine.

"She did say something about that, but I pointed out that James was a better fighter than me, and she seemed happy at that."

"So Wimbledon eh? Did you go down to speak to Chloe Simmons?"

"How did you know where she lived?"

"Patrick must have told me," Nealey Dean said as she flopped out on the sofa opposite Kennedy's chair. Kennedy noted from the arrangement of the cushions, the close proximity of a smoked glass coffee table bearing a couple of coasters - one with her hardly touched glass of wine

- a script, a Penguin Classic copy of *Madame Bovary*, and a copy of *The Telegraph*, that this must be the young actress' favourite position in her apartment.

"I hope your day was better than mine," she said as she closed her eyes and took a generous sip of wine.

Kennedy remained quiet, allowing her to enjoy her moment of repose.

Eventually she said, "Somehow the press have found out I knew Patrick, and they were outside the studio all day long."

Kennedy thought of ann rea, knowing she probably would have been aware of that fact.

"Luckily I was able to leave by the back exit and got back here without any of them knowing, but it's only a matter of time. It sets a bit of an atmosphere around the studio."

"I knew someone once who was a journalist..."

"Oh, that's such a sad way to put it, Christy," Nealey said, springing back to life again.

Christy forced a smile.

"It's fine, Nealey. If I'm honest, it had been coming for quite some time, but the point I was going to make was that ann rea reckoned that all you need to do to stop the press chasing you is to stop running. The pack mentality disappears when you face them, smile, and even say something like, 'I'm sorry, but my solicitor says I mustn't say a word to you.' She figured that once you make yourself available, even briefly, you're no longer of interest to them."

"I'll remember that," she said. "Are you hungry?"

Kennedy hesitated just one beat too long.

"Oh, I'm a terrible hostess."

"No, I'm fine. I'll get something on the way home," Kennedy protested.

"Well, I do need to eat something myself..."

"Okay, do you have any eggs?"

Twenty-three minutes later they were sitting back in their places to enjoy Kennedy's version of an omelette with peas (Nealey insisted on some greens), some toasted brown bread, and a second glass of wine.

"I'm impressed, Christy. Any chance you could give James a few tips in the kitchen," she said as she cleared their plates.

"I'm afraid that's the extent of my repertoire."

"You're kidding me."

"Well, at a push I could probably scramble some eggs as well," he admitted.

"Mothers feeding their boys; I'd hazard a guess that's probably where most of the problems start and finish."

"Nealey, just how well did you know Patrick Mylan?"

She looked at him with a bemused look.

"That's a funny way to ask a question, Christy. It's like you already know something."

Christy told her what he had discovered in Mylan's secret room - at least the part about her photograph.

"Oh that. That's been on the Internet for quite some time now. It was taken by one of the silly bugger crew members who thought he'd make a fortune with it. He soon discovered that Victoria Beckham or Anna Friel I am not, nor would I ever want to be… well, at least not Victoria. So in one way, I am shocked that Patrick would want to do that - in fact it totally grosses me out to even think about it - but I can assure you I didn't pose for him or anything close."

"I never thought you did."

"I didn't think so. So this will all come out now as well? James will… ah," she shook her head violently at the thought.

"Well, maybe not," Kennedy replied, and then explained what he had done with the large photo.

"I can't believe you'd actually do that for me. OhmiGod, isn't that meddling with evidence or something?"

"It's still there," Kennedy insisted.

"Will James ever see it?"

"I don't believe so."

"OhmiGod, is there something I can do for you in return, like fix you up with an Anna Friel or Victoria or someone?"

They both laughed.

"Going back to Patrick for a moment, Christy… you are aware, of course, that whatever he may have had going on in his head…"

"No, I realise that, but you would have thought that being in his company so much, he'd at least have asked you on a date."

"Go figure. He seemed more interested in fixing me up with Tim."

"Did he know you were in a relationship with James, with a policeman?"

"I believe I might have said that there was someone in my life, but I don't believe I would have mentioned that he was a policeman," she replied, looking as if she were trying to flash through all the relevant conversations she'd had with Mylan.

"What about Chloe? Why did you think he mentioned Miss Simmons to you?"

"Well, I've admitted I love finding out about people. His telling me might have been more me bulldozing my way in there like a bull in a china shop... or..."

"Or?" Kennedy asked eventually.

"Or maybe that was Patrick's way... his way of pulling me in, getting to know me better or something. I don't know, Christy; I'm trying to figure this out. Did Chloe say how she came to meet Patrick?"

"Over a long period of time," was as much as Kennedy was comfortable giving.

"Did she like go on a date with him or something and then it developed from there?"

Kennedy grimaced.

"Okay, I know there is a limit to what you can tell me at this point, and goodness, Christy, don't think I'm ungrateful after what you've already done for me."

"What about the other people at Mr Mylan's dinner parties: did they ever hint at anything about him?" Kennedy asked.

"Nothing. Maggie Littlewood was always very protective of him, always very sweet to him, but other than that, it was just your average group of people gathering together for a dinner party...ohmiGod!"

"What? Have you thought of something?"

"No, I've just thought that I sat beside him, drinking wine with him, as close as I am to you now, and all the time he'd a large, life-size photo of me with my kit off up in his attic. Oh, disgusting, totally disgusting!"

Nealey shuddered.

"And on top of that," she grimaced, crunching her chin to one side and then the other, "you've seen me in the... ah... even James hasn't ever seen me like that."

"Really?" Kennedy said involuntarily and then immediately regretting it. "Sorry, no, it's none of my business."

"No, of course not. I don't have that kind of a relationship with James - not yet... and probably not ever now. I'm totally off men,

Christy, no offence! Let me get us another bottle of wine."

"Did you really think I was sleeping with James?" she asked as she returned to the room with a freshly opened bottle of Sancerre. "Did he say anything to you?"

"Not at all," Kennedy said. "I don't think men talk about women they care about in that way, and other men don't really want to hear what goes on with the looser type of women."

"Which means they do want to hear what happens with the women they care about, or their mates care about, which means…"

"No, it doesn't," Kennedy protested.

"It's a funny relationship I have with James… you must swear you will never tell him we discussed this."

"Of course I wouldn't," Kennedy quickly confirmed, because he really wanted to hear what she was going to say.

"I like him, I like him a lot. He's very funny. We get on well… it's just… you know, we don't seem to be going anywhere. We see each other once a week max, and because I'm busy and he's busy and our schedules get in the way. But I'm inclined to believe that if we wanted to, if we needed to find a way, we'd find a way. Christy, a girl likes to be swept off her feet. I suppose what I'm trying to say is, we don't always know when we're in love, but we sure do know when it's not love. Do you know what I mean?"

Kennedy thought that Nealey Dean had most probably said in a few seconds what it had taken ann rea five years to say. Actually, truth be told, ann rea still hadn't said it properly.

"I think you have to have this discussion with James as soon as possible."

"Yes, you're right. But you know what?" she said sadly, "If it hadn't been for our chat, I wouldn't have admitted this, even to myself. All this stuff with Patrick, harbouring these… whatever it was that he was harbouring, it's such a complete waste of time."

"If Patrick had invited you out, what would have happened?" Kennedy asked.

"Nothing. He's not my type. I like participators."

"Maybe he knew that."

"You're not suggesting this might have had something to do with me?" Nealey asked earnestly.

"No, no. I'm suggesting maybe Patrick didn't approach you romantically because he knew what the answer was, but at the same time, he couldn't give up on you, so he was happy to have you around."

"So he was waiting around hoping that a bolt of lightning would occur and I'd fall into bed with him?"

Kennedy was about to respond when she added, "I don't think so. But what do men think attracts women to them? I mean, for my part, I admit that it's not that I'm attracted by looks. At the same time, I'm definitely put off by scruffy, unshaven people with shabby shoes, wrinkled clothes worn a day or more too long, unkempt hair, stupid hairstyles, or people who try too hard. But you know, if you can get beyond that, well it's all down to personality, isn't it? It's just very weird to discover there was a man who was an acquaintance ogling at a photo image of me to get his rocks off. Am I wrong, or is that weird? What attracts you to a woman, Christy?"

Christy thought of lots of answers to her trio of questions, but he realised he just didn't know.

"If you look at what attracts a man and a woman, you'd have to say that the sexual act is not the most important part of the dance." He wondered exactly where that had come from.

"Why is it not?" she asked.

"Well, first we need to know what the most important part of the dance is."

"Okay, Christy, I'm biting: what is the most important part of the dance?"

"I'd say mystery."

CHAPTER THIRTY-FOUR

Kennedy caught a cab straight from Nealey Dean's apartment to his house. It was nearly nine o'clock by the time he got to Primrose Hill, and there, for the third night in a row, was Miss Chada waiting for him. He noticed a little distance in her eyes as he hopped into the car beside her.

"I can't believe you did that to me," she started, a little tremor barely noticeable in her voice. "Why must all men be so predictably disappointing?"

"Ah, look, I'm so sorry," Kennedy began, realising he'd missed his appointment with her at Unlocked for her to do some more work on his back. "I'm working on this case and I had to go to Wimbledon. I'm not long back in town."

"That's still very bad manners Mr Kennedy."

'Mr Kennedy?' That's a funny way to address your lover, he thought. But how did she think of him? Was he her lover? She was definitely more upset than one should be about him missing a professional meeting with her. Yes, he should have called, and yes, he had considered getting Irvine or King to make the call on his behalf when he got tied up, but then he'd become so preoccupied with his work he just forgot. She sat beside him sulking. Okay, he'd made a major social gaffe, and she was going to make him pay for it.

"Do you fancy going back to your great restaurant again tonight?" Kennedy offered in the hope of a thaw.

"You shamed me in front of my colleagues," was her only reply.

"Look, Sharenna, I am soooo sorry. I really am."

"I didn't think you were like that."

"I'm not, normally," Kennedy said. He started hesitantly, realising that, "I don't usually do that" would only dig him an even deeper hole than the one he was already in.

He regretted turning down Nealey Dean's invitation to join her in another bottle of wine. He'd really enjoyed his conversation with her. There were no overtones or undertones between them. They might become friends, where being friends, for both of them, wouldn't be a second-best state. However, he realised that if he had stayed at Miss Dean's, Miss Chada would probably have continued to sit outside his house waiting for him and stewing even more fervently than she had.

"Sorry, Sharenna. The only reason the appointment slipped my mind was because you've done such an amazing job on my back. Now if I had been going on a date with you, well, that would have been a totally different matter altogether."

She diverted her eyes to him from the parked cars ahead for a split second without turning her head. He noticed her body relax a little, just a little. This was a completely new experience for Kennedy. Even when ann rea was mad at him, or mad at herself for being with him, she'd never behave like this. She'd always, but always, remain civil. Miss Chada's actions bordered on… well, the word that kept floating into Kennedy's head was "childish."

"I was worried. I didn't know what happened to you… your work… anything could have happened to you," she eventually said, showing the thaw had definitely set in.

"I am sorry. It is unforgivable," Kennedy said and meant it.

"I need you to ring Unlocked first thing in the morning and apologise. You have to pay for the missed session. They must not think that you are taking me for granted. They must not think we are anything but osteopath and patient."

She relaxed a little more, but still she made no move to get out of her car. For one moment, Kennedy felt she was waiting for him to get out of the car so she could drive off. Eventually she said, "What does a girl have to do to get a cup of coffee around here?"

Two and a half hours later, Kennedy walked her back to her car. As he watched her drive off, he reflected how the purity of their love-making had definitely been tarnished by their earlier scene. He thought back to his earlier conversation with Nealey Dean about the uniqueness of relationships. He wondered if, in all relationships, we stop making love to a beautiful woman, or a woman stops making love to her ideal man, at the point when one partner starts to deal with all the baggage the other partner brings to the relationship. Sharenna Chada had been, as usual, giving, and equally not scared to take, but for the first time, Kennedy had noticed that she hadn't got completely lost in their hunt for mutual pleasure. Something vital had changed. Kennedy, for his part, found it difficult to separate the owner of the perfect body, which had been entwined with his, with the person whose recent childish behaviour had shocked and continued to disturb him.

Perhaps that had been the sign ann rea had been looking for. Maybe she had been looking for the person she could be with where she wouldn't be preoccupied with the baggage element of the relationship. Could that have been ann rea's interpretation of love?

As he fell asleep, he began to wonder about how practical it would be to stop seeing Sharenna, romantically speaking, but to continue to see Miss Chada, professionally speaking.

CHAPTER THIRTY-FIVE

All things being equal, Kennedy's early morning Thursday meeting with his team was quite productive.

To kick off with, DS James Irvine had a copy of the preliminary report from the forensic accountant's team, and that certainly made for very interesting reading.

It appeared Maggie Littlewood had received a very large payment from Patrick Mylan just over two years ago. The amount was £85,000, and there was no information in relation to what it was for. Neither was there an invoice from her to Patrick for a corresponding amount.

Rodney Stuart was barely keeping his head above water and had several borrowings from Mylan. The forensic team still had to ascertain whether or not Stuart had approval for these amounts or if he had simply helped himself - a practice which, if the red-top newspapers were anything to go by, happened a lot these days, particularly in the music business. The noticeable thing about these payments was that they always coincided with his monthly invoice.

As per Kennedy's request, via Irvine, the FA team had gone through the Mylan/Dickens deal with a fine-tooth comb, and they were able to confirm that now Mylan was dead, all rights reverted (at the next accounting period) back to Tim Dickens.

Kennedy was digesting this information with DS Irvine when DC Dot King arrived back into the room.

"We've just had the report back from the examination of Mr Mylan's clothes. There were no stains of any kind on his underwear," she announced confidently.

"Which means?" Irvine asked, still distracted by the accounting report.

"Which means, Detective Sergeant Irvine, that our Mr Mylan did not reach sexual fulfilment in his final endeavours," King replied, attracting everyone's undivided attention.

"Which means?" Allaway seemed compelled to ask. Kennedy couldn't be sure if the DS was distracted by the current thread of the conversation or if he was enjoying drawing King further down this murky road.

"Which most likely proved that he *didn't* commit suicide," King stated.

"I don't think you can say that absolutely," Kennedy maintained.

"But it does *suggest* he didn't," King said, "or that at the very least his death wasn't an accident. The reason AEA people die is because they are so committed to sexual fulfilment they lose both control and consciousness."

"It most likely wasn't an accident," Kennedy conceded, "and the news is that our accounting detectives have moved three suspects up to the top of our list.

"Maggie Littlewood, for some reason or other, received £85,000 from Mylan. Rodney Stuart's company is in a bad way, and he appears to have borrowed heavily from Mylan. Our friends on the forensic accounting side have also confirmed the key man clause in Tom Dickens' deal with Patrick Mylan. That is to say, no Patrick Mylan, no deal."

"This case is turning out to be a little like DS Allaway's fantasies," King suggested devilishly: "nothing for ages, and then three come along at the same time."

Kennedy, although amused by King's comment, ignored it. "Let's get stuck into two of our leads. DS Irvine, you take DS Allaway and go and visit Rodney Stuart, and DC King and I will pay Maggie Littlewood another wee visit."

***

Like a coquettish girl, this year's summer was playing hard to get; you would get brief glimpses and hints of her full glory, but the dark clouds seeking to hide her beauty were never too far away. Kennedy had been looking forward to dallying in Roger and Maggie Littlewood's wonderful garden. If pushed, he might even have admitted it was the lure of some more tea and scones in the same garden that had biased his decision to interview Maggie Littlewood instead of the accountant, Rodney Stuart.

On the journey to Church Street in Hampstead, he was trying to figure out the best way to separate Maggie from her husband. She'd certainly seemed to be more informative on the previous occasion when she and Kennedy had been alone. As luck would have it, Roger was out. Unfortunately for Kennedy, the current rain shower, light thought it was, had put pain to his wish for tea and scones in the garden. Kennedy and King followed Maggie straight into her small kitchen, where she started to busy herself preparing some tea and cake. Sometimes, although not all of the times, Kennedy felt you could be more successful in your interviews if the subject was distracted with something like a manual task. It seemed to work better though with men, because they always appeared, to Kennedy at least, not to be as successful as the fairer sex in the multi-tasking stakes.

"Maggie, we've come back to talk to you about a payment Mr Mylan made to you a couple of years ago," Kennedy started.

"Have you indeed," Maggie replied, as she refilled and switched on the silver electric kettle. "Well then, it's very lucky for me that Roger isn't here."

"Oh?" King said in surprise.

Although Maggie efficiently continued on her criss-cross journey in her kitchen, Kennedy noticed Mrs Littlewood didn't prepare all the cups of tea in the same manner. She haphazardly added either the hot water or milk first or second. He wondered, hoped, if this was because she was preoccupied trying to come up with a reason for the £85,000 payment.

"Okay," she began as the three of them sat down at the small kitchen table. "Roger and I have always kept our money separate. When we started up together, we just continued with our separate bank accounts. He has never known what I have, and I … well, I've always had a fair idea of his finances, but I've never had to go to him for a sub, and he's never had to come to me for one."

Maggie, growing uncomfortable, was trying to hide her discomfort by biting into her delicious carrot cake.

"Anyway, after he retired, I started to get worried that he didn't have as much money as I though we might need," she continued, nodding her head to the beat of her speech. "I mean, it's so difficult, isn't it? You can never know how much money you're going to need.

You haven't a clue how long you're going to live, and what a hundred grand is worth today is obviously not going to be what it's worth in ten years' time. Anyway, I started to panic. A friend of my brother was a successful bookie."

Maggie stopped talking and stared at King for a few seconds. "I saw that judgemental look in your eyes, young lady."

"No," King protested, "I didn't mean anything."

Maggie Littlewood puffed up her perfectly permed hair before continuing, "It's okay, because you are right in your assumption," she laughed nervously. "Barry, Barry Colburn, was his name. He was a good friend of the family, and he'd always had an eye for me. Nothing like that," she directed at King. "He's been happily married for donkey's years as well. Anyway, every now and then he'd ring up for a chat - you know, a family update - but he'd always say at the end of his conversations, if you've a few bob to spare, put it on so and so at such and such race. Well, over the years I'd followed his advice, and I picked up a good bit of pin money. I think we all know where this is heading, don't we? After Roger retired, I found myself putting a bit more money on Barry's tips. I found myself ringing Barry up more frequently just so I'd pick up his tips. Have you ever backed the gee-gees?"

Both King and Kennedy shook their heads.

"It's such a rush. It's not dissimilar to gambling on the stock market, which is what we all do, but the rush is so much more intense. Eventually, for matters of convenience, I opened an account with Barry, and at first I was doing great. At one stage I was twenty-five grand up. However, once I started to lose money and dropped into the red, Barry stopped giving me tips. So I went looking for my own and... well, I don't need to bore you with the all details. I'll tell you this, though: never listen to the tipster on the early morning sports break on Radio Four. It could have been a lot more than eighty-five grand if Barry hadn't closed my account at that stage and refused me further credit."

"And Mr Mylan stepped in?" Kennedy asked, wanting to spare her further embarrassment.

"And Patrick, God bless him, stepped in. He had one demand though. He said he would only give me the money on condition I never paid it back. He wrote the cheque immediately, made no fuss whatsoever, and I'll never forget what he said to me as he handed it over:

'This is the only time having money is of any real use, so you can help your friends.'"

As Maggie Littlewood was giving DC King the bookie Barry Colburn's details, she pleaded with them, head nodding away more furiously than normal, not to tell her husband.

There was still something that was troubling Kennedy.

"I don't believe we'll need to advise Roger about this, but I would strongly recommend you do," he said as they moved to leave. Then, surprising himself, he asked, Colombo style, "Tell me this, Maggie, do you know a young lady by the name of Chloe Simmons?"

Maggie reacted like a woman who'd been swimming desperately to a life raft only to find when she reached it that the raft was nothing more than an illusion made by paper floating on the water.

"Yes, as it happens, I do. I went to school with her mother."

∗

King couldn't wait to get back into the privacy of their pool car to discuss this development.

"How did you ever figure that one out?" she said the moment she could shut her door.

"I had a feeling," was all Kennedy would say.

"I'm shocked that you don't seem excited by the news?"

"How so?"

"Well, don't you think Patrick could have paid her the £85,000 for setting him up with her friend's daughter, Chloe?" King offered.

"And?" Kennedy encouraged.

"Well... well, maybe..." King struggled to put a shape to her thoughts. "Well, maybe she was trying to get more money from him... or maybe... yes, that's it, maybe it was going to come out that she set her friend's daughter up as her best friend's mistress for eighty grand, so Maggie Littlewood either murdered Patrick or had someone do it for her to make it look like an accident."

"I don't believe so," Kennedy replied as he studied the road before them.

"Really," King said, disappointed. "Why on earth not?"

"Well, for starters, she gave us Barry Colburn's full details, and it will

be easy enough to check out her gambling story, if that's where the
£85,000 Mylan gave her went."

"But you still think she fits into this some way, don't you?" King
asked.

"Well, did you notice some of the photos on her dressing table and
desk? She looked liked she was a very sensual, beautiful forty-year-old."

"But surely all of Mylan's girls had to be younger than him?"

"Yes, mostly I'd agree, but then someone would have had to teach
Mylan the art in the first place."

"*Maggie Littlewood?*" King hissed in disbelief. Kennedy was convinced that if they hadn't been stopped at a red traffic light on Chalk
Farm road, DC Dot King would most likely have crashed the car at
that point.

CHAPTER THIRTY-SIX

Back in Camden Town Mews, Detective Sergeants Irvine and All-away were trying to gain access to Rodney Stuart's office.

Irvine could hear voices (well, at least one voice) from inside. He was convinced it wasn't a radio, so he continued banging loudly on the silvered oak door. Rodney Stuart opened it a few minutes later, still wearing his telephone headset and still rabbiting away to someone about how it's always important to hold your nerve, particularly when all around you are losing theirs. He blinked dismissively at the two member of Camden Town police force and shooed them in with an "oh, if you really must" glare.

As Stuart, looking decidedly more unhealthily (if that were possible) than he had been on the last visit, chatted away ten to the dozen on the phone, Irvine made a song and dance about removing several files from his tattered, but much-loved, briefcase and elaborately laying the contents all over Stuart's already crowded desk.

Stuart - who was pacing up and down his office, his hands-free facility allowing him to appear like Marcel Marceau on speed - suddenly stopped dead in his tracks as he noticed the contents of some of the pages now covering his desk.

"What the fu…" he started. "No, not you, sorry. Let me ring you right back," he snapped as he disconnected the phone. "How the eff, you, sea, Kay did you get my bank statements?"

"I thought they just might get your attention, Mr Stuart; they make interesting reading, don't they?"

"They don't mean anything. I invoice him regularly."

"And you ripped him off frequently," Irvine continued seamlessly. "You weren't even subtle enough to tie your payments into your invoices."

"You know nothing," Stuart shouted, lifting one of the bank statements. He seemed to be trying to figure out if it were an original or a photocopy. "I was always paying out on Paddy's behalf."

"Yes, we noticed that as well," Irvine claimed, "but we still figure there's nearly two hundred thousand pounds of Mr Mylan's money has gone into your account that has not been properly accounted for. Our forensic accountants were shocked, not at the amounts you were taking, but by how careless you were about trying to cover your tracks."

"You haven't a clue, have you?" Stuart whined. "This goes on all the time between an accountant and a client. It's called doing business together, and every few months we do an update with each other and settle up."

"That's certainly one explanation," Irvine said, lifting one of the statements again, "but according to our figures, you owe Mr Mylan at least two hundred grand, yet our boys worked out you're still nearly half a million in the hole, so can you explain to me how those sums were ever going to be resolved? Because, Rodney old chap, you're right; I certainly haven't a clue how you could possibly reconcile that."

Stuart said nothing. He continued studying the statements. It was as if he were waiting for some divine intervention from them. Some message would surely be sent from on high to help him.

"Rodney, the way we see it," Irvine began in a gentler, kinder, and less sarcastic voice, "Mr Mylan caught you with your hand so seriously in the till you were in danger of losing your fingertips. He threatened to expose you. You murdered him. Made it look like a bizarre accident, or suicide, but did you seriously think we weren't going to discover this nugget of information?"

"Look, Dickens' next royalty statements are due on the 30th of September. All of this would have worked out in the mix when that one came in."

"You're seriously trying to tell us you were going to make two hundred big ones from his next record and publishing royalty cheques."

"That's chicken feed compared to what's in the pipeline. There's a good few million to come in. I was on 5 per cent," Stuart claimed.

"I thought you were paid by the hour?" Allaway said, looking up from his notebook for the first time in ages.

"I used to be, but Paddy realised he was depending on me so much to monitor this for him and to protect him in this deal that he cut me in for a piece," Stuart said through a "so there" smirk.

"And no doubt you have the paperwork to back that claim up?" Irvine asked in disbelief.

"That wasn't Paddy's style. No lawyers, we discussed and agreed, deal done. We shook hands concluding the deal the way gentlemen used to."

"Did Mr Mylan have a will?" Irvine asked, thinking it might provide back-up for Stuart's claim.

"No. I tried to get him to do one, but he refused point blank."

"Was anyone else aware of the deal you claim to have done with Mr Mylan?" Irvine asked.

"I don't know. I certainly didn't tell anyone."

"Was Mr Mylan aware you were helping yourself?" Irvine snapped.

"'Advances,' Sergeant Irvine. I prefer to consider them as advances."

Irvine suddenly thought of something, "So these statements, how often did they come in? Every quarter?"

"No. There are two accounting periods per year. The actual periods finish on 31st of Dec and 30th of June. The record company and the publisher then have 90 days to calculate the sales and the relevant income for that period. The deadline for them getting the statements and payments to us is the 30th of September and the 30th of March."

Irvine felt he had no other option than to read Rodney Stuart his rights and bring him in.

He didn't go quietly.

"You've got it all wrong, mate. I've told you, you need to look at Tim Dickens. He has a much bigger motive than me. Maybe he didn't do it himself, but Marcus can be very ugly when he wants to be."

When neither Irvine nor Allaway appeared to be taking any heed of Stuart, he blurted out, "And maybe Chloe Simmons isn't as sweet and innocent as even I first thought."

"Why Chloe Simmons?"

"Well, she told me Paddy had been seeing his ex again," Stuart continued desperately. He was now willing to dish the dirt on anyone, anyone who might divert the spotlight away from him, "and you, more than most, must know what these bitches in heat are like when they get jealous."

CHAPTER THIRTY-SEVEN

Kennedy wasn't unhappy that Irvine brought Rodney Stuart in for questioning. With the amount of money he owed, he was certainly a flight risk. He was going to hold Stuart for as long as possible before questioning him again. In the meantime, he instructed the forensic accountants to prepare their case. He commended Irvine and Allaway on their work and returned to his office.

Kennedy studied his noticeboard. He was unable to concentrate on it; he was distracted, and he didn't know why. He knew the feeling he enjoyed at the resolution of a case, and this wasn't it. The case still wasn't resolved to his satisfaction. He still had to figure out how Rodney Stuart, or person or persons unknown, had committed the crime.

He buzzed through to Dot King to check if the Scene of Crime team had turned up anything. According to the young DC, SOCO were still working on it.

"Fancy another drive to Wimbledon?" Kennedy asked. "Stuart claims Miss Simmons had a motive."

"Ready when you are."

"Say half an hour out front. I want to give DS Allaway a chance to finish his report of the recent interview with Rodney Stuart."

Thirty-five minutes later, they were driving through Regent's Park en route to the tennis capital of the world. Kennedy was engrossed in the report, and King was focusing on the road ahead.

"Let's drop in and see Tim Dickens on the way," Kennedy suggested, picking up something of interest in the report.

"What, without an appointment?" King mocked.

"I'll risk Alice Robbins' wrath if you will."

Alice Robbins, in all her Goth glory, was in residence at the Dickens' mews house. The songwriter was absent.

"We have a wee point we needed to clear up," Kennedy began, happy to remain on the doorstep of the white-bricked building.

"I'll try."

"On one of the occasions you and Mr Dickens' were interviewed, you claimed, at the time of Mr Mylan's death, you and Mr Dickens were in the building *alone* working on his royalty statements."

"Yes, that's correct."

"And you also said the reason you were here *alone* was because you'd just received royalty statements, one from your publisher and one from your record company," Kennedy continued, referring to his notes, hoping he was appearing distracted and equally hoping she was concentrating on his emphasising the word "alone."

"Yes."

"And that you needed to check the statements *alone* as soon as you received them, otherwise Mr Dickens could potentially lose a considerable amount of money."

"Yes, that's also correct," she confirmed confidently.

"Now, can you tell me this please: how on earth were you checking the new royalty statements when they're not in fact due until 30th September - nearly three months away?" Kennedy asked, happy that Allaway was a stickler for loading his reports with details.

Miss Robbins had the look of horror usually only seen on the face of Shay Givens whenever he let in a rare goal.

Kennedy let this sink in before continuing, "What I suggest you do, Miss Robbins, is contact Mr Dickens as a matter of great urgency and tell him we'll see him back here," Kennedy paused again to check his watch, "at one-thirty."

"I'm afraid that won't be possible, Inspector," Alice Robbins announced, regaining most of her lost composure. "Timothy has an important lunch appointment with Sir Terry Wogan that cuts across that time."

"Well, Miss Robbins, here's the thing. I'd suggest it would be much better if you interrupted him than it would be if we had to arrest him in the middle of his lunch with Sir Terence."

✳✳✳

Kennedy and King made good time down to Wimbledon and were happy to discover that Miss Chloe Simmons, unlike Mr Tim Dickens, wasn't otherwise engaged.

She looked as immaculate as ever and was dressed as though she might be expecting company.

"Look, Miss Simmons," Kennedy began, after being shown through to the sitting room.

"Chloe, please. I thought we'd agreed you'd call me Chloe."

"Sorry, of course I mean Chloe." Kennedy started up again a little shakily; he kept thinking she really was disarmingly beautiful. "It's been brought to our attention that Mr Mylan had been seeing... had been seeing your predecessor again, and that you'd been aware of this."

"Yes, I knew he was seeing her again, because Patrick told me," she admitted immediately, and before Kennedy could comment added, "but he wasn't seeing her in the way you think. She had made contact with him again and visited him twice to try and get back with him. Patrick said he agreed to see her because she sounded so desperate and he felt bad for her."

"Do you know her name or any of her details?" King asked.

"No. I believe the main reason Patrick told me about her was because he, once again, wanted to make it clear to me that one day, perhaps even one day soon, I'd be his ex, and that once I was his ex, it was over for good. I think he also wanted to make it clear that he was - how should I put this? - monogamous. He wanted to prove the point to me..."

"Because he wished you to be the same?" King suggested.

"Demanded it, in fact."

"And you really didn't have a clue who she was, or what she looked like?"

"Sorry, no, and Patrick would get really annoyed when I asked him about his exes."

"Is there any other reason why Patrick might have told you she was coming around again?" Kennedy asked.

She thought for a few moments, "Maybe he was afraid Jean Claude might have mentioned it?" she suggested.

"You think Jean Claude was aware of this other lady?" King asked.

"Well, if she'd been around to see Patrick, then he must have been."

"Did you..." Kennedy started, uncomfortable with the question he was about to ask her, "did you date anyone else during the time you were with Mr Mylan?"

"Christy, I'm shocked you'd ask me such a question," she said in apparent hurt.

"I had to ask."

"I realise that," she replied quietly.

"But I'd really like an answer," he continued.

"Why no, of course not. I thought I made it clear to you when we met first that I was his, and only his."

***

Miss Simmons offered to make them some lunch, but they politely declined, conscious of their impending meeting with Mr Tim Dickens.

Kennedy loved being driven through the streets of London, examining the buildings. He never tired of this and was intrigued by the difference in the buildings in the various boroughs. Wimbledon had grand, spacious, regal houses, particularly the ones around the common, whereas the nearby Tooting was, well, quite a bit closer, in more ways than one, to the Old Kent Road - that was if you were playing Monopoly.

King's mobile went off. It was James Irvine for Kennedy.

"Nealey has just rung to ask if it would be possible for you to meet Tim Dickens at her flat as soon as possible."

"We're on our way to interview him now," Kennedy said into the phone. "Did she say what it was about?"

"She said she couldn't really speak," Irvine replied. Kennedy couldn't be sure, but he thought his favourite DS was sounding a little annoyed, "but she asked that you come alone. She said that they would wait there until you arrived."

CHAPTER THIRTY-EIGHT

Nealey Dean was equally subdued when she answered her door to Kennedy.

"Please come in, Christy."

Nealey closed the door, and Kennedy followed her into the apartment.

Kennedy could hear voices in her living room; he'd only been expecting Nealey and Tim to be there.

However, there sitting on her large sofa were two men of similar size and age. Kennedy immediately recognised Dickens' distinctive hair and expensive clothing. The gentleman to Dickens' right looked familiar as well, and as Kennedy passed him side-on, he gasped as the stranger's face came into view.

"Thank you for agreeing to this meeting, Inspector Kennedy," Dickens started as both men stood up. "Have you ever met the Home Secretary, the Right Honourable Duncan Trower?"

"Pleased to meet you, Secretary," Kennedy said, surprised at the politician's grip.

"Yes," Trower said, drawing the word out, sitting down, crossing his legs and realigning the crease down the front of the trousers of his dark blue pinstriped suit, "Timothy here has got himself in a wee bit of a tizz, I'm afraid, so I called the meeting here to help clear it up. Come and sit down with us, Nealey."

Nealey started to join them and then had second thoughts. "Would anyone like a drink?" she enquired.

"I'd say," Duncan Trower announced, sounding very jolly in a forced kind of way. "I don't usually indulge before sundown, but I'll admit I could murder a gin and tonic. Nealey dear, could you make mine a stiff one, please?"

Kennedy opted for a glass of orange juice; Nealey and Dickens both went for the large G & T.

The Right Honourable Duncan Trower was a dead ringer for a
younger Michael Hessletine. He was slim and tall, maybe even a wee bit
taller than Dickens, and had longish greying hair, perfectly styled to
sweep back and totally cover his ears, but never at any place capable of
soiling his politician's ever-fresh shirt. Kennedy wondered if the House
of Commons had its own high-speed laundry service to accommodate
this look. Every single politician couldn't possibly afford to have a brand
new shirt every day of his or her life. He should have checked *The Daily
Telegraph's* exposure on politicians' expenses closer.

From the distance of television and newspaper photos, Trower
looked much younger than he did in real life. He had a habit of sweeping his hair back by running the long spindly fingers of his right hand
through it, and every time he did so he'd adapt a pose, turning his head
slightly to the left, tilting it down, so that his eyes had to look up, and
opening his mouth slightly. Kennedy figured this movement must come
from the days when his hair was long enough for Trower to swish it
back with merely a flick of his head.

"You would report to Superintendent Thomas Castle, wouldn't
you?" Trower asked Kennedy directly in his perfect diction. Word had
it that Trower had risen though the political ranks on the strength of his
oratorical gifts alone.

"Yes, that's correct," Kennedy replied, thinking he, not Trower, was
the one sounding a wee bit nervous.

"Yes, a good man Thomas. His wife, Maureen, is good at rallying the
troops for us in Highgate. I always try to get up to at least one evening
of their choir season. She's got quite a passable voice, you know."

Dickens coughed. Kennedy couldn't be sure, but he thought it could
have been a signal to Trower to get on with it - to get on with what this
meeting was about.

Trower took a long drink of his G & T and seemed to be fortified
by it. He uncrossed his legs as he set the drink back down on the coffee table, crossed them again as he relaxed back into the sofa and went
through the previous ritual of realigning the crease in his trousers. He
even threw in one of his right-hand-through-his-hair-and-twitch ges-
tures for good measure.

"Detective Inspector Kennedy, I'm told you're one of the good
cops." Kennedy blinked to distract himself from the person who was

complimenting him - well, either complimenting him or circulating hot air. "I'm also told you're a first class detective, an honest chap and a no-nonsense but fair Ulsterman." Trower paused, managed to catch Kennedy's stare and hold it for a few seconds. "Isn't it funny what people think of us and say behind our backs? I dread to think what they say about me."

Another cough from Dickens, but this time followed by, "Dunc?"

Silence.

Nealey Dean raised her eyebrows.

"Christy," she began, "Duncan and Timothy have something very important they need to discuss with you."

"Now that would be very interesting," the Right Honourable Trower said starting up again, but totally ignoring Nealey's efforts. "You know, Nealey dear, what people would say behind your back."

"Okay, Christy," Tim Dickens began hesitantly, "the reason we asked you here…"

"The reason we asked you here," Trower interrupted, taking up the slack again, "is to clear up this little mess. You see, young Miss Alice Robbins, in her endeavours to protect her boss, her boss whom she is madly, possessively in love with, actually managed to drop her boss in even bigger trouble when she claimed they were both together at the time of Mr Mylan's sad demise. Alice, who's frightfully out of her depth…"

"Dunc!"

"Well, she is, Timothy, and it has to be said, sometimes you're too loyal for your own good. Anyway, be that as it may, the reason Alice told you she and Timothy were together on Saturday was not because she didn't want you to think he was off murdering Mr Mylan at that point. Heaven forbid. What she really didn't want you to discover was that at the time of Mr Mylan's death," and here Trower paused to break into a Miss Marple impression, actually more like an Irish Miss Marple on speed, "the old queen was in my arms."

"Dunc-can," screamed Nealey Dean at the top of her voice.

"Dunc," Tim Dickens shouted, but in a quieter voice than Dean's, and broke into a smile.

"But the thing is, Christy, for obvious reasons, outside of this room Timothy and I need to be frightfully discreet about this," Trower continued, obviously pleased as punch with the furore he'd created.

"I thank you for your candour, sir," Kennedy said, hoping he wasn't batting the proverbial eyelid. "Exactly what time did you meet up?"

"I sent my driver to pick him up from Blake's at seven o'clock on Friday evening, and then they picked me up at my Chelsea residence at about seven-forty. We were on the M40 en-route to the Cotswolds by eight-thirty, which is the perfect time to be on that road. You either have to leave before three o'clock or after eight."

Trower had changed his tone and was now delivering his information in a very serious voice.

"Where is your house in the Cotswolds?"

"Minster Lovell," Trower said.

"Where is that exactly?"

"*Exactly* midway between Burford and Witney. Do you know the Cotswolds at all?"

"I used to know someone in Fulbrook," Kennedy said, realising that Trower was doing his political spin on him and trying hard to turn the interview into a friendly conversation.

"But they moved on?" Trower continued.

"Yes, in fact they did."

"Yes," Trower agreed and broke into his Miss Marple voice again. "It's a very beautiful little village, very picture postcard, but eventually everyone moves on from Fulbrook. It's absolutely always heaving with tourists, don't you see."

Kennedy was aware he still had some housekeeping to do.

"When did you return to London?" he asked.

"We got in quite late," Trower replied, returning to his diction-perfect voice. "We wanted to have the benefit of the full day in the countryside. I believe it would have been just before midnight on Sunday."

"Would anyone have seen you while you were there?"

"Oh yes," Trower smiled. "I've a permanent staff of three, all paid for out of my own pocket, mind you." He paused and slipped into his Miss Marple voice. Kennedy wasn't even sure if Trower realised he was doing it, "I wouldn't want to risk distressing our loyal tax payers."

"We don't hide away like hermits," Dickens said, offering his first comments for a time.

"Hark, she's woken up at last!" Trower laughed, "He's correct, absolutely so, but we are discreet. When we want to go out to dinner, we merely borrow the wives or girlfriends of a couple of chums and head out in a gang. Um, Inspector, it's important you know, this is not a fling or anything. We're happily in a very serious and loving relationship, but it's just that we're both pubic figures, and…"

Dean and Dickens started to snigger at the same time. Kennedy had managed to let Trower's slip pass, but when Dean and Dickens started to snigger and then break into a full laugh, he too couldn't help but join them.

"What, what's the matter?" Trower said smiling, but wanting to know what they were laughing at, "You should hear yourselves, you're sniggering in harmony. Are my flies undone or something?"

This in turn caused the other three to laugh even more. Kennedy felt part of Dean and Dickens laugh was based on the sheer relief and subsequent release they were now enjoying in having, at least in their book, cleared the matter up.

"Do you not realise, Duncan, than when you were proclaiming from the rooftops your genuine love for Timothy, you said, 'We're both *pubic* figures…?'"

"I did not? I didn't, did I? Oh my God," Trower protested and broke into a hearty, earthy laugh. Then, on queue, he slipped back into his Miss Marple voice to say, "Oh my Lord, and here I am blaspheming as well."

Kennedy broke up the small talk with, "Just one thing that's been troubling me, Mr Dickens. When DS Irvine recently interviewed Miss Alice Robbins and yourself individually about your alibi for Saturday afternoon, DS Irvine confirmed that your alibis overlapped identically. How did you manage that?"

"Devious but simple," Dickens admitted. "When I was being interviewed in the studio, I'd left the talkback microphone on. Alice was lurking by the door of the control room and could hear every single word of our conversation clearly over the talkback system."

"No doubt Miss Robbins was the author of that particular idea."

"Duncan," Dickens chastised quietly, and that was all it took for Trower to apologise.

Kennedy left the apartment about five minutes later. The three of them seemed to be relaxing into a nice bottle of Merlot. Nealey got up to lead Kennedy to the door, but Trower signalled a "no" to her, indicating that he would do it. Nealey rose and kissed Kennedy good-bye anyway, inviting him to come back some time when they could enjoy a drink. Dickens shook Kennedy's hand furiously, and such was his relief and gratitude that the singer eventually broke into bear-hugging him.

"Christy, I'm sorry we had to meet under these circumstance," Trower announced as he and the Ulster detective reached the front door, "but on the positive side, were it not for these circumstances, we probably would never have met."

"You're not wrong there, sir," Kennedy replied, admiring his honesty.

"Nealey assures me you will be very discreet about this, but let me also say that if in the course of your investigation you're put in a position where we need to revisit this, we'll just have to deal with it. I think Timothy worries about my position a lot more than I do."

Trower shook Kennedy's hand using both his hands. He very smoothly removed one of his hands from the grip and, in one beautiful manoeuvre, dipped into the breast pocket of his suit jacket and deliver to Kennedy's free hand a business card.

"My private number is on there, Christy. Use it any time you need to."

CHAPTER THIRTY-NINE

Kennedy decided to walk back to North Bridge House. Marylebone High Street was a great walking area, Regent's Park was en route, the weather was great, and he was glad of the extra time to think.

Quicker than he thought possible, he was leaving Marylebone Basin, crossing and travelling east along the ultra busy Marylebone Road, the feed road for the M40, which the Right Honourable Duncan Trower and former pop sensation Tim Dickens had used to escape to Trower's weekend getaway.

Kennedy knew he'd have to check with Trower's staff at Minster Lovell, but it was a safe bet they'd confirm the Home Secretary's claim. Realistically, in these troubled times for those in public office, he had too much to risk by stepping forward with a bunch of lies.

So Timothy Dickens was out of the frame. Kennedy wondered about Marcus Urry. Could he, unknown to Dickens, have been responsible for Mylan's death? Or perhaps Dickens knew of his employee's intentions, maybe even directed them and got out of town over the weekend in question for that very reason. Kennedy felt those were slim pickings too. Dickens, as well as his lover, had just too much to lose. He beat himself up a bit over this assumption, realised his team would do likewise, but would be ready to readdress it if necessary. He wasn't unhappy about losing Tim Dickens from his suspect list. Besides Dickens' being a friend of Nealey Dean, Kennedy knew that sometimes the process of elimination was the most efficient method of honing in on the guilty person.

Rodney Stuart was, in more ways than one, an unattractive suspect, but at the moment he seemed to be the best Kennedy had. Irvine's approach had been 100 per cent correct: at the very least Rodney was definitely guilty of fleecing his client, and taking the accountant off the street was going to prevent him doing a runner, just in case he had murdered his client in order to hide his embezzlement.

Kennedy thought about Chloe Simmons as he nipped up York Gate and crossed York Bridge, which took him into the park at the tranquil Queen Mary's Gardens. Bizarre though the liaison might be, she boasted that Mylan saw her and *only* her during the term of their relationship. She seemed to set great store by that. Perhaps the monogamy offered Chloe the little bit of specialness everyone needs to feel. Sometimes it's being in love; sometimes it's being in lust; sometimes it's friendship; sometimes it's companionship. When none of the above is a compromise and is purely the basis of the connection, it is possible for the relationship to exist. However, take away this foundation, for instance in this case with the reappearance of the previous concubine, then the relationship collapses. So what might someone as young and as beautiful as Chloe Simmons do when the only sexual relationship she had ever known collapsed? But, if she sought vengeance, then surely the previous concubine, and not Mylan, would have been the main target.

Maybe, like Kennedy's team, Chloe had been unable to find her predecessor, so Mylan came back into the frame again as her target.

The garter belts Mylan was wearing when he died flashed into Kennedy's mind. From the first moment he'd spotted them on the victim's corpse, Kennedy had felt they were a sign - a sign of humiliation.

The sign said: *You should not have disrespected me.*

Chloe Simmons, a fatherless daughter, had been playing around with her emerging emotions for the last few years as she'd first been groomed by Mylan and then used by him to satisfy his carnal needs, and all of this happening at a time when she should have been falling hopelessly in and out of love on a weekly if not daily basis. Who was to say what she'd be capable of when she felt she might be about to lose the only stable relationship she'd ever known?

Sooner than he wanted to, Kennedy had emerged from the park at Albert Road, and he headed down towards the top of Parkway.

Before he could interview Chloe Simmons again, and he certainly knew that he must, he needed to uncover more about her predecessor. Chloe still was Mylan's "concubine," but what of the ex? Just how desperate had she been in her endeavours to start serving Mylan again? And, more importantly, when her efforts had been thwarted, what exactly might this mysterious unknown woman be capable of? Maybe even ending Mylan's life in a totally humiliating way?

Kennedy added Jean Claude Banks to his list of people in need of revisiting.

He stormed into North Bridge House.

Sgt Flynn wasn't at his desk. And why would he be every time Kennedy walked in? Yet Flynn's presence centred Kennedy's thoughts and his day. Kennedy didn't know who Mylan's last mistress was. (He preferred, even mentally, to refer to her as a mistress rather than a concubine, even though Simmons didn't seem to take the same offence from the title as Kennedy did.) So he was trying to work out if he was annoyed about the mistress's identity, Flynn's absence, or the fact that his favourite desk sergeant's replacement was greedily tucking into a box of doughnuts.

It would appear that this salt of the earth, overtly friendly, covertly bulky, Caucasian woman was to be the new face of North Bridge House. "Salt of the earth my arse," Kennedy said under his breath very uncharitably. "Give me the aging Flynn any day of the week. At least he hasn't got *all* of his tricks from watching *Hill Street Blues.*"

"Oh, Detective Inspector Christy Kennedy, a pleasure to make your acquaintance again," she giggled, like a schoolgirl on her first date, "I've got an envelope here for you; I believe it's the phone records of a certain Mr Patrick Mylan."

CHAPTER FORTY

Kennedy had several things he needed to do, all of which would in turn uncover several other things he needed to do. He decided to do what he normally did at times like these, and that was to address the first thing that grabbed his attention. Reviewing Patrick Mylan's mobile phone records for his last days on this earth would be a start, and it would be at the very least one thing less for him to attend to.

As he scrolled through the list, he noted the names and telephones numbers of Mylan's acquaintances he and his team hadn't already interviewed. The first page, the most recent one, only threw up one name. Four pages on as he turned on to the final page, the page containing the oldest calls, he still only had slim pickings, three names in total. On the final page, he spotted a name about three quarters of the way down that stopped him in his tracks. He genuinely felt he'd been kicked in the chest by the back legs of a stallion. Had he been on his feet at that point, his legs would most surely have given way under him.

Sharenna Chada had rung Patrick Mylan several times, and Mylan had rung her twice on that particular day.

CHAPTER FORTY-ONE

Kennedy's mind flashed through all of the permutations he knew everyone, including Miss Bleedin' Saltoftheearth, would flash through. Not one of the scenarios looked good for him.

In his heart he knew that although Sharenna must be involved in this in some way, she couldn't possibly have murdered Patrick Mylan because she was in bed with Kennedy during Mylan's guessed time of death and several hours either side. Or could she?

His brain went into over-drive as he tried to work out how she could possibly be involved and how he could now get hold of her. Rather than scroll back through the phone records, Kennedy remembered the note she'd given him with her mobile number. He still had it in his pocket, tucked safely in his credit card wallet along with the Right Honourable Duncan Trower's business card.

Monday.
I'm happy you came to see me. I hoped you would.
Ring me on 07972 147738 whenever you finish work
and I'll come and see you.
                                               S.

Kennedy started to dial the number. He set the phone back down again. Was he just overreacting? Was Miss Chada really Patrick Mylan's last concubine? *No, scrap that,* Kennedy thought; *was she really Mylan's last but one concubine?* He needed to think about what he'd say. Kennedy and Miss Chada didn't have the kind of relationship where they would just ring each other for a chat.

He set the phone back down again, this time banging it down in frustration. If he rang using his office phone, there would be a record of a connection between the two of them. He was annoyed for thinking like a criminal. He was shocked at how easily and quickly he'd switched to another mindset.

Should he just go to Castle now and lay everything on the table for his superior? At the least, there would be an inquiry. These days there had to be. Well, on closer consideration, maybe not. Maybe he didn't have anything he needed to admit to his superior. As of that moment, the only thing, the only *single* semi-incriminating thing was the fact that Miss Chada and Mr Mylan had telephone contact. What on earth was wrong with that? She was a masseuse. Mylan lived locally to Un-locked, her practice, so there was at least some percentage of a chance that Mylan could also have been one of her clients. Kennedy blew out a long sigh of relief.

Of course Partick Mylan could have been seeing Sharenna Chada in a professional capacity. So why shouldn't Kennedy ring her? He'd just discovered her name on his telephone list; of course he had to ring her. And he didn't need to sneak out of North Bridge House to ring her from a coin box.

He lifted the phone. He thought through the consequences again. He set the phone down again. What was the proper and professional way to do this? Well, he could get either DC Dot King or DS James Irvine to follow up that particular lead and dispatch them to interview Miss Chada. He could wait until he went home that evening; she'd been to see him every single night since the weekend. In fact, now that he came to think of this, she'd been with him or he'd been with her, whichever way he or Castle would want to put it, every day since Mylan had been murdered.

"Okay," he said out loud in his empty office, calming himself down, "what exactly is it that you think you have done wrong?"

"Nothing," he replied to himself, thirty seconds later. "You'd a bad back; Miss Chada successfully treated it for you. Then she seduced you. You were totally unaware of her involvement in the Mylan case at any time you were intimate. Where you *would* be wrong," he lectured himself, "would be if you were now to continue seeing her knowing that she might, just might be involved in your current case."

Yes, that makes sense, he thought, *a lot of sense*.

That was the key to this, wasn't it? He wasn't aware of her involve-ment. But now that he was aware of her *potential* involvement, should he continue to be romantically involved with her, then and only then could he find himself in a compromising situation. On reflection, he wasn't actually romantically involved with Miss Chada. The actual fact was that he was physically involved with her. He had to tell her immediately that they could not continue with their relationship due to the new set of circumstances he was now aware of. Was he being grossly unfair to her? Did she deserve to be dumped, just because he was a cop and her name had surfaced on his current investigation? The bottom line was that she might be totally innocent and Kennedy, by his actions, was ruining any chance of their having a future relationship.

Then the cop brain clicked back into gear. He went through the timings of his encounter with her the previous Saturday. What if she *was* involved? What if she seduced him so she could have an alibi for the time of Mylan's death?

All he succeeded in doing was winding himself up again. This time it felt more like a donkey's kick than a stallion's kick.

He rose from his desk, put on his black windbreaker and departed North Bridge House. He had made his decision.

He was going to Unlocked to see Miss Chada. He would ask her if she was seeing Mylan in a professional capacity or if she had once had a relationship, of sorts, with him. If she answered yes to the latter question and no to the former, then he would have to hand over at least her part of the questioning to Irvine or King. If at that stage, it looked as if Miss Chada might be in any way involved in this, then he would have to stand down from the investigation and declare his conflict of interest.

He could hear Castle ask, "And what, pray, would your conflicting interest be, matey?"

"Oh," he'd have to answer truthfully, "I was actually having sex with her at the time Mylan was murdered."

CHAPTER FORTY-TWO

Seven minutes later, he was walking through the front door of Unlocked. Before he had a chance to speak, Jan, the chirpy receptionist, announced, "Oh, Mr Kennedy, I'm afraid you're out of luck. Miss Chada is not in today."

"Oh, ehm, any idea when she'll be back?" he asked crestfallen.

"She wasn't best pleased with you, Mr Kennedy. She hates no-shows," Jan continued, totally ignoring his question.

"Yes, yes, I have already apologised to her. When did you say she'd be back?"

"Well, that might be a lot longer than we both might want. She always had next week blocked off, but before she left yesterday, she had me settle up with her, saying she needed a longer break. She said she'd let me know later when she was coming back. I thought she must be going to work somewhere else, maybe Neal's Yard, but she said no. She gave me her word that when she returned she would come back here and give us first refusal. She asked us to recommend our other practitioners to her clients, and I have someone perfect lined up for you, Mr Kennedy. Hans Van Pullman. He's Swiss, very strong and does excellent deep tissue work."

"Have you any idea where Miss Chada is?"

"No. Miss Chada keeps herself to herself. She never socialised with the rest of us. She's never been to anyone's crib, nor we to hers."

"Surely you must have an address for her, for cheques and forwarding letters and so forth?"

"I've a mobile number which I'm happy to give you, but that's it."

They compared numbers; it was the same one Kennedy had.

Miss Chada, it appeared, had agreed to take a smaller than normal percentage from Unlocked on condition she always receive cash.

This was not looking good.

When Kennedy returned to North Bridge House, he rushed to his office and quickly dialled Miss Chada's number.

"I'm out of town for quite some time. Don't know when I'll be back again. Please speak with Jan at Unlocked about on-going treatments," Miss Chada said unemotionally on her message.

Kennedy focused in on her line, "Don't know when I'll be back again." Kennedy knew it was from a song, he didn't know which one.

He typed the line in to Google, and John Denver's name beamed back at him. The next line to the lyric and the title to the song was: "I'm leaving on a jet plane."

Hardly a Freudian clue, Kennedy thought.

He went straight to Superintendent Thomas Castle's office and filled him in on the facts so far.

"Christy, I'm happy to see you're keeping your head. You've done everything by the book. I'll put this meeting in my report. If there is really nothing else you need to tell me, I'm happy for you to continue to lead this investigation. Apart from anything else, matey, you're going to have a much bigger incentive than anyone else to catch this Miss Chada."

That was it. No fuss, no need to worry. Castle was being Castle and doing what he always did, which was to support his team.

Just as Kennedy was about to escape his office, Castle did have a wee farewell for him: "You're a bit of a dark horse, matey."

CHAPTER FORTY-THREE

Kennedy quickly returned to Castle's office to address a bit of house-keeping business he'd forgotten. Permission granted, he went and sought out Sgt Tim Flynn, who was "doing a bit of much needed filing in the basement," brought him back up to the reception. He then instructed Miss Custard Filling "to arise, take up your doughnuts and walk," and sent her flustering, while still maintaining her political correctness, away from public view to the basement to do "a bit of much needed filing."

Flynn, back firmly in his proper place at *his* North Bridge House reception desk, immediately contacted New Scotland Yard, as per Kennedy's request, and asked them to use their channels to see if a Miss Sharenna Chada was booked on an international flight any day soon.

By the time Kennedy returned to his office, his phone was ringing. Flynn already had the news for him that a Miss Sharenna Chada had flown Upper Class that very morning at eleven-thirty to San Francisco on Virgin Atlantic Flight number VS019.

"San Francisco," Kennedy said aloud to himself. "Why San Francisco?"

Then he remembered something Jean Claude Banks had said at their first meeting about Mylan having a property in California.

He wanted to interview Rodney Stuart but he couldn't, because poor Rodney was already under severe interrogation from the forensic accountants.

Kennedy sought out Irvine and together they walked around to Patrick Mylan's house. On the journey, Kennedy explained in detail what had happened between himself and Miss Chada. Irvine was non-judgemental and took on board the information just as he might any other details on this or any other case.

They arrived at Mylan's house just as Jean Claude was about to head off on his Vespa. The Frenchman happily took Kennedy and

Irvine into the house and brewed up a coffee for himself and Irvine. Kennedy settled for mineral water. When they were all settled in the conservatory, Kennedy described Sharenna Chada in great detail for the Frenchman.

"Ah yes, you mean Miss Chada?"

"Yes," Kennedy agreed. "You know her?"

"*Mais oui,* she was Mr Mylan's woman before Miss Simmons."

Frustrated, Kennedy asked himself why he hadn't pushed Jean Claude Banks further in that area on Monday morning. Of course it still would not have prevented what had happened between himself and the brown-skinned woman over the weekend.

"Do you know where she lived?" Irvine asked.

"*Non.*"

"Did you know her?" Kennedy knew Banks' years with Mylan pre-dated Miss Chada's.

"But of course."

"But you never knew where she lived?"

"When she was Mr Mylan's woman, she had an apartment in Albert Mansions overlooking the park."

"Not too far from here then?"

"In fact, no," Banks agreed, "but when she and Mr Mylan's paths diverged, she sold her apartment and moved out of the area."

"You told us Mr Mylan had a property in America in California. Did you mean San Francisco?" Kennedy asked, surprised by how detached he was. Somehow he'd managed to totally focus back in on the investigation.

"But of course, San Francisco."

"Was Miss Chada aware of this property?"

"Mr Mylan and she visited there three times to my recollection."

"Do you know exactly where the property is in San Francisco?" Kennedy pushed, remembering some friend of his father's lived in San Francisco.

"I wouldn't know that. Mr Stuart, I assume, would know that. He'd need to take care of the bills, wouldn't he?"

✳✳✳

Kennedy and Irvine had returned to North Bridge House by three-forty on Thursday afternoon. Miss Chada wouldn't have landed yet at San Francisco airport, but equally she'd be a long time gone out of UK airspace and jurisdiction. Kennedy realised he didn't have enough time to do the necessary paperwork to have someone pick her up at San Francisco airport. It was frustrating, but it also meant he didn't have to use the embarrassing line, "We suspect she may have been involved in the death of Mr Patrick Mylan. However, at the time Mr Mylan was dying, Miss Chada was in bed with me."

Mr Stuart was still being interviewed. The forensic accountant's team claimed they were happy for the interruption, which would give them a rest while keeping the pressure on Stuart.

Stuart was an easy interviewee; maybe he was just relieved that the accountants were giving him a rest. He was low on energy, and he answered each question he was asked and even volunteered the information that Mr Mylan's parting gift to Miss Chada had, in fact, been the property in Half Moon Bay, which was on the outskirts of the sprawling San Francisco. He hadn't seen Miss Chada for over two years, and he had no idea of her current whereabouts.

Kennedy phoned his father and received the usual, "Is everything okay, Christopher?"

"Totally, Dad. You know that friend of yours in San Francisco?"

"Yes, Don Nolan. What about him? Are you going over for a holiday? Do you need his details? His number is…"

And on and on Kennedy's dad went in a one-sided conversation, very near a monologue, where Kennedy had all the information he required and hardly needed to ask a question in order to get it.

Kennedy went to see Castle and told him he'd like to fly out to America first thing the next morning.

Castle laughed, but at least he didn't call him "matey."

"It'll take at least a week before we can get the paper work lined up."

Kennedy returned to his office and immediately called the Right Honourable Duncan Trower.

Trower was as good as his word about Kennedy's ringing any time he needed anything. He took the call immediately, seemed happy with Kennedy's news. At the very least, the recent development served to take the pressure off his lover, Tim Dickens. Trower promised he would sort out all the necessary paperwork and introductions as quickly as possible.

Trower was back on to Kennedy within the hour, and his office contacted Superintendent Thomas Castle shortly thereafter confirming all the details. Trower's office had booked Kennedy on a Virgin Atlantic flight for the following morning, and in Upper Class. Castle was informed that Kennedy could be expected to start immediately into the investigation following an eleven-hour flight, so they didn't consider Kennedy's travelling in coach to be most advantageous to their joint endeavours.

***

So exactly twenty-four hours after Sharenna Chada had fled the country and hightailed it to America, Kennedy was on a flight heading in the same direction. He was 100 per cent legit, although extradition papers, if they proved necessary, were going to be a different matter altogether. Trower's office had, however, fixed up the relevant stateside contacts for him should they be required.

Kennedy considered the work he'd left for Irvine and King. He needed them to interview Maggie Littlewood by herself again. Kennedy was now sure she was the concubine connection in all of this. She knew Chloe's mother and probably introduced Mylan to the Simmons family and consequently Chloe herself. Kennedy felt sure there must be a connection between Maggie Littlewood and Sharenna Chada. He also suspected that his theory that Maggie and Mylan had once been lovers themselves was not as far-fetched as it had at first seemed. He suggested to Irvine that he speak with Roger Littlewood again. If there was a chance that Maggie was once Mylan's lover and was now his procurer, was there also a chance that Roger had discovered this and sought his own revenge? King and Irvine also needed to do follow-up interviews with Chloe Simmons and with Marcus Urry. There was still a slight chance that Urry, even without his boss's knowledge, had some involvement in Mylan's demise. He was going to California to follow up just one lead, Kennedy reminded his team. They still had the majority of the work to do in Camden Town.

He thought about Miss Chada and his relationship with her. The question was not so much how she fit into his life but more how he fit into hers; and when and how exactly she had decided to involve him in this, whatever *this* was. He thought of her indisputable beauty, and he thought of their five days of passionate love-making. There had been several times during that period when she had given herself to him so unselfishly and so completely that it was nearly impossible to reconcile that person with the person whom he now suspected of being involved in the death of Patrick Mylan. It seemed unthinkable for her to have had any hidden agenda. He sincerely believed it would be totally impossible for any human to betray her soul so.

He'd worked pretty much the whole way through the Thursday night and Friday morning and then come straight to Heathrow. Soon he was airborne, and then before he knew it he felt his eyes grow heavy. The word "concubine" and what one may or may not be capable of seemed to float in and out of his mind.

When he did start to drift off, he gave himself to the blissful unconsciousness willingly.

PART THREE

HALF MOON BAY

CHAPTER FORTY-FOUR

Flew in from Miami Beach BOAC,
Didn't get to bed last night.

Well, Kennedy had actually flown in from Camden Town, and when the Beatles had written "Back in The USSR," they hadn't experienced the pleasure of the Virgin Atlantic Upper Class fold-out bed. As a result of that, and no doubt aided considerably by the little bag of goodies the in-flight staff had given him, Kennedy arrived totally refreshed.

It was Friday, *still* Friday, but Sharenna Chada had a clear twenty-four hours head start on him.

Kennedy walked off the plane into what had once been the new frontier. Even now, a century and a half later, the smell of the newness, of being totally alive with excitement, managed to hit him smack clean between the eyes. The unique smell came from the heat and the lack of damp. Not that it didn't rain in America, particularly in the San Francisco area, but the moisture didn't instil itself into the atmosphere as it did in Kennedy's native Ulster or, to a much lesser degree, in his adopted home of Camden Town.

Kennedy, though a policeman himself, found himself acting guilty in the presence of the immigration officers. Maybe he was acting strangely while trying to appear innocent. Kennedy reckoned the more seasoned guards probably factored this into their assessment; otherwise 99 per cent of all queues would be detained for further questioning.

He needn't have worried, because right at the back of the extremely long immigration queue was a police officer, one in a different uniform from the immigration officers, holding a card with Kennedy's name clearly printed. Kennedy went up and introduced himself to the officer, who took Kennedy's paperwork and passport and whisked him through a VIP channel.

So far so good.

"You been stateside before?" The patrolman, who'd introduced himself as Kevin MacCormac, "but everyone calls me Mactoo," started just after they'd cleared passport control.

"A few times; not for a good while though," Kennedy replied.

"This coast?"

"No, just the East Coast, mostly Boston."

"All right," Mac replied, drawing out the two syllables to emphasise his discovery. "That's the Chief Donald Nolan connection."

"Yeah, he's a good friend of my father's brother."

"Who'd be your uncle?" Mac asked. He'd a wonderful, deep, radio-friendly voice. Mac was tall and thin with the only visible body hair being a dark triangle just under his bottom lip. He smiled easily and frequently.

"Well, yes," Kennedy replied, wondering if he had phrased his reply so in order to give credit to his father rather than his uncle.

"No, no, I meant, who would *want* to be your uncle, you know, having the chief as a friend - but I was just kidding, of course."

By now they'd reached the pavement outside the terminal. They small-chatted their way into and through San Francisco's dramatic skyline.

Kennedy wasn't really tuned in to the conversation, so immersed was he in the visual distractions thrown at him on his first visit to this vibey West Coast city. They say America looks different from the UK due to the "look" of American TV shows, which apparently has something to do with the number of lines on their screens. Kennedy mentally compared *West Wing* to *East Enders;* he wished he hadn't. But he felt it was more than just a small screen development. To Kennedy's eyes, America, in the shape of San Francisco, *looked* different because it was different. It was colourful, energetic, distracting. It was people friendly, and its people were friendly. It was a consumer enticing colony. It was engaging and embracing. America didn't know the meaning of the word shy.

"We're nearly there," Mactoo announced as he dodged in and out of heavy traffic, mostly taxis and buses. Eventually they turned into Sixth Avenue. "So tell me this: you're from England; how the hell did someone like Dave Beck*ham* ever get back into the national side? To get away with that kind of stupid you'd have to have a genius behind you.

I know, I know, we paid millions for him, but we still haven't got the hang of this soccer shit yet, so we've got a reasonable excuse, right? But I'd really love to know who negotiated him back into the team after his sell-by date. If I ever found out, and I could hire them, I'd have the confidence to go ahead with a divorce."

Football wasn't the best subject for Kennedy, but luckily enough they had reached their destination. They pulled off Sixth and into the courtyard of a modern red-brick building, the Richmond station house, which was in the Golden Gate Division. Somewhere in the building was Police Chief Don Nolan, an old friend of Kennedy's uncle.

Kennedy was expecting the police station to be a mad house. He must have watched too many episodes of *NYPD Blue*, because although it did turn out to be very busy, it was also civilised and extremely modern.

Police Chief Don Nolan was tied up, so Kennedy had to kick his heels for about an hour, during which he heard officers deal with a man in his early twenties who'd been assaulted by two known acquaintances who'd "disrespected" him. From what Kennedy could gather, the three had been involved in auto theft - *Auto theft sounds so much better than stealing a car*, Kennedy thought - when the "disrespecting" took place. Given the circumstances, it seemed to be a weird charge for the young victim to be making, so his listlessness and vacant look were perhaps due more to self-induced chemical abuse than to physical abuse from others.

Another victim had been preparing to get out of her car on the eight hundred block of Clement Street when a stranger suddenly appeared at her door and sprayed her in the face with pepper. The stranger manhandled her out of the car before jumping into it himself and driving off. An ambulance was called to attend to the victim, who sat no more than six feet away from Kennedy, telling her case officer that the suspect was fifty to sixty years old, wearing sun glasses, had a light-coloured hat, blue jeans, and had forgotten to remove his name-tag, which also provided the details of the store where he worked. The officer seemed more interested in the woman than in her plight.

Another woman, sitting at a desk the other side of the open plan office, was telling a young and enthusiastic officer that she'd been jogging on Post Street near Scott Street listening to Tom Waits singing

"In the Neighbourhood" on her iPod. A suspect walked up to her, tapped his wrist indicating that he wanted to know the time. When she was distracted, looking down at her watch, the suspect nicked her iPod and fled west on Pond Street. The suspect was male, dressed in a silver windbreaker and a light blue Van Morrison T-shirt. The victim wondered aloud if the insurance company would spring for a complete set of Tom Waits CDs, so she'd have a bigger selection to download from. The victim was informed, helpfully, that if she didn't ask she'd never find out.

Yet another victim was advising his case officer that he'd been standing on the corner of 26th Avenue and Geary, minding his own business, when a man came along pushing his car west on Geary. The suspect waved the man over and asked for his help. A few difficult, laborious, and sweaty steps later, the suspect asked the victim if he could borrow the victim's cell phone to call for help instead. The victim, happy for the rest, willingly obliged. Then the suspect jumped into his supposedly ailing car, a sky blue Mustang, and miraculously drove off, a cell phone the richer.

So, another day in downtown San Francisco, Kennedy thought; *not all that different from Parkway in Camden Town.*

Which was when he heard a voice summoning him into Chief Nolan's office.

As the Ulster-born detective walked into the chief's office, just before six o'clock, two thoughts hit him. One, back in Camden Town it was now two o'clock the following morning; and two, his carry-on wheelie suitcase was still in the boot of Mactoo's patrol car, and goodness knew where Mactoo was now. Somehow this didn't seem to bother him as much as he thought it should.

Chief Nolan's mid-Atlantic accent did not disguise his Ulster roots.

"Christy," he said, enthusiastically shaking Kennedy's hand, "great to meet you. I've heard all about you from your uncle Harry."

"And I've heard a lot about you too," Christy replied, happy to get his hand back.

"Aye, they're all very proud of you," Nolan announced, inviting Kennedy to take the chair opposite his desk and facing a wall of Nolan's forty-odd year law enforcement career in photographs, diplomas, and awards. Kennedy wondered how proud his own family would be of him once they discovered that he'd been sleeping with a murder suspect.

Chief Don Nolan was a fit, muscular, dark-haired, clean-shaven man, about five foot ten inches in height - a no-nonsense kind of guy. His uniform was immaculate and so wrinkle-free it looked as if he'd put it on and had it pressed on him.

"So," Kennedy enquired, impatient to get on with what he'd come here for, "any progress on apprehending my suspect?"

"Or your 'person of interest,' as we refer to suspects here," Nolan smiled. He then opened a file in front of him and announced, "Sharenna Chada."

"Yes, that's her." Kennedy decided to come clean and jump right in and tell Nolan the whole story. "Less than a week ago…"

"Hold it right there," Nolan ordered, as he held up his hand in a stop sign. "I, hmm… I just wanted to greet you and say hello and invite you over to our house for Sunday lunch. The wife, Maddee, would love to meet you. She's a big fan of your Uncle Harry. In fact, and I'll tell you this for nothing, if I hadn't been as quick on my feet, she might have been your auntie today. Anyway, that's by the by. But getting back to this Miss Chada of yours, she's not actually on my patch. Word has it she's down in Half Moon Bay, Patrolman MacCormac's patch, and…"

Kennedy remembered the Half Moon Bay Police Department motif on the door to Mactoo's patrol car. Right beside that was the banner bearing the legend: "Serving Our Community With Pride." He remembered it clearly because the style of the script typeface of the lettering had made Kennedy originally misread it as "Sewing Our Community With Pride." The crest on Mactoo's uniform jacket also boasted a Half Moon Bay motif. Apparently this was the very same Half Moon Bay where Patrick Mylan had bought the house he'd eventually given to Sharenna Chada as a gift in full and final settlement for services rendered; with Mylan's emphasis on the word "final."

"… he," Nolan continued, "just popped you in here so we could meet up face to face. He's going to take you back down to Half Moon Bay to meet his chief, Edward Donohue. He's a good man, and he's going to look after you."

Chief Nolan was a friend of the family and had just wanted to extend his hospitality personally. Kennedy would have preferred to use the time to start working on the case, but he tried not to let his disappointment show.

***

"Tell me this," Mactoo asked in his best DJ voice as they hopped back into his two tone patrol car: "Christy - is that a real name or a madey-uppy name?"

"It's short for Christopher," Kennedy replied.

"Ah, and I can see why you'd want to use Christy as a handle," Mactoo replied after a few seconds' consideration. Then they commenced the seventy-minute, conversation-free journey. Kennedy wasn't being rude, but once the car started to move, his jet lag kicked right in and he fell asleep.

***

"She's got an airtight alibi. We can't just pick her up," Chief Ed Donohue said in genuine disbelief.

It was later that evening and they were in Chief Donohue's office at 537 Kelly Avenue in downtown Half Moon Bay. In attendance were Officers Kevin MacCormac, Grace Scott, and Detective Inspector Christy Kennedy. Chief Donohue, a slim-framed man with a chiselled, serious face but gentle eyes, was a dead ringer for the famous fifties' cowboy actor, Randolph Scott. He was a little north of six foot. His greying to white short hair made him look wise, as opposed to old.

Grace Scott looked preoccupied. The only feminine signs she betrayed were wisps of copper-colour hair escaping from the side and back of her Half Moon Bay Police Department baseball style cap. Kennedy figured she'd be in her early thirties. She was married (although the white ring of skin of her wedding finger showed she preferred not to wear her wedding ring while working) and, as it was now twenty-past-eight in the evening, she was most probably anxious to get home and have dinner with her husband and children. *And then again maybe not*, Kennedy thought. She didn't look like a mother, but perhaps motherhood was something she also had to leave at home with her wedding ring to be able to do her job properly. She and Mactoo seemed to be giving each other a lot of space.

In the centre of Chief Donohue's tidy desk lay the Patrick Mylan file and case notes, all officially rubber-stamped by the Home Office. The chief had obviously studied the file very closely, because he quoted relevant facts from the case without once checking the file.

"What *is* her alibi?" Grace Scott asked.

Donohue flashed her a "that was a dumb question" look, but she just glared at him. To Kennedy they were behaving like a man and a woman with a history, where the niceties of gently discussing their way through things they disagreed on gave way straight to the 'let's do battle' approach.

"She was with me at the time Patrick Mylan was being murdered."

"Okay, right," Scott started up again, this time turning on Kennedy. "So you thought you could arrest her and extradite her, *why?*"

"I..." Kennedy started.

"Look, let's back up a bit here," the chief ordered, glaring furiously at Scott.

"Yeah, you're right, Chief," Scott replied, but the intensity of her voice was still charged. "Inspector Kennedy, what exactly were you and this Chada woman doing at the time Mylan was being murdered?"

"Grace," Donohue shouted. Mactoo perked up as if he'd got the best seat in the house for the final seconds of a tied basketball game.

Kennedy, perhaps something to do with his hunger and jet lag, didn't feel uncomfortable, figuring he was being used as bait for another of their confrontations. But then again, there looked to be a good thirty years between them; they couldn't possibly be a couple, could they?

"Look," he said, staring directly at the very earnest Grace Scott, "I might as well tell you..."

"Inspector, you don't have to," Donohue cautioned.

"I was in bed with the suspect," Kennedy admitted near enough simultaneously.

"Right," Scott spat in sheer liquid disbelief, "and so then you know she nipped out, killed the victim, and then nipped back into bed with you. I've heard all about these cosy crimes you English have..."

"Irish," Kennedy interrupted.

"Sorry?"

"I'm Irish actually, Northern Irish."

She just shook her head and glared at Kennedy in disgust.

Kennedy felt Mactoo was either going to nip out for some popcorn or break into applause.

Scott stood up, turned to Donohue and hissed, "I can't believe you took me off my case to work on this."

On the word "this," she slammed her open right hand down with all her might on Mylan's file and turned and stormed out of the office. Mactoo blew a visible sigh of relief. Kennedy wondered if he had been expecting it to develop into blows.

The chief rushed to the open door and called after Scott, "I'm advising you for the final time, you don't have another case. You're working on this. You and MacCormac are detailed to Inspector Kennedy for the duration."

By this time Scott was nearly outside the building, so Kennedy couldn't be sure what she said in reply, but he thought there might have been a word thrown in repeatedly that rhymed with the word "luck" and prefixed with "dumb."

"MacCormac," Donohue started up again a few seconds later, "would you take Inspector Kennedy out for dinner and then take him back to the guest cabin up on my ranch?"

"Are you sure?" Mactoo replied, his disbelief obvious.

"No, it's fine," Kennedy offered. "I'm fine to stay in a hotel."

"No, you won't. MacCormac just meant there was someone else already staying in the guest cabin, didn't you, MacCormac?"

"Oh yeah," Mactoo smiled largely.

"There are always people coming and going there," Chief Donohue continued, "and there's more than enough room for a whole squad of police. You'll probably never even see the other guest."

Kennedy went to protest but was cut short by the chief.

"I insist and that's it, Inspector. Take it as a direct order. Now go with MacCormac here, and he'll set you up with a good supper."

***

It was now nearly five o'clock the following morning on Kennedy's body clock.

He found it difficult to concentrate on his comfort food - the all day breakfast he ordered in a restaurant cum bar on the waterside.

He remembered his wine being undrinkable and Mactoo having a cheeseburger and quite a few bottles of beer. He also remembered Mactoo looking at him and smiling a lot, as though he knew something Kennedy didn't. He also recalled Mactoo listing the top ten golden rules of avoiding jet lag:

1. Immediately set your watch and your mind to USA time.
2. If you've got a sweet tooth, now would be a good time to hit the Hershey bars.
3. Eat your meals only at USA meal times.
4. Never lie on a bed or sit in a chair for a rest.
5. Never lie on a bed or sit in a chair and watch TV.
6. Keep both brain and body active all the time.
7. Stay up as late as possible for the first couple of nights.
8. No matter how little sleep you get during the night, still get up early.
9. Don't drink alcohol in the afternoon.
10. Don't sleep with murder suspects.

Mactoo apologised for point number ten, but that was only after he'd laughed the whole way home on it.

By the time they reached Donohue's ranch, it was dark and surprisingly cold. They pulled in beside the other Half Moon Bay patrol car parked away from the main house by a grove of trees and waited as Chief Donohue, dragging furiously on a ciggy and backlit by the cream-coloured light from his kitchen, wandered over to them. He was now out of uniform and looked every bit the Randolph Scott about to hitch up and ride out to right some wrong. Maybe not Kennedy's wrong though; that would have to wait until tomorrow.

Kennedy was so zonked at that stage, he didn't remember much else save Donohue instructing him, in whispers, as to where the bathroom, kitchen, and the spacious bedroom were located and to treat the wooden building as his own. He flopped out on top of the bed and fell asleep immediately.

CHAPTER FORTY-FIVE

Kennedy woke up with a start, totally disorientated. It took him a few seconds to reorient himself to his new surroundings. He felt like he'd been sleeping for over twenty-four hours and it was the following evening. He checked his watch, which he'd reset to local time. It was ten forty-five and still dark outside. It must be the following evening. He couldn't possibly have been asleep for only half an hour, could he? His sleep had felt so deep. But the date on his watch confirmed that was exactly what had just happened. He felt hungry. He felt grubby. He had a crick in his neck from lying face down on top of the bed. His neck discomfort reminded him of Miss Chada.

As he showered he thought of Sharenna. She was also somewhere among these rolling, tree-covered hills. What was she doing just now? He wasn't allowed to arrest her. Truth be told, he knew he wasn't quite ready to arrest her. He still had to figure out how she could have pulled off Mylan's murder. But what should his plan of action be in the morning? Should he show up on her doorstep and let her know he knew where she was and he was on to her? Should he just keep a low profile until he solved the puzzle of this crime? In his now charitable moment, he did acknowledge how clever she'd been. Who better than a copper to give you a cast-iron alibi? He had been well and truly duped. Could it be that the reason he'd been keen to get out of Camden Town so quickly was not as much to apprehend the suspect as to avoid being in Camden Town when his colleagues discovered what had happened?

The power shower was exactly what he needed. It invigorated him and washed away the doziness from his brain. Now totally awake and alert, he decided to investigate the accommodation. The second he opened his bedroom door, he thought he heard someone crying and saw someone sitting over by the fire place, the grate aglow with burning logs. Kennedy loved the smell of burning wood.

The other guest was aware of his presence but surprisingly seemed unable to stop crying. Kennedy wondered if this was a cultural thing. In England people would go out of their way not to be seen crying in the presence of strangers. The Americans were meant to be more in touch with their feelings; could this be the living proof?

Kennedy considered what to do. He could just disappear back into his bedroom or he could walk across the large log-walled room and offer some comfort. He returned to his bedroom, but no sooner had he closed the door than he chastised himself under his breath, opened the door again and walked across the room in the direction of the fire.

Okay, Kennedy thought, as he noticed the vibrant copper-coloured hair of the woman sitting rocking gently back and forth in the sofa in front of the fire, *this is weird.* It was Officer Grace Scott. Not only was the chief having a scene with her, but he was also putting her up in his guest cabin, which probably meant his wife was still alive and installed in the main house. No wonder Chief Donohue had been forgiving of Kennedy's indiscretion back in Primrose Hill.

Why was Officer Scott sobbing so uncontrollably? Had the chief dumped her? Still, neither Scott nor Kennedy acknowledged each other. Kennedy felt he was now intruding on her space. Just as he was about to return to his bedroom, she swung her head around in his direction, her hair arcing out in a fiery copper umbrella as she did so.

"Ah, Inspector," she announced, using the palms of both hands to aggressively wipe the tears from her face and eyes.

"Sorry."

"No, no, it's fine. Come on up and take a seat. Even better, get yourself a glass from the liquor cabinet behind you; no one likes to drink alone."

"Sure," Kennedy replied as he did as bid.

She poured him a generous glass of a Napa Valley red, which Kennedy found very agreeable, maybe even too agreeable. He sat beside her in the sofa, which was bigger than some of the Camden Town bedsits he'd been in.

They both sat sipping silently, looking deep into the low flames.

"Okay, Inspector, I appreciate that."

"What?" he prompted, when it seemed she wasn't going to complete her thought.

"Oh, you know, Inspector, that you didn't say, 'Come on now, it's going to be okay.'

"Christy will do."

"But unprofessional to superiors."

"I'm a visitor, a guest. I'm not a superior. I've no rank here."

"My dad says you are, and that I've got to 'yes sir, no sir, three bags full sir' you."

"Your dad?" Kennedy said, wondering why she'd think he'd have a connection with her father.

"Chief Edward Donohue."

"He's your father? But I thought… sure your name is Scott? And you swore at him?"

"You thought *what* exactly, Inspector?" she said turning to face him for the first time.

Kennedy could mutter nothing more than, "Oh, ehm..."

"Wait… you don't mean to say you actually thought I was here… unbelievable…you didn't actually think I was shacking up with the chief…" and she burst into a fit of embarrassed laughter, but the more she laughed the less she was embarrassed, until eventually she was in the middle of a very infectious full-blown holler.

Kennedy even joined in, initially in the hope of defusing a potential international incident, but then he also saw the funny side of the situation.

"Oh, my goodness, Inspector, I needed that. Let me tell you something. It's true what they say: never drink alone late at night."

Grace Scott had a very pleasing voice, more Jennifer Connolly than Keira Knightly. Out of her uniform and even in her black trainer bottoms and the large bright red woollen jumper she was presently camped in, she looked a lot more feminine than she had when he'd first met her.

She obviously didn't want to discuss herself, because she kept throwing questions at Kennedy until he stopped giving her one-word answers.

"So how have you ended up here, Inspector?"

"As in my career generally, or specifically this current mess I seem to be in?"

"Let's start with this current mess of yours."

"Okay," Kennedy sighed, taking quite a large gulp of the delicious wine, "I was on a case and ah, I got stabbed and it didn't heal the way everyone hoped it would. I started to be troubled by my back, and then my girlfriend…"

"Are we talking girlfriend-girlfriend, or the suspect in your current case?"

"I'm getting to that," Kennedy replied, trying to navigate his way through this awkward situation. He decided the best way was not to dress it up, just tell it like it was. "My then girlfriend, ann rea, before she dumped me, sought out a specialist to give me back treatment. This specialist turned out to be Miss Sharenna Chada. I've been seeing her professionally speaking for around a year, but we hardly spoke. I'd address her as Miss Chada, and she'd call me Mr Kennedy. Anyway, in recent months my back has been giving me more and more trouble until, in fact this time last week…" Kennedy paused as he allowed the magnitude of the previous week's developments to sink in. "I was pretty much immobile in bed. Actually, make that I was immobile on the floor. It's the worst I've ever been; I was in sheer agony. Miss Chada came around and worked her magic and ended up staying the night and the next day as well. At the same time as she was with me, Mr Patrick Mylan was being murdered."

"But surely, all joking aside, she can't have been involved?" Grace said, refilling both their glasses. She looked a little unsteady and she'd started to slur some of her words.

Kennedy then proceeded to spend a good few minutes talking Grace through the Mylan case to date. Even though she was feeling the effects of the wine, she got right into the history, throwing questions and suggestions at Kennedy as he delivered his tale.

"So then, after you'd given her her cast iron alibi, she dropped you like a hot potato?"

"Well, no."

"Don't tell me you had a repeat performance?" she laughed.

"Yes," Kennedy admitted quickly. If Grace Scott was going to be working with him stateside, it was important she felt he had nothing to hide.

"How many times?"

"I saw her every night until she fled here the night before last, or was it last night."

"So did you think it might have developed into a relationship?"

"No, it was a physical thing."

She raised her eyebrows.

"No, honestly, it really was," Kennedy protested, "although…"

"Although you found you had feelings for her," Scott offered. Kennedy felt she was ribbing him.

"No. She seemed very concerned when I didn't show up for a professional appointment with her. She felt I was slighting her in front of her colleagues."

"Okay, let's get back to your girlfriend," Scott said with a new degree of enthusiasm. "How long from when she dumped you until you ended up in bed with your osteopath?"

Kennedy then explained the long on/off relationship with ann rea.

Scott seemed impressed by Kennedy's conviction that ann rea had been the perfect girl for him.

"It's brilliant when you meet someone and you know they're the one," she said, and then looked at Kennedy for agreement before adding, "Yep, I suppose it's much easier though when *both* parties have that feeling."

Something about the look of sadness creeping over her face betrayed she was thinking of her perfect partner. Obviously, due to her current emotional state and her name change from Donohue to Scott, she'd very recently split up with her husband.

"The first moment I saw Steve, I just knew he could be the perfect man for me. I started to wonder about him, and his likes and dislikes, and if it would be possible for us to be compatible. No matter the packaging, you just don't know, do you?"

"Yeah, but it's good discovering."

She went on to tell Kennedy how she had met and married her husband, Steve Scott, another officer in the Half Moon Bay Police Department.

She told Kennedy they had clicked immediately, discovering they shared a lot of each other's interests, and were married within six months. On their first wedding anniversary, they were making plans about when she would retire to concentrate on their planned family.

"Then on the 13th of April this year, on the eve of our second wedding anniversary, his body was discovered by the side of Pilarcitos Creek…"

"Oh, my God."

"…and just under the bridge at Main Street," she continued totally ignoring him.

"I'm so sorry," Kennedy said quietly.

"And then," she continued very shakily, trying to catch her breath enough to allow her to get her words out, "it was like my life was over too. It was like the person I waited my entire life for, the person I was convinced was out there and looking for me at the same time was gone, stolen from me, and this thing that I had, this hook I had on the meaning of life, my life, Steve and my life, was gone, not only gone, but, by its absence, mocking me. It was as if someone had wanted to show me just how perfect it could be, like… that it could be better than I'd ever dreamed it could be, and then, like a thief in the night, he was stolen right out from under my eyes… It was like…I was being forced to grieve my own death."

Then Grace Scott broke down and started to sob again, the wail of complete and utter loss and emptiness. Tears were streaming down her face now, her nose was running, and she turned to look at him, her eyes beseeching him to do something, anything, to help her.

Kennedy moved slowly across to her and he awkwardly, self-consciously, started to put his arm around her shoulder. She snuggled into him, and he raised his other hand to secure her in a grasp. They sat there gently rocking back and forth in silence for nearly half an hour. At one point, he felt she drifted off to sleep, but then from out of nowhere she whispered, "I've never been able to talk to anyone about this."

She sat up in the sofa, disentangling herself from Kennedy's arms, but still remaining close by his side. Once again she used her hands to clean her face and nose.

"We've only just met, and you're most likely jet-lagging out of your brains, and here I am dumping on you."

"Actually, to be fair, you know, I think I started to dump on you first."

They both tilted back into the sofa.

She finished off her wine. So did Kennedy, but at a much slower speed.

"Okay, that's as much as I can allow myself," she said, slapping both her cheeks with her hands. "I need to get to bed, and so do you. Good night, Inspector."

She replaced the fireguard and staggered off to her corner of the cabin.

Kennedy returned to his bed. It was five o'clock in the morning, and he imagined he wouldn't get to sleep again before daylight arrived.

Half an hour later he was lying in bed still wide awake when there was a knock on his door. He didn't answer. He didn't know what to say. She opened the door anyway.

"Are you still awake?" she asked

"Yes," Kennedy replied, wondering why he was whispering.

"If I lay beside you, could you just hold me, please?"

"Of course," Kennedy replied, and held open the covers for her.

She hopped in beside him. He lay on his back with her head resting in the crook of his arm, and she snuggled up close to him. They lay in silence for about twenty-minutes until the morning light started to invade the room.

Kennedy turned his head slightly to study her face. He hadn't realised how naturally beautiful she looked. As if realising he was looking at her, she said in a voice not much above a whisper, "You know, when you cuddled me out on the sofa, I definitely started to feel a little better, a bit safer, and then when I went into my bedroom I started to feel bad again, but now, like this, I feel safe again."

Grace Scott stuck her thumb in her mouth, and within a few minutes he could hear she'd drifted off to sleep.

CHAPTER FORTY-SIX

When Kennedy woke up sometime later, the sun was up and Grace Scott was gone. The indent her head had made on the opposite pillowcase and her lingering scent were the only proof that he hadn't been dreaming. He could hear music in the living area and he could smell food. He was trying to decide what to do when his door swung open and there she stood, ready to bang two tins together. She looked a million dollars and not at all like a woman who'd been up most of the night crying.

Grace Scott was wearing a knee-length, high-neck, loose fitting, royal blue dress and a pair of ornate cowboy boots. In the daylight, her copper hair looked a more vibrant ginger, and Kennedy could now see her stunning features clearly for the first time. The light shining through her dress betrayed a fine figure of a woman. *Very fine,* Kennedy thought, managing to avert his eyes before being discovered.

"Morning, Inspector," she said. "How's your head?"

"I'm fine, thanks, and yours?"

"I'm feeling good," she replied, and then dropped to a quieter voice, "the best I've felt for some time. Fancy some breakfast?"

"Time for a shower?" Kennedy asked.

"You already smell good, Inspector," she said as she turned on her heels. "Come on out here before it gets cold."

Kennedy made a quick pit stop in the bathroom. He cleaned his teeth, washed his face and pulled on his light-coloured Chinos and a clean Jackson Browne T-shirt from his wheelie suitcase, while the smell of food led him by the nose into the main room.

In the daylight, he could see how majestic the main room of the "log cabin" really was. The cabin, the size of a small gym, boasted a high vaulted roof supported by dramatic wooden beams. Apart from the four bedrooms and en suite bathrooms along one side, the remainder of the space was open plan, with the bedroom block creating a landing for the library cum study above.

The matching rich-coloured wood on the floor, doors, doorframes, and skirting boards gave the room a very warm American Arts and Crafts look. The main room was generously peppered with antiques and artifacts from the Wild West, with lots of Fredrick Remington prints and sculptures of cowboys on horses. There was even an old saddle, restored, heavily polished, and placed on what looked like a small section of a varnished wooden fence.

"Come on," she ordered impatiently, "you can check out the crib later."

Kennedy checked the spread on the dining table. It was still only seven-twenty. Grace Scott must have been up at least an hour getting this all together, meaning she couldn't have slept for more than an hour.

Kennedy helped himself to a large glass of freshly squeezed orange juice, which was a revelation to drink compared to the insipid coloured wallpaper paste that passed for orange juice back in Camden Town.

"Jackson's the man," she declared as she broke two eggs into the pan. "How do you like your eggs?"

"Not too runny, not too hard," Kennedy replied, as he wondered aloud about the Jackson statement.

"Okay, just so you know, and because I'm not going to do this every day for you, when you're in a diner, your order would be eggs over medium."

"Right," Kennedy replied.

"That's one of my favourite albums of all time," she continued, referring to the cover of Jackson Brown's amazing first album on the front of his T-shirt, which ann rea had bought him. She returned to the table with her pan and served his eggs and several rashers of bacon, cooked crispy, exactly the way Kennedy liked them. Then it got even better: Grace took a tray of hash brown potatoes from the oven and carefully placed them on the table in front of him. The only thing missing for the perfect breakfast were some baked beans by the eggs over medium.

They then settled into enjoying their breakfast and discussing their preferences in music. She was into Jackson Browne; Neil Young, who lived very near by; Van Morrison, who used to live not too far away in Mill Valley; Bonnie Raitt; Karen Carpenter; Alison Krauss; Crosby, Stills, & Nash; Huey Lewis and the News; Tom Waits; and

Leonard Cohen, whom she'd seen quite recently. It had been the last concert she and her husband had attended together, in fact. Her favourite movies were *Butch Cassidy and the Sundance Kid; The Paper Chase; Dances with Wolves; Frankie and Johnnie; All The Presidents Men; Gran Torino;* and anything staring Clint Eastwood, Kevin Costner, Al Pacino, or Michelle Pfeiffer. She didn't read a lot of books, and when she did find the time, they were always biographies or true crime books.

Kennedy stuck to the OJ, and Grace drank her coffee. She tried to pour him a cup and then seemed to remember something. "Oh yes, Ed said you'd most likely be a tea man."

Kennedy was amused that his visit had been discussed to some degree in advance.

Kennedy insisted on filling the dishwasher with their breakfast dishes as they continued their conversation. He was surprised by how incredibly comfortable they seemed with each other. He was very happy that there didn't appear to be any hints of anything other than friendship from either side.

"Okay, Inspector," she began, when he'd finished packing the dishwasher and she'd showed him how to start it, "I've got a proposal I want to suggest to you."

"Right," Kennedy smiled, wondering how long her thoughts had been brewing.

"I admit I thought breakfast would be a good meal to present this to you over. So, as I said, don't think you're going to get the works every morning." She paused to smile - to check, he supposed, that she hadn't lost him with her admission. She took a large breath. "Okay, you need help with your investigation, and I'll admit I've been ordered to give it to you. But I've also got my case..."

"Your husband?"

"Yes," she replied, "and I'd like to suggest that we work together on both cases. I mean, if we manage to get Sharenna Chada and Ed allows us to arrest her, then there's going to be a good chunk of time before the extradition paperwork is finalised."

Kennedy thought about it.

"Look, Inspector, it's true I've hit a wall on my investigation into Steve's murder. Ed thinks it was a simple case of Steve being in the

wrong place at the wrong time, and because of this there was no motive, so we're only going to find the guilty party by happenstance. Conviction of the same would be even more difficult."

"Have you any leads at all, any suspicions?" Kennedy asked.

"I'm sorry to say, I don't. I mean I have a few thoughts, but I don't
want you to think that I've any real leads or anything. As my father
keeps saying, it's one of those cases that doesn't hold the heat."

"Sorry?" Kennedy said.

"Well, you know, you can get pans or whatever, and no matter how
much you put it on the fire or on the stove, it just never retains the heat.
You have to keep warming it up. Well, Chief Donohue reckons cases
are the same. Some cases, he claims, hold the heat. You can progress
from one point to another logically and work it out. But, with a case like
my husband's... well, the chief would claim you have to go back to it
each day and heat it up again and start from scratch."

"Right," Kennedy agreed, amused by the comparison. "Have you
got a case file, or whatever you call it here?"

"You mean a murder book?" she said through a smile.

"Is that really what they call it?"

"Only in the movies," she replied, disappearing into her room and
shouting back through to him, "apart from which, the file I have is
barely thick enough to be a dust-jacket."

She reappeared with a foolscap manila file, which she handed over
to him. She continued to look at it once it was in his hands. There was
something very protective about her, as if she were not sure whether or
not to trust him with something so precious to her. This file contained
her last memories and notes on her late husband's life.

As Kennedy studied the contents, she wandered around him nervously. He kept reading; she kept pacing.

Basically, her thirty-eight-year-old husband, Officer Steve Scott, had
been found face down in a local creek. There were traces of chloroform found in his blood, and he had suffered a massive head trauma.
The resultant indentation on the back of his head could have been
made by some smooth object, such as a baseball bat. There was no evidence found on the bank of the creek. The water had been very high,
so if there had been evidence by the body it could have been washed
away. However, the lack of evidence around the body led the author

of the report to believe Officer Steve Scott had been thrown off the bridge and perhaps banged his head on the way down. This was listed as an alternate to the baseball bat theory. Subsequent investigations into Officer Scott, his life, and the cases he'd worked on produced no suspects

"I think I'm up to speed," he said eventually, thinking that from the file, at least, this case certainly held no heat, "so what should we do next?"

She gave a little jump in the air, waving both her arms furiously and then became a little self-conscious.

"You mean… you'll do it? You mean you'll help me?" she said, appearing very emotional, perhaps even close to tears.

Kennedy nodded.

"Well, smack my mamma," she declared and rushed over to Kennedy. "Oops, sorry…" she said as she pulled herself up short, "hugging moment. Would you mind if I hugged you?"

Kennedy opened his arms. Her body felt good through her light dress.

"Okay, now the difficult part," she said as she disentangled herself in a more businesslike manner. "Now I have to go and see if I can get my dad's blessing."

"Do you want me to go along with you?" Kennedy asked.

"Would you mind?" Grace replied, a split second too quickly.

Five minutes later they were on the way back to the cabin, her spirits still high. "That was too easy," she said when they were out of earshot of the main house.

Kennedy was too distracted by the beauty of the landscape to be paying proper attention to Grace. It was nothing short of spectacular, with the sun maybe bleeding out a wee bit too much light from the colour of this picture postcard scene. He fully expected the Cartwrghts of *Bonanza* fame to ride out of the trees in the distance and right up to them. To the right of their cabin, the land sloped down towards a large meadow, which flattened out into a corral busy with frisky horses. Grace kept muttering. Kennedy kept drinking in the rich scenes right under his own nose.

"That was so easy," she repeated, "that if I was cynical, I'd say that he had planned this from the beginning."

"Really?" Kennedy said, desperate to wander down towards the horses.

"Yeah, like even up to the part where he said, 'It's probably better if I take MacCormac off this,'" Grace said, her green eyes semi-closed as she recalled her father's words.

"Were you and Mactoo ever involved?"

She crunched her face into a horrible contortion, mortified at the suggestion, "Nooo way, José!"

"He close to the chief?"

"Not particularly. He was Steve's partner occasionally though," she said. "Okay, so what's our plan?"

"First off, I'd like to have a shower, and then I'd like to go and visit the scene of the crime."

"But we're talking over two months old here, Inspector. There's cold, and then there's freezing, and then there's this."

"Christy, please."

"Okay, Inspector, whichever you prefer," she said. "I'll meet you out in front of the cabin in ten minutes." She sauntered off in the direction of her father's grand house, her cowgirl boots crunching their way through the dry, stony, rock-hard earth.

CHAPTER FORTY-SEVEN

Half Moon Bay on a Saturday morning felt, to Kennedy, like a throwback to the good old days when cowboys would have ridden into town, scattering the tumbleweed to the four winds, tied their horses to the hitching posts outside one of the grand Spanish-style buildings, and nipped into the bar for a wake-u-up special. Unbelievably there was such a bar, San Benito House, or at least it appeared so from the outside. The shops were colourful, maybe a wee bit too touristy. The sidewalks were filled with a mixed aroma of brewing coffee and baked breads very recently drawn from the oven. Kennedy reckoned the majority of people on the sun-drenched streets were outta-towners getting the first tick marked off on their daylong list of things to do and see.

Grace Scott dropped Kennedy off on the corner of Main Street and Kelly Avenue. Pointing Kennedy in the direction of the bridge under which her husband had been found, she said she had some things she needed to attend to down at the station. Perhaps she preferred to find something to do rather than revisit the site that had pretty much ended life as she knew it.

Kennedy nipped into Moon News, the bookstore on the right just before the bridge, to look for a book on the area. The storeowner, a slim sophisticated hippie in her late forties, chatted freely to Kennedy for ten minutes solid, stopping only to sell customers, mostly tourists, newspapers.

"Do you remember an incident a couple of months ago when…" Kennedy ventured when he eventually found a customer-free space.

"You don't mean when Grace's poor husband Steve was found dead, do you?" she said, her face immediately losing what little colour it possessed.

"Yes, actually," Kennedy replied. He hadn't intended to ask any direct questions, but he was happy the conversation was developing naturally. "Do you remember exactly when it happened?"

"Like it was yesterday. You're not a journalist, are you?" she asked, her warmth quickly receding.

"No, no, I just met Grace and her father... I'm Christy Kennedy. I'm a policeman myself, over in London."

"Oh that's okay then," she said, returning to her friendly self. "I'm Jennifer, Jennifer Rainbow," she continued extending her hand. "Actually, it was a Saturday morning. It wasn't as nice a day as today. It had been raining really hard the day before, as it has a habit of doing here occasionally, more frequently than we'd like."

"I've been warned," Kennedy laughed, trying hard to keep the tone conversational.

"I was opening up the bookstore, just before nine o'clock, and I heard a bit of a commotion down by the bridge. I locked the store again and ran down there. Coach, that's Coach Goldberg, he's retired, gets his *New York Times* from me every morning... He's usually my first customer of the day. Anyway, a tourist had spotted the body while taking some photographs over the bridge. Coach came along, just as a crowd was building up. He phoned Chief Donohue and took charge of the area. He used to be a lawyer in Boston, so he knew what to do."

"Was Officer Scott in his uniform?"

"Now that I come to think of it, no, he wasn't,"

"Would Coach Goldberg have known Officer Scott?"

"Normally, yes, but the body," Jennifer Rainbow's voice became shaky and she dropped to a whisper, "was found face down. The upper part of the torso was in the water and the remainder of the body on the bank, but also water-soaked."

Kennedy was worried about asking too many questions and appearing suspicious himself.

"How long have you lived here?" Kennedy asked, deciding to take his questions away from the crime.

"I was born and bred here, Christy. I moved into San Francisco for a while after I got married. My husband worked for BGP..."

When Kennedy's eyebrows shaped a "who?"

"BGP stands for: Bill Graham Presents, the name of the company. Bill Graham was a concert promoter and manager with a great eye for detail. My husband was on the road too much, so we split up; we're still good friends. Bill Graham was killed in a helicopter accident. BGP as a company kept going for a while, but eventually they sold out - to the devil, some say. All the key staff members were tied into the deal and well looked after. My husband in turn looked after me as well in our settlement, and I bought this place."

"It's a great bookstore," Kennedy said, looking around the shelves.

"Yes, it's become harder, but we're doing okay, and it gives me a great social life. Funny thing, well I suppose I really mean sad thing, is that the incident down by the bridge brought a certain type of crowd flocking to Half Moon Bay and, I hate to admit this, but we've done very well since the body was found."

Great, Kennedy thought, *she's opened up the door to the topic again herself.* "I suppose there wouldn't be a lot of crime in Half Moon Bay?"

"Well, not murders. I think I could recall two other murders in recent years."

"A long while ago?"

"A good few years," she replied.

A customer came into the store then. Kennedy browsed "casually" around the shelves for a bit, but within five minutes there were four other customers in the store, so he decided to leave. Perhaps he'd have a chance to talk to her again later in the day. He imagined the bookstore being a bit of a centre for the local community. He figured she got to hear a lot of the local gossip, but she wasn't likely to share it with him on their first meeting.

Kennedy was walking towards the bridge, thinking that it would be a good idea to try to have a chat with Coach Goldberg, when his thoughts were interrupted by a horn honking continuously. Kennedy looked around and couldn't spot anything except for a battered green Ford pick-up truck with a "My Other Gun Is a Winchester" sticker on the bumper. He had to admit he was very disappointed by the cars on the streets of Half Moon Bay. They were all, without exception, the characterless, boring shapes ever present Europe-wide. Kennedy had expected the classic cuts of the Chevrolets, Mustangs, Corvettes, and Thunderbirds, which had all been ever visible in the American movies he loved when he was growing up.

His disappointment lifted the moment he spotted Grace Scott. She had been honking, trying to get his attention, but she'd been blocked in on the other side of the truck with the rifle sticker, which is why Kennedy initially couldn't see her. She'd swapped her patrol car for a black Mustang, the vintage Mustang Kennedy had been longing to see. She did a U-turn and nearly ran over Kennedy as she shouted, "Hop in quickly."

Three silent, white-knuckle minutes later they were out of town, turning left off Main Street on to Higgins Canyon Road and closing in on a traditional white, tongued-and-grooved New England saltbox, complete with freshly painted green window shutters

"This is the James Livingston House," she announced as they pulled up in the gravel car park in a cloud of dust.

"Right, and can I ask who is Livingston and why are we visiting his house?" Kennedy asked.

"James Livingston was a Scot who came to San Francisco during the 1849 Gold Rush. He did well in property, bought 1,162 acres in this neighbourhood, and he and his brother Thomas drove 800 head of cattle from Ohio to the new ranch. James married his Spanish sweetheart in 1852 and built this house with hand-sawn redwood in 1853. These days it's owned by a New Age collective, and I have reason to believe your Miss Chada may be working in there as a masseuse."

CHAPTER FORTY-EIGHT

Kennedy and Grace were sitting in the car park of the Livingston House. Kennedy had been keen to get out and go looking for Miss Chada, but Grace advised him it would be more advantageous to stay where they were. She tuned the radio into a classic country rock station whose programmer seemed trapped in the 1980s.

"This James Livingston fellow, did he make his money illegally?" Kennedy eventually asked, if only to distract himself from the music.

"The chief always says that most great fortunes start with a crime."

Kennedy laughed.

"So what was Livingston's crime?"

"I'm not even sure there was one, but if there was, in those days it would most likely have been smuggling."

"So not prostitution then?" Kennedy asked.

"I can see where you're coming from," she laughed, "but this isn't a brothel; it's a legit establishment. I was going to circulate Miss Chada's photo around the city, but Ed persuaded me to go about it a bit more subtly. So I visited various members of the Chambers of Commerce, the majority of whom are, believe it or not, women. When I visited the station house this morning, there was a message from Pam Johnston, also a Scot. Anyway, a new girl started work yesterday. Pam said the new girl fitted the description of Sharenna Chada, but there was a more definite giveaway on top of that."

"There was?" Kennedy asked, trying to stare a hole through the pure white wall of the house.

"Yes," Grace said, avoiding Kennedy's eyes, "she called herself 'Sharenna Chada.'"

"No!" Kennedy jested.

"Yes," Grace replied, "how brazen is that?"

"Believing you're innocent - not acting the part, becoming the part" Kennedy offered, "is always the best way to play this."

"Well, Pam also said they knew your Miss Chada very well. Apparently she's visited them several times over the last couple of years, and she frequently talked about moving here. According to Pam, Miss Chada is the best masseuse any of them have ever met."

Kennedy opened his mouth to say something. Grace stopped him with, "There's more."

"There is?" he replied, turning around to look at Grace for the first time since they'd arrived.

"Yes. According to Ruth, this Miss Chada of yours is very beautiful and has a body to die for."

Just then a cab pulled up, honked it's horn, and about thirty seconds later the small white front door of the Johnston House opened, and out into the sunlight stepped Miss Chada, the brown of her skin highlighting the starched white of her pristine nurse style top and trousers uniform.

Kennedy went to open the door but forgot his seatbelt. In one quick motion, Grace Scott removed her Half Moon Bay Police baseball cap, shoved it down over Kennedy's head so the peak hid his eyes and secured his seatbelt clip in place with one hand while she slammed her trusty Mustang into gear with the other. She screeched around the car park, took a left and a right on to Main Street and back towards Half Moon Bay.

"I take it that was your Miss Chada?"

"That was her. I need to speak to her, Grace."

"Yes, but not now. You know where she is. She doesn't know you're here; let's keep it that way for now. The chief reckons we've got one shot at getting her extradited, so let's not blow it. Let's get all our wee, as you call them, soldiers lined up neatly in a row."

"But what if she does a runner?"

"Look, Inspector, as far as I can tell, Miss Chada thinks she's got away with it Irish free…"

"Sorry?"

"It was just a private joke Steve and I had. Our name was Scott, so when anyone said someone was getting off Scott-free, we'd always change it to Irish-free."

"O-kay," Kennedy replied in an "I get it" tone.

"Anyway, as I was saying, if she is guilty, your Miss Chada thinks she committed the perfect murder back in London. Maybe, from what you say, she had been planning it for the last year. She figures no one will think it was her because she has the perfect alibi. I believe she's more concerned now about starting off her life again. Do you think there is any chance that Miss Chada was responsible for the deterioration in your back over the last couple of months?"

"In that she was making me dependant on her so I'd unwittingly be her perfect alibi? Oh yes, I definitely think that could be the case."

"I say we let her get on with her new life. Pam has promised to keep an eye on her for me while you and I get our case together, and then Miss Chada will enjoy neither Scottish nor Irish freedom."

Grace turned up the volume of a track, which had just come on the radio.

"Who's this?" Kennedy asked.

"It's Alison Krauss," she answered after a moment. Kennedy couldn't be sure, due to the loud volume of the radio, but he thought he heard her voice break a little with emotion.

"Fancy a bit of sightseeing?" she eventually asked, quite a few seconds after the song eventually finished.

"Actually, if you wouldn't mind, I'd quite like to go back to the bridge and have a look around there."

She looked surprised, pleasantly surprised, and a large smile dissolved the dark cloud which had recently descended over her.

She parked outside Coastside Net, a computer and Internet access shop, and they walked along the sidewalk on the direction of the bridge. Everyone seemed to know her and had the time of day for her. "What can I tell you, Inspector? It's a small town."

Kennedy observed her new quietness as they walked on to the bridge.

The central, vehicle section of the 111-year-old bridge was coated with the traditional tarmac surface and marked by double (no turning or overtaking) yellow lines along the centre. The vehicle section of the bridge was partitioned from the public boardwalk on both sides by a white picket fence, which looked as if it had been reinforced to withstand the impact of a vehicle. The boardwalk was protected from the drop to the creek by a sturdy, solid white fence. Kennedy and Grace Scott turned away from each other.

Kennedy opened the Scott file and studied it as he walked the scene. He looked over the side of the bridge and marvelled at how high and furious the waters below were. It was hard to make out the submerged riverbank line. He wasn't going to get a chance to examine the crime scene in detail until the water had subsided substantially. He crossed to the other side of the bridge, the town side and walked back toward the bridge. Due to the roadside safety-fence at either end of the bridge, he couldn't walk straight across. He looked back into town, down Main Street, which ran straight out of the bridge. Half Moon Bay was now getting a little busier, and Kennedy found it hard to believe that a man had maliciously lost his life in such a gentle, small-town, hippie setting. He turned and looked in the opposite direction where the road curved quickly to the left once clear of the bridge.

At some point, Kennedy became aware that Grace Scott was now studying his every move.

"You were so lost in your own world there I didn't want to disturb you," she eventually said, when she joined him on his side of the bridge. "Several people came and stared at you, and you didn't even seem to notice them, I bet."

Kennedy smiled but didn't comment.

"And another thing," she added as he continued studying the bridge, "I don't know if you're aware of it or not, but the more you concentrate the more you flex the fingers of your right hand." By the time Kennedy looked down at his hand, his fingers had already stopped their furious subconscious flexing.

He stood looking up and down the bridge for a while, and then he went down on his hunkers. He stood up again and walked along the side and leaned over the fence, focusing back on the spot where he knew, from the police report, that Steve Scott had been found face down, head and shoulders in the waters.

Grace kept looking at him, examining his face as if looking for a clue about what he was thinking.

"Okay," Kennedy eventually said, "there's not much more we can do here until the river drops."

"And your thoughts?"

"Well, the report says he was thrown from the bridge…Sorry, Grace, are you okay with this?"

"Yes," she smiled, "I'm fine. To be any good to Steve, I've had to detach myself…you were about to say something about the report."

"The report said Officer Scott was murdered somewhere else and then dumped over the bridge."

"Yes."

"I don't think so," Kennedy said, turning back towards the centre of the road. "That ornate yet effective picket fence would have made it impossible just to drive up and throw the body straight over the edge of the railings into the river. Even if they'd tried, they would have blocked the bridge and risked getting caught. Their other option would have been to park at one end of the bridge, but they would have had to park too far away to avoid the side fences and then carry the body back to throw it over the edge. But it's too public here. Someone would surely have seen the killer or killers. Only an idiot would have risked it. They could have just driven out of town to somewhere more discreet. No, I doubt your..." Kennedy pulled himself up short. "I doubt Officer Scott would have been thrown off the bridge."

"Why did my guys miss this?" she said, as much to herself as to Kennedy.

"You know, a fellow officer goes down, not everyone thinks by the book, Grace," Kennedy said, feeling the scars on his lower abdomen, which proved his point.

Chapter Forty-Nine

They did little else on either case for the remainder of Saturday. Grace gave Kennedy the tourist view of Half Moon Bay and the surrounding area.

During the course of their three-hour trip, she filled in a little of the history of Half Moon Bay. Snugly located in the nook between Pilarcitos Creek and Arroyo Leon Creek, the picturesque town is sheltered beneath the rolling hills. Until the turn of the twentieth century, it was known as Spanishtown, a farming community of Italian and Portuguese specialising in artichokes and Brussels sprouts. Business picked up during prohibition when it became a safe harbour for Canadian rum runners. It was a Bay area suburb, famous for pumpkins plus pseudo-Cape Cod cluster developments along Highway 1. There were amazing "dangerous," Grace claimed - icy thirty-five-feet high surfing waves at Pillar Point. The commercial highlight of the year happened during the third weekend of October when they celebrated the Annual Half Moon Bay Art and Pumpkin Festival, which an average of 250,000 people attended. The normal population was 12,499 plus Neil Young.

She also told Kennedy a little more about herself. Like Kennedy an only child, she also didn't have many friends. After she and Steve Scott met, all they needed was each other. They knew this would wear off, but at the time of his death it still hadn't. Her dad had two brothers: one in politics in the city and an older one who had retired to wine country a few years previously. The chief himself had planned to retire four years ago, but before he'd a chance to his wife, Grace's mother, had died after a long brutal fight with cancer. Grace had never considered anything other than detective work as a career. Now that Steve had passed, her career was her life, rather than just a part of it.

Kennedy found it easy to talk to Grace. She was a person who didn't mind showing her feelings, and he felt they were becoming friends.

Kennedy didn't have many real friends. He liked and got on well with his trusted detective sergeant James Irvine, but when push came to shove, would he consider him to be a friend? He found himself discussing things with Grace that he'd never discussed with anyone before - well, anyone except ann rea. He wondered if this was because he was so far away from home, but even in London he was also still far away from home.

Before Kennedy knew it, they'd reached the end of the day, and Grace insisted on taking him to dinner. She picked her favourite restaurant in the area, Pasta Moon, which was midway between the bridge and Moon News, where Kennedy had started his day. She ordered butternut squash and mascarpone ravioli and persuaded the gastronomically unadventurous, sweet-toothed Kennedy to do likewise. He didn't regret his decision; it was like having a desert for a main course, and the glass of house red hit the spot big time. At the end of the meal, tiredness hit him like an out-of-control juggernaut. While they were waiting for the bill which she insisted on paying, he found he was having great difficultly keeping his eyes open.

They got back to the cabin shortly after eight o'clock. Kennedy opted for a dander to walk off the wine. Grace was "bushed" from the night before and retired immediately. Kennedy strolled down to the corral and stroked a couple of horses though the fence. The friskiest horse was pure white and reminded him of Silver, the Lone Ranger's trusty steed. Kennedy reckoned his fascination with America had probably started with watching the Lone Ranger on television back home in Portrush.

The cabin and the chief's house now in the distance, Kennedy walked on to make sure he had at least a chance of sleeping the whole way through the night. He barely made it back to the cabin. He could quite easily have lain down on the earth, curled up, and gone to sleep. He was so tired his eyes stung as if someone had rubbed them with sandpaper.

As he walked up the incline towards the house and cabin compound, he saw someone leaning into Grace's Mustang. At first he though it was Grace; but then, hearing Kennedy's footsteps, the person stepped back from the vehicle. The shape was too full-figured for Grace or her dad. The light was fading and Kennedy's eyes refused to focus for him, but, from the body language, it appeared that the man was behaving as if he were doing something he shouldn't have been.

"Hello?" Kennedy called out.

The figure ignored Kennedy. *A bad sign.*

Kennedy quickened his step. As he drew closer, he realised the figure was definitely that of a middle-aged, overweight male, unshaven, dressed in a denim shirt, jacket, and jeans and a reversed green baseball hat. The mystery man continued to futter around in the back seat of Grace's car, but when he was still about fifty feet away, Kennedy broke into a run. The man turned on his heels and ran as well.

As Kennedy sped up, he saw that the intruder had something in his right hand. He recognised it was a file, the Steve Scott case file he'd been examining during the day. Kennedy figured he'd easily catch the overweight man, but then what? Kennedy was a visitor; he couldn't just go around beating people up, no matter how strangely they were behaving. From about three feet away, he took two more large strides. Using his right foot, he clipped the stranger's right ankle, which in turn caught on his left foot, and the intruder clumsily tripped himself up. Kennedy came on him too fast, and he too tripped and fell over. The file and contents scattered out around them both.

The stranger uttered several profanities as he scampered to his feet. Kennedy was going for the file as he noticed a flat-back truck race towards them both. In the nick of time, and only just, he managed to roll quickly three times to the right and out of the line of the truck. The stranger, huffing, puffing, and swearing, hopped on to the back of the truck. As it roared away, its grubby white-walled wheels spun up a cloud of dust that covered the entire yard.

Kennedy was winded but not seriously hurt. As he was coming to his senses, he became aware of a vision in white emerging from the cloud of dust.

"Inspector! Inspector!" Grace Scott screamed, ignoring her modesty as her long T-shirt filled with wind and rose. In her excitement she was going too fast and collided with Kennedy, knocking him over again. "Well, smack my mamma," she said as she regained her composure and her modesty. "What the heck was that all about?"

"Someone was trying to steal the file on Steve's case," Kennedy told her, averting his eyes.

"Are you okay?" she asked as she started brushing Kennedy down. She turned him away from her and nudged him to lead the way back into the unlit cabin. "Okay, Inspector," she said once inside, very slowly and deliberately, "I need you to promise not to look. I need you to stare at the floor."

Kennedy did as he was bid.

"Damn and blast, I've only gone and ripped my T-shirt the whole way down the side. Of course it's nothing you've never seen before, but I don't know you well enough to share mine. But don't be getting any ideas. I don't mean that when I get to know you better, I'll share… oh shit, help! I didn't mean I wouldn't, or for that matter that I would… Shit, if Ed sees us like this, you're done for, Inspector. God, shut up, Grace. Right, I'm stopping talking now. This is me not talking, well… about to not talk. Oh God, I can't believe the state I'm in with you, and I barely know you. Well we did sleep together. I'm digging myself into this hole deeper and deeper, aren't I?"

"Ah, that would be a yes," Kennedy replied, still in the dark but highly amused.

"Shit, shut up Grace," she ordered herself again. "Right, eyes closed Inspector. I'm going to my room."

In a few minutes she came running back into the main room of the cabin.

"Can I open my eyes?" Kennedy asked.

"Yes, of course."

She had pulled on a grey sweatshirt with the Grateful Dead skull on the front, and she was still zipping up her jeans, which were so tight she had to hop from foot to foot to accomplish her task.

"Are you okay, Inspector?" she said, rushing over to him and using a master switch to turn on all the lamps in the room.

"I'm fine, Grace, just winded; the only thing that's injured is my pride."

"What happened out there?"

Kennedy recounted his nocturnal adventure, and then for the first time since the strangers had sped off, he realised he still had the file, with its pages untidily spread within, clasped in a vice-like grip in his right hand.

Grace fussed around Kennedy for a few minutes, examining him carefully to make sure he wasn't injured. She seemed genuinely concerned. She was so close to him he could smell her hypnotic blend of scents.

"This means we're… you're on to something," she said, growing more excited by the second. "Don't you see, someone saw us, obviously saw you today down at the bridge. A someone who must have something to hide."

She strode across the room to the drinks area and poured them each a generous glass of wine. She was now animated, charged, prowling bare-footed, her flowing ginger mane looking like a halo of fire.

She's morphed into a completely different woman. Kennedy felt she was giving off a sexual energy for the first time. Equally he knew it had nothing whatsoever to do with him.

"Sometwo. There were two of them," he offered: "the driver and the overweight chap with the green baseball cap who was hoaking around in the back seat of your car."

"Hoaking?"

"Sorry, Ulster word for searching."

"Right. Two of them, but that is also good. Ed always says that if two people are involved in a murder, there is twice the chance of catching the culprits. What do you think? This is good, isn't it? Can we talk about it or are you tired?"

"I'm too wired to sleep at this particular moment," Kennedy replied, as he took the glass of wine offered and followed her towards the empty fireplace. He was about to sit on the stool across from her, but she patted the cushion beside her in the ginormous sofa she'd just flopped into. It seemed to Kennedy that she was happy to live in that corner of the sofa when she was in the cabin. She had her little table for coffee, drinks, food, and the CD, television, and DVD remotes. In front of her and to the right of her side of the sofa, she had a magazine, a paper, and a book rack all within arm's length. It reminded Kennedy of Nealey Dean's quite similar set-up in her Marylebone apartment.

"Inspector, I can't believe it," she began after a generous gulp of wine. "This really is the first sign, break, whatever, since Steve was murdered. There's been absolutely zero before now. I know Ed loves me, but I've been so obsessed with this, I'm sure he has been thinking I'd lost it. The more people churned out the old cliché about Steve being in the wrong place at the wrong time, the more it drove me on."

Two large glasses of wine later, Kennedy's eyes started to feel heavy again. He'd fully intended to go through Steve's file again that night and see what the thieves had been after, but though the spirit had been willing, the flesh had been weak. They bid their goodnights and retired to their rooms.

Just as Kennedy was starting to doze off, while thinking of Grace and the last twenty-four hours, there was a knock on his door.

"You still awake, Inspector?"

"Barely," Kennedy muttered.

"Would you just hold me again tonight? Last night was so comforting. Today was a great day. I don't want to cry again. I really…"

"You're very welcome," Kennedy offered, and as he opened one eye he noticed she'd changed back into a long white T-shirt again. He held the cover up for her and she jumped in.

This time she spooned Kennedy, and he felt she snuggled up much closer to him than on the previous night. He was thankful that his back was towards her, since this way no one but himself was going to be aware of the potentially embarrassing development.

CHAPTER FIFTY

Kennedy woke to what sounded like loudly crackling flames either on the other side of the ceiling of his bedroom or just outside the window. He lay listening to the sound for a minute. If it was a fire, why hadn't he smelled any smoke? Doctor Taylor had once informed him that one of the flaws of the human body was that we can't smell when we're sleeping. Apparently it would interfere with our sleep. Kennedy was sure the crackling was getting louder. He suddenly had a vision of the overweight, denim-clad man returning in the night to torch the cabin to ensure Steve Scott's file was destroyed one way or another.

Grace Scott was still sleeping peacefully, sleeping contentedly with her thumb securely in her mouth. Kennedy slowly and carefully slipped out of the bed, picked up his clothes and, as quietly as possible, opened the bedroom door. He quickly and carefully closed the door behind him.

He pulled on his chinos, blue shirt, and socks. Now the sound was under the main roof. He was convinced the noise of the fire above was growing louder. He decided it was best not to open the main door in case the flames were contained just outside the door. There was no tell-tale smoke in the cabin, so, worst case scenario, he felt he could, if it was necessary, save Grace and avoid the wrath of Chief Ed Donohue.

It was still only five-fifty, but it looked a lot darker than it had been the previous morning when they'd just been turning in. As he pulled the drapes open at the far end of the main room, he realised the fire that he was going to bravely save Grace from was in fact a furious cloud-burst. The torrential rain was falling so heavily that he could barely see the corral at the foot of the meadow, let alone the tall trees that rose up with the hills at the far side. Rain or no rain, it was a glorious scene. Kennedy pulled over a chair in front of the panoramic window and just sat there contently. There was going to be no chance of being able to examine the banks of Pilarcitos Creek today either.

Then the clouds broke, and the new sun came shining through and fully removed the darkness. The transformation in the scenery was nothing short of spectacular. The hills, with their thick, tree-lined foliage wore now fully in view and looked visibly refreshed from their recent shower. Those proud trees lived a life of luxury. They remained static while everything was brought to them: heat, light, water, food, and even the deposits he was sure the trees would avoid if they possibly could.

Kennedy sat for another thirty minutes, transfixed by the transformation from the need for shelter from wintry gloom to summer enticement for the outdoors. He loved this part of the day; when it was young, fresh, and unspoilt. He fancied a walk, and ten minutes later he was down as far as where the line of trees bordered the fields beyond the corral. The air felt unused and invigorating, and even in spite of the recent vicious showers, it still smelled like America.

From out of nowhere, Sharenna Chada came into his mind and seriously disturbed his peaceful thoughts. Could Grace be right? Could Miss Chada really have thought she'd gotten away with the murder of Patrick Mylan and was now in Half Moon Bay settling down into the next part of her life? He knew Grace and her father were right; he did need to have a cast-iron case before he confronted her. Kennedy was pretty certain it was Miss Chada, mainly due to the phone records, using him as an alibi, and her skipping town. He had honed in on the motive, and all that needed to be resolved now was the how.

He calculated it was early Sunday afternoon in the UK, and DS James Irvine would soon continue the London side of the investigation by interviewing Maggie Littlewood again first thing tomorrow morning. Kennedy regretted not pushing Maggie further when he'd interviewed her. Come to that, Rodney Stuart had obviously known much more than he admitted. But only with the advantage of hindsight did Kennedy know what questions Mylan's longest friend and accountant should have been asked. Even Banks wasn't at all reluctant to give up information on Sharenna Chada when Kennedy had *eventually* quizzed him about it. "Yes," Kennedy admitted, to himself and the trees, aloud, "while questioning it always pays dividends to go on fishing expeditions." By the time Kennedy contacted London, he hoped to be able to read the details of Irvine's current interview with Maggie.

Irvine had set Kennedy up with an idiot-proof account with GoTo-
MyPC, where he, Kennedy, could sign into his North Bridge House
computer from anywhere in the world. He'd yet to try it out, and
Kennedy had clocked that the Coastside Net store was probably the
most private route for him to keep contact with North Bridge House.

By this point, Kennedy realised he was lost. He thought about it for
a while and decided he was thoroughly enjoying the feeling. Eventually
he came across a river.

"No," he corrected himself out loud, "this is a creek."

The recent downpour had filled the creek to dangerous levels, and
the fast-flowing waters looked very vicious. He thought this must probably be the border of the chief's land, so he backtracked a bit and then
followed the slope of the hill back down again to the fields just beyond
the corral.

It was now seven o'clock, and it was his turn to make breakfast, so
he strolled back to the cabin, only to meet the chief returning from
somewhere.

"Early morning stroll, Christy?"

"Yeah. It's amazing here. Unbelievable. I got lost in the trees for a
while." Kennedy was worried that his inability to string a sentence together was making him sound too much like a hippie.

"Do you ride?"

"Sadly not, Chief," Kennedy replied.

"You should get Grace to take you out on a trail on one of the quiet
horses. She's been on horses since she was six. She's a brilliant horse-
woman; she'll look after you well."

Kennedy panicked at Grace's name. What if the chief went in and
found her in Kennedy's bed! No amount of explanation would suffice.

"Is Grace up yet?"

"She wasn't up when I came out for a walk," Kennedy replied, picking his words carefully.

"Any progress? I heard you were down by the bridge yesterday?"

"A few observations, but nothing solid yet," Kennedy replied. He
was having bizarre flashes of being in a cowboy movie and having a
conversation with Randolph Scott.

"Well, London speaks very highly of you, and hopefully Grace will
be satisfied when you conclude your investigation."

"Chief, do you know what Officer Scott was working on when he died?"

"Officer MacCormac has already rechecked all those avenues for the city police; you should talk to him."

"So there's absolutely nothing suspicious there?"

Chief Ed Donohue broke into a hearty laugh. "Look, Christy, we're not LA or New York here. Heck, we're not even San Francisco, We don't really get a lot of major crimes going on. We're more peace-keepers, dispute settlers, a stepping stone on the career paths for some of our more ambitious officers. We're plagued with robberies, domestics, disturbance of the peace, but for the most part that's all we get. Recently, it's taking all of our resources to prevent teenagers from beating the living daylights out of each other. It's the girls who are the worst offenders."

Kennedy only nodded.

"You're not shocked?"

"I'm afraid it's the new culture," Kennedy replied.

"Okay," the chief said, moving on and now acting a little self-conscious, "Grace came to see me yesterday and, ah… Christy, I have to tell you, you don't know how wonderful you're making her feel by taking her seriously. I have to tell you I, ah …feel very good about that."

Kennedy wondered how Randolph Scott… how good the chief would feel about Kennedy if he knew that his daughter and the Ulster detective had shared the same bed for the previous two nights.

The chief, hands deep in pockets, tried to free a stubborn stone from the path way beneath them. Kennedy felt their chat was over.

"So, how are you sleeping?"

"Not bad last night," Kennedy replied, hoping he wasn't blushing.

"What are you up to today?"

"Chief Nolan has invited me over to his place for lunch."

"MacCormac mentioned that. He was worried he'd have to take you over, but Grace saved his bacon by volunteering to chauffeur you instead." The chief reached over and shook Kennedy's hand. "Right, you have a great day, and if I don't see you later, I'll see you down in Kelly Street tomorrow morning."

As the chief walked away, Kennedy started to worry about his progress. Here he was, at great expense to Camden Town CID, in America for two nights already and venturing into his third day with nothing to show. He knew his Ulster upbringing and work ethic were at the root of his guilt. He knew how he could quickly kick the guilt into touch for the moment: he'd prepare breakfast for Grace Scott.

Kennedy noticed that even though she'd prepared the full works for him yesterday, Grace had only taken scrambled egg on rye toast herself, so twenty minutes later he walked back into his bedroom with a tray bearing his special recipe for scrambled eggs, toast, OJ, and coffee. He remembered she liked her coffee strong and black.

"Oh, Inspector, a girl could get used to this," she said sleepily.

She said she'd been woken by Kennedy and her dad talking outside the window next to the bed. She too had been worried that the chief would come in and discover her in Kennedy's bed. Not so worried that she had scampered back to her own bedroom though, Kennedy noted.

"I drifted back off to sleep again," she explained, as if reading Kennedy's mind. Then mid first bite, she continued, "Oh my goodness, not just a pretty accent. Where'd you ever learn to make scrambled eggs like these?"

"My dad," Kennedy admitted. "Just melt butter in a pot and crack the eggs into the butter and mix, but be careful when you take them away from the heat; if anything, you should be too early and let the heat of the pot do the final cooking."

"No milk?"

"No milk."

"Listen to us would you? Domesticated or what?" she said as she laughed. She paused from eating her eggs to catch her fiery hair in a long tail and expertly restrained it by a colourful elastic band she had around her wrist.

Kennedy looked at Grace Scott, sitting up in his bed, smiling but still with a hint of that ever-present sadness not too far away. The last thing he thought about was domestication. She was so attractive it was unbearable.

"I'll get my eggs before they go cold," he said sheepishly as he departed the room.

"Good," she said after him, "I'll just luxuriate here before I have my shower. We should head over to Chief Nolan about eleven-thirty. You don't mind if I stay in your bed do you?"

"Not at all," Kennedy said, remembering that technically, as Ed Donohue's daughter, it was more her bed than his anyway. "Can I get you anything else?"

"What time is it?" she called out to him.

"Just before eight."

"Oh good, you wouldn't do me a big favour, would you, after you've had your breakfast? Would you nip over to the front porch of the main house? *The San Francisco Chronicle* and *The New York Times* will have been delivered there. Mine will be the two left on the swing seat. I love nothing more than lying in bed reading the Sunday papers."

"No problem, give me a couple of minutes."

Five minutes later Kennedy had finished his breakfast and done his chore. Grace had obviously nipped into her bedroom and put on a red sweatshirt and black sweat pants and was now lying on top of the bed awaiting her papers.

Kennedy couldn't believe the size of the papers. He imagined a fair sized tree or two from Donohue's forest would have to have been felled and pulped just to supply the pages under his arm. She patted for him to sit on the bed.

"New York or San Francisco?" she asked.

"San Francisco," Kennedy said, thinking local knowledge would be better for him.

"Okay, so will you do me a favour, Inspector? What I love to do..." Her voice went quiet and broke slightly. "What I miss so much doing every Sunday morning is reading the papers... with... Steve and then talking about each other's papers when we went out for a drive. I miss our ritual so much. I miss him..."

Her voice grew stronger towards the end of her sentence.

"Anything to save me reading two papers this size," Kennedy said.

"Go and get your tea or OJ and join me."

By the time Kennedy had returned with his OJ and fresh toast, she'd turned on the bedside radio. It was tuned to a country station. Not the purveyors of Kennedy's favourite kind of music, or so he thought. However he did find himself enjoying track after track. Occasionally she would put down her ever-spreading pages to stop to listen to a particular song.

Before he knew it, a couple of hours had passed with nothing more than a wee giggle here or a "damn fool" here, or "well, smack my mamma" there or an "oh" nearly absolutely everywhere. Kennedy's comments were all restricted to "hmph."

Kennedy noticed Grace grimaced when a song came on that started with what sounded like someone hitting a biscuit tin. Before the vocals started, he recognised it from the song on the radio she was moved by on the previous day. The vocal started off with what sounded like one of those extremely tight-trousered, American, male, rock singers soulfully delivering a plaintive lyric:

> *"I've spent my life looking for you*
> *And finding my way wasn't easy to do*
> *But I knew there was you all the while*
> *And it's been worth every mile*
> *So lay down beside me*
> *Love me and hide me*
> *And kiss all the hurting*
> *Of this world away*
> *Hold me so close*
> *That I feel your heart beat*
> *And don't ever wander away"*

Then from out of nowhere, and beautifully low-key at first, came a female voice so pure it stabbed you right in the heart as she delivered:

> *"Mornings and evenings all were the same*
> *There was no music till I heard your name*
> *I knew when I saw you smile*
> *And now I can rest for a while*
> *So lay down beside me*
> *Love me and hide me*
> *And kiss all the hurting*
> *Of this world away*
> *Hold me so close*
> *That I feel your heart beat*
> *And don't ever wander away"*

Kennedy had never *ever* heard a line delivered with such devastating effect as when this girl sang:

I knew when I saw you smile.

He didn't dare look at Grace from then on for fear she would see his eyes were welling up. He needn't have worried; tears were literally streaming freefall down her cheeks.

The DJ with the rich deep American voice announced that they had just been listening to, or, Kennedy would more accurately claim, been destroyed by, Alison Krauss duetting with John Waite on a song called "Lay Down Beside Me," a song, the DJ claimed, perfectly written by Don Williams.

Later when they were driving into San Francisco, Grace admitted that she'd never been so affected by the track before.

"It was weird though, Inspector. Although I was bawling my eyes out, I wasn't feeling bad; it was just such a joyful experience."

It turns out that Alison and John Waite were partners, which might have accounted for why the performance was so highly charged.

"Do you have a song that does that to you, Inspector - you know, gets under your skin?"

Kennedy thought about this for a while before saying, "Well, I have this old 8-track at home..."

"Back up there, Inspector. What exactly is an 8-track?"

"Oh I always thought they were more popular in America?"

"Blind spot for me I'm afraid," she admitted.

"It's kinda a large cassette. They were in use in the seventies, and the magic of them was that you don't have to turn it over like a real cassette. We're talking way before CDs, and then probably CD development came along, and the good old 8-track didn't really take off,"

"Now there's a surprise," she muttered.

"Anyway, I have an 8-track by Planxty, an Irish traditional band, and it's got this song on it called 'Thousands Are Sailing.' I mean, I haven't been able to listen to it in years because they don't make eight track players any more. But I remember it as being a really beautiful song..."

"I think you may be viewing the song through rose-coloured glasses," Grace said, cutting him off. "That's very depressing, Inspector. You're making me wish I'd never asked."

"Yeah, you're right," Kennedy admitted, "your song was probably better."

Much and all as Kennedy and Grace Scott had enjoyed the song, they played safe on the journey into San Francisco in that she retuned the radio from the country station KBWF (The Wolf) to Free FM, a local talk radio. They enjoyed quite a bit of banter between themselves as a result of the input from some of the callers into the station. Kennedy came to the conclusion that it might be San Francisco, but it was just like London or Camden Town in that people liked to bitch and moan about: the price of gas; various taxes; disappointment in a particular team's performance; drug dealers; the insolence of youth; the loss of love; annoyance at their favourite novice artist being voted off a talent show; and the chutzpah of Lady Mucca, Heather Mills McCartney, continuing to covet the spotlight. Thankfully she seemed to be succeeding less and less.

San Francisco just seemed to go on and on. That's not to say he didn't enjoy the journey. It was a glorious June day with the sun shining brightly, he was in great company and enjoying the chat, so much so that the hour flew by. Before he knew it, they were pulling into the driveway of a magnificent townhouse on Vallejo Street in Pacific Heights. Chief Don Nolan was out in the driveway warmly welcoming them both before Grace had even a chance to turn off the ignition.

Madeira, his wife, greeted them both like they were family.

"Please call me Maddee," she said while still hugging Kennedy. "How's your Uncle Harry?"

"He's grand," Kennedy said, realising that although he was not exactly hamming up his Ulsterness, he was using an "Orish" phrase he'd never use at home. He'd noticed himself doing it a few times with Grace.

"This is an incredible house, Chief," Kennedy said.

"Yeah, Maddee's family have lived here for a few generations now," he replied, "I'd hate to try to buy a house in this neighbourhood now though."

Maddee Nolan wore a headscarf, presumably to protect her hair, face, and neck from the hot midday sun. The overall effect with her dark green, high-neck dress and her scarf meticulously wrapped around her neck and over her crown was so sophisticated it spotlighted her classic looks. There's something very refined, very Audrey Hepburn about a woman wearing a headscarf that way. In fact here was a lot Audrey Hepburn in Mrs Madeira Nolan.

Maddee Nolan was impish and teasing as well; from the moment out in the driveway she kept telling Kennedy and Grace Scott, whom she knew, that they were such a beautiful couple. Kennedy seemed more awkward about Maddee's comments than Grace.

Maddee acted very pleased when Kennedy selected an OJ as his pre-lunch drink. Not a word was said, but she nodded to herself approvingly as Kennedy refused offers of something stronger. Also attending the lunch were the chief and Maddee's three sons, their two wives, and a girlfriend, plus two daughters - one of whom was a twin to the youngest son - and their two husbands. There were various children running around as well, but as the adults sat down to lunch all the children seemed to mysteriously disappear.

As they took their places at the table, it was the chief's turn to give a private nod of approval when Kennedy opted for red wine. Kennedy was happy being seated beside Grace, at Maddee's end of the table. The chat generally centred around Ulster. The chief's children seemed greatly amused by, and interested in, tales of this mystery man, Uncle Harry, whom they'd obviously heard mentioned throughout their lives. They seemed very happy to be able to quiz someone who actually knew the famous Harry Kennedy. According to the youngest daughter, Collette, her mum, when annoyed with her dad, would always say, "Oh I do wish I'd married into the Kennedy clan." Then Chief Nolan would protest that Harry Kennedy had nothing whatsoever to do with, and certainly wasn't related to, Boston's old Joe Kennedy's branch of the family.

Kennedy couldn't help eating too much; the food was delicious, and Maddee kept heaping more on his plate. Afterwards, Grace persuaded him to go for a walk to help his digestion. They headed off up Vallejo Street, took a very quick right into Gough Street, and headed down towards the stunning San Francisco Bay. To Kennedy it was like walking along familiar streets, thanks entirely to his lifelong fascination with American movies. By the time they returned to the Nolan house just before four o'clock, there were a lot more vehicles parked around the house and the nearby multi-storey apartment block.

"They're showing you off, Inspector," Grace whispered, pulling him closer with their interlinked arms.

"Maddee's a wonderful woman, isn't she?"

"You were wondering what would have happened if she'd married your Uncle Harry, weren't you."

"Yes," Kennedy admitted, surprised.

"I saw it in your eyes."

It turned out that Chief Don Nolan had invited most of his force and their partners and, consequently, their kids to the after-lunch drinks party.

Maddee paraded Kennedy around introducing him to everyone. At one point, he and Grace got split up and the chief sidled up to Kennedy and invited him to go outside where the lads were shooting a few hoops.

Kennedy was transfixed by the way the chief kept bouncing the ball in the shape of a V. He looked like he was having trouble getting the basketball to do his bidding.

"Any progress on your Camden Town murder case?" the chief asked as he took a shot from what looked like an impossible distance to Kennedy. The ball barely touched the net on its way through. Kennedy could only stand, stare, and marvel.

"Well, Grace found out where Miss Chada's working, and we're monitoring that. Hopefully by tomorrow morning I'll have more information on the case from London."

"Chief Donohue tells me you're also helping Grace look into her husband's murder," the chief continued, passing the ball to Kennedy.

"Well, I figured I could look at it. Of course I'm not suggesting I'll find something the locals might have missed," Kennedy said, spending too much time trying to take aim with the ball.

"Don't aim," Chief Nolan ordered. "Bounce the ball - bounce, bounce."

Kennedy did as ordered. The ball seemed a bit sluggish.

"That's better," the chief continued in his coaching. "Now keep bouncing, don't look at the ball, keep looking at the net, and when you feel it, when you feel comfortable with the ball, take a shot."

Kennedy did as coached, and there was no one more shocked than he when the ball, after a severe bit of rattling around the hoop, eventually dropped through.

The chief retrieved the ball, caught it mid bounce and squeezed it between his two large hands.

"Ah, I thought so; it's got a slow leak. It'll be okay for today though; we'll get another hour of it at least. Now where was I? Oh yes. Don't worry about pulling anyone's nose out of joint by interfering in the Scott case. Because it was a homicide, It was the city police who looked into it. They couldn't find anything, so they were pulled off It to attend to all the other craziness of our wonderful city. So a different set of eyes, a different mind to consider the details would be greatly appreciated. Apart from which, Edward tells me your willingness to look at the case has taken Grace out of herself again. You know this is the first time she's been out since Steve died?"

"I didn't," Kennedy admitted. He spotted Grace at the other side of the garden, being hit on by a rubber man who was unsubtly pawing her.

"Excuse me, Chief," Kennedy said, as he walked off towards Grace.

Grace clocked Kennedy and nodded to him not to interfere.

"Come on, Chip," she was hissing, under her breath, "what about Joan and the kids? You're better than this."

"Joan pulled up the drawbridge ages ago, and you're without a man. Come on, Gracie."

She backed Chip towards the hedge bordering the garden. Grace put her left hand on Chip's cheek in a outwardly compassionate manner. Anyone who was looking on would focus on this. Meanwhile, grabbing a handful of Chip's goolies with her other hand, she squeezed until Chip seemed to want to buckle at the knees and sink to the lawn in sheer agony. Refusing to let him drop, she squeezed until tears were streaming down his face.

"Okay, Chip?" she said, still retaining her gentle compassionate tone, "have we had enough?"

Chip nodded his head furiously in an attempt at "Yes!"

Grace then moved her left hand from the side of Chips face, placed it smack bang centre on his nose and, as she let go of his goolies, shoved with all her might, sending him sprawling into the thick of the hedge.

To the rest of the party crowd, it just looked as if someone had had too much to drink and had fallen over. But Kennedy doubted good old Chip was ever going to be a proper man again.

Nothing seemed to be dampening Grace's spirits though. On the way back to Half Moon Bay, she was quite magnanimous about Chip.

"You know, our officers, they go out in the morning and they never know if they're going to catch a bullet before the end of their shift, so most of the ones who are honest about it try to pull like it might be their last time."

They reached the Donohue ranch shortly after ten.

As they were going through the front door to the cabin, Chief Donohue came out of his house and called after them, "You two seem to have had a nice day. Fancy a nightcap?"

Kennedy shied away, claiming he wanted to make an early start. Grace, after a moment, said, "I'll take you up on your offer, Chief. Make mine an Irish coffee. Let me grab a jacket and I'll be over in two minutes."

When they were in the cabin, she whispered, "Listen, Inspector, I won't be long, but I've a favour to ask."

"Okay."

"Can I sleep in your arms again tonight, please?"

"That's… perfectly… you know, I'm fine with that."

"It'll be the last night I promise," she said through a smile, grabbing a brown leather jacket from the back of the door and heading off towards her father's house.

CHAPTER FIFTY-ONE

Monday morning saw Grace up first and a full breakfast already prepared for Kennedy.

"Okay, what's our plan of attack today?" Grace asked, when they were clearing the dishes into the dishwasher.

"First off, I need to check my messages from London. I thought I could do it at Coastside Net."

"You can use my computer at the station house," she said.

"No, I need you on that one going through Officer Scott's last few cases."

"I'm sure the chief could set you up with a system of your own."

"I'll be fine; I'd prefer to use Coastside Net."

"No problem," Grace said.

"Then I'd like us to meet up and interview Officer Mactoo and then Coach Goldberg," Kennedy said, mentally working his way through his list, "and then I've a bit of research to do on my Camden Town case."

"You've come up with something on that too?" Grace asked, looking impressed.

"Something Chief Nolan said to me, but I need to do some serious checking," Kennedy replied, sounding a wee bit impatient now. "Right so, if you'll go put on your uniform…"

"That was the reason I took up the chief's offer for a nightcap last night. As I'll be working with a New Scotland Yard inspector for a few days, I was checking if it would be okay to dump my uniform for now. He agreed, as long as we travelled in the patrol car."

Today, with her checked shirt over a white T-shirt, denim jeans, leather boots, and a leather jacket in her hand, she looked more cowgirl than policewoman. Her one concession to the Half Moon Bay Police Department was her trusty baseball cap proudly bearing their crest.

Grace Scott dropped Kennedy at Coastside Net at eight-thirty.

Kennedy figured it was four-thirty in the afternoon in Camden Town, still time to sign on, pick up messages, and then nip down to Kelly Street station house to call James Irvine. One slight problem; Coastside Net didn't actually open until nine o'clock.

Earlier on the way down Main Street with Grace, he'd noticed a growing crowd of men at a small space known as Mac Dutra Park, at the junction with Kelly Avenue. They were waiting for an infrequent supply of pick-up trucks that would pull up by the pavement on Main Street to, Kennedy assumed, take them off to do some casual, cash only work. He stared at all the faces for as long as was socially acceptable, hoping to see the overweight intruder with the green baseball cap from the other night, but no luck.

At eight fifty-seven, he headed back towards Coastside Net. They still weren't open. Kennedy walked on up Main Street as far as the bridge under which Steve Scott's body had been found. The earth on the bank looked more solid today. He would have a closer look later.

He pulled some dollars from a hole in the wall using his credit card. He liked the feel and look of the dollars. There was something reassuring about having the same notes in your pockets as the cowboys did, back in their day.

He considered going to visit Jennifer Rainbow at Moon News, but noticed a white van with the legend Coastside Net displayed on the side pull up outside the Internet store.

Five minutes later, Kennedy was up, albeit on fawn-like legs, on the World Wide Web. The reason he didn't want to use a computer down at the Half Moon Bay police department on Kelly Avenue was because, still a novice in this arena, he found he got on much better without people looking over his shoulder. There was a pile of junk, several New Scotland Yard circulars, and messages from DS James Irvine, the Home Secretary's office, DC King, and even one from ann rea.

DS James Irvine had interviewed Maggie Littlewood in the company of her husband Roger and, according to DS Irvine, Maggie - prompted by Roger - admitted that not only did she "introduce" - "introduce" was apparently the word Maggie used to describe her pimping, posh pimping but pimping nonetheless - Miss Chada and Miss Chloe Simmons to Patrick Mylan. She had also introduced him to the pervious concubine before Miss Chada, who was called Gina Webb, and before that Patrick Mylan's woman was the very same

Maggie Littlewood herself. Roger's theory was that when Patrick "outgrew" Maggie, which happened just before Roger and Maggie met, she continued to love him through the girls she procured for him. Irvine's theory was Maggie was doing it to pay off her substantial gambling debts.

Kennedy thought it wasn't the first time in a case that people like Maggie tried to head the police off at the pass by giving them relatively harmless information like, in this case, the tale about her bookie friend, in the hope of hiding a bigger secret. Maggie could have saved everyone a lot of time. Although it wouldn't have solved the case immediately, it would have helped Kennedy and his team rule out a lot of unimportant information.

Maggie Littlewood also admitted to Irvine that she had been very happy when Mylan had moved on from Chada to Simmons, claiming that Miss Chada was obsessive and appeared to be gaining some kind of hold over Patrick Mylan.

The email from the energetic and resourceful DC Dot King advised Kennedy that she'd tracked Gina Webb, now Mrs Gina Perfect, down to an address in the suburbs of Chicago, where she'd been living for the last ten years, happily married and bringing up a family.

Dot King also advised Kennedy that ann rea had been on to North Bridge House wanting to know how to get a message to Kennedy. King had suggested email would be the best route, and assuring her it would be completely private. The Camden Town journalist also wanted to know when Kennedy would be back in Camden Town. King, honestly, told Miss rea she didn't know.

The email from the Home Secretary's office was friendly, asking Kennedy how he was getting on with his investigation, giving him more information on the extradition process and requesting that Kennedy keep them in the loop.

Kennedy had saved ann rea's email until last.

"Hi, Kennedy," she started. "I hear you're in the USA, you always said you wanted to do that. Anyway I recently went to see the Blue Nile perform at Somerset House, and when I got home I wrote this to you. It's not really a letter, in that I need or want a reply. Think of it more as a journal page I wanted to share with you. I needed to get it to you before I lost my bottle. I think the note says things, important things I've not been able to say. It's helped me come to terms with us.

I've scanned the actual page and attached it - here's hoping you've
managed to master the art of opening attachments.

That's all."

Kennedy opened the attachment. Not only could he open it but he
also printed off a copy for himself. He folded the copy, put it in his
pocket, paid his very reasonable bill to Steve and headed out into the
hot Half Moon Bay morning.

He wandered back down Main Street into the town and found a
seat on a street bench opposite the Spanish style Half Moon Bay Inn.
Although the sun was hot, there was a pleasant breeze. He opened the
copy of ann rea's email and read:

> *Christy, Sunday past, I forced myself to go to the Blue Nile Con-*
> *cert at Somerset House. It was just so spiritual. He (pb) opened his*
> *mouth and I almost melted, it was like the perfect concert, the per-*
> *fect final concert to see and I'd quite happily stop doing everything*
> *after being allowed to experience that. I thought of you Christy in*
> *every word he sang. When I heard him sing I knew we were all over;*
> *I knew you had to be the last true love of my life. Equally I knew and*
> *accepted that due to my lack of trust or belief in what we had I'd shat-*
> *tered something fragile, precious and although I was afforded enough*
> *of an insight into what we had, I knew we could never get it back. The*
> *thing that scares me most about love Christy is how close success and*
> *failure are. As Paul Buchanan sang not so much about lost love, as*
> *about losing the ability to love, you knew he knew that happiness*
> *was not always something to be desired; sometimes there's just too*
> *great a price to pay. I know I'm waffling but during the concert all my*
> *thoughts were collected in perfect order and I could see this flawed*
> *perfection that he sang about - wipe the tears from your face - and I*
> *really experienced something special. But then... you come out of*
> *the concerts and you feel your jeans are too tight; you feel you should*
> *have washed your hair before you left home; the first two buses are*
> *packed so full you can't even get on, even to stand; someone hits on*
> *you and you seriously wonder do these people really believe that*
> *anyone with even half a brain will react to them; the taxi driver does-*
> *n't want to take you because he's going in the opposite direction and*
> *then it rained and rained and rained and I just sat down on someone's*
> *doorsteps and cried and do you know why I cried Christy? I cried*

*because I didn't have you to come home to. With you to come home
to all of the above is just the daily crap that you brush out of your way.
Without you to come home to all of the above becomes your life, my
life. I swear to you I couldn't stop crying and then this man with grey
hair and wearing a leather jacket came up to me. He was very gentle,
quietly spoken with a Scottish accent and he sat down beside me. He
didn't say anything obvious like, 'it's going to be okay.' I think he actually said, "I wonder what Wayne Rooney feels when he misses an
open goal?" He just sat with me and stayed with me until I stopped
crying. When I stopped crying he helped me up and he whistled at the
top of his lungs until he found a cab that would stop for him and then
he put me in it and he waited until I gave the driver the instructions
and when he was satisfied that the driver was going to take me home
without complaint he closed the door. But as he closed the door we
looked each other in the eye for the first time since we met. And he
nodded a gentle, "I know." That was it, just, "I know." And as he
closed the door and the cab pulled away from the pavement I realised
it was Paul Buchanan. I turned around and looked out the back window of the cab just in time to see him pull up the collar of his coat and
head off into the crowd and the wind and the rain.*

Kennedy reread her words two more times and realised why she'd
been so desperate to get a copy to him. Her note, the page from her
journal, or whatever it was, really summed up what they had and,
equally, what they didn't have. Without actually saying it, she'd spelled
out that there was no sense in trying to get back to what they had and
she put the blame firmly at her own door step.

He felt a weird sensation; he felt so far away from both Camden
Town and ann rea. But he acknowledged he didn't feel sad. He found
himself more preoccupied by what was ahead of him rather than what
was behind him. He realised that he and ann rea probably started to
deal with their break-up from the moment they got together, which was
probably why it took so long to get it together in the first place.

Kennedy had always figured men and women say more about
themselves by what they do rather than by what they say.

When Kennedy met up with Grace ten minutes later in the Half
Moon Bay station house, he didn't tell Grace about the note from ann
rea. He tried to work out what that said about himself.

Chapter Fifty-Two

"Good, you're here," Grace said enthusiastically when she spotted him walking into the reception area of the station house. "Mactoo is waiting for us, and then we're treating Coach Goldberg to an early lunch."

"Now tell me this," Mactoo said by way of greeting Kennedy, "how come every time you guys go to the elections, you always, but always, pick the wrong guy, and the only time you didn't pick the wrong guy was when you picked a woman?"

"Why don't you ask me one on cricket," Kennedy suggested.

"Funny you should bring that up," Mactoo replied, looking as if he were moving in for the kill.

"Kevin, for heaven's sake, can we get on with this *please*?" Grace pleaded.

"Sorry, Officer Scott," Mactoo backtracked. "Please fire away with your questions, Inspector Christopher Kennedy."

"Christopher is it?" Grace said, raising her eyebrows. Kennedy sank his head, "Sorry, sorry Inspector, but you have to admit it's a funny name."

"How long had you known Officer Steve Scott?" Kennedy asked.

"Since we were kids." When neither Kennedy nor Grace stopped him he kept talking. "Okay, there were three of us, three buddies, that's Steve Scott, Don Miller and me, and we were all the same age. When we were nine we used to go and search for these beautiful Japanese glass floats. Don Miller's mother collected these floats, which were used to buoy fishing nets. Anyway, for some reason or other these glass floats, some very big and like balls and some smaller and oblong like large sausages, would always float in with the first spring shower. So we'd all take a day off school and go to the water over at Princeton, and on the way we'd stop at the bakery in Half Moon Bay, collect a few bottles of milk, a few bottles of buttermilk, and a few chunks of butter. We'd take off our shoes and socks, roll up our trousers and walk the beach looking for the Japanese floats. At the same time, we'd collect the cork floats that had come off the local fishermen's nets, and we'd trade those back to the fishermen for crab meat, and then we'd nip back into Half Moon Bay and get some freshly baked bread - still hot from the oven - and we'd sit on the pier, butter our bread, eat our crab meat and bread with the butter now melted into it, and drink our milk. I can actually taste it now. Those were the best days of my life, and Mrs Miller used to be so happy when we managed to get her some of the Japanese glass floats."

"I never knew that story, Mactoo," Grace whispered.

"You know, I'd forgotten it myself, Grace. It was just when the inspector here asked me how long I'd known Steve, the scene of the four of us, Steve, Don Miller, his mum, and me, sitting on the pier enjoying our feast flashed into my mind."

"Good. Thank you," Kennedy continued, happy for the insight into the young Steve Scott's life.

Kennedy felt that too often on cases, the victim is sadly nothing more than a corpse. He felt it was vitally important that in someway, he give them back a bit of their lives again, if only so people outside the immediate family would be allowed to steal a glimpse of the magnitude of the life lost and how devastating for the loved ones the loss can be. Too often the focus of attention falls on the family of the murderer, while those family members of the deceased try, mostly unsuccessfully and in total obscurity, to cope with the fact that their lives will never, ever, be as enriched as they were before the loss.

"Mactoo," Kennedy began, "would you mind talking us through the last few cases you worked on with Officer Scott?"

"Your run of the mill Half Moon Bay stuff." Mactoo consulted his notebook through his wire-framed spectacles. "We both went to a disturbance up on Spindriff Way, just off Highway One, where two female senior citizens, neighbours, both well in their seventies, who should have known better, were physically fighting with each other. One of them had a truckload of topsoil delivered so she could reseed her garden. The truck driver tipped his load across the border of both their properties, and the lady who was doing her garden took her time clearing her soil from her neighbour's garden. The other woman started spraying the first woman and her pile of dirt with her hose. The wet woman started shoving the other woman around, and that's apparently when the scuffle broke out. We arrived and separated both ladies, and both filed battery charges against each other which we had to forward to the district attorney's office."

Noting that Kennedy's new notebook was still unused at the end of Mactoo's information, Mactoo agreed, "Yeah, you're probably right, nothing there."

Kennedy experienced a quick flash that Mactoo might be the person behind the intruders up at the chief's ranch. *Now that would make sense*, Kennedy thought, as Mactoo continued to study his notebook. He could know of something in the case file that he felt was for some reason incriminating and he needed to get rid of. Kennedy couldn't believe anyone outside of the Half Moon Bay Police Department would be aware of his endeavours. But then, if Mactoo were aware of something, surely Chief Donohue must have access to the same information? If the chief and Mactoo were sitting on something, that might account for the case's not being solved.

"Here's a bad one for you," Mactoo announced, breaking into Kennedy's thoughts. "On Friday, March 24th of this year, Officer Scott and myself were called out to investigate a brutal attack by one teenage girl on another."

"The Florence Asher Case?" Grace said, her face growing very serious.

"Yes, that's the one." Mactoo continued, glancing at his notes. "It happened just after school, outside City Hall by the bus stop. A local girl pulled another girl off a bus and beat her up really badly using her fists and a hardback reference book. There were several other adults and teenagers around at the time of the incident, but no one seemed willing to interfere.

"By the time we got there she'd run off, but enough people had identified her as being one Florence Asher, and we had no trouble tracking her down to a coffee house on the opposite side of the street. When we arrived, she was offering a BJ to one of her male classmates to give her an alibi for the time of the beating. The negotiations were still going on when we arrived."

"Jesus," Grace said, "I hadn't heard about that bit."

"It was all a bit stupid. She still had the reference book with her other books, and it was visibly splattered with blood on the cover. On top of which, several people had positively identified her. We arrested her, took her to the station house where she was charged with assault. She didn't even spend a night in jail. Her dad's lawyer worked away efficiently behind the scenes, and she was released later that evening."

"Her father is a big IT man," Grace started to explain, "a billionaire a few times over."

"Was Officer Scott annoyed about her being released without charge?" Kennedy asked.

"I think we were both more bemused by the whole incident."

"What happened when it came to trial?" Kennedy asked.

"It didn't," Grace declared.

"Word around town was that Mr Asher paid off the other girl's family. They went away quietly, refused to press charges, and claimed the stress of going to court would disrupt the victim's forthcoming exams."

"Did you discover what the beating was about?"

"A boy," Mactoo claimed.

"A boy?" Kennedy said. "What age was Florence?"

"Sixteen," Mactoo replied. "The boy was Aaron Mullkerin. He's from a good family here in the town. A nice lad, good at basketball. He was apparently more attracted to the less sexually experienced victim than the promiscuous Miss Asher."

"Would it be possible to see the case notes?" Kennedy asked.

"Of course," Grace replied before Mactoo had a chance to consider the request.

When Grace went away to fetch the file, Kennedy took the opportunity to ask Mactoo, "Would these kids have been doing drugs?"

"A bit of dope; maybe they'd been very adventurous and dropped an E at a weekend party," Mactoo replied. "I'd say the alcohol might be a bigger problem though. Apart from anything else, it's much easier to get. All they need do is steal it from their parents' liquor cabinets."

"Would such violence, amongst girls, be unusual in Half Moon Bay?"

"Five years ago - what am I talking about? - *eighteen* months ago it would be unheard of, but the girls these days... well, it's become part of their culture."

"Right," Kennedy said, happy to move on. "Any other cases you and Steve were working on?"

"Traffic violations, shit like that; nothing happens here. We're the city (beside the city) that time, and criminals, have forgotten."

"Were you Officer Scott's primary partner?" Kennedy asked.

"Not really. It doesn't work like that here," Mactoo began. "There are eighteen sworn officers here - that figure includes a reserve of auxiliary officers - and three non-sworn officers. We're all competing with each other to see who can find and caution the litter louts first."

"Have you had any theories about Steve's death yourself, Mactoo?"

"At first I thought it must have had something to do with drugs," he started; "you know, drug dealers. Taking out a police officer is a serious crime up here, so someone wouldn't have lightly made the decision to kill him. But then when we didn't turn anything up - and I have to tell you for about three weeks this place was crawling with city police officers - and not even the slightest clue was turned up, I started to think that maybe Steve had just found himself in the wrong place at the wrong time."

"I want to ask you about the men who hang around Mac Dutra Park, on the corner of Main Street and Kelly Ave."

"Yeah," Mactoo said with a sigh, "they're all Hispanic, mostly Mexican."

"Are they legal?" Kennedy asked.

"I would guess that most are in the country illegally."

"I saw about thirty of them there this morning. Are there many more in the group?" Kennedy asked.

"Probably about fifty tops," Mactoo answered, doing a mental head count.

"Would any of them be involved in anything illegal?"

"I wouldn't think so, Inspector Kennedy," he replied quickly. "The vast majority of these men are hard-working, law-abiding citizens. When we do discover illegal aliens that are gang members or who we know have committed crimes, we have to use the Immigration and Customs Enforcement (ICE) Agents to deal with them."

By the time Officer Grace Scott had returned, MacCormac and Kennedy had finished their chat. Mactoo left, claiming he had the rest of the day off. Grace had the case notes for Florence Asher's assault.

When they were by themselves, Grace said, "You don't know how hard it is for me not to ask if you learned anything?"

"I'm glad you're not," Kennedy said, "but in exchange I promise to keep you up to date."

"Deal," she said, offering Kennedy a high five. When he didn't respond she added, "We're outta here," before he had even a chance to open the file. "We're meeting Coach Goldberg in five minutes for lunch."

"With all this eating, how do you manage to keep your figure?" Kennedy said innocently.

"You shouldn't have noticed," she replied very seriously and quietly. If it hadn't been for the obvious exaggeration in her swagger, Kennedy would have put it down as a reprimand.

CHAPTER FIFTY-THREE

By the time they reached Barbara's Fishtrap up at Princeton, Coach Goldberg was already seated in a booth in the bar section sucking on a bottle of Heineken. Police officers and taxi drivers seemed to be comfortable in the bar. The décor was naturally rustic, the space was comfortable, the food was great, the jukebox played an amazing selection of music, and tourists were rarer in the bar section than water hydrants in the streets around Tiger Woods' home.

"You know, with your condition, you really shouldn't be drinking at lunchtime," the tipsy middle-aged woman was saying to Coach.

"Oh, I don't know," Coach Goldberg replied. "I often come in here for a Heineken. I find it helps me mind my own business. Would you like one?"

"What condition is this, Coach?" Grace asked as they joined Coach in the booth.

"Oh, apparently I suffer badly from a disease known as retirement. I have it on very good authority it's terminal."

Grace shoved him playfully on the shoulder.

"Careful, Grace," Coach shouted. "Mind my retirement."

Eventually, introductions over, Kennedy and Coach ordered the salmon burger while Grace opted for a mixed salad. She also extended further restraint, not to mention decency, by not looking down her nose at Kennedy when his order arrived with a very generous portion of chips.

"You were first on the scene when Officer Scott's body was found?"

"Actually, there were a couple of tourists who spotted Steve first," Coach began. "A bit of a crowd was building up, and I was worried about securing the scene of crime. Then I realised I couldn't be 100 per cent sure that Ste… that Officer Scott was dead, so I ran around into Stone Pine Road, straight into the park and down through the bushes to the river to see if I could help him. As I got closer, I could tell from the greyish colour that he was dead."

"Was he cold?" Kennedy asked.

"Totally, his skin was very cold to the touch. He'd been dead a while."

"How long had Steve been missing?" Kennedy asked Grace.

"Overnight," she said plaintively. "It was his gym night, so he was off there after his shift. He was due in late. I'd pulled an early shift, so I didn't wait up. When I woke up the next morning, I realised he hadn't come home."

"Did you notice any footprints around the body?" Kennedy asked Coach.

"Not that I could see, but the whole area was waterlogged, and the creek was still quite high. What with that and all the bushes, there wasn't a lot of standing room on either side of the water."

"What did you do next?" Kennedy asked.

"Once I realised I couldn't help Steve, I stood back carefully. My shoes and the bottom of my pants were soaking, so I went to higher ground and rang Grace's dad at the station house and supervised the area until he could get the troops down."

Coach had a very honest smile. Kennedy noticed that he wasn't scared to eyeball the person he was speaking to.

"Did it look to you as if Officer Scott had come off the bridge?"

"No, it didn't," Coach replied without hesitation, "nor were there any visible marks or bruises on him."

"I believe the top half of his torso was in the river, but his legs were on the bank. Did you notice if his trousers were wet?"

"All his clothes were soaking," Coach replied immediately. "It was like he'd jumped into a swimming pool fully dressed."

"Have you any theory about how he might have ended up there?"

"Well, the water was very high and was flowing furiously. I imagine he was probably put in the river upstream. Then as he came around the corner just before the bridge, the momentum he'd built up on the way down deposited him on the bank."

"But why would they do that?" Grace wondered aloud. "Why dump him in the river? If they'd buried him up in the hills, he'd never have been found."

"Laziness, I imagine," Kennedy suggested. "It's a lot more work than you'd imagine burying a body; all that digging, then moving the body. Maybe they panicked…"

"Or were disturbed before they a chance to hide the body properly," Grace interrupted, "so they just dumped him in the river hoping he'd be carried to the sea."

"Where does Pilarcitous Creek run into the sea?"

"Up at Elmar Beach," Coach and Grace replied at the same time.

"How far away is that?" Kennedy continued.

"A bit over a mile, at the max, up the coast," Coach replied solo.

"Which properties does the river run through?" Kennedy asked.

Coach looked at Grace.

"My father's ranch, Asher's Triple W ranch, and Highland's Baywood Park."

✳✳✳

As they were leaving, Coach said to them, "Most people, particularly men, are very territorial about their fries, yet Grace here was picking from your stash. You both appeared very comfortable with that."

"And your point?" Grace asked, good-humouredly.

"No point," Coach said with a wry grin, "just an observation, kids. But remember: platonic is only passion with the brakes on."

CHAPTER FIFTY-FOUR

Kennedy and Grace left Coach to return to doing what he'd been doing when they'd arrived: sucking on his beer and minding his own business. It didn't take them long to nip back into Half Moon Bay.

"Okay. What I'd like to do," Kennedy started as they got out of the patrol car just outside of the Half Moon Bay Inn, "is to go down to the bank of the creek and then either work our way back up the river, or drive up and work our way down."

"Sounds like an idea. What size are you?" Grace said hopping back in the patrol car.

"Sorry?"

"Your feet, Inspector. What size are your feet?"

"Oh right," he said. "Nine, I'm a nine."

"Okay, dainty feet, that's a size eleven in the US. I'll go down to the station house and pick us up a couple of pairs of waders. I'll leave the patrol car down there and we can walk up the creek and get my car back down."

"Or walk back down."

"Or, as you say, walk back down, country boy," she said through a false sweet smile.

Kennedy walked down Main Street towards Highway 92 and turned right at Stone Pine Road and into the park. Kennedy felt that the word "park" was more than a little generous to honour the overgrowth. He had to fight his way through dense bushes in order to get to the water's edge of the creek. He walked downstream about twenty yards until he was level with the bridge again and approximately in the spot where Patrolman Steve Scott's body was found.

Coach had been right; there wasn't much room to manoeuvre. Coach had also been correct that it would have been impossible to deposit the body on the bank. Kennedy still reckoned the body hadn't been thrown off the bridge, which meant, by process of elimination, that Coach's theory made sense: the body was dumped in the creek upstream, was carried downstream by the current and eventually banked under the bridge. He searched and searched for the ten minutes it took Grace to return but could find nothing of interest from his position on the bank.

Five minutes later, both Grace and Kennedy, decked out in all-in-one fisherman's waterproof trousers, were wandering out into the middle of the creek. Even though the sun was shining, Kennedy felt the coolness of the water through his waders. At its deepest mid-creek, the rapidly flowing water came to just above Kennedy's mid-thigh.

Grace studied Kennedy studying the location. "You look like you have an idea," she said eventually.

"No, not at all," Kennedy admitted, as he continued his examination.

"What are you looking for then?"

"I'm looking for an idea," Kennedy said. "The scene where the body was found may not give up any clues of its own, but that in itself could be a clue. It also means we can now eliminate the scene from our investigation."

"I think I get you," she replied as she hunkered down on the other bank and continued to examine Kennedy examining the scene. "No, sorry, I don't, Inspector. What *exactly* do you mean?"

"Well, if there are no clues here, then it raises the question: why is the body here?"

"Well, there wouldn't be any clues here anyway, because the high water of the creek would wash them all away," she offered.

"Exactly, and that could be our clue. The body could be here because someone wanted the water to wash away the clues."

"Okay, that makes sense," she replied, nodding her head. "Am I bothering you asking you these questions while you do your work?"

"No, not at all," Kennedy replied, although normally he liked to do this part of his work alone with his own thoughts. "I find it helps to eliminate as much as possible. According to the gospel of Sherlock Holmes, 'Eliminate the impossible; whatever remains, however improbable, must be the truth.'"

"But what about your suspicions and a detective's legendary gut instinct?"

"It's been my experience that gut instincts only get in the way. The investigation must be about amassing information and then, when you've collected all the information possible, you stand back and see how it all fits together."

Grace nodded to herself.

"Let's move upstream," Kennedy suggested a few minutes later.

Grace called out the names of Johnston Street and San Benito Street as they passed them. Next landmark was where Arroyo Leon Creek flowed into Pilarcitos Creek from the south. Kennedy stopped at the junction and studied it in great detail.

"Coach was right," Kennedy announced eventually, "the body definitely came down Pilarcitos Creek. Look, it got caught in those bushes..."

"That's a piece torn from Steve's shirt," Grace said in shock. "How did you know it was Steve's shirt?" she eventually asked in a controlled voice.

"It's in the report," Kennedy replied. "If he had come out of this side of the creek," Kennedy continued, pointing up Arroyo Leon Creek, "he'd have been carried too wide by the current to have hit here. So his body must have come from further up Pilarcitos Creek."

"How did my people miss all this?" she asked herself as much as Kennedy.

"You have to be looking for something before you can miss it," Kennedy replied, "but in fairness it would be logical to assume the body had been thrown off the bridge. Your people were personally involved in the case and with Steve, so the temptation is to focus in on 'Who did this to Steve?' They were concentrating on the bigger picture. Whereas I always find it best to..."

"Just chase the small clues first?" she offered, sounding upbeat.

"Exactly."

The creek was shallower but trickier the further they travelled upstream. As it veered to the left, Grace announced, "Okay, there's my dad's ranch to the north, and Asher's to the south on the right."

The creek twisted and turned through the two ranches for about three quarters of a mile, until eventually Kennedy said, "The creek is too shallow now to carry a body. The body must have been placed in the creek somewhere between here and back down at the bridge."

"So the body came from our ranch or the Archer ranch," Grace stated. "But why would Steve have needed to be on the Archer's ranch?"

Kennedy smiled. "What I'd like to do is to walk back down the creek again. You can study Archer's bank and I'll study your dad's bank, and we'll see if we can spot any movement of earth, stones, or branches - anything that might suggest recent activity."

"But why bother with our side of the creek?" she asked, and then, "Elimination, I get it, elimination. I like this approach, Inspector. It's tiring, wading through all of this water and all, but I like the approach."

"But what about this though," she said after five more minutes of wading downstream: "what if, and I am talking hypothetically here, what if my dad was involved? But... being a policeman he was aware someone would be doing this, checking the bank, so he was clever enough not only to tidy his side of the bank, but also to tamper with Asher's bank so it appeared a body had passed through it?"

"Good question and very valid, so we must view the evidence accordingly."

"And you have already been doing that?"

"Why, yes," he replied.

Half an hour later they arrived back at the Arroyo Leon Creek junction.

"Still nothing my side, Inspector."

"Nor mine."

"There were a couple of sections back there though, with high banks, rocks and stuff, where I couldn't really tell. I'd need to be up on the edge of the bank to see for sure," she said as they climbed out of the creek.

"Similarly on your dad's side."

"Okay, what next, Inspector?"

"I'd like you to walk along the creek until it reaches the ocean at Elmar Beach."

"Looking for what?"

"You'll know when you see it," was all he'd say.

"And what are you going to do?"

"I'm going to have another chat with Chief Donohue."

CHAPTER FIFTY-FIVE

"I heard you took some time out to go fishing," Chief Donohue laughed as Kennedy was shown into his office.

"Sorry? Oh right," Kennedy stuttered, as he sat in the seat directly in front of the chief's desk.

"Do you do a lot of fishing, Inspector Kennedy?"

"After a fashion," Kennedy replied. "I'm always fishing for information."

"So how can I help you?"

Kennedy was a little surprised the chief hadn't asked him if he and Grace had turned up anything.

"I wanted to ask you about...Asher."

"Okay. Any particular reason?"

"Officer Scott and I discovered that Steve's body had been put in the creek somewhere between your two properties."

"How did you discover that?"

Kennedy went on to describe how he and Grace had come to their conclusion.

"That also means the body could have come from my side of the creek."

"Yes," Kennedy replied. He was impressed that Donohue didn't hesitate to put this topic on the table. "I'd like to get your impressions on Steve Scott, sir."

"Reminds me of this story I always tell Grace about a couple of old friends of mine. They had four boys, all born within a period of six years. The older three had black hair and dark eyes. The youngest had red hair and blue eyes. On his deathbed, my friend turns to his wife and said, 'Sweetie, please be honest with me. Is our youngest boy my child?' The wife, hand on the old, well-thumbed family Bible, replied, 'I swear on everything holy, he is your son.' A few minutes later my friend passed away a contented man. The wife then said through her tears, 'Thank God he didn't ask about the other three.'"

Kennedy laughed.

"It's always important to ask your questions specifically, Inspector," Donohue continued, dropping his feet from the corner of his desk and pyramiding his arms under his chin on the desk, "but it's vitally important to ask the correct questions. So, just for the record, Inspector," Donohue stated firmly, "I had no problems with my son-in-law. He was a good guy, and he and my daughter were happy and in love. They were good together. He was good at his work, considerate of his fellow officers, and got on well with everyone."

The chief paused for a few moments then flicked through his large, brown, leather-bound desk diary. "On the night in question I was in San Francisco. Yes here it is, April 12th. Of course I know where I was, but I just wanted to show you my journal entry as well. I was at a meeting with a lot of my fellow chiefs about our on-going zero tolerance war against drug dealers. The meeting finished, as ever, late. I had dinner with a few of them, stayed overnight in the city, and my driver drove me down here the following morning. I just got in the door here on Kelly Street when the call came in from Coach Goldberg down at Pilarcitos Bridge."

"Thanks for being so candid with me," Kennedy said.

"And while we're on this love-fest," Donohue replied, "thank you for not shying away from getting into this. Grace says you're a straight-up guy. Anyway, that over, where are you with all of this?"

"We need to find a way to view the creek from Asher's bank."

Donohue didn't volunteer any solutions himself; he waited for Kennedy to talk him through it.

"Do you know Asher well?" Kennedy asked.

"He's not one of the locals, and he's not a community man. He's new money. It appears he made his fortune buying and selling something that doesn't exist. Having said that, he sold a big piece of his company for half a *billion* dollars, so he must have been doing something right. He's got expensive lawyers with political clout. He's forty at the most, divorced, never short of girls up at the ranch, I hear. He's got one daughter. Liz in reception at the station here says she's got a mouth on her."

"Do you know any of his staff up on the ranch?"

"Never been invited around there, Inspector, and never had cause to pay him a visit."

"What's the protocol if I want to pay him a visit?"

"Just make sure Officer Scott is with you; that makes it official."

"Is it okay with you if I chat with Liz on the way out?"

Donohue looked at his watch, "It's six already, you just missed her. You'll have to wait until the morning."

"Okay," Kennedy replied.

"How are you getting on with your own case?"

"I think I've got a lead, something I picked up over the weekend, and I have a piece of evidence from London hopefully being delivered here tomorrow."

"Have you spoken to your person of interest yet?"

Kennedy loved the American-speak for suspect. He had heard Grace use it a few times.

"We'll leave it until I've worked out a bit more of the case. We know where ... where our person of interest is," Kennedy replied, trying the phrase out for the first time. It sounded good in an American cop show kind of way. "And Grace thinks it's better not to tip our hand until we've something more to go on. She reckons Miss Chada feels she's gotten away with it, so she's going nowhere fast. We know where she is, and Grace has a tap on her."

"Okay, you two seem to be turning into quite a team, and it seems to be a two-way street," Donohue said, a hint of pride evident. He rose on his side of the desk, showing the meeting was over. "Keep fishing," he continued. "Keep me posted, Inspector, and if you guys need anything, just give me a holler."

***

Kennedy walked back up into town feeling foolish that he hadn't organised a meeting point and time with Grace. He used the time to visit Half Moon Bay's several taverns to see if he could spot either Green Cap or his pick-up, with no joy. Kennedy suspected that the locals probably had their own non-tourist hangouts somewhere on the outskirts of the town.

As he sat on a creaky community chair under the veranda over the boardwalk opposite The Half Moon Bay Inn, he wondered about Sharenna Chada and how she was fitting into her new life. Kennedy found that away from home you quickly fell into a routine. Having things to do at certain times gave you the security that came naturally when you were in your own town.

Kennedy didn't know how long he sat there lost in his thoughts, but he noticed the sun was going down, it was getting cooler and the last of the tourists had long since disappeared. Even in the fading light, Grace Scott's translucent, fiery hair screamed out for attention as she wearily waddled up the street in her waterproofs. She was still a vision to behold.

"You," she called out when she reached the Half Moon Bay Inn opposite him, "you're going to treat me to a slap-up meal in Pasta Moon."

"Done," Kennedy said.

"Could you bear to have dinner with me if I don't have a shower? I'm soooooooo exhausted, I just don't have the energy, and we're old friends by this stage."

"Anything that keeps the flies your side of the dinner table is all right with me," Kennedy said.

"Inspector, that was hardly gallant."

"You're not sitting where I am," he said. "Just kidding," he added just in the nick of time. She broke into a large warm smile and ruffled her fingers through his hair in a matey kind of way.

Twenty minutes later, and both refreshed to some degree in the restrooms at Kelly Street station house, they were sitting down to dinner in Pasta Moon. They both had the same delicious meal as last time. Kennedy brought her up to speed with the details of his conversation with her father.

"And you?" he asked.

"Not a lot to report," she replied, as if she were recalling every painful watery step, "except that the creek was deep enough for the water to go the whole way out to the sea. So, if Steve's body hadn't beached under the bridge on Main Street, we'd probably *never* have discovered it."

She stopped talking at that point as if to let the drama of the statement register with both of them. Their glasses of white wine and the breadbasket arrived.

"You know, there are a few tunnels that come up from the seafront under the town. One comes in under the Half Moon Bay Inn actually."

"Tell me more." Kennedy, intrigued, felt she might have come up with a new angle.

"They were most likely built in the 1920s to help the rum runners get their contraband off the beach quickly and safely. Then, during World War II, the Italians were banned from the south side of town. We didn't want them running down to the beach and giving signals to the Japanese. The Italians used these tunnels to move and hide, or to illegally get into their favourite bars when the police or military were in town searching for someone."

"Are the tunnels used for anything today?"

"Nope. They're mostly blocked up, but I was thinking it might have been another way they could have got Steve's body down to the beach without being noticed. Dumping him in the creek still doesn't make sense to me."

"But there's no connection between the tunnels and the flow of the creek?" Kennedy asked, as he noticed there was something very delicate about Grace Scott's hands and fingers.

She agreed reluctantly. "I just had to come up with some theories to fill my time." Then her face grew serious. "Do you miss ann rea?"

Kennedy was just about to answer when she interrupted him.

"It's just I was wondering about this as I was walking down the creek, on my *very long walk* down to the sea. You know, with Steve, he's dead and I miss him desperately, but I'm officially allowed to grieve him. But with ann rea, well, that's most certainly as big a loss from your life, but she's still there. I was wondering if I had ever been given the choice of Steve being out of my life but still being alive, or him being dead, which would I have chosen?"

Kennedy returned his fork to the table. He thought that was just such a sad thing for her to be thinking about, and he felt guilty for leaving her by herself in the creek.

She saw all of this in his eyes.

"Inspector," she protested, "this was about how *you* feel about losing ann rea. Please answer me that. It's important."

"Well, for me, the weirdness in ending a long-term relationship is that I feel I know all about her life, but I'm no longer allowed to be part of that life. I can still feel her closeness, but I'm not allowed to share it. And you know what the really annoying thing about it is?"

"Tell me?"

"I still can't find anything wrong with her. I mean... I mean she was perfect," Kennedy said, admitting something he'd never admitted to anyone, even himself before.

They were silent for a full minute before Kennedy spoke again.

"You know," Kennedy said, as much to himself as to Grace Scott, "the thing I loved most about ann rea was the fact that she was the only one out of the two of us who knew we couldn't work, and she went to a lot of trouble and pain to let me down easy."

"Look, Kennedy, as we've had a few glasses and are making our confessions, I just need to tell you how much it means to have you as a friend. It was bad enough to lose Steve, but that's what could destroy me. And I know that's not what Steve would have wanted. He would not have wanted my life to end as well! I felt I'd lost a connection with everyone. That's why it was great when you came along, just in the nick of time. Maybe it was just because you were jet lagged out of your brains, but you didn't treat me with kid gloves. You made it clear you enjoyed my company, but you never for a second suggested there would be the usual trade-off cost for your company."

She playfully punched him in the arm.

"I even noticed my dad look at me as if to suggest, 'It might still be too early for you to be playing the merry widow role, Grace,' because you'd made me happy again. Look, Inspector, I don't want to get laid, but I do appreciate the company. Steve and I lived in a bubble, and I gave up everyone else. Well, maybe I didn't exactly give them up, you know… but then he died, everything went to zero overnight, and then you came into town and you treated me with respect; that's all I wanted to say. Now pay the freakin' bill, Inspector, or I'll kick your ass."

CHAPTHER FIFTY-SIX

Tuesday morning arrived much too quickly for Kennedy. He considered a night's sleep to be like a train journey where you pulled into the station of a new day. Only on this particular Tuesday, it felt as if he'd not got all his gear packed, ready to disembark the train when it pulled into the station, and was panicking to have time to get off the train before it pulled out again with him on board.

Chief Edward Donohue was the reason for his panic. For the first time since Kennedy had arrived in Half Moon Bay, the chief had entered the log cabin. Even before he'd opened his eyes to greet the new day, Kennedy could hear Chief Donohue walking backwards and forwards in the main room, and it sounded like he was outside his door.

Big trouble in little Half Moon Bay, Kennedy thought. To be found in bed with the chief's daughter in the chief's own home… This was not going to be an easy one to get out of.

Kennedy felt for Grace on her side of the bed. "On her side of the bed," Kennedy whispered to himself in his semi-conscious state. "Would you just listen to yourself: 'On her side of the bed.'"

He felt nothing.

Then he remembered, and allowed himself the luxury of a large breath. When they'd returned to the cabin from Pasta Moon on the previous evening, Grace kept her promise from Sunday evening. Claiming she was totally bushed, she gave Kennedy a brief peck on the check before retiring, without any great fuss or drama, to her own room.

Funny that this was also the morning the chief chose to disturb the sanctuary of the cabin. "Well, maybe not so much funny, as lucky," Kennedy said as he hopped out of bed and searched in his wheelie for a change of everything.

By the time he'd showered, dressed, and entered the main room, the chief and Grace were at the table hugging their coffee mugs.

"Ah, there he is," Donohue said.

"Good morning, Inspector," Grace said, adding her wonderful smile.

Kennedy couldn't figure out if she was smiling because she was happy, glad to see him, or just relieved the chief hadn't arrived twenty-four hours earlier and found them in bed together.

"Good morning to you both," Kennedy said, and then, addressing Grace, "How did you sleep?"

"Best for ages, Inspector, best for ages. There's tea in the pot for you, and I've got some toast on the go."

"Toast, toast!" Donohue near shouted. "The man needs a proper breakfast, Gracie. You've just been saying how much you like him being here, so we don't want him checking into a hotel, now do we?"

"Nah, I'm good, Chief; tea and toast would be great. We'd a big dinner last evening in Pasta Moon."

"Okay, but I find I can't get into my stride if I don't have a proper breakfast."

Kennedy poured his tea and honeyed his wheaten toast, sensing the chief watching his every move closely while also observing his daughter's reactions.

When the chief seemed convinced that Grace was genuinely ignoring Kennedy completely, he went on, "I have business in the city today, Inspector, but I just wanted to advise you before I go that the Home Office has a package for you. It's going to take another day to get through the system. In the Blair/Bush days it would have flown straight through to you, but our side aren't as keen on Cameron, so all they'll do now is send you a message saying it's on its way. Is that the package you were waiting for?"

"Hopefully," Kennedy said, slightly disappointed.

"Our guest here," Donohue continued for the benefit of his daughter, "has got friends in high places. There's a personal note in the package from the Home Secretary to our Inspector Kennedy."

"For heaven's sake, you didn't open it, did you?"

"Of course not. His office details are on the address sticker."

"We better let him get to his tea then, Dad. We don't want to risk an invasion just because he's teed off with us for letting his tea go cold."

The chief drained his own cup of coffee, bade his goodbye, and wandered off muttering something to himself about the Boston Tea Party.

It was still only seven-forty, but Grace was raring to go.

"What's first today, Inspector?"

"I want to talk to Liz, down in the station house," Kennedy replied.

"Okay," Grace replied slowly, "and that would be why?"

"From what the chief said yesterday afternoon, Liz seems to know Florence Asher."

On the journey down to the station house, Grace said, "I feel great today, Inspector."

Liz hadn't arrived when Kennedy and Grace Scott reached the station.

Mactoo was in residence though, and he shot the breeze with Kennedy for a few minutes.

"Tell me this, Inspector," Mactoo said as Grace wandered off somewhere, "Brillo Pads. Did we invent them or did you guys?"

"I haven't a clue," Kennedy replied, amused and wondering where all this man's bizarre thoughts came from. Grace maintained he'd taken too many mushrooms in his youth.

"No, me neither, but I always figured that if a man went to all that trouble to invent something like a Brillo Pad, then I should at the very least buy some now and again in appreciation."

Grace heard the end of the conversation as she returned and laughed, "You don't mean to tell us you've gone all domesticated on us, Mactoo?"

"Heck no, that's the FPO's domain," he protested, hands to the sky.

"That's the Fun Prevention Officer, a.k.a. his wife," Grace clarified for Kennedy's benefit.

"But I have got a shelf full of them in my study," Mactoo continued, completely ignoring Grace. "Twenty-four boxes stacked six high, four along, together. Looks pretty cool to me. I'm thinking of framing them - you know, a variation on the Andy Warhol vibe?"

At which point the black-haired, slim-framed receptionist arrived in the lobby where Mactoo, Grace, and Kennedy had been discussing Brillo Pads.

"Can we talk to you privately, Liz?" Grace asked.

"Yes, sure. Did I do something wrong? Am I in some kind of trouble?"

"No, no, nothing like that," Kennedy replied. "We're just collecting information."

The all-American Liz seemed to relax a little as they entered the interview room. Grace sat on the same side of the table as Liz. Kennedy felt the gesture was to relax Liz even more.

"We wanted to talk to you about Florence Asher," Kennedy started. "Do you know her well?"

"I don't actually know her at all; I only know *of* her."

"Oh," Kennedy said in surprise, "I understood from the chief you felt she was, ah, rude."

"Oh that," Liz replied, on the same page at last. "I was here one evening when she came into reception, bold as brass, and demanded to see Officer..." she stopped mid-sentence and turned to look at Grace.

"What is it, Liz?" Grace asked gently.

"Well, she was asking for Steve, your husband."

"Okay," Grace said, processing the information. "That's okay, and did you know what she wanted him for?"

"It was around the time she attacked that poor girl up outside the Town Hall," Liz continued, still sounding a little hesitant. "I think it was about two or three days after she was let off. That would make it the end of March or early April. It's in my desk log. So she comes in, asks to see Officer Scott. I say I need to know why she wants to see him, you know, for my log. She says, 'Fuck that, do you know who I am?' She thought she'd got swagger. You know, rocking back and forth as she spoke, pointing the horn fingers, the sign of the devil, on you. Giving it lots of major attitude, but designer attitude..."

"I know exactly what you mean, Liz," Grace said, nodding at her to move on with her information.

"So, I'm not having any of it. She's with this other girl, Sophia Lawrence; her dad works up at Livingston's."

Kennedy and Grace both froze and stared at each other. If there had been a soundtrack running it, would have gone Dang de Dang Dang at that point.

"Anyway, Sophia is saying, 'Let's split.' She was putting on more front than Walmart, but you can tell inside she's crying for her mommy. Florence won't budge. She was swearing like a trooper and demanding this and demanding that and saying, 'Do you realise who I am?'"

"Did she get physically aggressive or violent towards you?" Kennedy asked.

"She was coming over all tough, but I could have handled both of them with one hand tied behind my back."

"And that's a fact," Grace told Kennedy.

"Asher was getting cruder and bluer by the second," Liz continued, "saying what she and her friend could do to me and Officer Scott. Eventually Officer Scott came out, figured it was nothing more than a bit of trouble-making and said, 'Okay, Miss Asher, if you need to speak to me, can you please make sure your lawyer is present. Now you both please get out of here before you're arrested for disturbing the peace,' and with that he winked at me and strode out of the station house. The girls giggled and swooned a bit, swore at me and then ran out."

"Did they chase after Officer Scott?" Kennedy asked.

"Don't know. I couldn't see, and then I got distracted by something else."

***

"That meeting wasn't in the Florence Asher case file," Kennedy offered as they followed Liz from the interview room. He hung back just enough so she wouldn't hear them.

"It didn't need to be," Grace said, a bit defensively. "It wasn't part of the case, and the visit was logged in Liz's desk file."

By the time they caught up with Liz in the reception area, she had checked her log. The meeting between Officer Steve Scott and Miss Florence Asher took place, or more importantly, didn't take place, on April 3rd, ten days before he was found face down in the creek.

"I think we need to talk to Florence Asher," Grace Scott said as she and Kennedy walked towards her patrol car.

"I think we really need to speak to Sophia Lawrence first," Kennedy replied. "Do you know where she lives?"

"Yeah, they're in that real nice colonial style house up on Main Street."

"What does her dad do at Livingston's?" Kennedy continued.

"He's an accountant."

Five minutes and several very beautiful and colourful historical houses later, they pulled up outside the Lawrence house.

"I think you'll get a lot more from her than I will. You should go in alone."

"You're probably right, but we need to do this the right way. What I suggest is you sit with her mother as far away as possible from the girl, but always keep us in view, and then if anything comes out of it, we can rightfully say that a female police officer and a guardian were both present at the interview."

The mother, who looked too old to be Sophia's mother, was nervous of the police visit, yet she was friendly, openly concerned, and co-operative.

Grace and Mrs Lawrence went through to the other end of the large, open-plan kitchen cum dining cum lounge area to make tea while Sophia and Kennedy made themselves comfortable in the television section of the room where Sophia had been dallying when they'd arrived. She'd offered to turn it off, but Kennedy suggested they merely turn it down a bit.

"Sophia, do you know why we're here to talk to you?"

'That's a funny accent? Are you Scottish? My friend Lolly, whose parents are divorced… well, her mother has a new boyfriend and he's Scottish. He likes to drink."

"Nope, I'm not Scottish, but it is a common mistake. I'm from Northern Ireland."

"Oh, where U2 come from?"

"No, that would be the other side of the border. They're from Dublin. Van Morrison is from Northern Ireland," Kennedy offered hopefully.

"Who?"

"Ah, I think he'd be to your mum and dad what U2 are to you."

"What are you talking about!" Sophia whined loudly. "U2 are sooooooo yesterday. Jay Z and Beyoncé, now they're truly wicked."

Kennedy was still having trouble hearing street slang from a middle-class white girl, in her parents' beautiful house, but he kept his own counsel.

"Sophia," Kennedy began again, realising that trying to talk her language would not work, "I've something very serious I need to talk to you about…"

She froze.

"Oh shit, nothing's happened to my dad, has it?" she said with such genuine concern and fondness that Kennedy was heartened.

"Goodness, no; nothing like that, Sophia," Kennedy said compassionately. "No, what I need to talk to you about is the evening you and Florence Asher visited the Half Moon Bay police station on Kelly Street."

"Yeah, that was just a bit of fun," she said, the wind back in her sails of bravado again. "Well, it started off as a bit of fun."

Sophia signalled the end of each of her sentences by raising her voice slightly and making it sound like a question. He could hear a muttering from the TV, and he could hear a conversation from Sophia's mother and Grace, but he could not make any of it out. Sophia should feel she could enjoy the privacy both he and Grace felt she would need. Even so, she dropped to a whisper for her shocker statement:

"Ever since the time, you know, where she beat up that girl over the boy?"

Kennedy nodded that he knew exactly what she was referring to.

"Well, Flo had the hots for," and here she paused to mime the words, *Officer Scott.* "She thought he was just... just awesome."

When Kennedy didn't make any observation, she obviously thought she was on safe ground, because she continued, "Well, he was hot, wasn't he? Flo has been having sex for longer than any of us, and she's mad for it. My other best friend, Carrie - she lives two houses up - she says she thinks Flo is a nymphomaniac." Sophia broke into a large knowing smile.

"She was after everyone," she continued, and then she dropped to yet another conspiratorial whisper. "I know three teachers she's been with, and only two are male."

"And Officer Steve Scott?"

Pointing her right hand in the shape of a gun at Kennedy, she pulled the trigger twice and let the hammer of her thumb fall, saying in time to the beat of her thumb, "Bang! Bang! He shot her down. Man, did he ever shoot her down."

"Was this outside the police station?"

"Yes, first off, Miss 'I've got so much long black healthy hair I don't know what to do with it' wouldn't let us in to see...," and then she paused to mime the word *Steve* again. "Eventually he came out, and then we didn't want to make it too obvious. I mean, he was married and all, so we hung around the reception winding up Miss Long Black Hair again, then we split. Steve was still out in the parking lot. We wandered over, you know full of attitude, giving it loads, like you do, but Steve's not biting. Flo takes the lead. She says, 'You're fit, I'm fit, are you fit for it?' He blanks her; she says something about him going to the gym. He hadn't a clue what she was talking about. It's just downright sad how quickly men go off when they get married. Are you married?"

"No," Kennedy replied.

"Divorced?"

"No," Kennedy replied, desperate to get back to the main topic.

"Gay, are you gay? That's cool. Flo says gay men are very fit."

"No to that one too."

"At least you didn't say, 'But some of my best friends are.' I can't stand that 'Look how liberal I am' shit."

She paused to look over at Grace and her mum again. *Good.* Kennedy thought, *she's going to get back to Flo and Steve.*

"Are you a widow hag? You know, you like them in mourning?"

"No," Kennedy hissed. "For goodness sake, her husband's only dead."

"I didn't mean Officer Scott's wife, I meant generally, but you meant her, didn't you? Awesome. That shows you're thinking about her. What the hell is it about her? What exactly is it that she's got that you're all after?"

"How do you mean?" Kennedy replied evenly, hoping they might return to the subject at hand.

"Well, Flo eventually came out and said it to Steve. She said, 'We'll blow you in the back of your car if you want.' I mean, she didn't actually mean 'we' as in me and her. She just said it that way so if he didn't go for it, she could save face. I mean, I would never ever do that, never," she said, shuddering. "Ask my boyfriend."

Kennedy nodded that he accepted that it wasn't something Sophia would ever do.

"So what did officer Scott say?" Kennedy whispered.

"His actual words were, 'I see what you're after. Let me tell you something. I have the greatest wife in the world. She is an absolute goddess. And I am so in love with her it's a daily joy to me. You're nothing more than a teeny-bopper, and you insult my wife by coming on to me. If you don't crawl back under the rock you came from, I'm going

to arrest you for impersonating a member of the female species!' With
that he slammed his car door closed and drove off."

"What did Florence do?"

"She ran after the patrol car shouting, 'Jerk,' 'Boring old fart,' and
screaming curses like you've never heard. Like I'd never repeat," she
added demurely as her mother and Grace Scott walked across with tea,
coffee, and cookies for all of them.

Before Officer Grace Scott and Inspector Christy Kennedy had left
the Lawrence household, Mrs Lawrence declared that her daughter
was banned from ever seeing or fraternising with "that Asher tramp"
again. If she ever caught Sophia with Florence again, her daughter
would be grounded forever, or at least until the arrival of her daughter's
first-born.

"But mum, if I'm grounded, I'll never ever meet a boy, and so there
never ever will be a first-born."

"Exactly," her mother replied firmly.

***

"She said he said that?" Grace cried, barely managing to get the
words out.

They were a few streets away from the Lawrence house, and
Kennedy was recalling what Sophia Lawrence had told him in the
course of the interview. Grace had been so overcome with raw emotion
she had to pull over.

"I'm good, Inspector," she eventually managed to say through her
sobbing. "Tell me again, please, exactly what Steve said."

"He said, 'Let me tell you something. I have the greatest wife in the
world and she is an absolute goddess. And I am so in love with her it's
a daily joy to me. You're nothing more than a teeny-bopper and you insult my wife by coming on to me. If you don't crawl back under your
rock this very moment I've going to arrest you for impersonating a
member of the female species!'"

She leaned over and hugged Kennedy and whispered, "Thank
you. Thank you, thank you, Inspector, that means so much to me.
I mean, I believed he was faithful to me as I was to him, but when I
hear someone tried to tempt him away and he, he... he just didn't."

She broke down and started to cry again.

"This is stupid. But... I'm just so happy," she began, composing herself again, "Look, Inspector, I think I would like to take some time out to be by myself ... by... myself with my thoughts about Steve. I need some time for him," she said, struggling to find some words to capture what was in her heart. Eventually she said it very succinctly, "I'd like to take some time out to be with my sweetheart."

CHAPTER FIFTY-SEVEN

So tell me this, Inspector," Mactoo announced, as they cruised along Highway 1, forty minutes later, "how many bullets are there in the cylinder of a six shooter?"

"That's obviously a trick question, but in the spirit of cooperation, I'll still go with six."

"Some of the time, but not all of the time, Christopher. If we're talking about a true gunslinger, he would only use five. And do you know what he would save the spare chamber for?"

"I'm still biting: what would he save the spare chamber for?" Kennedy asked, now slightly regretting having to have a driver take him up to the Asher property.

"He saved it for a twenty dollar bill," Mactoo continued, happy to have a new audience for his material, "and the twenty dollars was there so if the gunslinger should lose the draw and meet his maker, there would be twenty dollars for liquor at his funeral to make sure he got a good send-off."

"I wonder," Kennedy said after a few moments consideration, "how many times sacrificing that sixth bullet would have cost a gunslinger his life?"

"Now that is a good question, Inspector. Let me get back to you on that one," Mactoo mused, looking as if he'd have taken a puff on his pipe at that point, were one available. "In the meantime, here's the Triple W Ranch."

The WWW Ranch was in fact named after the worldwide web and was run on money rather than ingenuity. It had more of the feel of a corporation than a farm. Quickly checking all the vehicles in sight, Kennedy couldn't find one that was as much a crock as Green Hat's pick-up that had nearly run him over. All these vehicles were pristine, aqua in colour, with the WWW Ranch logo displayed in white on the doors.

As Kennedy went up to the front door of the grand, white wooden house, he regretted that Grace wasn't with him. The house, which looked like it was repainted at least once a week, was like the setting for a Ralph Lauren photo-shoot. It was set into a big bank of trees, and Kennedy figured the rooms at the back were probably very dark. He much preferred Chief O'Donohue's less cultivated landscape and house.

Mactoo rang the doorbell. The door was opened by a uniformed maid who looked as if she'd come straight from duty at the Ritz Carlton a little further up the coast.

"We've come to see Mr Asher," Mactoo announced.

"He's up in San Francisco today," the maid answered. She was about to say something else when she was interrupted by another voice coming up behind her.

"I'll deal with this, Ellie," the girl said dismissively as she swaggered up to the two police officers, literally shooing the maid away. "I haven't seen you around before," she continued, looking directly at Kennedy.

"Miss Asher, this is Detective Inspector Christy Kennedy, who is helping us on one of our current investigations," Mactoo announced.

"And which particular investigation would that be?"

"We're looking into the death of Officer Steve Scott," Kennedy said, and he was just about to add, "but we'll come back when your parents are here," when she said, "I thought that investigation was all over. Anyway, it had nothing to do with me. I'd a rave here that night. It was an awesome party. There must have been over a hundred people here. I got so out-of-it, totally hammered and off of my face. We wrecked the place. My dad grounded me for a day. He said the clean-up and repair work cost him $50,000."

As Kennedy considered how bizarre this statement was in light of his unobtrusive introduction, he studied the girl. She was really well developed for a sixteen-year-old. She wore skin-tight jeans, which looked as if they'd been pulled on over a red one-piece bathing suit. Her ensemble left absolutely nothing to the imagination, which Kennedy realised was her desired effect. The "putting it all on a plate" jailbait effect had never done anything for Kennedy, but he noticed she was most certainly ringing some of Mactoo's bells. Her make-up was generously applied, and she probably visited her hairdresser once a day. The overall effect was picturesque but soulless.

Kennedy experienced a shudder of extreme sadness when he wondered what the wee girl beneath all the make-up and swagger was really like. She was trying too hard to either please her dad or, perhaps for her dad, trying to emulate her mother.

"We need to examine the bank of the creek on your property, please?" Knowing he couldn't get permission from a minor, Kennedy added, "Who's in charge of the ranch in your father's absence?"

"I believe you'll find you need a warrant for that, Mr Kennedy," she replied cockily, proving she wasn't as immature as Kennedy had assessed.

"Nonetheless, we need to officially ask whoever is in charge," Mactoo said, allowing his brain to reactivate again, "and then, if we're turned down, we have to go to the courts and seek a search warrant."

"Gee, I'd really like to help you," she said in her best Marilyn Monroe whisper, "but if I let you on the property, my dad would go totally ape shit with me and probably ground me for... oh... maybe as much as ten minutes."

She laughed loudly at her own attempt at humour.

"Florence, we'll be back, don't you worry, and I can personally see you getting grounded for ever," Mactoo said in as serious a tone as Kennedy had ever heard from him.

"Yeah, bring it on, big boy, but I've got over one hundred witnesses who will cover for me," she snarled as she slammed the door in their faces.

"Mactoo, can we drive around, pretending to find our way off the ranch. Green Hat and his mate's beat-up truck must be around here somewhere."

"No, Inspector, we need to do this very officially and by the book. We need to be seen to be leaving here the very second we were refused permission. The chief will never forgive me if I mess this up." Then he added as an afterthought, "And Grace will never forgive you."

The second they exited the grand gates of WWW ranch, Mactoo seemed to relax

"Did you know," Mactoo eventually said, settling back into his relaxed homespun style, "if you put a little whisky on a scorpion's tail, it will run around crazily until it stings itself to death?"

Kennedy's mind was elsewhere.

"Well," Mactoo continued, as he sped along the dangerous streets at over twice the speed limit, "I think we just dropped some whisky on Miss Florence Asher's tail."

The minute they walked into the station house, Liz shouted to Kennedy that he was to ring the chief immediately at the number she handed him.

In the office Grace had commandeered for both of them, Kennedy quickly dialled the number, imagining the worst. Were his wings about to be clipped?

"Hi, Chief, I just got back to the station."

"Inspector, I've just had Asher on the phone to me huffing and puffing and trying to blow our station house down. Please tell me what happened; spare me nothing."

Kennedy recalled the encounter with Miss Asher, leaving absolutely nothing out.

"She said that," the chief barked, "that she had a hundred witnesses?"

"She actually said she had *over* a hundred witnesses," Kennedy clarified for the record."

"Well, I kinda figured by the storm Asher was blowing up, threatening to have me thrown off the force, if you don't mind, that you and Mactoo must have been dong something right. So what do you want to do?"

"I want to get on the property as soon as possible and inspect the bank from the positions where it might have been possible to throw a body into the creek. I also want to check the property for the guy with the green cap, his mate and the beat up truck..."

"You mean the same guys who nearly ran you down up on my ranch?" The chief interrupted.

Kennedy could hear his brain tick over the telephonic static for a few seconds

"Okay, leave it with me. I'll speak with the judge and see how quickly I can get a warrant issued," the chief eventually said.

Where was Grace? Did she and Steve have a special place they went to? He thought about her classic looks and how she did her best, not exactly to hide them, but pretty close. And then he thought about Florence and how it appeared her dream would be to be like Grace. If she had Grace's beauty, though, she'd be sure to tout it to death.

When the phone on the desk rang, he picked it up on the second ring.

"Okay," the chief said, dispensing with all small talk, "here's what I've got. We can go back to the property and look for the two men and their vehicle. That's based on their alleged trespass and attack on my property. We can't check the bank of the creek, not just yet anyway. However, if we discover any information on our initial search that gives justification to examine the bank of the creek, the judge will rule on granting a further warrant for a more extensive search. But please, under no circumstances, go near that creek bank."

"Agreed," Kennedy replied.

"Just so you know, we are going to the Triple W because we have reason to believe they may be harbouring two people who a) trespassed on my property and b) while on my property attempted grand theft, and c) drove in a manner which endangered the lives of others, i,e. namely you and Grace. Okay "b" is very important. If you find your two men, the attempted grand theft will tie them to the murder of Officer Scott, in that they were trying to steal his file. A pair of complete idiots, Inspector. Like we're not going to have computer back-up of our files! If it wasn't so sad it would be funny."

"Unbelievable," Kennedy agreed. "Thank you, sir."

"No problem. Look, this should just take half an hour to set up. Grace should be back before then."

"How is she?"

"I've spoken to her and she's fine. She needed some space, and now she's raring to go. Tell Mactoo to take every officer he can put his hands on up there. We might not have a lot of time. Once Asher gets his hands on the warrant, his very expensive team of octopuses (they have hands in everyone's pockets) will spring into action."

Forty minutes later, five patrol cars, fourteen officers, and Christy Kennedy (body armoured up to the eyeballs) came screeching into the forecourt of Asher's grand ranch house.

Asher himself had mysteriously reappeared from San Francisco - probably something to do with the helicopter, blades still silently turning, on the front lawn, Kennedy reckoned.

Asher greeted them affably on the front steps of his house. As Asher read the warrant, Kennedy studied him. He was slim, looked to be around forty, was going prematurely grey and had had vanity surgery done to his face, most noticeably around his eyes. He wore a Ralph Lauren blue and black striped Polo shirt; reddish orange pants with a white belt. The combo Kennedy would never have had the courage to wear, even for a bet, was completed with dark blue socks and genuine looking moccasins.

When Asher reached the end of the warrant, Mactoo shouted, "Right, boys, you know what you're looking for."

Florence Asher arrived at her father's side, more soberly dressed now in a less revealing dark brown summer dress, her face still red from the severe scrubbing she'd endured to remove all her make-up. Without it, she looked surprisingly...plain.

Kennedy and Grace rushed straight to the row of six garages at the right of the house. Once they gained access, they were stopped dead in their tracks. Before them, in the open-plan garage, were six of the most beautiful classic US cars Kennedy had ever set his eyes on. Sadly, though, there was no beat-up truck.

"It's obvious Asher is not going to permit any bangers around his house," Kennedy started.

Mactoo entered the garage behind them. When he clocked the cars he gasped, "Three of these are priceless, totally priceless, and the other three could be exchanged for a good chunk of the national debt."

"To heck with the priceless cars, Mactoo. Let's find the pick-up, before we're pulled out of here!" Grace hissed.

One of Asher's staff ran into the garage, obviously to supervise the search and protect the cars.

"Michael, I didn't know you were working up here," Grace said.

"Yep, sure am, Grace. It pays my way through Berkeley."

"Mactoo, watch the door," she ordered. "Michael, we're here because of what happened to Steve. Please help us," she pleaded. "Where does Asher keep the farm vehicles?"

"Up on the back lot where the old farmhouse used to be. The farmhands live up there as well," he replied very quietly.

Mactoo returned to the garage and silently nodded his head towards the outside of the building. Michael scarpered to the opposite end of the garage and pretended to ignore the police officers.

"Let's take the patrol car up to the back lot," Mactoo said when they were out of earshot of Asher on the way back to the main house. Kennedy was grateful for both the ride and the air-conditioning. It was the hottest part of the day, and the body armour was not only slowing him down, it was making him sweat. He didn't like feeling trapped in clothes.

Kennedy and Grace couldn't believe their luck as they drove up to the badly neglected old farmhouse. There, parked outside, was the battered pick-up truck that had nearly run Kennedy over up at the chief's ranch. Kennedy immediately clocked the "My Other Gun Is a Winchester" bumper-sicker and kicked himself for not including that vital detail in the search earlier.

Mactoo signalled them to be quiet and led them to the back of the shotgun style farmhouse through a beautiful natural garden with a multi-coloured variety of flowers and plants. Drawing his gun and opening the teak door silvered by age, he entered the house gingerly. Grace followed suit and ordered Kennedy to stay by the door.

Every few seconds he heard doors slam open and heard them shout, "Clear!" and more footsteps. Next he heard them climb the stairs, shouting, "Clear!" for every empty room they checked. And then Kennedy heard what sounded like additional footsteps. He clearly heard Grace shout, "Down on the floor, face first, now, hands behind your head!"

He heard her scream the same order with greater volume. He heard someone scurrying about as Grace's person of interest seemed to be doing as commanded. Next, from what seemed another part of the house, a part closer to him, he heard the sound of running bare feet. Then the sound of heavier feet, someone in shoes or boots chasing, then Grace ordering, "Go after him. I've got this one."

Kennedy heard the sound above him of a window opening and someone scampering on to the porch roof directly above him, someone of generous proportions, if the sound of the creaking of the supports of the porch roof was anything to go by. He lifted the broom lying on the porch beside him.

First he saw the bare legs, then the chubby, wobbly bare thighs, then the... "Oh no, you're not totally nude," Kennedy whispered to himself. It was not going to be a pretty sight. Then, after his privates, the first of his three bellies and then the rest of the body eventually followed thanks to the laws of gravity. After the thud of the fall, where Kennedy actually felt a tremor in the earth beneath his feet, he realised that the person of interest wasn't totally nude after all. He was still wearing his green baseball hat.

Kennedy hoped that the fall had broken Green Cap's ankle and that he would be spared having to chase after Green Cap. Sadly that did not prove to be the case, as Green Cap wobbled to his feet and started to head for the bushes.

Kennedy had a theory that balance was all about confidence. Look how thin our ankles are. Then consider how much weight those thin an kles have to carry. We should fall over between each step. But it's confidence and the momentum that keeps us going.

Kennedy wasn't as close to Green Cap as he'd been on the night outside the log cabin when he was able to trip him up, but at least this time he was armed. He came out from the shadows of the porch and carefully aimed his brush, handle first, between the lower regions of Green Cap's wobbly wee legs. The brush landed right where Kennedy aimed it. First Green Cap's right ankle hit the brush shaft, which in turn hit his left ankle, which in turn turned the brush shaft ninety degrees, whereby the brush shaft clattered with the front of his foot. This, in turn, proved Kennedy's theory: remove the momentum and the confidence and the human body collapses - in Green Cap's case in an unsightly mess.

Kennedy rushed to the clothes line and retrieved a drying, ratty, Michael Bolton T-shirt, which he threw at Green Cap so Grace Scott's, rather than the person of interest's, blushes might be spared.

"Good job, man," Grace shouted as she, Mactoo and their prisoner exited the back door.

Mactoo raced back upstairs and returned a few minutes later with trousers, shirts, some mismatched socks, and two pairs of shoes for the two men who had been sleeping off a heavy night of drinking.

Kennedy and Grace bundled the two in the back of two separate patrol cars to keep them apart while they were transferred to Kelly Street police station. Mactoo volunteered to stay behind and guard the pickup and see what else he might discover in the meantime.

As Grace drove her patrol car down the main sweeping driveway, Kennedy could see, in the wing mirrors, Asher and his daughter standing in the grand porch of their virgin-white house. This time though the daughter was holding her father's hand very tightly.

CHAPTER FIFTY-EIGHT

It turned out that Green Cap, a.k.a. Dustin McClelland, and Bobby Cohn were still too drunk to be questioned.

Mactoo said, "We were very lucky Bobby was out of it. He's a great boxer when he's sober. He'd have to be with a nose like that."

Despite the risk that Asher's lawyers would have them out by morning, the chief decided that they would not be questioned until the next day. The chief figured that Asher seemed more interested in his daughter's liberty than the freedom of two of his workforce.

The pick-up truck was put on a trailer destined for San Francisco, and Grace volunteered herself and Kennedy to take it in to the city immediately. She said they needed to kill time until they could interview the two persons of interest.

By the time they reached San Francisco, the forensic mechanics said they couldn't get to the vehicle until first thing the following morning, which was how Grace Scott and Christy Kennedy were to be found later that evening in the Great American Music Hall up on O'Farrell Street, listening to the fine music of Ry Cooder and Nick Lowe as they, along with drummer supreme, Jim Keltner, enthralled a packed house.

Kennedy liked the Great American Music Hall. The chips were good but the burgers were amazing. The finest San Francisco music venue reminded Kennedy of a smaller version of the Irish ballrooms back home. The Great American Music Hall was obviously not as large as the Arcadia in Portrush - where the younger Kennedy had enjoyed many a fine evening's entertainment - but it was very funky in a Americana kind of way.

Kennedy and Grace had great fun; they chatted intensely about nothing at all and continued their conversation all the way back to the chief's ranch.

She persuaded him to make them both a cup of his tea, just to see what the fuss was all about.

As he was making it, she said, "Your Miss Chada has been behaving herself, you know, Inspector. I went to see her today, treated myself to a massage. She does have magic in them fingers of hers. She didn't say a word to me. I asked her a few general questions, but only got one word replies."

"She didn't know who you were?"

"Hadn't a clue. I took the Mustang and was in my street clothes. But I'll tell you this, Inspector, she's one beautiful woman. I've never known anyone before who has made love to a goddess. You must be smoother than you pretend. But what is it about her, Inspector?"

Kennedy shrugged.

"I remember you told me she totally gave herself to you, and I thought that was a funny thing to say. She gave herself to you, so what were you meant to do? Trade her in for another model? Sell her on?"

Kennedy laughed.

"No, I'm serious, Inspector," she said as she sampled his tea, "Oh yes, now this is really good. It's not at all like the tea we make. But Miss Chada. I looked at her in the mirror as she massaged me, and I wondered about her, and I wondered about Florence Asher and about myself even. Do we all unconsciously put on show to get what we need? To catch our mate?"

"I think we all put on a show of whom we think we need to be, in order to be attractive to the person we're trying to attract."

"You know, some women will take excuses for men to their beds," she continued, appeared not to have registered Kennedy's response to her earlier question. "Why is that?"

"Could it be because they can't find anyone else?"

"Or perhaps because they don't feel entitled to anyone better?" she offered. "But I think I'm getting away from my point. I'm tired and I want to go to bed, but the point I was trying to make was, Miss Chada gave herself totally to you, yet you admitted you weren't at all interested in her beyond the physical side."

"But she was sleeping with me to facilitate her alibi," Kennedy said.

"But she kept on sleeping with you, even when she had her alibi and it was potentially dangerous to continue to see you. The time you said you felt Miss Chada gave herself completely to you, was that the first time she slept with you or one of the later times, you know, after she already had her alibi."

Kennedy thought about it for a few seconds, quite a few seconds.

"I'd have to say it was perhaps the fifth or sixth time," Kennedy admitted.

"After she had secured her alibi?" Grace pushed.

"Yes."

"That's what I find so sad, that she would give herself to you like that and you wouldn't be affected by it."

"Grace, let's not forget, we are talking about my one and only person of interest here."

"I know, Inspector, and that's what I mean," she said, sounding like it had all fallen into place for her at that precise moment. "How did she end up in that place where she felt she had to do what she did?"

Kennedy went to sleep that night with that very thought in his mind.

CHAPTER FIFTY-NINE

Wednesday midmorning they discovered Green Cap and Bobby Cohn had been as useful as ashtrays on a motorcycle when it came to wiping the truck clean. There was yet another tear and threads from Officer Steve Scott's red-checked shirt discovered deep in the flatbed, as well as quite a few hairs and several fibres, which Kennedy guessed would match up with the deceased. Even with this information and evidence in the bag, Kennedy still wanted to take the interview slowly.

Assume nothing, he always thought, *and you won't be disappointed.*

Chief Donohue had been wrong when *he'd* assumed Asher would leave his boys to fend for themselves just as long as his little girl was okay. Green Cap was all lawyered up to the peak of his grubby cap when Grace and Kennedy sat down with him.

The first words out of Green Cap's mouth were, "I want my own lawyer."

Asher's lawyer looked like someone had just saved him from having to wipe dog-do off his shoes and was out of there quicker than it took the American nation to forget George W. Bush. The smile slowly disappeared from Grace's face.

Dustin McClelland, a.k.a. Green Cap, had to be returned to his cell so the court could appoint a lawyer. His only condition was that it wouldn't be any of Asher's lawyers and that he didn't want to share a lawyer with Bobby Cohn.

"Is this a good sign or a bad sign?" Grace asked her father as they were waiting in his office to find a lawyer for Green Cap.

"Could be good or it could be bad, Grace. The only thing I've learned is to never second-guess situations like this. When you do, you're in danger of being sucker punched."

"Do you think we can make this stick?" she then asked Kennedy.

"It's better we go into this looking for the truth, rather than trying to make something stick," Kennedy replied.

Grace and her father nodded in agreement.

The Chief only agreed to allowing his daughter to be present at the interrogation on the strict condition and even stricter promise that she did not actually partake in the interview.

Manny Langenstein, the lawyer eventually appointed to Green Cap, seemed like a down-home kind of guy. Maybe in his late fifties and dressed like a stouter Colonel Custer with a bow tie, he looked healthy enough, but when he wheezed, it sounded like a death rattle. Too many years of lunch being nothing more substantial than coffee and cigarettes, Kennedy figured, seeing his nicotine-stained fingers. Langenstein took half an hour with his new (paid for by the state) client and then advised Grace he was ready for the interview to start. Manny paid Grace his respects and showed her the courtesy of holding out her seat for her.

"Why'd you change lawyers, Dustin?" Kennedy asked, once the formalities for the tape and video recorders were respected.

"I don't want to be tied to that bitch..."

Manny held up his forefinger to signal his client to stop. *Oh no,* Kennedy thought, *Green Cap is going to be nursery-stepped through every sentence.*

"Dustin, I'd like to remind you," Manny began in his slightly camp drawl, "there is a lady present, and I don't want to hear that kind of language in these proceedings. Now, please answer the inspector's questions."

"I don't want to be tied to Miss Asher. She's going straight to hell," Dustin replied immediately.

"Are you prepared to admit that you and Bobby Cohn attempted to steal something from Officer Grace Scott's property two nights ago?" Kennedy asked.

"Is Bobby Cohn being questioned too?" Dustin asked.

"Yes, sir," Kennedy replied, not admitting that the interview with Cohn wouldn't take place until after this one.

Dustin looked at Manny. Manny nodded. Dustin then looked back at Kennedy.

"Yes, sir, that was me and Bobby Cohn," he admitted.

"What were you after?" Kennedy pushed.

"That file with all the information on the death of Officer Scott's husband," Manny continued.

This was going better than Kennedy hoped. He prepared himself for the sucker punch.

"Why did you want that file, Dustin?" he continued.

"Miss Asher saw you down by the bridge studying it. She said there was information in there we needed to make sure you didn't see."

Manny Langenstein rolled his eyes to the heavens. Grace Scott started to take deep breaths.

Florence Asher had obviously thought her visit, with Sophia Lawrence, to the Half Moon Bay station house was recorded in Officer Steve Scott's file, and that this would lead the man from Scotland Yard directly to her.

Kennedy felt he was walking on eggshells. He knew that if he asked the wrong question now, he could derail this. He decided to draw Dustin in a bit more, get him to incriminate himself more before stepping up to the big stuff.

"So, Florence Asher sent you up to Chief Donohue's ranch to steal this file?"

"Yep," Dustin said, looking at Manny who didn't protest.

"Did Miss Asher ask you to do anything else, Dustin?"

"On that particular night?"

"Well, let's start with that particular night," Kennedy replied.

"No, that's all we had to do for her that night," Dustin replied.

"She didn't tell you to hurt me? I mean, come on, Dustin, you nearly ran me over."

"We thought you were gone for a walk and Mrs Scott had gone to bed. You surprised us. We were just trying to get out of there; we weren't trying to run you over."

"Okay, Dustin, I accept that," Kennedy said to Green Cap's visible relief. "Did Florence Asher tell you why she wanted that particular file?"

"Well, she said she'd been told you were a hot-shot Scotland Yard detective brought over to solve a case the locals hadn't been able to. She said if we got the file, you'd have nothing to work with."

Kennedy could hear Grace taking deep breaths beside him. He realised how painful this must be for her. All she probably felt like doing was to jump across the table and kick this fool's head in, but outwardly at least, she remained calm and collected.

"Okay, Dustin," Kennedy continued slowly, "so, here now, in front of your lawyer and Officer Scott and the tape and video recorder, are you prepared to admit to attempted robbery?"

Dustin looked slightly relieved.

"Yep, I'm prepared to admit to attempted robbery."

Kennedy said, "Do you mind if I just step out for a moment."

Everyone agreed, and Grace announced his departure for the benefit of the tape.

Kennedy went straight to Chief Donohue who was monitoring the interview.

"Do we now have enough to get a warrant to go up and search Asher's side of the creek?"

"Yes," The chief replied.

"Can we get an officer now to secure the site until such time as Grace and I can get up to inspect it? I've told Mactoo roughly where we think it might be."

"Done, Inspector. Now get back in there. There's not been a single word said since you left."

Grace announced Kennedy's return for the recordings.

"Okay, Dustin, did Miss Asher pay you and Bobby Cohn to carry out this robbery?"

"Attempted grand theft," Manny corrected.

"Yes. Sorry. Did Florence Asher pay you and Bobby Cohn to carry out this attempted grand theft?"

Dustin, whose faithful battered green baseball cap had been placed on his knee in Kennedy's absence, looked at Manny. Manny nodded positively to him.

"Miss Asher blackmailed us to rob you."

Grace Scott visibly winced. This was the sting in the tail; this blackmail angle was Dustin's way out.

"A wee schoolgirl blackmailed two fine examples of the male species such as yourself and Bobby Cohn?" Kennedy hammed.

"A wee schoolgirl, I don't think so," Dustin sneered back.

"Did Florence Asher blackmail you into murdering Officer Steve Scott?" Kennedy asked. The blackmail angle worried him. Had that been the reason why lawyer Manny Langenstein had been persuading his client to cooperate? The new and apparently unexpected pressure was reddening up Dustin's face something terrible.

"We didn't do murder, no, sir," he replied immediately, his voiced rising in volume quite a bit. "She did that all by herself."

Grace Scott let out the breath she seemed to have been holding for twenty minutes.

"You're saying Miss Asher murdered Officer Steve Scott?" Kennedy asked, as Manny nodded silently.

"I'm not saying she meant to, but that's what happened, and Bobby Cohn, no matter what you offer him, will say exactly the same thing, because that's the goddam truth."

"Okay, Dustin," Kennedy continued as he heard a lot of rushing around in the corridor outside the interview room. Chief Donohue was probably on his way to arrest Florence Asher. "Tell us exactly what happened, please."

"Well, Bobby and I were in the old farmhouse and we got a call..." Dustin paused to collect his thoughts. "No, it's better I go back to the start. What happened was Miss Archer was arrested for beating that girl up, you know, down on Main Street?"

"Yes, we know all about that, Mr McClelland," Grace replied in a clear, measured voice. Kennedy nodded to her to keep her promise with her father by not adding to the proceedings. He couldn't work out how she was holding it together. Someone had just on-record accused another person of murdering her husband. Of course, he might only be doing so to save his own skin, but either way, somewhere in the middle of this scenario between Bobby Cohn, Dustin McClelland, and Florence Asher lay the truth.

"Okay, Florence got off, like she always does, but during the investigation she met Officer Scott. I guess she took a fancy to him. Apparently he wasn't interested, and he also humiliated her in front of her best friend, Sophia Lawrence.

"Bobby met her on the farm early the next morning, and she was still hopping mad. She told Bobby she wanted to come and see him and me that night down in the old farmhouse and to make sure no one was there. She turned up half smashed, with three bottles of wine, looking more like a thirty-year-old hooker than a billionaire's teenage daughter.

"And then we went up to Bobby's room and...."

"As I said, Dustin, there is a lady present. I'm sure we don't need you to draw pictures," Manny interrupted.

"Well, all I'll say is, I didn't know half the things she was up to. How does a teenager..."

"Dustin, let's say for the sake of this conversation, she seduced both of you and move on from there, okay?" Manny suggested.

"Okay," Kennedy replied.

"She took both our mobile numbers, said she needed the numbers for when she felt like a bit more action, and that was it.

"Next day we both get a text from her with a video she managed to take on her phone the night before of the both of us with her. What she had done was real smart, because on the night she was in charge, telling us what to do to her, but on the video it looked like we were the ones taking advantage of her.

"She said in the text that she would pick us up in her car that evening after work. When she did, she said she had something to do that she needed our help with. Bobby started to paw at her, and she said, 'There'll be no more of that, mister, and if you don't do what I say, my father will get a copy of the video with our cosy little get-together last night. As I'm still a minor, I imagine he'd want to go straight to the police with it. That is after he's kicked a new...'" Green Hat paused and looked at Grace before continuing, "'kicked a new back end in for both of you.'

"She drove around town until we saw Officer Scott, and we did that every night for a week, checking out his routine. The next Tuesday, she told us to bring our pick-up and some rope. She brought ski masks as well. We'd worked out... she'd worked out, that every Tuesday he went to the gym."

"That's right, and I'd always had dinner with my dad on Tuesday evenings," Grace said with a start, as if she was just realising where this was going.

"We parked right next to his car in the parking lot, and as he was about to get in his car, Bobby came around from the back of our trailer and shoved a cloth she'd soaked with chloroform over his face. He passed out immediately."

"Where did she ever manage to get chloroform from?" Grace asked in spite of herself.

"From Craigslist, she said," Dustin replied. His lawyer nodded for him to continue with his confession. "We tied Officer Scott up, gagged him, and hauled him into the back of the trailer, and she had us drive him straight into the big barn at the back of the old farmhouse.

"When he was still unconscious, she slutted herself up again, to, she said, make him realise what he'd been missing. That's when we found he'd dissed her in front of her friend the previous week. She was after revenge. She was still seething. He took a long while to come around, and all the time she was drinking from a bottle of wine. Bobby and I kept to the other side of the barn; we were shitting ourselves. On the one hand, we'd kidnapped a police officer; and on the other hand, we were both looking at statutory rape, at the least. As he came around she went through this rap with him about realising he'd only said no to her because there was a witness, but now they were alone she would give him one more chance.

"She removed his gag and tried to kiss him. 'Don't worry,' she said, taking another swig from her bottle of wine, 'we'll get there.' She took off her skirt and blouse and danced in front of him. When she moved her body up close, Officer Scott spat at her and started to yell for help. He was hollering at the top of his voice. She screamed at him to keep quiet, 'You're going to ruin it,' she said. He called her a pathetic child and started to shout for help again. She warned him to shut up. She called for us by name, the idiot. We stayed where we were, behind the hay.

"All of a sudden we heard an almighty thud, and the officer stopped shouting.

"She cussed at us, calling us cowards and ordering us to come over and help get rid of him. She said it was an accident. She claimed she'd only tapped him on the head with the wine bottle to shut him up, and she'd just knocked him unconscious. She told us we should throw him in the creek, and when he woke in the morning he'd forget all about it. All he'd have would be a sore head. She kept saying no one had ever said no to her before.

"Officer Scott didn't seem alive to me, but Florence insisted he was. We backed the truck into the barn, threw him in the back and drove over the cre. We trailed him over to the high bank and rolled him in.

"I said, 'What if he drowns?'

"She said, 'I read somewhere that drowning is the best way to murder someone, because it's so difficult to prove it wasn't an accident.' No sooner was his body in the creek than she'd started to text all her friends, using the excuse of her dad being away to get them over to her house for a party so she'd have an alibi."

"One final thing," Kennedy said; "did Miss Asher help you lift Officer Scott's body into the truck?"

"Yes. Me and Bobby were making hard work of it, and she had a hissy fit, calling us mommy's boys. She might not look it, but she's real strong."

"Then when you drove the truck over to the creek, did she help you take Officer Scott off the back of the truck and over to the trailer?" Kennedy continued. It was vitally important they get this information on record now before her lawyers got involved.

"Yes. She helped us trail Officer Scott over to the creek, and then she seemed to enjoy rolling him into the creek by herself."

Dustin McClelland stopped talking. He seemed relieved to have gotten the confession off his chest.

Manny Langenstein half-heartedly tried to plea bargain for his client.

Kennedy, who knew he was way, way outside his jurisdiction, said a point blank, "No!"

"I might be better to throw my client to the mercy of the court," Manny continued.

"I believe when the video of Dustin, Bobby, and Florence is shown in court, you may not find much mercy there," Kennedy suggested. "I would recommend your client plead guilty to all his involvement."

Which is exactly what Dustin McClelland did.

Bobby Cohn painted a fairly similar, if equally unpalatable, picture.

CHAPTER SIXTY

Kennedy was standing in the interview room as Officer Grace Scott led a legal parade up the corridor towards him. She held a cuffed Florence Asher by her arm, followed very quickly by two expensively suited lawyer types, followed by Officer Kevin MacCormac. Back at the opened front door stood Florence's father on his cell phone, obviously making calls to every politician he'd ever supported trying to call in a favour for his daughter.

Grace nodded Kennedy back into the interview room.

"Someone shut the door or we'll have a blowback," Grace shouted, as she came right up to the interview room. "Whoops!" she shouted as the door in front of Kennedy banged shut so quickly it caught Kennedy by surprise. He couldn't be sure, but it looked as if Grace Scott, with a subtle nudge at the last possible second, presented Florence Asher's face, nose first, to the vicious backswing of the door.

"My nose, you fucking bitch," Florence screamed as her cuffed hands rose to the crimson blood now flowing from her nose. "You've ruined my beautiful nose, my best feature!" she screamed as the lawyers fussed around her.

"Oh don't worry, sweetie," Grace said. "Your daddy can buy you a new one, but I'd have him wait for, say, twenty-five years until you get released. I have a feeling that by the time you get out there are going to be several other body parts in need of replacement from wear and tear, if you see what I mean."

The lawyers were kicking up a storm, mentioning private hospitals, specialist surgeons, transferring over the bridge, and "immediately!"

"We have a good local doctor who'll do just fine," Grace announced. "We've got a cop killer here; she's not getting out of our sight for one second, mister. The next time she'll be free from us will be when we hand her over to Governor Olin G. Blackwell."

When it all cooled down and Asher's lawyers had assured Florence and her father that Alcatraz had long since closed down, they eventually got around to the inevitable discussion about a plea bargain. Chief Scott turned them down flat with, "No deals, gentlemen. We're going for murder uno. If she pleads guilty, we'll mention this to the judge. He's instructed to take guilty pleas into consideration when passing sentencing."

The lawyers suggested fighting it out. Of course they would; they'd receive bigger retainers and pay cheques for themselves.

Mr Asher advised his lawyers and Chief Donohue that his daughter would plead guilty. The chief realised Asher most likely had some other end game up his sleeve, but for now he and his daughter would settle for the plea of guilty.

***

The chief took Grace, Kennedy, and Mactoo to Cockney Corner for about an hour for a couple of drinks. They all knew they'd won, but there was no one really in the mood for celebrating. Officer Steve Scott, the thirty-eight-year-old, blue-eyed husband of Grace Scott, née Donohue, was dead, and no victory was ever going to bring him back. The scales of justice never really balance out.

"You know, I thought about this last night when I went to bed," Grace started, following a few minutes silent contemplation as they all stared into their drinks. "The saddest thing about death is how close it is to living, and then today when I was thinking about this some more, I realised that if that tramp Asher had fancied Mactoo here instead of Steve, then Steve would be here tonight having a drink."

"Hold on there, Grace," Mactoo protested. "I'm not sure I go along completely with you on this one."

"I didn't mean that Mactoo had to sacrifice his life. I just meant that if Florence Asher had been attracted to Mactoo instead of my Steve, he would have been happy to take that particular teeny-bopper bullet for us, wouldn't you, Mactoo?"

"Yeah, well, of course," he replied, "anything to help with my divorce. Of course, sir," he said, addressing his chief, "I wasn't for one moment suggesting I would, you know, go off with a sixteen-year-old."

"You're okay, Mactoo. The chief knows you wouldn't look at any-one a day under seventeen," Grace teased.

"Oh good, that's okay then," Mactoo said.

As Kennedy and the chief carried a weary Grace into her bedroom an hour later, he whispered to Kennedy, "Oh yes, I forgot to tell you, Inspector, that parcel of yours from the Home Office cleared customs this morning. It's in my office waiting for you."

CHAPTER SIXTY-ONE

Kennedy and Grace entered the main room of the cabin simultaneously at seven twenty-five the following morning. It was Thursday already and the end of his first full week in America, the land of the free (except for Green Cap, Bobby Cohn, and Florence Asher) and the home of the brave. Kennedy immediately thought of Steve Scott. Why did so many of the brave have to die?

"Good day's work yesterday, Inspector," was Grace's upbeat greeting. "I think you deserve one of my special breakfasts."

"Thanks," Kennedy said, "but I think I'd prefer to scoot down into town, pick up my parcel, check my emails, then check how the forensic guys are getting on up at the Triple W..."

"But you've got your confessions, Inspector," she interrupted.

"Hard evidence trumps words from criminals any day of the week, Grace. Lawyers have learned how to eloquently argue that black really can be white," Kennedy said. "I thought we'd get some breakfast on the way, my treat."

"You're the man, Inspector. Give me fifteen for a shower," she said as she disappeared back into her bedroom.

Superintendent Thomas Castle, DS James Irvine, DC Dot King, and the Home Secretary had all sent email messages to Kennedy. His team had only sent one each, as opposed to the Home Secretary's three. Well, he did have a vested interest and had probably gone out on a limb in his efforts to get Kennedy to the USA so quickly.

Kennedy sent them all polite replies about his work in progress, and he asked Irvine to email him photographs from the scene of the Patrick Mylan crime.

Incredibly (to Kennedy), the photos came back attached to the return message from Irvine, whose only other bit of information was that he was "well chuffed" that Manchester United's Ryan Giggs, BBC's

Sports personality of the year the previous year, had just been awarded a knighthood in the Queen's birthday list. Photo attachments success-fully printed, Kennedy dandered down Main Street to the cafe where Grace waited for him.

On the three-minute walk, Kennedy considered how easy it was to be in Half Moon Bay. He knew he hadn't been there that long re-ally, but he'd expected to be feeling some pangs of homesickness. Per-haps if ann rea were still in Camden Town waiting for him and Grace Scott not currently waiting for him up in her favourite coffee house, the pull of NW1 would have been stronger. He realised that the longer he was away, the less would be the interest in the developing news stories he'd left behind.

Grace had secured her favourite back corner table, ordered their breakfast, and had her nose stuck in her paper, coffee by her side. Kennedy had a chance to observe her undetected. She looked... happy was too strong a word, but she looked contented. She had an air about her, as if she were regaining her strength or power again. He couldn't believe how stunning she looked, basking in the flicker-ing shadows of the airy, cinnamon-smelling building, lost in her own wee world. Unconsciously she was giving off a vibe of "Stay away from me. Leave me to my thoughts." If he hadn't known her, no mat-ter how beautiful he thought she looked or how attracted he was to her, he would never have gone up to her and started a conversation from zero.

Then when she saw him approach, her attitude changed immedi-ately. She had such a big smile for him, she seemed genuinely happy to see him. He couldn't believe it was true. He knew in his heart it wasn't really true. He knew her feelings for him had initially been based on the fact that he was going to help her find out what happened to her husband. Now those feelings had most probably changed to gratitude for helping her find her husband's killers.

No sooner had Kennedy sat down than their food arrived. He was-n't a big breakfast fan back home in Primrose Hill, but this crispy bacon, two eggs over easy, hash browns, and OJ were a major treat. Yes, they still didn't boil water hot enough in their tea preparation, but come on, he jested to Grace, "Sure youse have only had two hundred years practice."

After breakfast, they went down to Kelly Street station to pick up Kennedy's package from DS James Irvine.

Kennedy asked Grace if there were any old fashioned bicycle shops. The closest one, Wheels On Fire, was over in San Mateo. En route they stopped at the Triple W Ranch and found the forensic team hard at work on the bank of the creek and in the barn. Tyre tracks and Dustin "Green Cap" McClelland's description had helped them select the correct locations. The officer in charge, Sergeant Chris O'Donnell, informed them that they'd picked up several pieces of vital evidence, assuring Grace that they had all they needed, including Florence's offending wine bottle which the sergeant reckoned would have both Florence and Officer Scott's DNA on it.

Next they stopped at the chief's ranch to swap Grace's Ford patrol car for her Mustang, and just under an hour later they were pulling up outside Wheels On Fire. The ornery owner eventually stopped jibbing Kennedy long enough to admit that he did have some of the old style repair kits for the "inner-tube" as he called it ("tube" as Kennedy called it) of the tyre. The Ulster detective also purchased a hand pump. Kennedy was like a kid who couldn't wait to get home to play with a new toy.

"This is a new side to you," Grace said, pulling up outside the log cabin.

"Fingers crossed it'll work," Kennedy began, as he unpacked the deflated twenty-four inch diameter, orange exercise ball. "Could you do me a major favour and get me a large bowl of water?"

By the time she returned he had attached the bicycle pump and pumped the ball up to 50 per cent of its potential. The half-filled basin she returned with was a bit too small for Kennedy's idea to work.

They searched for alternatives. A rain barrel was too dark for Kennedy's needs. The sink in the bathroom was also too small. There were only showers in the log cabin. The shower basin was big enough but couldn't hold enough water.

"I know," she said. "There's a place up on the creek where we used to go swimming. It's in the sun, and the water is very clear and about waist deep."

"Perfect," Kennedy said.

"We'll have to go by horseback," she said.

"I can't ride," he admitted.

"You can hop up with me," she insisted. "Let me quickly change."

Kennedy figured the only thing Grace must have changed was her mind, because she came out of the cabin a few minutes later dressed in exactly the same dark blue jeans, a pink shirt and her sensible, on-duty shoes.

It took a bit longer than expected for Kennedy to get up behind her. In fact, truth be told, he didn't master the manoeuvre at all. She had to dismount, assist Kennedy into the saddle and climb up behind him, all the time controlling the horse, Boots (because his brown turned to white just six inches above each hoof), from behind Kennedy. Then just as he was getting cosy, he realised he'd forgotten to take the orange ball with him. So she had to get down and fetch it for him along with his pump and mending kit.

They (particularly Kennedy) enjoyed the fifteen-minute trot to the creek, although he ached a little when they dismounted. Then he realised he'd forgotten to bring waders. Very quickly thereafter he also realised that Grace had indeed changed when she went into the cabin. She undressed to reveal a vibrant red bikini.

"Okay, now we're going to see what you've got. Off with your clothes, Inspector," she ordered.

"Nah, it's okay," Kennedy said bashfully, trying to avert his eyes from her perfect figure. "I'll just take off my shoes and socks and roll up my trousers." He thought of all the similarly dressed men on the beach at Portrush's West Strand, the majority of whom had had knotted handkerchiefs on their head as makeshift sun hats.

"Just kidding, Inspector," she said playfully. "In the back pocket of my jeans there, you'll find a spare swim suit of my dad's. You can change in the bushes; promise I won't look. Actually I think it's quite sweet that you're so shy."

Kennedy forgot his modesty as he remembered why they were up at the creek in the first place. As Grace swam smoothly in the creek, Kennedy pumped some more air into the ball. Then he joined Grace in the creek. The water, cooler than he'd expected, took his breath away as he went waist high.

"Okay," he began, "now the important part. I need you to help me look for bubbles coming out of the ball."

He submerged the ball and started to squeeze on it.

At first Grace found it hard to be serious, but pretty soon she began to follow his lead and concentrate at the underwater section of the ball as Kennedy slowly rotated it.

"Okay, Grace," Kennedy eventually said, "we need to be very still. We're creating our own air bubbles with our bodies."

"So that's what we're doing," she said playfully, but it went straight over Kennedy's head.

They kept looking for another full five minutes until Grace eventually shouted in excitement, "Bubbles, I saw bubbles; they're very small Inspector, but I saw them."

"Brilliant," he shouted and he squeezed a bit harder on the ball.

"There they are again, Inspector," she said laughing with genuine excitement, "lots of them."

"Okay," he said, "put your finger on the ball where the bubbles are and keep it there until we get out."

They looked like they were involved in one of those bizarre *It's A Knockout* games and were making great progress as they carefully made their way out of the creek. Then Grace slipped on the bank and fell totally back into the water. Kennedy immediately dropped his precious ball and plodded in after her, worrying she'd hit her head on a rock. He pulled her up towards him, without taking any care where he was grabbing her.

"You got me, Inspector; you saved me again," she gasped as she resurfaced. "Now can I have my left breast back again please?"

"Oh goodness," he stammered, "I'm sorry. Of course I didn't mean to..."

"I'm only kidding, Inspector," she laughed, "it's only natural that your eyes would occasionally focus on my body. I don't think you should force yourself not to for fear of getting a crick in your neck from not looking at me. At least you're not letching."

They returned to the creek, repeated the process of locating the bubbles and then, this time, successfully negotiated the slippery bank. Grace held her finger on the location of the bubbles while Kennedy fetched a magic marker from his trousers and marked the location of the puncture.

Grace and Kennedy had one more stop to make. This time it was back in San Francisco, where Grace had organised a friend in the forensic lab to examine the ball for them. An hour and a half later, they were driving back from San Francisco content with the additional bit of information her friend had discovered.

"Okay," Kennedy said as they drove up Main Street over Pilarcitos Bridge, "I believe it's finally time for us to pick up Miss Sharenna Chada."

Chapter Sixty-Two

It wasn't to be as easy as that. According to the receptionist in Livingston House, Miss Chada was taking her first day off since she'd arrived from London. Kennedy was looking forward to seeing the house that Patrick Mylan had bought and then passed on to Miss Chada. He still hadn't worked out the connection between Patrick Mylan and Half Moon Bay. Chief Donohue's theory was that Mylan, like hundreds before him, had been driving either up from LA or down from San Francisco and had happened upon the picturesque town and, on an impulse, had stopped and fallen in love with something or other and decided to put down roots there.

If the chief's theory were accurate, then it showed a side of Mylan Kennedy had never imagined before.

Grace rang her contact in Livingston House, who told her that Miss Chada had taken the day off to visit San Francisco to see an accountant and a lawyer in order to set up her business model. It appeared she was hoping to remain in America permanently.

Maybe it was because Kennedy had received several messages from various people back in London about his progress, but he decided in the end not to, as Grace suggested, leave it until the following morning, choosing instead to visit Miss Chada's house and wait there in the hope of picking her up that night.

They drove out in the general direction of Half Moon Bay Airport, and Grace turned off just before Princeton by the Sea at El Granada and headed up Dolphine Avenue until they found a modern house built into a steep, tree-lined hill, with amazing views out over the ocean. It looked too big for one person. For the first time Kennedy wondered if Miss Chada had a partner; an accomplice in Mylan's murder perhaps? Kennedy chastised himself for not considering this option before. The house looked very tidy and well maintained, but the small, tell-tale concrete garden suggested an absentee owner. Grace reckoned the hill house wouldn't have a single back window, and she figured it would have set Mylan back at least one and a half million dollars.

At eleven-forty, they abandoned the idea of waiting for Miss Chada. Grace's point, and a valid one, was that the minute they arrested her, the clock started running. They would only waste the first twelve hours as they wouldn't be allowed to interview her until the morning anyway.

Kennedy spent a very restless night, while only several feet away in her own room, Grace slept the sleep of the contented.

***

Seven o'clock Friday morning, Kennedy was up noisily preparing their breakfast in the hope of disturbing Grace and stealing an hour on the day. Now that Kennedy felt he had solved the puzzle of the crime, he was keen to confront Sharenna Chada.

As he heard noises from Grace's room, he thought how much slower a pace he was working at while in America. The days just seemed to disappear on him. Maybe it was because he was away from home and didn't have all his creature comforts and office and team around him, but it still seemed to take longer to accomplish things over here. Like yesterday for instance; although in one way it was a breakthrough day, it was also frustrating because they couldn't start to question Miss Chada.

"Ah something smells good out here," Grace shouted as she positively sprang from her bedroom.

Kennedy's disappointment was too visible when he noted she was still in her sleeping T-shirt and shorts.

"Inspector, there are a lot of men out there who would give a month's wages to see me like this first thing in the morning."

"No, no, sorry I didn't mean it like that. *Of course* I like to see you undressed," he drooled, making it apparent he was drooling.

"Okay, now you're just weirding me out," she said, grabbing the slice of toast she just had raspberry-jammed. "I get the picture. I'll get some clothes on, and then we're outta here."

A few minutes later Grace Scott, her hair still wet but at least properly dressed, and a relieved Christy Kennedy were driving off in the direction of Half Moon Bay, leaving their half eaten breakfast still on the table.

***

Miss Chada wasn't at her house when they called, but she was at Livingston House, where she was making up for yesterday's trip into San Francisco by starting very early.

Kennedy thought it weird that as he and Grace Scott were shown through to Miss Chada's treatment room, she didn't look shocked to see him. If anything, she looked as if she'd been expecting him. If she was surprised about anything, it was Inspector Christy Kennedy from Camden Town CID being accompanied by a beautiful woman whom he introduced as "Officer Grace Scott from Half Moon Bay Police Department." If Miss Chada recognised Grace from her earlier visit for treatment, she wasn't letting on.

"Ah Mr Kennedy," Miss Chada asked, "is your back troubling you again?"

Kennedy decided not to beat about the bush. "Miss Chada, I'm here to arrest you on suspicion of the murder of Mr Patrick Mylan."

Grace Scott then read Miss Chada her Miranda rights.

"But Mr Kennedy you know where I was when Mr Mylan was murdered," she offered with a confident smile.

"We're going to bring you in to Half Moon Bay police station for questioning," Grace Scott announced. "Shall we cuff her?" she asked Kennedy.

"It's entirely up to her," Kennedy replied.

"That won't be necessary," Miss Chada said. "I will offer you no resistance. I have the conscience and confidence of the innocent."

There was then a bit of a pantomime in the car park outside Livingston House where Grace Scott put Miss Chada in the back seat of her patrol car. Kennedy then went to take his normal seat in front with Grace.

Grace took him to one side and whispered, "You're supposed to sit, child locked, in the back with our prisoner. You know, so she can't harm herself or interfere with the driver."

"Right," Kennedy replied, slightly embarrassed. "Got it." He hopped in the back of the car beside Miss Chada.

Seven minutes later, just as he was getting out of the car at the police station, Miss Chada leaned over after him and, quick as a flash,
used both her hands to aggressively manipulate something in the small
of Kennedy's back. When he stood up beside Grace on the pavement,
he immediately collapsed in a painful heap.

Grace Scott's first instinct was to go to the aid of her fellow officer,
and she was distracted enough in that split second for the agile Miss
Chada to dart out from the back seat and run right past her in the general direction of freedom. Well, freedom in as much as freedom was
the arms of Officer Kevin MacCormac, who was on his way out of the
station house and had observed the entire incident. Miss Chada swat-
ted Mactoo out of her path the way one swats flies. All, particularly
Grace, were amazed by her strength.

Mactoo rolled over twice, coming back into Chada's path; they collided and ended up in a heap on the road.

"Miss Chada, I presume," Mactoo announced, as he cuffed her and
dusted his uniform and his pride down. "A pleasure to meet you, I'm
sure. I've heard so much about you. Now tell me this, I've got this
shooting pain, which starts in my hip and works its way back down into
my ankle. It only happens when I stand around a lot. Any treatment
you would recommend?"

With that Mactoo frogmarched her into the Kelly Street station,
keeping her securely at arm's length in front of him.

Kennedy was back in sheer liquid agony. He felt as bad as he had
felt two Saturday mornings ago in his house in Camden Town when he
quite literally found it impossible to bear the pain. Kennedy realised
how guilty he had been of taking his better health for granted. When
he felt bad, he promised himself that he'd look after his back properly;
he'd get preventive treatment regularly; he'd never ever let it get into
the state it had been before. That was then. But recently he'd grown totally unaware of it. That probably had a lot to do with being in the company of a certain Grace Scott.

Grace was now doing her utmost to take care of him. She was trying to help him, but the reality was she couldn't. He couldn't stand, he
couldn't sit; he couldn't lie down without experiencing excruciating
pain. Kennedy didn't want to feel as bad and as helpless as he felt in
anywhere else but his home. Illness is always somewhat more difficult

to endure when away from one's home. At that moment he longed for his cosy house in Primrose Hill more than he had ever done.

"Okay, Inspector," Grace said gently, "this is going to hurt, but I can't think of anything else to do. I'm scared if I don't get you some treatment you'll be permanently crippled." With that she hauled Kennedy up from the pavement. The pain was so unbearable that tears freely flowed down his face. Grace, as determined as she knew how to be, decided she was going to have to keep hurting him if she was to be of any help. She nudged him into the back of her car and pulled him face down across the back seat. She kept repeating, "I'm sorry, Inspector, I'm really sorry."

Eventually she had him sprawled fully across the back seat. By dropping his left knee over the edge of the seat down towards the floor and keeping his head face down as opposed to the left or the right, he was slightly more comfortable. The only problem with that position was he was nose down directly where Miss Chada had been sitting, and her unique blend of aromas infused his nostrils.

Kennedy's panic subsided a little at that point. He'd managed to get himself into a position where the pain was manageable. That was of course until the vibration caused by Grace closing the car door set off his trouble again. She gingerly put the car into gear, and Kennedy could feel every pebble in the station house car park as she drove over them. She hit a bump and Kennedy screamed out in pain again.

"I don't know any other way to do this, Inspector," and with that she slammed the car into the next gear and stuck her foot down. For three minutes Kennedy was in sheer agony again and covered head to toe in a film of sweat, but at last they were now where she wanted them to be. He could hear her get out of her car. Thankfully she didn't close the car door. He could hear her running away. All Kennedy could see was the dark leather of the back seat of her patrol car. He imagined she had taken him to a hospital, and soon help and relief would be with him.

Then he got a panic attack. He surely wouldn't be in a mental or physical state to interview Miss Chada for at least a few days, maybe longer. How long could the Half Moon Bay police keep Miss Chada in custody without either charging her or letting her go. It was probably the same as the UK - two days - and then they could go to court and apply for an extension. But they'd have nothing to use to get an extension granted. Even if Grace had the suss to charge Miss Chada with grievous bodily harm, a good lawyer would get her out on bail, and then she'd be off into the wilds of the United States of America. She'd never be found.

He heard feet running towards him, then Grace saying, "Please be careful, he's in very bad shape."

Kennedy heard a new voice in the back of the car with him.

"Christy, my name is Pam. I'm a friend of Grace, and I need you to trust me, okay?"

"Okay," Kennedy whispered. He even found it painful to talk.

"Now don't be alarmed," she continued in a gentle soothing voice. "I'm going to gently touch your back, and I want you to guide me to where Sharenna put her hands when she hurt you, okay?"

"Okay," Kennedy whispered.

She was so gentle Kennedy could barely feel her hands on his back.

"Lower," Kennedy whispered.

Her fingers continued to feather over him. He could sense but not see Grace near by, monitoring Pam's every move.

"Ah! There!" he screamed.

"Okay, Christy," she continued when he'd calmed down, "I think I know what she did. We're gong to need to get you out of the car before I can help."

Kennedy didn't want to move. Not an inch.

"We can give you an injection which will help the pain until we can fix it," Pam offered.

"No," Kennedy replied. He'd always been told never to accept injections for back pain.

"Okay, we have what we call a surfboard; we can slide that underneath you and lift you out."

The exercise wasn't as painful as Kennedy imagined it would be, and eventually they lifted him clear of the car and into a standing position. Pam got behind him, put her arms under his oxters and brought her hands up behind his head where she interlocked her fingers.

"Now I need to wait here until one of my team fetches me something from inside."

Kennedy relaxed, thinking that treatment, pain, call it what you will, was probably some time away; but the second she felt him relax into her arms, she quickly leaned backwards and swept him off his feet.

Kennedy heard a loud crack. He saw a flash of white light. He felt heat in his neck and in the small of his back. He felt sure he was going to pass out with the pain.

He saw Grace Scott directly in front of him, the look of concern obvious in her eyes.

Pam disentangled herself from Kennedy. Thinking he would fall over, he reached out for Grace to steady himself and was surprised when he found he didn't need her support.

"A miracle, Inspector," Grace said with obvious relief as she slowly let Kennedy go.

"That was very cruel, Grace," Pam said. "She dislocated the nerve between his second and fourth lumbar vertebrae. I just stretched it back into place. You're good to go, Christy, just no gymnastics or any...any strenuous exercises for a few days, okay?" she said, now glaring at Grace.

CHAPTER SIXTY-THREE

When Miss Chada was shown into the interview room in Half Moon Bay police station, Kennedy was already standing against the wall and Grace was sitting on one of the only two chairs in the room, one either side of the table.

After Grace had introduced the proceedings for the sake of the tape and video recorder and had asked Miss Chada to confirm, for the benefit of the recording equipment, that she was giving up her right to a lawyer, Kennedy made a bit of a stage fuss over there being only two chairs in the room.

"Not to worry," he said. "I'll nip out and fetch one."

Grace announced this interruption, again for the benefit of the expensive equipment, and thirty seconds later, "Inspector Kennedy has returned to the interview room with a... with an object to sit on."

"My new masseuse says this is good for my back," Kennedy announced as he brought the fully inflated orange exercise ball back in with him, plonked it down at the end of the table between them and balanced himself carefully on it.

Miss Chada would have made a good poker player; her face gave nothing away. Well, it was more that she appeared like she was giving nothing away. But that was it, Kennedy thought: she looked like she had something to give away and she was carefully ensuring that her body language didn't betray her, which in a way of course it did.

"Okay, Sharenna, first off I should tell you, you needn't worry about my back. Thanks to Pam at Livingston House, it's better than it's ever been. But it's interesting that you ran."

"I was within my rights to run. I thought I was being kidnapped."

"Yeah, right," Grace snarled. "How many people get kidnapped and taken to a police station."

"This has nothing to do with you," Miss Chada snapped back

viciously at Grace. "Did your new man tell you where he was when Mr Mylan was being murdered?"

"Actually, that was the very *first* thing he told me," Grace said.

"Then how could I possibly be responsible?" Miss Chada replied. "This is no sense," Miss Chada continued, focusing intently on the tape recorder.

"For the record," Kennedy said, as he ripped the patch he had carefully affixed yesterday to the now fully inflated exercise ball beneath him, "here's how you managed to be in both places at once.

"You rang me two Saturday mornings ago around ten o'clock to set me up. You already knew, because of your, shall we say, manipulation, that I would be in a bad way with my back. You told me you could come and see me after two-thirty at my house. You'd never been to see me in my house before, but for your plan to work you had to.

"You said you had a very busy morning's work ahead of you before you could come and see me."

Miss Chada didn't reply. She occasionally stole a glace at the exercise ball Kennedy was sitting comfortably and safely on.

"You knew that Patrick Mylan, as a creature of habit, liked his Saturday mornings to himself, so you knew he would be alone."

"You enticed him into the swimming pool. Maybe you also got him drunk; there was certainly a lot of alcohol found in his blood. Mrs Littlewood said you were the only one who had the power to control him. She claimed he always had a weakness for you. We've been advised by more than a few people that Mylan always, but always, fell into a deep sleep after sex. You made love to him beside the pool, maybe even on this very ball I'm sitting on. True to form, Mr Mylan immediately fell asleep. You suspended him by a belt around his neck. The belt was attached to a hook on the back of the swimming room toilet door.

"You'd removed several items of his clothing, but put other items on him in order to humiliate him when he was found. You carefully positioned the body and left him hanging there as though he were involved in an autoerotic enterprise."

Grace raised her eyebrows at Kennedy's bizarre choice of words.

"But then, if he'd choked himself on his belt then..." Miss Chada asked, again stealing another glance at Kennedy's seat, "how come he died later when I was with you? I believe as was the case?"

"You're 100 per cent right, and that is a very good question, Miss Chada," Kennedy said largely. "So we both agree what you needed to do was to find some way of delaying his choking until you could be elsewhere. In this particular instance, in fact, you were with me, securing your alibi."

Kennedy smiled, Grace smiled, and even Miss Chada smiled. Kennedy smiled because Miss Chada was still maintaining that she *couldn't* have done it and not that she *didn't* do it. Grace was smiling, Kennedy figured, because the penny had finally dropped with her and she had figured it out. Miss Chada was smiling Kennedy figured, because Kennedy had just admitted in front of a witness just how watertight her alibi was.

Kennedy was rolling around aggressively now on the ball, and the more he moved around, the more he expelled air from the balloon and the more he expelled air from the balloon, the lower he sank.

"Now, say you were to have an exercise ball, such as this exact exercise ball, for instance, and you were to put a few pin holes in it, as in say five small pinholes in a small circle, and you were to place Mr Mylan seated on the ball with his back to the door and his neck strung up to the coat hook using a belt…"

Miss Chada twitched a little, but only a little.

"Securing Patrick Mylan in this position, you could then nip around the corner to me to establish your alibi, while leaving poor Mr Mylan to suffer by the laws of physics and gravity until, eventually, sometime later that day when we were in bed and the air had run out of the exercise ball until it was totally deflated and Mr Mylan had sunk accordingly and was choked to death."

"That's just plain stupid Mr Kennedy," Miss Chada shot back indignantly, shaking her head from side to side several times before continuing. "How a detective with a reputation such as your own could suggest that I entered Patrick's house, enticed him into the swimming pool, made love to him, waited until he fell asleep, undressed him, put suspender belts on his legs, hung him up from a coat hook on the back of the door to the toilet, sat him on an exercise ball, punctured the exercise ball with a pin, and then left him to die… please, that is just so stupid. I have lost all respect for you and I think I will be going."

Kennedy had never heard Miss Chada say so much at once, or use so many commas in all the time he'd known her. He was so shocked by the duration of her statement that he nearly missed the most important part of the statement altogether.

"Could you please play Miss Chada's last answer back for me, Officer Scott?"

Grace rewound the last few minutes of the tape and hit the "play" button.

"...entered Patrick's house, enticed him into the swimming pool, made love to him, waited until he fell asleep, undressed him, put suspender belts on his legs, hung him up from a coat hook on the back of the door to the toilet, sat him on an exercise ball..."

This time Kennedy jumped up from his deflating exercise ball, stopped and rewound the tape, but not quite so far as Grace had before he hit the "play" button, to hear: "...undressed him, put suspender belts on his legs, hung..."

Kennedy pressed the stop button.

"Sharenna, how did you know about the suspender belts?"

"You said it to me just now," Miss Chada claimed, fright now visible in her lonely, sad eyes.

"No I didn't," Kennedy claimed, and he replayed his part of the tape to prove the point. "That particular bit of information is not public knowledge, Sharenna. You only knew it because *you* were the one who put the suspender belts on him to humiliate Patrick Mylan further when he was discovered."

Miss Sharenna Chada had pride. She looked less annoyed than shocked and surprised that he'd actually worked out how she had done it. She was now finally ashamed of her action. Was that part of the secret of a successful murder, Kennedy wondered? People don't feel the massive guilt and consequences of what they've done because they think they've been clever enough to get away with it. Consequently, they don't feel bad because they don't feel accountable. Like Miss Chada, perhaps they only felt accountable when someone else knew for sure that they did it.

CHAPTER SIXTY-FOUR

Miss Chada confessed her guilt, chose a Jesuit priest and the court appointed lawyer - Manny Langenstein stepping up again for his busiest couple of days in years - to make her full and frank confession. She chose not to fight extradition on condition Kennedy would agree to visit her daily, by himself, until her paperwork was processed. Chief Edward Donohue could not agree to that, so eventually a compromise was reached where Kennedy's daily visits to Miss Chada would be "supervised" by an officer other than Grace Scott.

As Kennedy had suspected, it was Maggie Littlewood who'd made the initial introduction. Maggie and Sharenna's mother had taken a night class together and had become good friends and frequent visitors to each other's houses. Around that time, or shortly thereafter, Maggie started dating Patrick Mylan, and he would accompany her to visits to the Chada's house. When Sharenna had first met Patrick, she was thirteen years old. She went to great trouble to ensure Kennedy knew that nothing untoward happened with Mylan until after she was twenty. In the meantime, it appeared, Mylan and Maggie Littlewood ceased to be romantically involved but continued to be friends. Kennedy figured Sharenna was Mylan's second concubine after Gina Webb, and he groomed and prepared her, just as he had with Chloe Simmons and Gina Webb. He also imagined the relationships with his three concubines were different from the relationship Mylan had enjoyed with Maggie Littlewood, which would be the reason why they were still friends.

Again, as was the case with Simmons, Patrick Mylan was generous, courteous, and honest, in that he never pretended their relationship was anything other than what it was. That is to say, convenient and sexual.

And, as was also the case with Chloe Simmons, when it came time to cross that line from pupil to concubine or lover, call it what you will, Sharenna was the one to take the initiative.

"I reached a point where I couldn't resist my desires any longer," Sharenna whispered, but not shyly. "It just became impossible for me to delay the act of pleasuring him for the first time. I didn't have his patience. Afterwards I wished I'd resisted my urges just a little longer so that I would have had more memories to savour and heighten my enjoyment in my many replays."

It became clear that Mylan changed his concubines not, as Kennedy first thought, when he tired of one, but when his new concubine, or mistress, was ready. What Mylan hadn't figured on was the fact that Sharenna would fall deeply in love with him. Yes, he'd invested several years in teaching her how to love him, but the only love he wanted from her was physical.

Miss Chada said she hadn't seen the end of her relationship coming. Perhaps, Miss Chada claimed, if Mylan had let her down easier, maybe allowed her time to wean herself off him, the situation would have been different. She admitted she should have been prepared for it. He had always told her that eventually she would be replaced; it would have nothing to do with her, but all to do with his inability to share a love with a woman.

From the little she'd been allowed to learn of his early life, Miss Chada guessed that when Mylan's father and mother died and he'd gone to live with his uncle and aunt, they had neither shown love nor affection for each other, let alone for Patrick. The farm and the animals always took preference over human relationships, maybe even to the point that having relationships was a sign of weakness, a weakness that could not be tolerated on his uncle's farm.

Her biggest problem was that for several years - "Seven," she said, "if you count from the time he awoke my desire to love him and please him" - he had been completely her life. Nothing else really existed for her apart for Mylan and keeping him happy for those seven years.

Kennedy reflected on how Chloe Simmons, with all her other "outside" interests, had chosen an easier path. She wasn't to be a concubine for life. It was as a way to give her a good, well actually "great" would have been a better word, leg-up on her life's path.

Miss Chada claimed that for her the breaking up with Mylan was all over in a week. Patrick mentioned that he was going away on a trip in ten days and that when he returned they would no longer see each other.

She pleaded with him: was she doing something wrong? Was there something more or different she could do?

He explained to her that she was just perfect, and that was the way he always wanted to remember her. He did not want to reach a point where he went off her, tired of her. Never for one second did he imagine she might tire of him.

She saw little of him in the final week, and even when she did it was just to talk through details. They were no longer intimate with each other.

The more they were apart, the more she hurt. She admitted that her original plan had been to seek out her successor and kill her. Miss Chada was shocked by how easily murder came into her area of consideration. Pretty soon she realised that if she were to have any chance with Mylan after she had gotten rid of her successor, she could not be connected to the crime. She said she really enjoyed plotting how she could get rid of someone without being connected to it. She grew preoccupied with the murder of her successor.

Around the time she finally figured out how to do it, she started to realise that her anger should be directed towards Mylan himself and not towards someone else, someone like herself for instance, who through no fault of her own found herself enslaved by this man.

She had pretty much worked out how to commit her murder when she decided to give him one final chance. She went back to see him and was both shocked and relieved that he wasn't as cold as she'd imagined he would be. But she soon realised why. One of his favourite treats was getting an underwater BJ; something Miss Chada had in fact turned him on to. Apparently, her successor (who Kennedy obviously knew to be Chloe Simmons) had never managed to master this feat of pleasuring him, and in fact at one point she had nearly drowned while attempting it.

After Miss Chada had preformed her few moments of underwater magic, Mylan, just before his customary nap, had once again reiterated why he and Miss Chada did not have a future. He suggested she should use the house he had given her in Half Moon Bay, in fact, as the perfect opportunity for a new beginning. A new life, he said.

Miss Sharenna Chada finalised and refined her plan. When she was working out her alibi, the seduction of Kennedy was just too obvious a choice for her to ignore. She manipulated Kennedy's back to the point where he became dependent on her and she knew he would be on hand as her alibi.

She also knew that one of the few things Mylan loved more than his Saturday's alone was her unique BJ, which he'd christened a UBJ. She visited him, told him she had taken his advice and was off to the West Coast the following Friday, and offered a UBJ as a parting gift.

It was a gift he was unable to resist.

She had given Mylan one final chance to take her back. He had said no and hadn't been particularly polite about it. He also insisted that she never ever come around again, when she returned to England, no matter how brilliant her UBJs were. She claimed that Kennedy was incorrect in that she hadn't got Mylan drunk. When he fell asleep contented, she injected some of Mylan's own neat whiskey directly into his bloodstream, choosing the very discreet location between his toes to do so.

Apart from that, Kennedy, she claimed, had worked out all the rest.

She was surprised, no shocked, at the release she felt by killing him. She had dreamed of a time when she wouldn't feel bad all the time, and when Mylan was dead that really happened; all her bad feelings disappeared.

"I thought I would feel differently in other ways when I killed him," she said in a gentler tone, looking directly into Kennedy's eyes. "I looked at myself in the mirror to see the change. There wasn't one. I was a murderer for heaven's sake; I believed I would look different. I remember thinking the whole experience was a bit similar to losing your virginity. You think everyone who looks at you realises you are no longer a virgin. I thought people would see I was a murderer. I certainly thought you, a policeman, would be able to see that I was a murderer.

She looked at Kennedy as if she expected him to say something. When he didn't she continued, "At the time I considered murdering my successor I was experiencing mental turmoil. I knew I could never do that. But when I addressed the issue of removing Patrick instead it seemed to me to be something I just had to do."

The other confession she made to Kennedy was that when she had been with him, he was the only other man apart from Mylan that she'd ever been to bed with. She found it weird being with someone who wanted to please her just as much as she'd wanted to please him. That was the reason she kept turning up at his house, even after she'd secured her alibi.

Kennedy told Grace Scott most of Sharenna Chada's confession. He omitted the last bit.

CHAPTER SIXTY-FIVE

Kennedy used most of the following week getting all the paperwork in place for Miss Chada's return to London. The process was quite speedy with the Home Office still involved. The Right Honourable Duncan Trower couldn't thank Kennedy enough for his endeavours. Kennedy still had more than enough time to hang out with Grace Scott, who kept saying, "Well smack my mamma, Inspector, I just can't believe how you tied that one up."

Five short days later, paperwork completed and prisoner secured by US marshals on the awaiting plane, Grace Scott brought Kennedy to San Francisco International Airport. She happily ribbed him about sharing his cabin, well not just his cabin but also his bed, yet nothing happening.

"You had your chance, Inspector. If you hadn't been such a gentleman that night they tried to steal our file up at my dad's, you could very easily have cohabited my lingerie - well, actually, that's not strictly true, you couldn't, because I wasn't wearing any."

"But you asked if I could just hold you," Kennedy said, with regret clear in his voice.

"Yes, and most men I've known would have just agreed tactically just so they could jump straight to home base, but as I said, you were such a gentlemen you kept your word... listen, Inspector, I was so wired that night I'd have even considered being another notch on wrinkly David Letterman's bedpost. And then..."

"And then..."

"Well, if we had made love that night, then that would have been the one and only time. I wasn't ready then. I would have been guilt ridden, and you would have been the one who'd have suffered, assuming that is, you'd have been interested in anything more than a quick roll in my bed."

"Grace…" he started.

"I know, Inspector," she said gently, looking deeply into his eyes.

It was nearly time for Kennedy to go through the security checkpoint. He shook her hand awkwardly.

Was that going to be it? After all they'd been through, a quick goodbye with a shake of the hand? Grace Scott had never looked so beautiful to Kennedy. There was always an undercurrent of sadness about her, but she was so full of life, so up for life, that she managed to beat the sadness into retreat. Kennedy wondered what to do. His instinct was to satisfy the powerful feeling he had for her in a kiss. But that would be unfair. That would be taking advantage of a grieving widow. Mind you, she told him, not in so many words, that solving Steve's case had allowed her to start to draw a line under that part of her life. Or could that have been just the conclusion he'd wished to draw from her words?

Should he kiss her? His ex, ann rea, and that was the first time he could remember considering her as his ex, had always said that when you have to spend too much time persuading yourself to do something, then the act in question was usually something to be avoided.

He shook her hand again. She squeezed his hand before finally letting it go.

"Goodbye, Grace."

"Goodbye, Inspector," she said with a beautiful smile.

He walked straight through the security checkpoint.

He turned to steal one final glance at her, but she'd disappeared. That was it. He was homeward bound, and he imagined her returning to the cabin he'd shared with her for the past couple of weeks. He could see her walking through the front door and flopping down into her gigantic sofa. Soon an ocean would separate them, and he'd never hear her say again, "Will you just hold me, please?"

But that's exactly what he thought he heard from somewhere behind. He turned and there she was, large as life, totally breathless, and positively demanding his attention.

"Sorry, Inspector, but I couldn't just let you go like that. Besides, there's no sense in being a police officer if you can't take advantage of your status occasionally."

Grace Scott ran up to Kennedy and hugged him. They hugged so tightly he could feel every curve of her full body through her light dress.

They had their heads over each other's shoulders, and she pulled her head back so she could look at his face. She put her cheek gently on his cheek, and they both closed their eyes. Their hugging grew tighter, but she sought out his lips with her lips and they kissed. It was a long, passionate kiss with neither holding back in either reserve or doubt. It was the kiss Kennedy had wished for from the very first time he'd seen her in the Half Moon Bay police station.

The kiss concluded naturally and gently.

They hugged again.

"Okay, shall I tell you what that was for?" she asked.

Kennedy nodded.

"I wanted you to know that I... I like you, Christy. I wanted you to be interested enough to come back to me and try and get to second base."

"I think we're way beyond second base," he replied, remembering the vision in the ripped T-shirt outside the cabin when Green Hat had tried to steal the file.

"You just might be right, Inspector," she said sweetly, "so much so that I would predict," and she paused and subtly moved sensually tight to him, "you're going to have great difficulty walking to your gate."

"Aye, the gate and all the way beyond to Camden Town," he declared, to her fit of contagious giggles.